STRAINING

Groag's mail-clad figure e~~~~~~~~~~~~~ ~~~~~~
long that poof Prince Del~~~~~~ *~~~~~~ ~~~~ ~~~ tame
magician was splattered all across the walls!* he
thought.

The brass container full of the magic exploding
powder was heavy in Groag's hands. He looked at the
armchair, then the bed, and decided to hide the magic
powder in the fireplace. He used a poker to scrape a
long trench in the pile of hot, white ash, then set the
container into the trench and carefully covered it
again. There was a whisper of sound behind him. He
turned like a great cat and met the wide, frightened
eyes of the maid who'd just opened the door.

"What are you doing here?" she demanded in a
squeaky soprano.

"Nothing *you'll* live to tell about!" Groag bellowed.
He leaped forward with the poker upraised.

There was a flash as red as the fires of Armageddon.
The blast was equally impressive, but Groag didn't
live to hear it. Joe reached his room as quickly as any
of the servants. The stench of burning feathers from
the mattress mingled with the brimstone odor of gunpowder. He snatched a lamp from a wall bracket and
plunged into his room. His feet slipped.

On Groag.

Groag had taken most of the blast, driving him into
the stone doorjamb. Joe couldn't be sure whether
Groag's clothes had been blown off his body, or
whether the body had simply leaked through the fabric after being strained through his chain-link
armor. . . .

—from "The Enchanted Bunny"

Baen Books by David Drake

DAVID DRAKE

ALL THE WAY TO THE GALLOWS

Copyright © 1996 by David Drake

A Baen Books Original

Baen Publishing Enterprises
P.O. Box 1403
Riverdale, N.Y. 10471

ISBN: 0-671-87753-4

Cover art by Bob Eggleton

First printing, December 1996

Distributed by
SIMON & SCHUSTER
1230 Avenue of the Americas
New York, N.Y. 10020

Printed in the United States of America

DEDICATION

To David Handler, and my sister Di
(whose six-year-old self watched in
puzzlement as I rolled on the floor)

CONTENTS

ACKNOWLEDGEMENTS

"The Enchanted Bunny" is copyright © 1990 by David Drake. First published in *The Undesired Princess and The Enchanted Bunny*.

"The Noble Savages" is copyright © 1993 by Bill Fawcett and Associates. First published in *The Harriers: Blood & War*, created by Gordon R. Dickson.

"Airborne All the Way!" is copyright © 1995 by Wizards of the Coast, Inc. All rights reserved. Magic: The Gathering ® and Wizards of the Coast ® are trademarks of Wizards of the Coast, Inc.

"Cannibal Plants from Heck" is copyright © 1994 by David Drake. First published in *Alien Pregnant by Elvis*, edited by Esther Friesner and Martin H. Greenberg.

"The Bond" is copyright © 1985 by David Drake. First published in *Far Frontiers, Volume III* edited by Jerry Pournelle & Jim Baen.

"Mom and the Kids" is copyright © 1990 by Larry Niven and David Drake. First published in *The Fleet: Sworn Allies*, edited by David Drake & Bill Fawcett.

"The Bullhead" is copyright © 1991 by David Drake. First published in *Old Nathan*.

"A Very Offensive Weapon" is copyright © 1995 by Bill Fawcett and Associates. First published in *Forever After*, created by Roger Zelazny.

Why Gallows Humor?

Okay, the name Lucrezia Borgia doesn't immediately conjure up images of her needlework, but for all you or I know she was very good at it. Likewise I'm not best known for my humorous writing.

Still, I laugh a lot. Without a great deal of subtlety, the way I do most things. I'm regularly located at parties in large houses by my peals of laughter. When I was eight years old I used to fall off my chair and roll around on the floor while watching the sitcom *Topper*. There was just something about a ghost St. Bernard guzzling everybody's drinks that broke me up.

A sense of humor can be painful. Our TV was in the unfinished basement. *You* try rolling around on a concrete slab.

It also hurt when I started to slide in helpless laughter between the theater seats while watching *Monty Python and the Holy Grail* at age 30. There isn't enough room between theater seats (and a good thing, too, given the state of the floors). It was the opening credits that destroyed me, by the way.

Therefore this is a collection by a person who laughs not wisely but too well. It's also a collection by a person who's better known for gritty fiction about war and the military. I sometimes cringe to remember things we laughed at in Viet Nam and Cambodia, but gallows humor is the only kind that exists in a war zone. There's a good deal of that attitude in these stories.

Finally, most of the stories are set in somebody else's

universe. If I choose a story premise it's generally pretty grim. (This isn't deliberate; it just happens.) When somebody else shows me a way to handle things with a lighter touch, I dive in with enthusiasm.

Herewith *All the Way to the Gallows*. I don't think I'll get an argument if I say these aren't stories that anybody else would have written.

—Dave Drake
Chatham County, NC

L. Sprague de Camp, one of the top writers of the Golden Age of Science Fiction (and still going strong!), was a great influence on me as an SF writer. Over the years I've encouraged Jim Baen to bring out new editions of some of Sprague's best work.

One of the pieces was "The Undesired Princess," a 1942 lead novel from John W. Campbell's legendary fantasy magazine Unknown Worlds. *While some of the stories that appeared in* Unknown/Unknown Worlds *were pretty darned grim, the magazine's keynote was intensely logical fantasy with a lighter touch than, say, stories in* Weird Tales. *"The Undesired Princess" could stand as the paradigm for the "typical* Unknown *story."*

The trouble with the piece is it's only 40,000 words long—too short for modern book publication. Jim said he'd republish the de Camp if I'd write a novelet in the same style to bind in with it.

I wrote "The Enchanted Bunny."

The Enchanted Bunny

Joe Johnson got into the little car of the airport's People Mover, ignoring the synthesized voice that was telling him to keep away from the doors. Joe was trying to carry his attaché case—stuffed with clothes as well as papers, since he'd used it for an overnight bag on this quick trip to see the Senator—and also to read the wad of photocopy the Senator had handed Joe in front of the terminal "to glance through on the flight back."

The Senator hadn't wanted to be around when Joe read the new section. He must have thought Joe wouldn't be pleased at the way he'd handled the Poopsi LaFlamme Incident.

The Senator was right.

Joe sat down on a plastic-cushioned seat. At least the car was empty except for Joe and the swarthy man—was he an Oriental?—the swarthy Oriental at the far end. When Joe flew in the day before, he'd shared the ride to the main concourse with a family of seven, five of whom—including the putative father—were playing catch with a Nerf ball.

The doors closed. The People Mover said something about the next stop being the Red Concourse and lurched into gentle motion.

Joe flipped another page of the chapter over the paperclip holding it by the corner. *It was about that time that I met a Miss LaFlamme, a friend of my wife Margaret, who worked, as I understand it, as a dancer of some sort. . . .*

5

Good God Almighty! Did the Senator—did the *ex*-Senator, who was well known to be broke for a lot of the reasons that could make his memoirs a best-seller—really think he was going to get away with this?

The publishers hadn't paid a six-figure advance for stump speeches and homilies. They'd been promised scandal, they *wanted* scandal—

And the Senator's rewrite man, Joe Johnson, wanted scandal, too, because his two-percent royalty share was worth zip, zilch, *zero* if *The Image of a Public Man* turned out to be bumpf like this.

"... stopping at the Red Concourse," said the synthesized voice. The car slowed, smoothly but abruptly enough that the attaché case slid on Joe's lap and he had to grab at it. More people got on.

Joe flipped the page.

—helping Miss LaFlamme carry the bags of groceries to her suite. Unfortunately, the elevator—

The People Mover shoop-shooped into motion again. Joe tightened his grip on the case. One of the new arrivals in the car was a crying infant.

Joe felt like crying also. Senator Coble had been *told* about the sort of thing that would go into the book. He'd *agreed.*

An elevator repairman at Poopsi LaFlamme's hotel had lifted the access plate to see why somebody'd pulled the emergency stop button between floors. He'd had a camera in his pocket. That had been the Senator's bad luck at the time; but the photo of two goggle-eyed drunks, wearing nothing but stupid expressions as they stared up from a litter of champagne bottles, would be *great* for the back jacket. . . .

Except apparently the Senator thought everybody—and particularly his publishers—had been living on a different planet when all that occurred.

"In a moment, we will be stopping at the Blue Concourse," said the People Mover dispassionately.

Joe flipped the page. *Unfortunately, pornographic photographs, neither of whose participants looked in the least like myself or Miss LaFlamme, began to circulate in the gutter press—*

And the Washington *Post*. And *Time* magazine. And—

The car halted. The people who'd boarded at the previous stop got off.

Joe flipped the page. *—avoided the notoriety inevitable with legal proceedings, because I remembered the words of my sainted mother, may she smile on me from her present home with Jesus. "Fools' names," she told me, "and fools' faces, are always found in public—"*

Damn! Joe's concourse!

The People Mover's doors were still open. Joe jumped up.

The paperclip slipped and half the ridiculous nonsense he'd been reading spewed across the floor of the car.

For a moment, Joe hesitated, but he had plenty of time to catch his plane. He bent and began picking up the mess.

The draft might be useless, but it wasn't something Joe wanted to leave lying around either. The swarthy man—maybe a Mongolian? He didn't look like any of the Oriental races with which Joe was familiar—watched without expression.

The car slowed and stopped again. Joe stuffed the papers into his attaché case and stepped out. He'd cross to the People Mover on the opposite side of the brightly-lighted concourse and go back one stop.

There were several dozen people in the concourse: businessmen, family groups, youths with back-packs and sports equipment that they'd have the dickens of a time fitting into the overhead stowage of the aircraft on which they traveled. Nothing unusual—

Except that they were all Japanese.

Well, a tourist group; or chance; and anyway, it didn't matter to Joe Johnson. . . .

But the faces all turned toward him as he started across the tile floor. People backed away. A little boy grabbed his mother's kimono-clad legs and screamed in abject terror.

Joe paused. A pair of airport policemen began running down the escalator from the upper level of the concourse. Joe couldn't understand the words they were shouting at him.

The policemen wore flat caps and brass-buttoned frock coats, and they were both drawing the sabers that clattered in patent-leather sheaths at their sides.

Joe hurled himself back into the People Mover just as the doors closed. He stared out through the windows at the screaming foreign crowd. He was terrified that people would burst in on him before the car started to move—

Though the faces he saw looked as frightened as his own must be.

The People Mover's circuitry shunted it into motion. Joe breathed out in relief and looked around him. Only then did he realize that he wasn't in the car he'd left.

There were no seats or any other amenities within the vehicle. The walls were corrugated metal. They'd been painted a bilious hospital-green at some point, but now most of their color came from rust.

Scratched graffiti covered the walls, the floor, and other scribblings. The writing wasn't in any language Joe recognized.

Joe set his attaché case between his feet and rubbed his eyes with both hands. He felt more alone than he ever had before in his life. He must have fallen and hit his head; but he wasn't waking up.

The car didn't sound as smooth as a piece of electronics any more. Bearings squealed like lost souls. There was a persistent slow jarring as the flat spot in a wheel hit the track, again and again.

The People Mover—if that's what it was now—slowed and stopped with a sepulchral moan. The door didn't open automatically. Joe hesitated, then gripped the handle and slid the panel sideways.

There wasn't a crowd of infuriated Japanese waiting on the concourse. There wasn't even a concourse, just a dingy street, and it seemed to be deserted.

Joe got out of the vehicle. It was one of a series of cars which curved out of sight among twisted buildings. The line began to move again, very slowly, as Joe watched transfixed. He couldn't tell what powered the train, but it certainly wasn't electric motors in the individual cars.

There was a smell of sulphur in the air, and there was very little light.

Joe looked up. The sky was blue, but its color was that of a cobalt bowl rather than heaven. There seemed to be a solid dome covering the city, because occasionally a streak of angry red crawled across it. The trails differed in length and placement, but they always described the same curves.

The close-set buildings were three and four stories high, with peak roofs and many gables. The windows were barred, and none of them were lighted.

Joe swallowed. His arms clutched the attaché case to his chest. The train clanked and squealed behind him, moving toward some unguessable destination. . . .

Figures moved half a block away: a man was walking his dogs on the dim street. Claws or heel-taps clicked on the cracked concrete.

"Sir?" Joe called. His voice sounded squeaky. "Excuse me, sir?"

They were very big dogs. Joe knew a man who walked a pet cougar, but these blurred, sinewy forms were more the size of tigers.

There was a rumbling overhead like that of a distant avalanche. The walker paused. Joe looked up.

The dome reddened with great blotches. *Clouds*, Joe thought—and then his mind coalesced the blotches into a single shape, a human face distorted as if it were being pressed down onto the field of a photocopier.

A face that must have been hundreds of yards across.

Red, sickly light flooded down onto the city from the roaring dome. The two "dogs" reared up onto their hind legs. They had lizard teeth and limbs like armatures of wire. The "man" walking them was the same as his beasts, and they were none of them from any human universe.

A fluting *Ka-Ka-Ka-Ka-Ka* came from the throats of the demon trio as they loped toward Joe.

Joe turned. He was probably screaming. The train clacked past behind him at less than a walking pace. Joe grabbed the handle of one of the doors. The panel slid a few inches, then stopped with a rusty shriek.

Joe shrieked louder and wrenched the door open with a convulsive effort. He leaped into the interior. For a moment, he was aware of nothing but the clawed hand slashing toward him.

Then Joe landed on stiff cushions and man's lap, while a voice said, "Bless me, Kiki! The wizard we've been looking for!"

"I beg your pardon," said Joe, disentangling himself from the other man in what seemed to be a horse-drawn carriage clopping over cobblestones.

It struck Joe that he'd never heard "*I beg your pardon*" used as a real apology until now; but that sure wasn't the *only* first he'd racked up on this trip to Atlanta.

The other man in the carriage seemed to be in his late teens. He was dressed in a green silk jumper with puffed sleeves and breeches, high stockings, and a fur cloak.

A sword stood upright with the chape of its scabbard between the man's feet. The weapon had an ornate hilt, but it was of a serviceable size and stiffness. Joe rubbed his nose, where he'd given himself a good crack when he hit the sword.

A tiny monkey peeked out from behind the youth's right ear, then his left, and chittered furiously. The animal wore a miniature fur cloak fastened with a diamond brooch.

The monkey's garment reminded Joe that wherever he was, it wasn't Atlanta in the summertime. The carriage had gauze curtains rather than glazing over the windows. Joe shivered in his cotton slacks and short-sleeved shirt.

"I'm Delendor, Master Sorceror," the youth said. "Though of course you'd already know that, wouldn't you? May I ask how you choose to be named here in Hamisch?"

Kiki hopped from Delendor's shoulder to Joe's. The monkey's body was warm and smelled faintly of stale urine. It crawled around the back of Joe's neck, making clicking sounds.

"I'm Joe Johnson," Joe said. "I think I am. God."

He clicked open the latches of his attaché case. Everything inside was as he remembered it, including the dirty socks.

Kiki reached down, snatched the pen out of Joe's shirt pocket, and hurled it through the carriage window at the head of a burly man riding a donkey in the opposite direction.

The man shouted, "Muckin' bassit!"

Joe shouted, "Hey!"

Delendor shouted, "Kiki! For shame!"

The monkey chirped, leaped, and disappeared behind Delendor's head again.

"I *am* sorry," Delendor said. "Was it valuable? We can stop and . . . ?"

And discuss things with the guy on the donkey, Joe thought. "No thanks, I've got enough problems," he said aloud. "It was just a twenty-nine-cent pen, after all."

Though replacing it might be a little difficult.

"You see," Delendor continued, "Kiki's been my only friend for eight years, since father sent my sister Estoril off to Glenheim to be fostered by King Belder. I don't get along very well with my brothers Glam and Groag, you know . . . them being older, I suppose."

"Eight years?" Joe said, focusing on a little question because he sure-hell didn't want to think about the bigger ones. "How long do monkeys live, anyway?"

"Oh!" said Delendor. "I don't—I'd rather not think about that." He wrapped his chittering pet in his cloak and held him tightly.

Joe flashed a sudden memory of himself moments

before, clutching his attaché case to his chest and praying that he was somewhere other than in the hell which his senses showed him. At least Kiki was alive. . . .

"Estoril's visiting us any day now," Delendor said, bubbly again. Kiki peeked out of the cloak, then hopped to balance on the carriage window. "It'll be wonderful to see her again. And to find a great magician to help me, too! My stars must really be in alignment!"

"I'm not a magician," Joe said in a dull voice.

Reaction was setting in. He stared at the photocopied chapter of the Senator's memoirs. *That* sort of fantasy he was used to.

"After you help me slay the dragon," Delendor continued, proving that he hadn't been listening to Joe, "I'll get more respect. And of course we'll save the kingdom."

"Of course," muttered Joe.

Kiki reached out the window and snatched the plume from the helmet of a man in half-armor who carried a short-hafted spontoon. The spontoon's ornate blade was more symbol than weapon. The man bellowed.

"Kiki!" Delendor cried. "Not the Civic Guard!" He took the plume away from his pet and leaned out the window of the carriage as the horses plodded along.

"Oh," said the guardsman—the cop—in a changed voice as he trotted beside the vehicle to retrieve his ornament. "No harm done, Your Highness. Have your little joke."

"Ah . . ." Joe said. "Ah, Delendor? Are you a king?"

"Of course not," Delendor said in surprise. "My father, King Morhaven, is still alive."

He pursed his lips. "And anyway, both Glam and Groag are older than I am. Though that wouldn't *prevent* father. . . ."

Joe hugged his attaché case. He closed his eyes. The carriage was unsprung, but its swaying suggested that it was suspended from leather straps to soften the rap of the cobblestones.

God.

"Now," the prince went on cheerfully, "I suppose the

dragon's the important thing . . . but what I *really* want you to do is to find my enchanted princess."

Joe opened his eyes. "I'm not . . ." he began.

But there wasn't any point in repeating what Delendor wouldn't listen to anyway. For that matter, there was nothing unreasonable about assuming that a man who plopped out of midair into a moving carriage was a magician.

The prince opened the locket on his neck chain and displayed it to Joe. The interior could have held a miniature painting—but it didn't. It was a mirror, and it showed Joe his own haggard face.

"I've had the locket all my life," Delendor said, "a gift from my sainted mother. It was the most beautiful girl in the world—and as I grew older, so did the girl in the painting. But only a few weeks ago, I opened the locket and it was a *rabbit*, just as you see it now. I'm sure she's the princess I'm to marry, and that she's been turned into a bunny by an evil sorceror."

Delendor beamed at Joe. "Don't you think?"

"I suppose next," Joe said resignedly, "you're going to tell me about your wicked stepmother."

"I beg your pardon!" snapped the prince, giving the phrase its usual connotations.

Delendor drew himself up straight and closed the locket. "My mother Blumarine was a saint! Everyone who knew her says so. And when she died giving birth to me, my father never *thought* of marrying a third time."

"Ah," said Joe. "Look, sorry, that's not what I meant." It occurred to him that Delendor's sword was too respectable a piece of hardware to be only for show.

"I'm not sure what father's first wife was like," the prince went on, relaxing immediately. "But I think she must have been all right. Estoril more than balances Glam and Groag, don't you think?"

"I, ah," Joe said. "Well, I'll take your word for it."

"They say that mother had been in love with a young knight in her father's court," Delendor went on. "Her father was King Belder of Glenheim, of course. But they couldn't marry until he'd proved himself—which he tried to do when the dragon appeared, in Glenheim that time. And it almost broke mother's heart when the dragon ate the young man. King Belder married her to my father at once to take her, well, her mind off the tragedy, but they say she never really recovered."

Kiki leaned out of the window and began chittering happily. Delendor stroked his pet's fur and said, "Yes, yes, we're almost home, little friend."

He beamed at Joe once more. "That's why it's so important for me to slay the dragon now that it's reappeared, you see," the prince explained. "As a gift to my sainted mother. And *then* we'll find my enchanted princess."

Joe buried his face in his hands. "Oh, God," he muttered.

Something warm patted his thumb. Kiki was trying to console him.

The measured hoofbeats echoed, then the windows darkened for a moment as the carriage passed beneath a masonry gateway. Joe pushed the curtain aside for a better look.

They'd driven into a flagged courtyard in the center of a three-story stone building. The inner walls glittered with hundreds of diamond-paned windows. Servants in red and yellow livery bustled about the coach, while other servants in more prosaic garb busied themselves with washing, smithing, carpentry—and apparently lounging about.

"The Palace of Hamisch," Delendor said with satisfaction.

Joe nodded. A real fairytale palace looked more practical—and comfortable—than the nineteenth-century notion of what a fairytale palace should be.

A real fairytale palace. God 'elp us.

The carriage pulled up beneath a porte cochere. Servants flung open the doors with enthusiasm to hand out the prince and his companion.

Joe didn't know quite how to react. He let a pair of liveried youths take his hands, but the whole business made him feel as though he were wearing a corsage and a prom dress.

Kiki jumped from Delendor's right shoulder to his left and back again. Joe noticed that each of the nearest servants kept a hand surreptitiously close to his cap.

The carriage clucked into motion. There was a stable on the opposite side of the courtyard.

"Your Highness," said the fiftyish man whose age and corpulence marked him as the palace major domo, "your father and brothers have been meeting in regard to the, ah, dragon; and King Morhaven specifically asked that when you arrived, you be sent—"

"Is my sister here yet?" Delendor interrupted.

"Yes," said the major domo, "the Princess Estoril has been placed in her old rooms in—"

As the carriage swung into the stables, the driver turned and smirked over his shoulder at Joe. He was the swarthy maybe-Mongolian who'd shared Joe's car in Atlanta.

"*Hey!*" Joe bawled as he took a long stride. His foot slipped on the smooth flagstones and he fell on his arse.

The coach disappeared into the stables.

Instead of making another attempt to run after the man, Joe stood and used the attention that his performance had just gained him to demand, "Prince! Your Highness, that is. Who was driving us?"

Delendor blinked. "How on earth would I know?" he said. "I just called for a coach, of course."

The nods of all the servants underscored a statement as obviously true as the fact the sun rose in the east.

Did the sun here rise in the east?

"Well, anyway, Clarkson," the prince went on, turning again to the major domo, "find a room for my friend here in my wing. I'll go see Estoril at once."

"Ah, Your Highness," the major domo replied with the fixed smile of an underling caught in the middle. "Your father did specifically ask that—"

"Oh, don't worry about that, Clarkson!" Delendor threw over his shoulder as he strode into the palace. "My friend Joe here is a mighty magician. He and I will take care of the dragon, never fear!"

Clarkson watched as his master disappeared, then sized up Joe. "No doubt . . ." the major domo said neutrally. "Well, we're used to His Highness' enthusiasms, aren't we?"

Joe nodded, though he was pretty sure that the question wasn't one which Clarkson expected him to answer.

Joe's room was on the third floor, overlooking the courtyard. Its only furnishings were a bed frame and a cedar chest. There were two casement windows and, in one corner against the outer wall, a fireplace which shared a flue with the room next door.

The fire wasn't set, and the room was colder than Hell.

Clarkson watched with glum disdain as a housekeeper opened the cedar chest with a key hanging from her belt. She handed out feather comforters to lower-ranking maids. They spread them over the bed frame in what looked like a warm, if not particularly soft, arrangement.

"Why isn't the fire laid?" the major domo demanded peevishly. "And there should be a chamberpot, you *know* what happens when there isn't a chamberpot. And on the courtyard side, too!"

"I don't know where the girl's gotten to," the housekeeper said with a grimace. "I'm sure it'll be seen to shortly, sir."

"Ah," Joe said. "Ah, Clarkson? I wonder if you could find me some warmer clothes? A fur coat would be perfect."

The major domo stared at Joe disdainfully. "That's scarcely my affair," he said. "I suppose you can talk to the chamberlain. Or to the prince, no doubt."

Enough was enough.

Joe set his attaché case down and stood with his hands on his hips.

"Oh?" he said, letting the past hour of terror and frustration raise his voice into real anger. "Oh? It doesn't matter to you, then? Well, Clarkson, does it matter to you if you spend the rest of eternity as a fat green frog in the castle moat?"

The maids and housekeeper scurried out of the room, their mouths forming ovals of silent horror. Clarkson's face set itself in a rictus. "Yes, of course, milord," he muttered through stiff lips. "Yes, of course, I'll take care of that immediately."

The major domo dodged through the door like a caroming pinball, keeping as far from Joe as he could. He bowed, spreading his arms—and grabbed the handle to pull the door closed behind him.

Which left Joe alone, as cold as fear and an all-stone room could make a man.

He stared out one of the diamond-paned windows. It was clean enough, but there was frost on both sides of the glass. Maybe one of the half-seen figures in the rooms across the courtyard was the maybe-Mongolian, who'd maybe brought Joe—

His door opened and banged shut again behind a slip of a girl in drab clothing. She shot the flimsy bolt and ran two steps toward the cedar chest before she realized Joe had turned from the window and was watching her in amazement.

Joe thought she was going to scream, but she choked the sound off by clapping both her hands over her own mouth. Through her fingers she whimpered, "Please help me! Please hide me!"

"Coo-ee!" called a man's deep voice from the hallway.

"Here chick-chick-chickee!" boomed another man.

A fist hammered Joe's door. "Better not make us come in for you, chickie," the first voice warned.

Great.

"Sure," Joe whispered.

The girl was short and rail-thin. Mousy brown hair trailed out from beneath her mob cap. She started for the chest again.

Joe grabbed her by the shoulder. "Not there," he said, raising his voice a little because the banging on the door had become louder and constant. He threw back the top comforter.

"*There*," he explained, pointing. She gave him a hopeful, terrified look and flattened herself cross-ways on the bed.

Joe folded the thick feather quilt over her. Then he slid up one of the windows—it couldn't possibly make the room colder—and drew open the bolt just as the doorpanel started to splinter inward under the impacts of something harder than a hand.

Two black-bearded men, built like NFL nose guards, forced their way into the room. They'd been hammering the door with their sword pommels.

Delendor's weapon had looked serviceable. The swords *this* pair carried would have been two-handers—in hands smaller than theirs.

They didn't even bother to look at Joe. "Where are you, bitch?" one shouted. "We were just gonna show you a good time, but by god it'll be the *last* time fer you now!"

"Look, I'm here as a guest of—" Joe began.

"*There* we go!" the other intruder boomed as his eyes lighted on the cedar chest as the only hiding place in the room.

He kicked the chest with the toe of his heavy leather boot. "Come out, come out, wherever you are!" he shouted.

His fellow rammed his big sword through the top of the cedar chest and splinteringly out the back. Its point sparked on the stone flooring.

Both men stabbed repeatedly at the fragile wood until it was quite obvious that the chest was empty.

They'd thought she was inside that, Joe realized. His body went cold. He'd already put his case down. Otherwise his nerveless hands would've dropped it.

"We saw 'er come in, so she musta got out the . . ."

one of the men said. He peered through the open casement. There was no ledge, and the walls were a smooth, sheer drop to the flagstone courtyard.

The two men turned toward Joe simultaneously. They held their bare swords with the easy naturalness of accountants keying numbers into adding machines.

"And just who the hell are you, boyo?" asked the one who'd first stabbed the cedar chest.

In what seemed likely to be his last thought, Joe wondered whether the FAA kept statistics on the number of air travelers who were hacked to death by sword-carrying thugs.

"He's the magician who's going to help your royal brother slay the dragon, Groag," said a cold voice from the doorway.

Which would make the other thug Glam; and no, they didn't show much family resemblance to Delendor.

Joe turned. The brothers had jumped noticeably when the newcomer spoke; and anyway, turning his back on Glam and Groag wouldn't make them *more* likely to dismember him.

"I'm Joe Johnson," he said, holding out his hand to be shaken. "I'm glad to see you."

Classic understatement.

The newcomer was tall, gray, and fine-featured. He wore black velvet robes, rather like academic regalia—though heavier, which this damned unheated building made a good idea. He stared at Joe's hand for a moment, then touched it in an obvious attempt to puzzle out an unfamiliar form of social interchange.

"My name is Ezekiel," he said. "I—"

"I think we'll go now," muttered Glam, bouncing off the doorjamb in much the fashion that the major domo had done minutes earlier. Groag followed him on the same course. Joe noticed that the brothers had sheathed their swords.

The room returned to normal size with Glam and Groag out of it. There were *some* advantages to being mistaken for a magician.

"Ah, thanks," Joe said. "I, ah . . . didn't like the way things were going."

"They're not bad lads," Ezekiel said with what seemed to be his universal air of cool detachment. "A little head-strong, perhaps. But I couldn't have you turning the king's elder sons into . . . frogs, I believe I heard?"

He raised a quizzical eyebrow.

Joe shrugged. Before he spoke—before he decided *what* to say—a train of servants streamed into the room, carrying furs; charcoal and kindling with which they laid a fire; and a chamberpot.

"I suppose," Ezekiel pressed, "you have your apparatus with you? You don't—" he paused "—plan to deal with the dragon unaided, do you?"

"I was wondering," Joe temporized, "if you could tell me something about this dragon?"

Ezekiel blinked. "I'm not sure what it is you want to know," he said reasonably enough. "It's a dragon more than thirty yards long and invulnerable to weapons except at one point on its body . . . which no one in recorded history has discovered."

He smiled coldly. "It digs a burrow deep in the rock and sleeps twenty years of twenty-one, which is good . . . but in the year the beast wakes, it does quite enough damage to ruin a kingdom for a generation. Glenheim has barely recovered from the most recent visitation . . . and this time, the creature has chosen to devour a path through Hamisch. As no doubt your friend Prince Delendor has explained."

The servants were leaving with as much dispatch as they'd arrived. They carried out the scraps of cedar chest with a muttered promise of a replacement.

The fire burned nicely and might even have warmed the room, except that the window was still open. Joe shut it.

"Delendor was too occupied with seeing his sister to give me much of the background," he said neutrally.

Ezekiel's face twisted with disgust, the first emotion he'd shown since he arrived. "Prince Delendor's affection for his sister is, I'm sorry to say, unnatural," he said. "The king was well advised to send Estoril away when he did."

His lips pursed, shutting off the flow of excessively free words. "I wish you luck with your difficult task," Ezekiel concluded formally. "It's of course an honor to meet so powerful a colleague as yourself."

He left the room, and Joe closed the door behind him.

Joe took a deep breath. Well, he was still alive, which he wouldn't've bet would be the case a few minutes ago.

"Ah," he said to the bed. "You can come out now."

The folded comforter lay so flat that for an instant Joe thought the girl had been spirited away—which fit the way other things had been happening, though it wouldn't've improved his mood.

"Oh, bless you, sir," said her muffled voice as the feathers humped. The girl slipped out and stood before him again.

She wasn't really a girl. Her face was that of a woman in her mid-twenties, maybe a few years younger than Joe. Her slight form and, even more, her air of frightened diffidence made her look much younger at a glance.

"I'll . . ." she said. "I think it's safe for me to leave now. Bless—"

"Wait a darn minute!" Joe said. He put out his arm to stop her progress toward the door, then jerked back—furious with himself—when he saw the look of terror flash across her face.

"Look," he said, "I'd just like to know your name—"

"Mary, sir," she said with a deep curtsey. When she rose, she was blushing.

"For *God*'s sake, call me Joe!" he said, more harshly than he'd meant.

Joe cleared his throat. His new fur garments were stacked in a corner. He donned a cloak as much to give his hands something to do as for the warmth of it. "And, ah," he said, "maybe you can give me a notion of what's going on? I mean—"

He *didn't* mean Glam and Groag, as Mary's expression of fear and distaste suggested she thought he did.

Joe understood the brothers well enough. They were jocks in a society which put even fewer restrictions on jock behavior than did a college dorm.

"No, no," Joe said, patting her thin shoulder. "Not that. Just tell me if what Ezekiel said about the dragon's true. And who *is* Ezekiel, anyway?"

"Why, he's the royal sorcerer," Mary said in amazement. "And a very powerful one, though nowhere near as powerful as you, Master Joe. It would take Ezekiel weeks to turn somebody into a frog, and I'm sure he doesn't know how to deal with the dragon."

"Oh, boy," Joe said. From the look behind Ezekiel's eyes when they talked, the magician had been contemplating the start of a multi-week project that would leave him with one fewer rival—and the moat with one more frog.

"I'm sure he must really hate you, Master Joe," Mary said, confirming Joe's guess. "Of course, Ezekiel doesn't really like anybody, though he does things for Glam and Groag often enough."

Does this palace even have a moat?

"Look, Mary," he said "is Delendor the only guy trying to kill this dragon, then? Isn't there an army or—you know, something?"

"Well, many brave knights have tried to slay the dragon over the years," Mary said, frowning at the unfamiliar word "army." "And sometimes commoners or even peasants have attacked the beast, but that didn't work either. So now there's . . . well, Glam and Groag say they've been spying out the dragon's habits, but I don't think anybody *really* wants to get near it."

A look of terrible sadness crossed the woman's face. "Except for Prince Delendor. He's serious. Oh, Master Joe, you *will* save him, won't you?"

Joe smiled and patted the woman's shoulder again. "We'll see what we can do," he said.

But dollars to doughnuts, there was damn-all a free-lance writer *could* do about this problem.

Joe waited in his room; at first in the expectation that Delendor would be back shortly . . . and later, because Joe didn't have anyplace better to go. Anyway, the scatter-brained youth *might* still arrive.

Joe carried the *Fasti* to read on the airplane. Ovid's erudite myths and false etymologies had at least as much bearing on this world as they did on the one from which the People Mover had spirited Joe away.

After an hour or so, Joe snagged the first servant to pass in the hallway and asked for an armchair. What he got was solid, cushionless, and not particularly comfortable—but it arrived within fifteen minutes of Joe's request. The men carrying the chair panted as if they'd run all the way from the basement with it.

The frog story seemed to have gotten around.

But nobody else came to Joe's room until a servant summoned him to dinner in the evening.

"It's so brave of you to return to Hamisch to show solidarity when the dragon threatens, Estoril," said Delendor. "Most people are fleeing the other way."

Kiki sat on the prince's head. When Delendor leaned forward to see his sister past his two huge brothers and King Morhaven, the youth and monkey looked like a totem pole.

Estoril was black haired, like Glam and Groag, but her fine features were at least as lovely as Delendor's were boyishly handsome.

"Or into the city," said the king gloomily. "We're going to have a real sanitation problem soon, especially because of the herds of animals."

"I don't think that will be a serious difficulty, Your Highness," said Ezekiel, beside Estoril at the far end of the table from Joe. "The creature demolished the walls of Glenheim within minutes on its previous appearance . . .

and, as I recall, made short work of the cattle shelter-ing there."

"Well," said Delendor brightly, "*that* won't be a prob-lem here, because I'm going to slay the dragon. Right, Joe?"

"Actually," said Estoril, giving Delendor a look that Joe couldn't fathom, "my visiting now had nothing to do with the dragon. Katya—that was Blumarine's old nurse—died. In her last hours, she told me some things that . . . well, I thought I'd visit again."

Ezekiel took a sip of wine that Joe thought could dou-ble as antifreeze. "I met Katya once," he said. "She was a wise woman of some power. Did *you* know her, Joe?" the magician added sharply.

Joe choked on a mouthful of stewed carrot.

"Uh-uh," he managed to mumble without spraying. The meal ran to grilled meat and boiled vegetables, both of which would have been okay if they'd been taken off the heat within an hour or so of being thoroughly cooked.

Estoril turned. Joe couldn't see her face, but there was steel in her voice as she said, "According to Katya, Blumarine herself was a powerful magician. Was that the case, Master Ezekiel?"

"My mother?" Delendor blurted in amazement.

"My understanding, dear princess," Ezekiel said in a deliberately condescending voice, "is that your step-mother may have been a student of wisdom; but that if she ever practiced the craft, it was on the most rarified of levels. At any rate—"

The magician paused to drink the rest of his wine with apparent satisfaction. "At any rate," he went on, "it's certain that she couldn't prevent the young knight with whom she was romantically linked from being killed and eaten by the dragon."

The table waited in frozen silence.

"I believe," Ezekiel concluded, "that his name was Delendor, too, was it not, princess?"

King Morhaven hid his own face in his winecup. Glam and Groag chuckled like pools of bubbling mud.

The hell of embarrassment was that it only afflicted decent—or at least partially-decent—people. "I wonder if any of you can tell me," Joe said loudly to change the subject, "about the kind of guns you have here?"

Everyone stared at him. "Guns?" the king repeated.

Well, they'd been speaking English until now. "I mean," Joe explained, "the things that shoot, you know, bullets?"

This time it was Delendor who said, "Bullets?"

Ezekiel sneered.

Right, back to words of one syllable. After all, Joe had worked with the Senator. . . . "What," said Joe, "do you use to shoot things at a distance?"

"Distance" was two syllables.

"Arbalests, of course," said Morhaven. He pointed to a servant and ordered, "You there. Bring Master Joe an arbalest."

"Or you can throw rocks," Delendor noted happily. "I met a peasant who was very clever that way. Knocked squirrels right out of trees."

"From what I've been told," Joe said, "I doubt that slinging pebbles at your dragon is going to do a lot of good."

"What?" Groag said to Delendor in honest horror. "You're going to throw rocks at the dragon instead of facing it with your sword?"

The servant was returning to the table, carrying a massive crossbow that looked as though it weighed twenty pounds.

And that meant, just possibly, that Joe *could* arrange for Delendor to kill the dragon!

"Why, that's disgusting!" Glam added, echoing Groag's tone. "Even for a little shrimp like you!"

"Hang on—" Joe said. Everybody ignored him.

"I said nothing of the sort!" Delendor spluttered, his voice rising an octave. "How dare you suggest that I'd act in an unknightly fashion?"

Joe snapped his fingers and shouted, "Wait a minute!"

The room fell silent. Servants flattened. Delendor's

brothers flinched as if ready to duck under the table to preserve themselves from frogness.

"Right," said Joe in a normal voice. "Now, the problem isn't knightly honor, it's the dragon. Is that correct?"

Morhaven and all three of his sons opened their mouths to object. Before they could speak, Estoril said, "Yes, that *is* correct."

She looked around the table. Her eyes were the color of a sunlit glacier. The men closed their mouths again without speaking.

"Right," Joe repeated. "Now, I know you've got charcoal. Do you have sulphur?"

The proportions were seventy-five, fifteen, ten. But Joe couldn't for the life of him remember whether the fifteen was charcoal or sulphur.

Everyone else at the table looked at Ezekiel. The magician frowned and said, "Yes, I have sulphur in my laboratory. But I don't see—"

"Wait," said Joe, because this was the kicker, the make-or-break. He swallowed. "Do you have potassium nitrate here? Saltpeter? I think it comes from. . . ."

Joe *thought* it came from under manure piles, but unless the locals had the stuff refined, he was damned if he could find it himself. He wasn't a chemist, he just had slightly misspent his youth.

"Yes . . ." Ezekiel agreed. "I have a store of saltpeter."

"Then, by god, I *can* help you kill this dragon!" Joe said in a rush of heady triumph. "No problem!"

Reality froze him. "Ah . . ." he added. "That is, if Master Ezekiel helps by providing materials and, ah, equipment for my work?"

"And *I'll* slay—" Delendor began.

"Father," Estoril interjected with enough clarity and volume to cut through her brother's burbling, "Delendor is after all rather young. Perhaps Glam or—"

"What?" roared Glam and Groag together.

"What?" shrilled Delendor as he jumped to his feet. Kiki leaped from the prince's head and described a cartwheel in the air. "I *demand* the right to prove myself by—"

"Silence!" boomed King Morhaven. He stood, and for the first time Joe was reminded that the hunched, aging man *was* a monarch.

The king pointed at Delendor and dipped his finger. The youth subsided into his chair as if Morhaven had thrown a control lever.

King Morhaven transferred his gaze and pointing finger to Joe. "You," he said, "will prepare your dragon-killing magic." He turned. "And you, Ezekiel," he continued, "will help your colleague in whatever fashion he requires."

The magician—the real magician—nodded his cold face. "I hear and obey, Your Highness," he said.

Morhaven turned majestically again. "Delendor," he said, "your sister is correct that you are young; but the task is one at which seasoned heroes have failed in ages past. You have my permission to try your skill against the monster."

The king's face looked haggard, but there was no denying the authority in his voice as he added, "And if you succeed in saving the kingdom, my son, then there can be only one suitable recompense."

Joe blinked. If he understood correctly (and there couldn't be much doubt about what Morhaven meant), then the king had just offered the crown to his youngest son for slaying the dragon.

No wonder everybody was staring in amazement as King Morhaven seated himself again.

The regal gesture ended with a thump and a startled gasp from the king as his fanny hit the throne six inches below where it had been when he stood.

Kiki, chirruping happily, ran for the door. The monkey dragged behind him the thick cushion he'd abstracted from the throne while Morhaven was standing.

Joe, wearing an ankle-length flannel nightgown (at home he slept nude; but at home he didn't sleep in a stone icebox), had just started to get into bed when there was a soft rapping on his door.

He straightened. The fireplace held only the memory of an orange glow, but it was enough for him to navigate to the door past the room's few objects.

"Yes?" he whispered, standing to the side of the stone jamb in memory of the way the brothers' swords had ripped the cedar chest.

"Please, sir?" responded a tiny voice he thought he recognized.

Joe opened the door. Mary, a thin wraith, slipped in and shoved the door closed before Joe could.

"Please, sir," she repeated. "If you could hide me for a few nights yet, I'd be ever so grateful."

"What?" Joe said. "Mary, for Pete's sake! I'd like to help, but there's nowhere—"

And as she spoke, the obvious thought struck him dumb. *No! She was the size of an eight-year-old, she was as helpless as an eight-year old, and the very thought— Ick!*

"Oh, Master Joe, I'll sleep at the foot of your bed," Mary explained. "I'll be every so quiet, I promise. I'm just so afraid."

With excellent reason, Joe realized. If the dragon was half as real and dangerous as Glam and Groag, then this place was long overdue for the invention of gunpowder.

And anyway, there wasn't much time to spend thinking about the situation, unless he wanted them both to freeze.

"Right," Joe said. "We'll, ah—"

But the girl—the woman!—had already eeled between the upper and lower comforters, lying crosswise as she'd hidden this afternoon. Joe got in more gingerly, keeping his knees bent.

"Ah, Mary?" he said after a moment.

"Joe sir?"

"Could King Morhaven make Delendor his successor under, ah, your constitution?"

"Oh, yes!" the muffled voice responded. "And wouldn't it be wonderful? But only when Delendor shows what a hero he is. Oh, Master Joe, sir, you're a gift from heaven to all Hamisch!"

"Or something," muttered Joe. But now that he'd thought of gunpowder, he was pretty confident.

Arnault, the royal armorer, was a husky, sooty man wearing a leather apron. His forearms were the size of Joe's calves; blisters from flying sparks gave them an ulcerated look.

"Yaas, master?" he rumbled in a voice that suggested that he was happier in his forge than being summoned to the new magician's laboratory.

Joe wasn't thrilled about the laboratory either. He was using the palace's summer kitchen, built in a corner of the courtyard and open on all sides to vent the heat of the ovens and grills during hot weather.

The weather now was cold enough that Joe wore fur mittens to keep the brass mortar and pestle from freezing his hands. On the other hand, the light was good; there was plenty of work space . . . and if something went wrong, the open sides would be a real advantage.

"Right," said Joe to the armorer. "I want you to make me a steel tube about three feet long and with a bore of . . ." *Forty-five caliber? No, that might be a little tricky.*

Joe cleared his throat. "A bore of about a half inch. Somewhere around that, it doesn't matter precisely so long as it's the same all the way along."

"Whazat?"

"And, ah," Joe added, beaming as though a display of confidence would banish the utter confusion from the armorer's face, "make sure the tube's walls are thick. Maybe you could use a wagon axle or something."

After all, they wouldn't have to carry the gun far.

"What?" the armorer repeated.

"I thought you wanted the tube to be steel, Joe," said Estoril. "Or was that one of the paradoxes of your craft?"

There were at least a hundred spectators, mostly servants. They crowded the sides of the summer kitchen to goggle at the magical preparations. He'd ordered them away half a dozen times, but that just meant the mass drew back a few yards into the courtyard . . . and drifted inward as soon as Joe bent over his paraphernalia again.

Of course, Joe could demand a closed room and bar himself in it until he'd finished the process—or blown himself to smithereens. That still didn't seem like the better choice.

Joe didn't even bother telling the members of the royal family to leave him alone. But if he had to do this over, he'd keep a couple frogs in his coat pockets and let them out at strategic times. . . .

The spectator weren't the immediate problem, though.

"Right," Joe said with his chirpy face on. "How thick are your axles here?"

"Waal," said the armorer, "they's aboot—" He mimed a four-inch diameter with his hands.

"But they're wooden!" said Delendor. "Ah, aren't they?" He looked around at the other spectators.

Ezekiel nodded silently. Joe thought he saw the magician's mouth quirk toward a smile.

"Right," said Joe. "Wood."

He swallowed. "Well, all I meant was that you need to get a round steel rod about this thick—" he curled his middle finger against the tip of his thumb, making a circle of about two inches in diameter "—and a yard long. Then—"

"Naow," said the armorer.

"No?" Joe translated aloud. His control slipped. "Well, why the hell *not*, then?"

"Whaar's a body t' foind so much stale, thaan?" the armorer demanded. "Is a body t' coot the edge fram avery sword in the kingdom, thaan?"

The big man's complexion was suffusing with blood and rage, and Joe didn't like the way the fellow's hands knotted about one another. The armorer wouldn't have to strangle a man in the normal fashion. He could just grab a victim's head and give a quick jerk, like a hunter finishing a wounded pheasant. . . .

"And after you have provided Arnault with the billet of steel, Master Joe," Ezekiel interjected—and thank goodness for the sardonic magician for a change, because he directed Arnault's smoldering eyes away from Joe. "Then I think you'll have to teach him your magical technique of boring the material."

The armorer didn't deign to nod.

"Right," said Joe, as though the false word were a catechism. Black gloom settled over his soul.

Joe didn't know anything about metalworking. If he *had* some background in metallurgy, he still wouldn't know how to adapt modern techniques to things Arnault could accomplish . . . which seemed to mean hammering bars into rough horseshoe shapes.

"Perhaps Arnault could weld a bundle of iron rods into a tube?" Estoril suggested. "About a yard long, you said?"

"Yaas, loidy," agreed the armorer with a massive nod.

"*No!*" gasped Joe.

Even Joe could visualize the blackened mass of weak spots and open holes that would result from somebody trying to weld a tube on a hand forge. Arnault wouldn't be making a gun, it'd be a bomb!

Joe's face cleared while the others stared—or glowered, in the cases of Arnault and Delendor's brothers—at him. "Estoril," he said, "you're brilliant! Now, how fast does this dragon move?"

"Yes, not only beautiful but wise beyond imagining," Delendor said, turning toward the princess. "I—"

"Del!" Estoril snapped, glancing fiercely toward Delendor, then looking away as if to emphasize that she'd' never seen him before in her life.

"For the most part, not very quickly," Ezekiel answered. Joe had already noticed that the magician was carrying out the spirit as well as the letter of King Morhaven's orders. "And it sleeps for long periods."

He smiled again. You didn't have to know Ezekiel for long to know what kind of news would cause him to smile.

"When the beast chooses to run, though," Ezekiel went on, "it can catch a galloping horse . . . as I understand *Sir* Delendor of Glenheim learned in times past."

Joe stared at Ezekiel and thought, *You cruel son of a bitch.*

Ezekiel scared him, the way looking eye-to-eye at a spider had scared him once. There wasn't anything in the magician that belonged in human society, despite the man's undoubted brains and knowledge.

"Right," said Joe as though he still thought he was speaking to a human being. "Would the dragon go around, say, a cast-iron kettle—" *did they have cast-iron kettles?* "—if it had a fuze burning to it?"

"The dragon walks through walls of fire," Delendor said. "I don't think we'll be able to burn it, Joe."

He sounded doubtful. Doubtful about his choice of a magician, Joe suspected.

"We won't try," Joe said in sudden confidence. "We'll blow the thing to hell and gone!"

His enthusiasm—the foreign wizard's enthusiasm—drew a gasp of delight and wonder from the assembled crowd; except, noticeably, for Ezekiel and Delendor's brothers.

"Now," said Joe, "we'll need to test it. What do you use for pipes here?"

"Poipes?" said Arnault.

"You know, Joe explained. "Water pipes."

"Pipes for water?" said Delendor. "Why, we have wells. Don't you have wells in your own country, Joe?"

"I have tubing drawn of lead, left over from my clepsydra," said Ezekiel.

He held up his index finger. "The outer size is this," he explained, "and the inner size—" he held up the little finger of the same hand "—is this."

"Perfect!" Joe said, wondering what a clepsydra was. "Great! Fetch me a six-inch length, that'll be enough, and I'll get back to making something to fill it with. Boy, that dragon's going to get his last surprise!"

Ezekiel stayed where he was, but Joe had more important things to deal with than enforcing instantaneous obedience. He hadn't gotten very far with his gunpowder, after all.

Joe had made gunpowder when in he was in grade school, but he'd never been able to make it correctly because of the cost. Now it *had* to be right, but cost didn't matter.

Charcoal was easy, then as now. As a kid, he'd ground up a charcoal briquette, using the face of a hammer and a saucepan abstracted from the kitchen.

Here, Ezekiel provided a mortar and a pestle whose sides sloped to a concave grinding surface which mated with the mortar's convex head, both of brass. Pieces of natural charcoal (which looked disconcertingly like scraps of burned wood) powdered more cleanly than briquettes processed with sawdust had done.

Joe poured the black dust into one of Ezekiel's screw-stoppered brass jars. He didn't bother wiping the pestle clean, because after all, he was going to mix all the ingredients at some point anyway.

Lumps of sulphur powdered as easily as bits of dried mud. Sulphur had been a cheap purchase at the drugstore also. The only complicating factor was that you didn't want to buy the jar of sulphur from the same druggist as sold you the saltpeter.

Saltpeter was the rub. Saltpeter was expensive, and it was supposed to provide seventy-five percent of the bulk of the powder; so Joe and his friends had changed the formula. It was as simple as that.

After all, they weren't trying to shoot a knight out of his armored saddle—or blow a dragon to kingdom come. They just wanted spectacular fireworks. Mixing the ingredients in equal parts gave a lot more hiss and spatter from a small jar of saltpeter than the "right" way would have done.

With his powdered sulphur in a second jar, Joe got to work on the saltpeter.

Ezekiel's store of the substance amounted to several

pounds, so far as Joe could judge the quantity in the heavy brass container. He didn't know precisely how much gunpowder it was going to take to blow up a dragon, but this ought to do the job.

The saltpeter crystals were a dirty yellow-white, like the teeth of Glam and Groag. They crushed beneath the mortar with a faint squeaking, unlike the crisp, wholesome sound the charcoal had made.

The spectators were getting bored. Kiki had snatched a hat and was now more the center of interest than Joe was. Servants formed a ring about the little animal and were making good-natured attempts to grab him as he bounced around them, cloak fluttering.

The spectators who weren't watching the monkey had mostly broken up into their own conversational groups. Delendor and his sister murmured about old times, while Glam and Groag discussed the fine points of unlacing a deer.

It had bothered Joe to feel that he was some sort of a circus act. He found that it bothered him more to think that he was a *boring* circus act, a tumbler whom everybody ignored while the lion tamer and trapeze artists performed in the other rings.

Almost everybody ignored him. As Joe mixed his test batch of powder—three measures of saltpeter and a half measure each of charcoal and sulphur (because he still couldn't for the life of him remember which of the pair was supposed to be fifteen percent and which ten)—he felt Ezekiel's eyes on his back. The magician's gaze was cold and veiled, like a container of dry ice.

And Ezekiel wasn't quite the only one watching with unabated interest as Joe went on with the procedure. Joe lifted his head to stretch his cramped shoulders. In a third-floor room across the courtyard—Joe's room, he thought, though he couldn't be sure—was a wan white face observing at a safe distance from Glam and Groag.

Mary's features were indistinct, but Joe felt the poor kid's concern.

He went back to mixing his ingredients. He felt better for the glimpse at the window.

"All right, Ezekiel," Joe said loudly to call *everybody's* attention back to him. "I'll need the tube now."

Ezekiel smiled and extended his hand with the length of lead pipe in it.

Joe was sure Ezekiel hadn't left the summer kitchen. The piece could have been concealed in the magician's sleeve all the time, but that left the question of how he'd known what Joe would want before Joe himself knew.

Being thought to be a magician in this culture was fine. Knowing a *real* magician was rather like knowing a real Mafioso. . . .

"Right," said Joe, staring at the pipe and thinking about the possible remainder of his life—unless he could find a People Mover going in the opposite direction. "Right. . . ."

Time for that later. He needed to close one end of the pipe before he filled it with powder. He could use Ezekiel's mortar to pound the soft metal into a seam, but that wasn't the job for which the piece of lab equipment had been designed.

Besides, the mortar's owner was watching.

"Arnault," Joe said briskly to the master armorer. "I need to close the end of this pipe. Do you have a hammer with you?"

"This poipe . . . ?" Arnault said, reaching out for the piece. When the armorer frowned, wrinkles gave his face almost the same surface as his cracked, stained leather apron.

He took the piece between his right thumb and index finger. When he squeezed, the metal flattened as if between a hammer and anvil.

Joe blinked. Arnault returned the pipe to him. The flattened end was warm.

Arnault didn't speak, but a smile of pride suffused his whole pitted, muscular being.

"Ah," said Joe. "Thank you."

Joe looked at the pipe he held, the glass funnel set

out in readiness, and the brass container of gunpowder. Either the cold or the shock of everything that'd been happening made his brain logy, because it took ten seconds of consideration before he realized that he was going to need a third hand. He glanced at the crowd.

Ezekiel was used to this type of work; Delendor was the guy whose life and career most depended on the job—

And Joe, for different reasons, didn't trust either one of them. "Estoril?" he said. "Princess? would you please hold this tube vertical while I pour the powder into it?"

Joe's eyes had scanned the window across the courtyard before settling back on the princess; but that was a silly thought and unworthy of him, even in his present state.

Estoril handled the pipe with the competence Joe already knew to expect from her. The spout of the funnel fit within the lead cylinder, so he didn't have to tell her not to worry if some of the gunpowder dribbled down.

The brass powder container was slick, heavy, and (when Joe took off his glove for a better grip) shockingly cold. He shook the jar as carefully as he could, dribbling a stream of the dirty-yellow gunpowder into the funnel and thence the pipe.

It sure didn't look black. Maybe he should've used more charcoal after all?

Drifting grains of sulphur gave the air a brimstone hint that reminded Joe of the immediately-previous stop on what had begun as a People Mover.

The tube was nearly full. Joe put down the items he held and took the tube from Estoril. "Arnault," he said, holding the almost-bomb to the armorer, "I'd like you to close this down to a little hole in the end. Can you do that?"

Arnault stared at the piece. It looked tiny in his hand. "Right," he said. "Doon to a coont haar."

Joe pursed his lips. "A little larger than that, I think," he said. "About the size of a straw."

Though, thinking about the sort of women who would

willingly consort with the master armorer, Arnault's description might have been quite accurate.

Granted that lead wasn't armor plate, it was still amazing to watch Arnault force the tube into the desired shape between the tips of his thumbs and index fingers. When he handed the result back, Joe couldn't imagine a machineshop back home improving on the job.

Nothing left to do but to complete the test.

Joe had been planning to take the bomb outside the walls of the palace, but now he had a better idea. The summer kitchen's three ovens were solid masonry affairs; and this was, after all, only a little bomb. . . .

Joe arranged it at the back of the center oven.

"Now, I want all of you to keep to the sides," Joe said, his voice deepened and multiplied by the cavity. When he straightened, he found everybody was staring at him from wherever they'd been standing before . . . except that Delendor and his brothers had moved up directly behind "the magician" to stare into the oven.

Ezekiel grinned.

Joe stuck his thumbs in his ears and waggled his fingers. "Back!" he shouted.

Kiki's four limbs gripped Delendor's head, completely hiding the youth's face. Glam and Groag hurtled into the crowd like elephants charging butt-first, doing a marvelous job of clearing the area in front of the oven.

"Right," said Joe, breathing heavily. "Now, if you'll all just keep it that way while I set the fuze."

From what he remembered, you were supposed to make your fuze by soaking string in a solution of gunpowder and letting it dry—or some damned thing. For this purpose, a bare train of powder would do well enough.

Joe dribbled a little pile of the foul-looking stuff at the base of the bomb, then ran the trail out to the mouth of the oven. Granted that he wasn't being graded on aesthetics, he still sure wished his black powder looked back.

"Now—" he said with his hand raised for a flourish.

Oops.

Joe screwed down the top on the powder container

and set it carefully on the ground to the side of the bank of ovens. All he needed was for a spark to get into *that*.

"Now," Joe repeated as the crowd watched him. "I'm going to light the fuze and—"

And neither he, not any of the people around him, had a match.

"Ah," he said, changing mental direction again. "Would somebody bring me a candle or—something, you know? I want to light the fuze."

"You want to light it *now*?" asked Ezekiel.

Joe nodded. He didn't understand the emphasis. "Ah, yeah," he said. 'Is there some reason—"

Ezekiel snapped his fingers. Something that looked like a tiny—no, it had to have been a spark—popped from his pointing index finger. The spark flicked the end of the train of gunpowder.

"Ge' back!" Joe shouted, waving his arms as he scrambled aside also. "Get clear, y'all!"

Ezekiel was smiling at him in cold satisfaction.

The pops and splutters of burning gunpowder echoed from the oven. Stinking white smoke oozed out of the door and hung in the cold air like a mass of raw cotton, opaque and evil looking.

Joe put his hands over his ears and opened his mouth to help equalize pressure against the coming blast. He wished he'd remembered to warn the locals that the bang would—

There was a pop. A stream of orange-red sparks spurted through the open oven door. Joe heard a whanging sound from within, a *whee!*—and the would-be bomb came sailing straight up the flue of the oven. It mounted skyward on a trail of white smoke and a rain of molten lead.

The crowd scattered, screaming in justified terror. Delendor picked up his sister and ran for the nearest doorway in a cloud of skirts. Even Ezekiel fled, though he did so with more judgment than any of the others: he flung himself into one of the cold ovens.

The rocket began to curve as the wall of the lead tube

melted unevenly. The only two people still watching it were Joe, in utter dismay; and Arnault, who stared out from the haze of his smoldering hair with a rapturous look on his face.

The rocket punched through one of the third-floor windows across from Joe's room. There was a faint *pop* from within. The remainder of the damaged window shivered outward into the courtyard.

Maybe a boxcar load of this "gunpowder" would daze a dragon. But probably not.

Arnault turned to Joe. The armorer's spark-lighted beard had gone out, but a wreath of hideous stench still wrapped him. "Moy, but yoor a cooning baastaard!" Arnault bellowed happily as he hugged Joe to him.

Joe squealed. His mother had always told him that if he persisted in playing with gunpowder he'd surely be killed, though he doubted she'd expected him to be crushed in an elephantine expression of joy. . . .

Arnault threw open his arms. Joe sprawled on the flagstones. He took a deep breath of the cold, sulphurous air and began coughing it out again.

Ezekiel crawled from the oven. His face was livid where it wasn't smudged with soot. For a moment, the magician stared upward toward the missing window, a gap in the array of diamond-paned reflections. A tiny wisp of smoke came out of the opening.

"You may think you're clever, destroying my laboratory that way!" he cried to Joe. "But it won't help your protegé against the dragon, you know. And *that's* what you're sworn to do!"

The magician turned and strode toward the door into the palace. His robes were flapping. The wisp of smoke from his room became a column. As Ezekiel reached the doorway, he flung dignity to the winds and began to run up the stairs.

Delendor reappeared, looking flushed and joyful. "Wow!" the prince said. "That's tremendous, Joe! My mother's spirit certainly led me right. Why, that dragon won't have a chance!"

"I'm glad you feel that way," said Joe as he got to his feet.

Joe's belly felt cold. What he'd done was sure-hell impressive . . . but it proved that he couldn't make gunpowder that would explode.

And that meant that Delendor was a dead duck.

There was a faint tap on Joe's door.

"Sure, come in," he mumbled without looking away from the window. The sun was still above the horizon, but in the shadowed courtyard beneath, servants and vehicles moved as if glimpsed through the water of a deep pool.

Mary slipped into the room. For a moment she poised beside the door, ready to flee. Then she asked, "Master Joe, am I disturbing you? If you need to plan all the little details of how you'll destroy the dragon, then I—"

Joe turned. The room was almost dark. The charcoal fire gave little light, and the low sun had to be reflected many times to reach Joe's leading-webbed windows.

"I *can't* destroy the dragon!" he said savagely. "I can't kill it, and I can't go home. And none of it's any fault of mine that *I* can see!"

Mary cowered back against the door. Her eyes were on Joe's face but her thin fingers fumbled to reopen the door.

"Aw, child, don't do that . . ." he said, reaching out— then grimacing in self-disgust when he saw her wince at the gesture. "Look," he said, "I'm just frustrated that . . . well, that I made things worse."

Mary began fussing with the fire, adding small bits of charcoal from the terra cotta container beside the fireplace. "And so now you want to leave?" she asked.

"I always wanted to leave," Joe said. He tried to keep the force of his emotion out of his voice. "Mary, I never wanted to *come* here, it just happened. But it doesn't look like I'll ever be able to leave, either."

"But Joe," she said, lifting her big frightened eyes to

his, "only a great magician could have done what you did this morning. I don't see why you think you're failing."

"Because I'm not a chemist," Joe explained.

He turned away from the pain in the maid's expression. The courtyard was still deeper in shadow. "Because I'm not much of anything, if you want to know the truth. I did the only thing I know how to do—from when I was a kid. And that's not going to help a damned bit if the dragon's half what everybody tells me it is."

Mary touched the hem of Joe's cloak diffidently. "I think you're something," she said.

"What I am," said Joe, "is the guy who told Delendor he'd fix it so he'd kill the dragon. Which was a lie. And Delendor's a decent kid who deserved better 'n that."

A four-horse carriage drove out of the stables across the courtyard. The streets would be pitch dark soon, so the lanterns on the vehicle's foreposts were lighted. They waked glimmers of vermilion lacquer and gilt on the carriage's polished sides.

"I'm sure you'll find a—" Mary began.

The carriage driver looked up at Joe's window. *Great god almighty! It was the Mongolian!*

Joe spun to his door. He had barely enough control to jiggle the latch open—it was simple but not of a present-day familiar type—instead of breaking off the slender handle that lifted the bar. His shoes skidded as he ran to the nearest staircase, but he managed not to fall.

At the back of Joe's mind was the knowledge that somebody—fate, the Mongolian, sunspots, *whatever*—might be playing with him. He could reach the courtyard and find that the coach had driven out the main gate and into the city . . . or simply had disappeared.

But Joe had to try. He should've had better sense to begin with than to think he could do any good in a world with dragons and real sorcerers. Since he'd screwed things up even worse, the only honorable course was to get himself the hell out of the way at the first chance that was offered.

Sure, that was honorable. And besides, it was surviv-able.

This was a servants' staircase, helical with stone steps that were just as slick as the floors. There wasn't any mamby-pamby nonsense about stair railings, either. By god, there were things Joe knew that he could teach these people . . .

Unfortunately, none of those things included dragon-slaying methods; and nobody in Hamisch was going to be much interested in staircase and bathroom designs from the guy who got Prince Delendor killed.

Joe swept down on a trio of maids. They flattened to the curving walls in terror when "the new magician" gal-loped past them.

The two long flights took him—well, Joe didn't know how long it took him. He knew if he slipped, he'd knock himself silly for sure; and he suspected that was just the sort of joke the Mongolian had in mind to torment a perfectly innocent ghostwriter.

He reached the ground floor between the laundry room and the buttery. A liveried servant dozed on a chair beside the courtyard door. Joe slammed past him, star-tling the man shriekingly awake as though the morning's rocket had been set off again between his coattails.

The carriage waited in the twilit courtyard. The swar-thy driver smirked past the coachlamp toward Joe. Vague voices drifted between the stone walls, and concertina music came from somewhere in the servants' quarters.

Joe put his foot on the carriage step and gripped the silver doorlatch. It was warmer than the surrounding air, but it wouldn't have stopped Joe if he'd thought the cold metal would flay the skin from his palm.

"Stop, Master Joe!" somebody wailed.

The carriage door started to swing open. Joe looked over his shoulder.

Mary had followed him down the stairs. Her eyes were streaming tears.

Her arms held out to him the attaché case he'd aban-doned when he saw his chance to go home.

Much the way Joe had abandoned Mary and his promise to Delendor.

"Right," said Joe. He hopped down from the carriage step and took the case from the maid.

"I don't think I'll need this for a while," he said to the sobbing woman. "But it may as well stay in my room for now. With me."

The driver clucked something to his horses. The coach began to move in toward the archway, but Joe didn't look back as he guided Mary into the palace.

As a result, Joe didn't see the clawed, skeletally-thin hand that pulled shut the carriage door from the inside.

A horde of minuscule demons was sweeping shattered equipment from Ezekiel's workbench. They suddenly froze in place, then formed a flying arrowhead which curved halfway around the laboratory before vanishing into the dimension from which the creatures had come. Their voices made a tiny eeping that persisted several seconds after the demons themselves disappeared.

"What's that?/What happened?" Glam and Groag blurted together in high-pitched voices. Each brother slapped one hand to his swordhilt and covered his face with the other, as though they thought the swarm of demons might flee down their throats—

As indeed the panicky demons might do, and much good the outflung hands would be in that event.

Ezekiel made one attempt to regain control by gesturing. Then he *heard* what the demons were wailing and stepped to an undamaged window—the center of the three casements was boarded up—to glance down into the courtyard.

"Great God!" he muttered as he jumped back again from the glass—and much good a stone wall would be if the *being* below chose to act against Ezekiel.

"What's going on?" Glam demanded in his full, booming voice. He'd regained confidence now that the flying demons were gone, and there seemed to be no room within his thick skull for wonder at what had frightened the horde away.

"I saw a . . ." the magician said. "A being. A being from the 7th Plane."

Groag strode over to the window Ezekiel had vacated and looked out. "You mean Delendor's tame wizard?" he said. "He don't look any great shakes to me."

"Joe Johnson is down there?" Ezekiel asked sharply. "You see him?"

"Yeah, sure I see him," Groag said, testy with his sudden fear and his present, false, assumption of safety. "He's getting into a carr—no, he ain't. He's going—" the big man squinted for a better look in the twilight "—back inside."

Ezekiel swallowed. The lingering smell of brimstone seemed sharper. "What is the—carriage doing?" he asked with as much nonchalance as he could muster.

"Huh?" Groag answered. "It just drove off, out the gate. Why?"

"Whadda ya mean, 7th Plane?" Glam asked. "You mean a demon?"

As though the word had been a summons, one of Ezekiel's pack of demons thrust its head back into the laboratory, then followed with its entire body. The creature was blue and more nearly the size of a gnat than a fly.

The demon gripped a shard of broken alembic and tried to lift the piece with a metallic shimmering of its wings. After it quivered vainly for several seconds, hundreds more of its fellows poured through the hole in the continuum and resumed their duties. Bits and pieces of wreckage rose and vanished.

"Not a demon," the magician said, speaking as much to himself as to the pair of humans with him in his laboratory. "Demons are beings of the 3d Plane, below rather than above ours. The inhabitants of the 7th Plane are—"

"But it's not this Joe character that we're supposed to worry about, then?" Glam interrupted.

"If he communes with creatures of the 7th Plane, then

you'd *better* worry about him!" Ezekiel snapped. The magician's vehemence straightened the two hulking princes like a slap. "The—folk of the 7th Plane don't meddle in human affairs, precisely . . . but they offer choices. They have terrible powers, but they won't be guided by humans. *Nobody* deals with them."

"Well then, what—" Groag said, his brow furrowing.

"Except," Ezekiel continued, "that the Princess Blumarine is said to have done so."

"You mean Delendor's mother . . . ?" Glam said in what was for him a considerable mental stretch. "But she's dead. Ain't she?"

"Blumarine couldn't save her beloved knight," Ezekiel said savagely. "And she won't be able to save her son, either. Do you hear?"

He glared around the room. *"Do you hear?"*

The waves of tiny demon wings rose and trembled with the amplitude of the magician's voice.

"Ah, good morning, Joe," said Delendor. "I was just wondering how preparations for my dragon-slaying are coming?"

Joe looked at the prince sourly. "You're up bright and early," he said.

"Well, ah, yes," Delendor agreed, looking around Joe's room with vague interest. "I *do* get up early, you know; and besides, Estoril and I are going on a picnic today."

Mary, wearing a sturdy pair of boots in place of her usual slippers, curtsied. She was blushing furiously. Kiki hopped from the prince's shoulder and chirped at Mary's feet, but the maid seemed unwilling even to admit the monkey was there.

"Ah, you're going on a picnic also, Joe?" Delendor added. His lips pursed. "But with an arbalest?"

"What we're doing," Joe said, "is taking a look at your blasted dragon."

"Really?" said Delendor. "Goodness. Why?"

"Because I haven't got a clue as what to do about a

damned dragon!" Joe snarled. "Because I'm not a magician! But I *might* be able to help if I had the faintest notion of what I'm supposed to be dealing with."

He didn't so much calm as run through the temporary enthusiasm that anger gave him. "And I, well, I'd really like to help things out here. Mary said she'd guide me. Apparently the dragon's pretty close to the city already."

Delendor nodded with his lips still pursed. "Yes," he said, "I wanted to go to the glade north of the walls where we picnicked when we were little, but Clarkson says that's not a good idea. But why the arbalest?"

The youth's expression grew tight and angry. "You're not planning to—"

"No, I'm *not* planning to shoot the dragon with a crossbow!" Joe blazed. "Though I sure as hell would if I thought it'd do a damned bit of good."

"*Oh!*" squealed Mary.

The maid had stuffed rags in her boots to line them down to the size of her tiny feet. Kiki grabbed the end of one and ran around in a circle, attempting to bind Mary's ankles together. Joe snatched at the monkey with his free hand.

Kiki bounded up the wall, off the ceiling, and back onto Delendor's shoulder in an impressive display of acrobatics—and judgment, given the fury that bent Joe's groping hand into a claw.

"Bad, bad monkey!" Delendor chided.

"Look, Delendor," Joe continued in an attempt to sound calm. "I just figured I ought to be armed if I'm going to look for this thing."

"Oh, well," the prince said, his face clearing. "Well, I'll loan you a sword then, Joe. It's more fitting to your position, though I suppose technically a magician isn't a—"

"No, I don't want a sword," Joe interrupted. "I don't know anything about swords except they're long enough to trip me if I need to run . . . as I figure I'll want to, pretty soon now."

"Ah," said Delendor. He didn't look as though he

would have approved if he understood. His eyes wandered; focused on Mary, who'd taken off her boot to restuff it; and snapped back to Joe.

"Delendor," Joe said, "I don't know anything about crossbows either. Or guns, if it comes to that. Arnault had to crank this—" he hefted the weapon in his right hand with some difficulty "—up for me."

Joe tried to smile as though he meant it. "Mary," he went on with a nod to the maid, "warned me not to put an arrow in the thing until I was out in open country. It's just a security blanket, but the good lord knows I need some security."

Delendor reached a decision. He nodded enthusiastically. "I understand," he said. "A very noble, if I may say so, undertaking. I'll tell Estoril that we won't be able to picnic today, because I'm going with my magician to view the threat to the kingdom first hand."

"Ah," Joe said. "Ah, are you really sure you want to do this?"

"I certainly do," the prince responded firmly. "And not only that, but we'll go on foot. The—fate—of Sir Delendor, my namesake, suggests that horses aren't to be trusted in the vicinity of the dragon."

Joe nodded. It just might be, he thought, that Delendor wasn't a complete airhead.

"Well, it's certainly a beautiful day to be out in the country, isn't it?" Delendor gushed. "Bright sun, crisp breeze . . . just cool enough to be bracing."

Joe sneezed. "No people around," he said. "Not a soul."

He looked back over his shoulder. The pennoned turrets on the city walls were still visible every time the road rolled upward. They'd set out on the main turnpike between Glenheim and Hamisch, so there should've been *some* traffic.

Unless the dragon was a lot closer than the farmers from outlying districts, now thronging the streets of Hamisch, had insisted.

It occurred to Joe that the farmers might be more

than a little upset about the lack of progress in dealing with the beast that was devastating their lands. If some of the nobles who were supposed to slay such threats could be enticed into proximity to the dragon, then one or the other was going to be killed.

And the farmers might think either result was a good one.

"I don't think we should be walking right up the road," Mary said, echoing Joe's next thought as it formed.

Delendor looked at the brush fringing the sides of the highway, then tapped the road's cobblestone surface with his green leather shoe. The edges of the road were apparently cut back every few years, but at the moment they were a tangle of saplings, bushes, and creepers—thick enough to provide concealment for somebody a few yards in, but not too dense to get through without a machete.

"Well, it might be more comfortable for walking," he said judiciously. "But my sword would catch. I don't think we'll do that."

"We'll do that," said Joe grimly as he forced his way into the brush.

Joe's legs were holding up—they'd walked less than a mile—but his arms were aching with the weight of the crossbow. The nut that held back the thumb-thick cord had a slot in it to grip the nock of the bolt. At least Joe didn't have the bolt falling off every time he let the weapon point down, the way he'd expected.

The bolt—the quarrel—had a thick wood shaft and three wooden feathers. The head was square and steel, with a four-knobbed face instead of a point. It looked dangerous as hell—

And if the dragon had shrugged off showers of similar missiles, as everybody assured Joe the beast had, then the dragon was Hell on four legs.

Kiki was having the time of his life, swinging around the three humans. He was so light that the branches of saplings, none of which were more than twelve feet tall, were sufficient to support his cheerful acrobatics.

Delendor, last in the line, had rotated his swordbelt so that the weapon in its scabbard hung behind him like a stiff tail. It didn't get in his way after all.

The prince's tasseled fur cloak, his ruffed tunic, and his ballooning silk breeches, on the other hand, seemed to cling and fray on every thorn. Delendor became increasingly—vocally—irritated about the fact.

"Joe," he called, "this doesn't make any sense at all. We could never escape if the dragon charged us, but the thorns wouldn't slow the beast a bit."

"We couldn't outrun it anyway," Joe said, doggedly forcing his way between a clump of saplings. "All we're trying to do is stay out of sight."

"The dragon stops when it makes a kill," Mary said. "The others will have time to get away while it eats."

The careless, matter-of-fact statement contrasted unpleasantly with the maid's timid voice.

"Well, perhaps in that case I should be in the lead," Delendor suggested. "Because my rank is—*drat!* Where do all these blackberry vines come from?"

If the prince had paid attention to what he was doing rather than to his concept of *noblesse oblige*, he'd've gone around those vines the way his companions had.

"You know," Delendor resumed a moment later, "this makes even less sense than I'd thought. We're making so much noise that we'll never sneak up on the—"

Joe froze with one foot lifted. He hissed, "Hush!"

"—dragon. I've done enough hunting to know—*ulp!*"

Mary had turned and clamped her hand over Delendor's mouth with surprising strength. "Oh, please, Prince!" she whispered. "*Please* obey Master Joe."

Joe put his foot down very carefully. Something that clanked and wheezed like a steam locomotive was coming up the road toward them. There wasn't much doubt about what the something was.

The dragon came around a sweeping bend only fifty yards away. Its color was the red of glowing iron.

The dragon probably wasn't any longer than the thirty-odd yards Ezekiel had claimed for it . . . but seeing a

creature of the unimaginably great size was very different
from hearing the words spoken.

No wonder the knights—and the crossbowmen—had
been unable to harm the thing.

The dragon was covered with bony scutes similar to
those of a crocodile, and the beast's general shape was
crocodile-like as well: so low-slung that the long jaws
almost brushed the cobblestones, with a massive body
carried on four short legs. The upper and lower rows
of the dragon's teeth overlapped like the spikes of an
Iron Maiden.

The dragon's claws sparked on the roadway. Its breath
chuffed out a reek of decay which enveloped Joe as he
peered from the brush in amazement.

Well, he'd come to look at the dragon to determine
what were its weak spots.

There weren't any.

They'd have to get back to Hamisch as fast as they
could—making the necessary wide circuit to avoid the
dragon. The beast would reach the city in a few tens of
minutes, and the only hope of the people inside was to
scatter. The walls wouldn't last a—

"*Kikikikiki!*" shrieked the monkey. It hurled a bit of
seedpod as it charged the dragon.

"Kiki!" cried Delendor in a voice almost as highpitched
as his pet's. The prince whisked his sword from its sheath
and crossed the expanse of brush between himself and
the highway in three deerlike leaps.

With Mary running after him, an equally athletic,
equally quixotic, demonstration.

"For god's sake!" Joe screamed. He tried to aim his
arbalest. A loop of honeysuckle was caught around the
right arm of the bow. "Come back! Come back!"

The dragon didn't charge, but its head swung with
horrifying speed to clop within a finger's breadth of Kiki.
The monkey's cries rose into a sound like an electronic
watch alarm.

Kiki hurled himself back into the brush. Delendor continued to run forward, with Mary right behind him—
casting doubt on the evolutionary course of intelligence.

"Get down!" Joe cried. "*Don't*, for god's sake—"

He slipped his bow loose of the vines and raised the weapon. He'd fired a rifle a couple times but the crossbow had a knob rather than a shoulder stock.

There weren't any proper sights. Joe tried to aim along the bolt's vertical fin, but the weapon's heavy muzzle wobbled furiously around a six-inch circle. The dragon was only twenty feet away, and Joe was going to miss it if he—

Delendor swung his sword in a swift, glittering arc. It rang on the dragon's snout as though it had struck an anvil. The blade shattered and the hilt, vibrating like a badly-tuned harmonica, flew out of Delendor's hand.

Delendor yelped and lost his footing. He hit the cobblestones butt-first, which was just as well in the short run because the dragon's jaws slammed where the prince's torso had been.

"*Get out of the*—" Joe shrieked.

"Take me!" Mary cried, waving her arms to catch the monster's attention as she stepped on Delendor's swordhilt.

Mary's foot flew in the air. She hit the ground in a flurry of skirts.

The dragon paused, faced with two victims ten feet apart. It opened its jaws wider. The maw was the size of a concert grand with the lid up. The interior of the dragon's mouth was as white as dried bone.

I'll never have a better chance, thought Joe as he squeezed the under-lever trigger of his crossbow. The muzzle dropped as the cord slammed forward.

Joe whanged his bolt into the roadway in an explosion of sparks.

The dragon snorted. It started to—

For Pete's sake, it was arching its short neck, then its back. Its monstrous, clawed forelegs were off the ground—

The sight should've been as ridiculous as that of *Fantasia*'s crocodiles doing *The Dance of the Hours* . . . but this close to the creature, it was more like watching an ICBM rising from its silo in preparation to launch.

The dragon was quivering in a tetanic arch, making

little whimpering sounds. Its belly plates were red like the scutes of its back and sides, but there were fine lines of yellow skin where the plates met.

There was a hole where the lower jaw joined the first plate covering the underside of the neck. The hole didn't look large, but blood was bubbling furiously out of it.

Joe's quarrel had ricocheted into what might very well be the only vulnerable point in the dragon's armor.

The dragon rose onto the claws of its hind feet. Its tail was stiff. The beast's armor squealed under the strain to which convulsing muscles were subjecting it.

Mary and Delendor sat up, staring at the monster that towered above them. Their legs were splayed, and they supported their torsos on their hands.

"Wow!" said the prince. Joe, fifty feet back in the brush, couldn't come up with anything more suitable for the occasion.

Kiki hopped onto Joe's shoulder. He made what were almost purring sounds as he stroked Joe's hair.

The dragon completed its arc and toppled backwards. It hit the ground with a crash.

Its limbs and tail continued to pummel the ground for hours, like the aftershocks of an earthquake.

Though there were eight yoke of oxen hitched to the sledge, they wheezed and blew with the effort of dragging the dragon's head, upside down, into the palace courtyard. The beast's tongue lolled out to drag the flagstones, striking sparks from them.

Prince Delendor sat astride the stump of the beast's neck. He waved his swordhilt and beamed as he received the boisterous cheers of the crowd.

"Must be the whole city down there," Groag said glumly as he watched from one window of Ezekiel's laboratory.

"Must be the whole *country*," Glam corrected in a similar tone. " 'Cept us."

"*Lookit* that!" said Groag.

"Then get out of the way and I will," snapped the

magician, tapping Groag on the shoulder and making little shooing motions with his hand. The big prince stepped aside, shaking his head.

The wreckage was gone from the laboratory, but neither the middle window nor the broken glassware had been replaced. A tinge of brimstone from the rocket still clung to the air.

The scene in the courtyard did nothing to improve Ezekiel's humor. King Morhaven was kneeling to Delendor, though the youth quickly dismounted as from a horse and stood Morhaven erect again.

The cheering rattled the laboratory's remaining windows.

"He'll make Delendor co-ruler as a result of this, you know," Ezekiel said. "And heir."

He turned and glared savagely at the two royal brothers. "You *know* that, don't you?"

Glam twisted the toe of his boot against the floor, as though trying to grind something deep into the stone. "Well," he said, "you know. . . . You know, if the little prick killed the dragon, I dunno what else the ole man could do. Lookit the *teeth* on that sucker."

"Don't be a bigger fool than god made you!" Ezekiel snarled. "Delendor didn't have anything to do with killing the dragon. It was that magician of his! That *damned* magician."

He made a cryptic sign. A swarm of twinkling demons whisked out of their own plane. Their tiny hands compressed globes of air into a pair of shimmering lenses.

Ezekiel stared through the alignment, then stepped back. "There," he said to the brothers. "Look at that."

Glam looked through the tubeless telescope, despite an obvious reluctance to put his eye close to the miniature demons who formed it. The lenses were focused on the dragon's neck. The wound there was marked with a flag of blood.

"Well," said Glam as his brother shouldered him aside, "that's where he stabbed the sucker, right?"

"Idiot!" Ezekiel said. "The wound's *square*, from a crossbow bolt. And who do you see carrying a crossbow?"

"Oh-h-h," said the brothers together.

Behind the sledge, almost lost in the crowd that mobbed Delendor, was the prince's magician—carrying a heavy arbalest. A servant girl clung to him, squeezed by the people cheering their master.

"I don' get it," Groag said. "Lots a guys shot it with crossbows before, din't they? I heard that, anyhow."

"Of course they did, oaf!" said Ezekiel. "This was obviously an enchanted arbalest which struck the one vulnerable part of the dragon's armor—even though a spot on the underside of the beast's throat *couldn't* be hit by a crossbow bolt."

He swung the telescope slightly by tapping the manicured nail of his index finger against the objective lens. Tiny demons popped and crackled at the contact.

Groag glared at the crossbow. "Don' look so special ta me," he said.

"I don' get it," Glam said. "If he got a crossbow ta kill the dragon, then what was all that stuff with the powder and fire t'other morning? Some kinda joke, was it?"

The magician grimaced. "I'm not sure," he admitted, glancing around his laboratory and remembering how it had looked *before* a rocket sizzled through the center window. "But I think. . . ."

Ezekiel had been shrinking down into his velvet robes. Now he shook himself and rose again to his full height.

"I think," the magician resumed, "that Joe Johnson has been brought here from a very great distance by a—7th Plane inhabitant. He initially attempted to use the magic of his own region here, but the correspondences differed. Rather than work them out, he found it easier to adapt *our* magic to the task."

"You promised us," said Glam in a dangerous voice, "that there wouldn't be no problem with Delendor. An' now you say there is."

"I can take care of your brother easily enough," said

Ezekiel in a carefully neutral tone. "But only after Joe Johnson is out of the way. Do you understand?"

Glam guffawed in a voice that rattled the window even against the cheering voices below. "You bet we do!" he said. "Cold iron's proof agin magic, right?"

"Ah, belt up," said his brother, staring through the telescope again. "You charge in like a bull in a boo-dwa, you just screw things up. *I'll* handle this one."

As he spoke, Groag marked carefully the servant to whom Joe Johnson gave his enchanted crossbow.

"And *you* said you weren't a magician!" Delendor crowed.

"Del, careful!" Estoril warned, but the prince had already jumped into a hell-clicking curvette too energetic for Joe's small room.

The feather in Delendor's peaked cap flattened against the ceiling. Kiki bounded from the prince's shoulder and caromed off the four walls before cringing against Joe's ankles.

Joe wrapped the quilt around him tighter. Servants had built up the fire next to which he huddled in his armchair. Despite that and the quilt, he still felt cold enough that the monkey's warm body was surprisingly pleasant.

He wondered where Mary had gone—and whether she'd be back tonight as usual.

He sneezed again.

"Bless you!" said Delendor, slightly more subdued. He sat down again on the cedar chest beside Estoril. "You know," he bubbled to the princess, "I just swung, *swish!*"

"I believe I heard that, yes," Estoril said dryly. Joe thought she winked at him, but he was blowing his nose and couldn't be sure.

Did Lancelot catch colds while carrying out deeds of derring-do? More to the point, did Lancelot's faithful servant catch colds?

"I didn't even know that I'd killed it until I saw it topple over backward!" Delendor continued, oblivious to everything but his own—false—memory. "Joe here's magic guided my thrust straight to the monster's throat! Except. . . ."

Delendor's handsome brow furrowed. "You know, I thought I'd *cut* at the dragon instead of thrusting." He brightened again. "Just shows how memory can play tricks on you, doesn't it?"

Joe sneezed.

Maybe now that the dragon was dead, he'd be able to go back home . . . though somehow, after the primary colors of life in Hamisch, even the Senator and his shenanigans seemed gray.

"But here, I've been doing all the talking," Delendor said, showing that he had *some* awareness of the world beyond him. "Essie, what was it you came back from Glenheim to tell us?"

Estoril looked at her hands, laid neatly in a chevron on the lap of her lace-fronted dress. "To tell the truth," she began, "I'm not sure. . . ."

"You know," the prince resumed, as though Estoril had finished her thought instead of merely her words, "when Joe arrived here, I really wanted him to find my enchanted princess."

Delendor fumbled within his puff-fronted tunic. "But now that you're back, Essie, I—well, I don't think about it very much."

He opened the oval locket and handed it to Estoril. From the flash of lamplight as the object passed, Joe knew it was still a mirror so far as he was concerned. He roused himself to ask, "Princess, what do *you* see in it?"

Estoril smiled. "My face," she said. "But the locket is very old—and it belonged to Del's mother."

She returned the locket to Delendor. "The Princess Blumarine was a very good woman," she said carefully. "But from what Katya told me, she was very—"

A sort of smile, wry but good-humored, flicked Estoril's mouth. "Powerful would be the wrong word, I think. The Princess Blumarine was very learned. I'm sure that the mirror shows her son whatever he says it does."

Delendor gave her a look of prim horror. "Essie!" he said. "Of *course* I wouldn't lie to you!"

Estoril glanced at the windows. They were again gray traceries of leading that barely illuminated the room. "Master Joe," the princess said, "would you like us to summon lamps?"

"Huh?" said Joe, aroused from his doze. "Oh, no—I mean . . . after you leave, that is, I think I'll just sit here and hope my sinuses decide to drain."

The problem wasn't just the cold breeze—and being out in it all day while the trophy was dragged to the palace. The shock of everything he'd been through today and the past three days had weakened Joe, leaving him prey to a bug.

"Well," said Estoril as she stood up, "we were just leaving."

"We . . . ?" said Delendor, though he hopped to his feet also.

"Are leaving," Estoril repeated. "And we're going to send some hot soup up to Joe."

"Oh, I'm not really—" Joe began.

"Which he will drink *all* of," the princess continued in a tone with as much flexibility as the dragon's armor.

Estoril opened the door and pointed Delendor into the hall; but then she paused. "Master Joe," she said softly, "the kingdom owes its safety to you. And I owe you Delendor's life—"

"Yes, yes," the prince broke in over Estoril's shoulder. "We owe it all to you, Joe."

"I wouldn't want you to think," Estoril continued as though there had been no interruption, "that *we* are unaware of precisely what you've accomplished. Or that we're ungrateful for your tact."

"It wasn't—" Joe said, but there was no way he could explain just what it *was* since he didn't have a clue himself. He started to get up.

"No, stay right there," Estoril ordered in her head nurse/mother persona.

"Kiki?" called Delendor. "*Kiki?*"

The monkey peeked out from between Joe's feet. Kiki had wrapped himself in a corner of the quilt also. After a moment, and with obvious reluctance, the little creature sprang across the cold floor and back on his master's shoulder.

"Remember to drink your soup," Estoril called as she pulled the door closed behind her.

Joe relaxed again. He missed the warmth of Kiki, though. Estoril was quite a lady. Smart and tough, but not cold for all that. She could've made the best ruler of anybody Joe had met yet in Hamisch, but it was obvious that wouldn't happen while there were sons around.

For that matter, Estoril probably couldn't get elected President, either, so long as there was some male boob with a fluent smile and the right connections to run against her.

Delendor wasn't a bad kid, and in a few years he wouldn't be a kid. He'd proved he had guts enough when he charged the dragon—like a damned fool! Maybe with his sister behind to do the thinking for the next while, Delendor could turn out to be a useful king.

Joe wasn't sure whether he was awake or dreaming. The coals in the fireplace were a mass of white ash, but they continued to give off heat.

If he got up and looked through the window behind him, would he really see the head of a dragon in the courtyard? Would he even see a courtyard?

But the warmth was good, and Joe really didn't want to move. Whatever reality was would keep. . . .

Something that sounded like a dropped garbage can came banging its way down the hall. The dragon's claws had sounded like that on the roadway—if there was a dragon, if there was a road. The claws hadn't echoed, but they'd been louder because the beast was so—

Joe's door burst open under the stroke of an armored hand. The latch flew across the room, bar in one direction and bracket in the other. A figure in full armor stood in the doorway with a drawn sword.

"You're in league with sundry devils, magician," the

figure boomed in Glam's voice—muffled by coming through the pointed faceplate of a pig's-head basinet. "But your time's come now!"

Joe's skin flushed as though he were coming out of a faint. He jumped to his feet, slinging aside the quilt—

And fell on his face in front of Glam.

A pane of the window behind Joe blasted into the room like storm-blown ice. There was a *blang!* many times louder than the sound of Glam knocking the door open. Joe twisted, trying unsuccessfully to get his feet back under him in the worst nightmare he'd had since—

Since jumping from that demon-wracked Hell into Delendor's carriage, a detached, analytical part of his mind told him.

Glam toppled over on his pointed faceplate. Amazing how much noise a suit of plate armor makes when you drop it to a stone floor. . . .

Delendor, Estoril, and a crowd of servants burst into the room—led by Mary with a lantern and a terrified expression.

"Stop right where you are, Glam!" Delendor shouted. The youth's right hand kept dipping to his empty scabbard. Lack of a sword hadn't kept him from charging Glam as blithely as he had the dragon in the morning.

"Oh, Master Joe," Mary said, kneeling on the stones as Joe managed to rise into a squat. "I saw Glam coming down the hall, so I ran to get help."

"You're all right, then?" Delendor said in amazement. He finally took in the fact that the awkward sprawl on the floor was Glam, not Joe; and that Glam wasn't moving.

Which surprised the hell out of Joe, too, now that he had time to think about it.

"You lot," Estoril ordered, gesturing to a pair of the huskier servants. "Stand the brute up again."

The princess had come running also; and it couldn't have been because she thought Glam in a rage would spare a woman. "Joe, what happened?"

"I'm damned if I know," Joe muttered. "Except that—"

He looked accusingly toward the prince's shoulder. Kiki cowered behind Delendor's head, then peeked over his master's feathered cap.

"—except that I know your little pet tied my shoelaces, Delendor," Joe concluded.

"Then you should thank him, Joe," said Estoril in a voice carefully purged of all emotion. "Because he seems to have saved your life."

She pointed. The fins of a heavy quarrel stood out slightly from the square hole in the center of Glam's breastplate. Crossbows here might not be able to penetrate dragons easily, but they sure punched through steel armor a treat.

Joe looked over his shoulder at the pane missing from the casement. The bolt that blew it out could've been fired from any of a dozen rooms across the courtyard, he supposed; but Joe wasn't in any real doubt as to whose hand had been on the trigger.

Not a bad time to fall on his face.

Delendor swept his hat off and bowed to Joe. The faces of all those who'd come to rescue Joe were suffused with awe.

"Through *iron*," the prince said, speaking for all of them. "What an amazingly powerful magician!"

"I did *not* tell you to kill the foreign magician, Groag," said Ezekiel. He pitched his voice in a compromise between being threatening and keeping anybody in the hall from overhearing.

"And I most particularly didn't tell you—you, a layman!—to attempt using a magician's own weapons against him!"

"B-b-but—" Groag said. His hands clenched into fists the size of deer hams. The tears squeezing from his eyes could have been either from grief for his brother or from rage.

Or from fear. In which case *both* the men in Ezekiel's laboratory were afraid of Joe Johnson.

"Although the thought of using the foreigner's magic

against him wasn't a bad one," Ezekiel added mildly, now that he was sure Groag wasn't going to pull him apart with his bare hands.

The magician's workbench had been partly refurbished into a production line. In a large glass vat, minuscule demons swam though a dark sludge. The demons' blue wings and scales sparkled as the creatures rose to the surface in waves, then submerged for another pass, thoroughly mixing the constituents of the thick mass.

Another work-gang of demons lifted tiny shovelsful of the sludge and spread it on a copper plate pierced with thousands of identical holes. Still more demons hovered and blew their hot breath on the bottom of the plate, keeping it just warm to the touch.

Groag stared at the operation for a moment. "Whazat?" he demanded.

"That," said Ezekiel, "was what you would have done if you'd had any sense."

"You din't tell—"

"You didn't ask!" the magician snapped.

He cleared his throat. "It was obvious to me," Ezekiel resumed in the dry, supercilious voice of a haughty lecturer, "that Joe Johnson's flame magic required some amendments to work here. I consulted my sources to learn the secret of those changes. Thus—"

Ezekiel gestured. "The ingredients were correct, though the proportions had to be modified slightly. Most important, they have to be mixed wet so that each *kernel* of powder retains the proper proportion of each ingredient."

Groag leaned to get a better look at the flowing sludge. His nose almost touched the surface. The wave of mixers broke upward just then; one of the demons yanked a hair out of Groag's nostril before resubmerging.

"Ouch!"

"After the mixing is complete," Ezekiel continued with a satisfied smirk, "the material is spread here—" he indicated the plate "—and dried at low heat. When that process is almost complete, my minions will form the material into kernels by extruding it through the holes in the plate."

Groag, covering his nose with his left hand, furrowed his brow and stared at the production line while a thought slowly formed. At last he said, "So what?"

The magician sighed. "Yes," he said, "I rather thought that might be the next question. Well, my boy, I'll show you 'what.' "

He gestured. A squad of demons whisked together the grains of gunpowder which had already been forced through the plate and carried them to a glass bottle of a size to hold a lady's perfume. When the demons were done, there was just enough room left for Ezekiel to insert the stopper firmly into the bottle's neck.

"When this batch is complete," the magician said as she picked up the bottle and walked to one of the undamaged windows, "there will be enough of the material to fill the brass container on the end of the bench."

He slid the casement up in its frame, then set the bottle on the ledge. A cold breeze rushed into the laboratory, making the oil lamps gutter. A glittering demon began to curvette above the bottle like a blowfly over a corpse.

"If you were to take that large container into Joe Johnson's room tomorrow evening while everyone is at dinner," Ezekiel continued as he stepped back, "you could conceal it under the chair in which he sits. And when Joe Johnson returns to his room—"

Ezekiel gestured. The demon shot straight down and reached a tiny arm through the bottle. When Ezekiel snapped his fingers, there was a spark from the demon's hand and the gunpowder detonated with a tremendous crash.

Groag bellowed in fear. Even the magician stepped backward, startled by the vehemence of what he'd achieved. His hand brushed his fine, gray beard and came away sparkling with slivers of glass.

Ezekiel cleared his throat. His ears rang.

He thought his own voice sounded thin as he concluded, "—*that* might happen to our foreign friend!"

The lock of Joe Johnson's door hadn't been repaired, so Groag didn't need a key to make a surreptitious entry into the magician's room.

Nobody would remark on Groag's absence at dinner. They'd just assume he was still sulking about the way the ole man fawned on Delendor. They'd 've been right any other time, too.

They'd see how long that poof Delendor lasted, once his tame magician was splattered all across the walls!

There was a small lamp burning in the room. It provided the only light, now, because Joe Johnson had tacked curtains over his windows. Was the magician afraid of another quarrel flying through the glass?

Groag shuddered under his chain mail even to think of aiming an arbalest at the cunning bastard. He'd been lucky his stupid brother came in the door just then. Otherwise Joe Johnson would probably 've turned the bolt around and it'd've been Groag with wooden fins growing out of his chest!

The brass container, its top screwed down tight on the magic powder, was heavy. Its surface was slick, and it kept turning in Groag's hands as though it wanted to slip away from him.

What if Ezekiel's magic *hadn't* been strong enough to counteract the power of the stranger?

Groag looked at the armchair pulled close to the fireplace. Its seat and legs were bare, nothing whatever to cover the shining container.

The comforter in which Joe Johnson wrapped himself was neatly folded on the bed. If Groag moved the quilt, that would be as much a giveaway as the obvious presence of the container itself.

Which left one sure hiding place. Groag stepped to the fireplace and used the poker to scrape a long trench in the pile of charcoal and hot, white ash. He set the magic container into the trench and carefully covered it again.

The mound was higher than it had been, but there was nothing to draw the eye in the few moments between Joe Johnson entering the room and his sitting down directly in front of the fireplace. . . .

Groag straightened, looking pleased. There was a whisper of sound behind him. He turned like a great cat and met the wide, frightened eyes of the little maid who'd just opened the door.

By god, it was the bitch he and Glam had been chasing the other day!

"What are you doing here?" the maid demanded in a squeaky soprano.

"Nothing *you'll* live to tell about!" Groag bellowed. He didn't bother to draw a sword. Instead, he leaped forward with the poker upraised.

There was a flash as red as the fires of Armageddon.

The blast was equally impressive, but Groag didn't live to hear it.

Mary lay on her back, across the hall from where white haze seethed from Joe's doorway.

Joe had left the banquet before the serious drinking began, so he reached the bomb site as quickly as any of the servants. Wind through the window openings drew orange flickers from the fire within; the stench of burning feathers mingled with the brimstone odor of gunpowder.

Joe knelt, cradling Mary's fragile body in his arms. She was unconscious but breathing normally.

Thank god!

Dozens of servants came running from both directions, many of them carrying firebuckets. Joe grabbed a sturdy-looking female, pointed to Mary, and said, "Watch her! I'll be right back!"

He snatched a lamp from a wall bracket and plunged into his room. His feet slipped.

On Groag.

King Morhaven's eldest son had taken most of the

blast. The shockwave blew Mary through the open door; Groag had been driven into the stone doorjamb instead.

Joe couldn't be sure whether Groag's clothes had been blown off his body, or whether the body had simply leaked through the fabric after being strained through his chain-link armor. He could be identified by the ornate hilt of his sword.

Confirmation came from the smoldering black beard hairs which clung to the bloodstained wall.

"Joe! Joe!" Delendor shouted as the young prince led a crowd up the stairway from the banquet hall. "Are you all right?"

Servants were tossing buckets of water on the flames, but that was pointless: there was nothing left in the room to save, and the wooden roof beams weren't yet in danger.

Joe grabbed a handful of burning bedding and flung it through one of the window openings. The mass drifted down into the courtyard. Blazing bits of cloth and feathers dribbled away like a slow-motion firework.

Others took over the job, hurling out even the shattered remnants of the bed frame and cedar chest. Nobody seemed to be too concerned about Groag.

Joe wasn't concerned either. He stepped out into the hall again, just as the thundering squadron of nobles from the banquet hall reached the scene.

Most of the nobles. Master Ezekiel wasn't among them.

"Is it . . . ?" King Morhaven called. "Is it . . . ?"

The king knew as well as anybody else did who was likely to be at the bottom of the current problem.

Joe opened his mouth to answer as bluntly as rage made him wish—but you couldn't blame the father for the sons, and anyway, there'd been enough outbursts of one sort and another this night.

"You'd better look for yourself," he said, and he handed Morhaven the lamp. The king, Delendor, and Estoril forced their way into the room through the mob of frantic servants.

"I'll take over now," Joe said as he squatted beside Mary again. A firebucket had been set nearby. He dipped his handkerchief in the water and began to sponge powder blackening and speckles of Groag from the maid's face.

The king came out of Joe's room. He'd aged a decade in a few seconds. Delendor and the princess walked to either side of Morhaven, looking worried and poised to catch him if he collapsed. Even Kiki seemed upset.

Morhaven straightened. "Very well," he said. "Events have forced me to the choice I'd already made. People of Hamisch, my successor shall be my son Delen—"

Estoril put one slim white hand over King Morhaven's mouth. "Father," she said in the shocked silence, "I wasn't sure that I'd ever repeat what Katya told me before she died. I think now that I have to."

"Katya?" Delendor repeated with a puzzled expression.

"Your mother Blumarine's nurse!" the princess snapped. "Don't you remember?"

Which of course Delendor hadn't, but he was used enough to the situation to nod wisely. His monkey aped his motions.

Estoril lowered her hand and looked Morhaven in the eye. "Father," she said. "Your Majesty. Princess Blumarine was secretly married to Sir Delendor. And her son Delendor—isn't your son, Your Majesty."

"Well I'll be!" said Delendor. If there was any emotion besides amazement in his tone, Joe didn't hear it. "Well I'll *be*. Then you're not my sister, Essie?"

"No," Estoril said, "but you *have* a real older sister." She took the locket from around Delendor's neck and snapped it open. "There," she continued. "That's your sister."

"Why," said Delendor. "Why . . . why look, Joe, she isn't a rabbit any more!"

He held the locket down to Joe. Instead of a mirror, it held a miniature painting on ivory of a young woman with lustrous blond hair. She was absolutely beautiful.

"*And*," Delendor added, rising with new excitement in

his voice, "that means there's no reason *we* can't be married. Essie, will you be my queen?"

"I think," said Estoril dryly, "that the proper question is, 'Del, will you be my consort?' But I think the answer is yes, either way."

She smiled. There was nothing dry about the affection in her eyes.

The woman in Joe's lap stirred. He looked down, his mouth already forming the words, "Oh, thank god you're all right, Mary—"

She wasn't Mary.

She was the woman in the locket painting.

"Good lord!" Joe blurted. "Who are you?"

The blond woman smiled. If there was a sight more beautiful than her face, it was her face with a smile wrapping it. "I'm Mary, Joe," she said.

Mary tried to sit. She was still dizzy from the explosion; Joe's arm helped her. "You've told my brother, then?" she asked/said to Estoril.

Even Estoril looked surprised. "Yes, and you're . . . "

"I'm your sister, Del," Mary said, "though for your sake and hers, mother kept it a secret. When the dragon appeared, I wanted to help you—but Katya put a spell on me to hide my likeness to you and prevent me from telling you the truth. She'd promised Blumarine . . . but I came to be near you anyway."

"And I broke the spell," Estoril amplified to Delendor's puzzled expression, "by telling you who your real father was."

Delendor blinked. Then his face cleared and he beamed happily. "Well, anyway," he said, "everything's settled now."

"No," said Joe in a voice that would have chilled him if it hadn't come from his own mouth. "There's one thing yet to be settled. Between me and Ezekiel."

He squeezed Mary's hand as he released her, but the woman didn't occupy a major part of his mind just at the moment.

Joe stood and picked up Groag's sword. The shagreen

scabbard had been blown away, and several of the jewels had been knocked out of the hilt, but the weapon was still serviceable.

It would serve.

With the sword in his hand, Joe began jogging down the hall. He was moving at a pace he was sure he could keep up until he reached Ezekiel's laboratory across the building.

Or wherever else the magician ran, this side of Hell.

Joe heard a crash of metal and breaking glass as he neared the last corner between him and the laboratory. When he rounded it, he saw the door of the laboratory open, a satchel dropped on the hallway, still spilling paraphernalia—

And a stairwell door still swinging closed.

Ezekiel had run from the banquet hall to his laboratory to pack the cream of his belongings. When he heard retribution coming, he'd abandoned even those valuables in his haste to escape.

Which he wasn't about to do.

"Hold it right there, Ezekiel!" Joe bellowed as he slammed down the stairs behind the fleeing magician.

The long sword in Joe's hand sang and sparked crazily as its point scraped the stairwell. Ezekiel's black robe trailed back around the stone helix, almost close enough to touch, but the unencumbered magician was able to maintain his distance ahead of his pursuer, past the first landing, the second—

Ezekiel banged through the door to the ground floor.

"Stop him!" Joe called to the servant there at the door by the pantry.

The fellow might have tried, but Ezekiel snapped his fingers. The servant froze with his mouth gaping like that of a surfaced carp. He blinked a moment later, but the magician was already past.

Ezekiel wasn't—*puff*—casting spells at Joe—*puff*— because he was sure—*puff*—that Joe was a greater magician than he was.

Ezekiel ran outside. Joe slipped and had to grab the jamb to keep from falling. A four-horse carriage waited in the courtyard.

The driver was a smirking Mongolian.

Ezekiel recognized the 7th Plane inhabitant also. "I'll be back to defeat you yet, Joe Johnson!" the magician screamed over his shoulder. He grabbed the latch and threw open the carriage door.

A clawed, hairy paw closed on Ezekiel's neck and drew him the rest of the way into the conveyance.

Joe stood panting, still clinging to the doorjamb as the coach drew away. It was accelerating faster than horses should have been able to move it.

Something flew out of a side window just as the vehicle disappeared into the arched gateway. It looked like a hand, but Joe didn't feel any need for certainty on the point.

Someone touched Joe's shoulder. He turned to see Mary, the new Mary, with a wistful smile on her face.

"It's over," Joe said to her, all he could manage while he tried to catch his breath.

"Mother—mother's friends, I suppose—brought you here to save my brother," Mary said, An attempt to make her smile a cheerful one failed miserably. "I suppose you'll go home to your own plane now?"

Joe grunted something that was meant to be laughter.

"I think that was my ride," he said, pointing his thumb in the direction the coach had disappeared.. "Believe me, *I'm* not getting in if it decides to come back again."

Mary wet her full, red lips nervously. "Are you disappointed?" she asked in a whisper.

"Do you remember what the king said upstairs?" Joe asked carefully. "About events making him do what he'd already decided he wanted to?"

Joe dropped the sword so that he could use both his arms to hug Mary.

He had a lot to learn about this world, but some things were just the same as they were back home.

Gordon R. Dickson and Chelsea Quinn Yarbro created a space opera series called The Harriers. The series was packaged by Bill Fawcett and sold to Jim Baen. I'm friendly with Gordy and Quinn, while Bill and Jim are very close friends indeed.

The framework of the series was not only light but politically correct: the Harriers are policemen who bounce around the galaxy righting wrongs without lethal weapons. Furthermore, each team has an alien commissar attached to make darned sure no villain's rights are trampled. Not to put too fine a point on it, I got dragged into The Harriers kicking and screaming that I was absolutely the worst person in the world to write a story in that construct.

When I really got into it, though, I realized I wasn't being asked to write a politically correct story: I was supposed to write about cops operating under strict politically-correct controls. That was something I could handle.

Some bits of the story's dialogue are cribbed from real conversations between Quinn and me as I was trying to understand the rules of the story universe. As for the night-blooming cereus—the one my wife planted in our bedroom bloomed while I was writing the story. The bloom is huge, gorgeous, and has a penetrating, peppery odor. I know it's traditional to name ships after leaders, cities, or large, hungry animals; but I tell you, a plant as striking as a night-blooming cereus deserves to have a super-dreadnought of its own.

The Noble Savages

"Ah, Guibert," said Officer Commanding (with Special Authority) McBrien from the depths of his malachite-lined office. "So glad you could make it. We don't chat often enough, you and I."

Right, thought Guibert. *My direct superior through about twenty levels of Magnicate bureaucracy "asks" me to his office, and I'm going to decide to wash my hair instead?*

The gold crests which dotted the malachite's ugly green were probably copied from McBrien's armorial bearings. Guibert's team joked that the Grand Harrier OC traced his ancestry back to Adam—though McBrien would have been offended at a comment that smacked of Patriarchal Religionism.

"Ah—" said McBrien. *He was nervous. Certainly not of me, a scruffy Petit Harrier team leader.* "Will you have a drink, Guibert? I've got a darling little liqueur from—"

"No thank you, sir." The huge office was filled with ancient and valuable furnishings. Guibert felt an urge, quickly suppressed, to undo his fly and take a whiz into one of the ormolu vases flanking the doorway.

"Ah," McBrien repeated. He was a tall man, straight-backed, with the aquiline face of a Roman consul. (There were probably Roman consuls in his chain of descent too.) "Well, Guibert, would you like to sit down?"

Author's Note: Poul Anderson is in no way responsible for this work; however, certain plot elements are a direct result of my reading his excellent *Planet of No Return* (aka *Question and Answer*) thirty-odd years ago.—DAD

"No thank you, sir."

McBrien's aristocratically pale visage flushed. "Sit *down*, Guibert!"

The chairs were Mission Style, black oak and leather. Guibert settled himself on one gingerly. It was so uncomfortable that it made him think of the cycle of torture and counter-torture which the Spanish and aboriginal cultures had inflicted on one another during the Mission Period.

"Ha-ha," McBrien said. "Sorry if I sounded abrupt, my good fellow. Pressures of command. I'm sure you know, being a commander yourself."

Commander of a four-man Petit Harrier insertion team and the commander of the Magnicate dreadnought *Night-Blooming Cereus*, the most powerful vessel in anything up to fifty light years. *You bet, obvious parallels.*

Speaking of Spanish/Aboriginal culture, McBrien's grin could have modeled for a sugar skull on the Day of the Dead celebrations. *Would that be Patriarchal Religionism—or an Aspect of Native Culture and therefore a compliment to the OC?*

"Ah," McBrien said. "You're sure you wouldn't like . . ."

Guibert wouldn't. Guibert was going to speak when ordered to, period. Guibert didn't have a clue about what he was doing in the OC's office, and he had a nasty suspicion that he wasn't going to be any happier about the situation when he learned what it was.

McBrien pursed his lips. He tented his fingers before him, then flattened his hands on the gleaming desktop in horror. He'd realized that he might have been thought to be indulging in prayer. Guibert waited, imagining wistfully though without real hope that the Grand Harrier would suddenly dismiss him.

"To tell the truth," McBrien lied brightly, "I've been thinking to myself, 'You know, Guibert looks like he needs some leave.' As a matter of fact, your whole team looks like it should have some time off, Guibert. You and, and . . ."

"Dayly, Karge, and Wenzil, sir?" Guibert said, volunteering information for the first time since he entered the OC's office. "Leave?"

McBrien relaxed visibly. "Exactly! Well, that's settled. I'm sure you gentlepersons will have a wonderful time on Sawick, a *wonderful* time. Have your team ready to go in half an hour, won't you? That's a good fellow."

Guibert blinked. "Sawick, sir?" he said. "Why in the name of the Nurturing Motherforce do you think we'd want to go there?"

McBrien drew himself up haughtily. He sniffed, a long sound in a nose as aristocratic as his. "Sawick is a favored destination among the *cognoscenti*, Guibert," he said. "Sawick provides a chance to view the sort of natural paradise from which our ancestors, sadly, turned millennia ago. The loss of that innocence is the root cause of the trouble and strife which have plagued our unfortunate race ever since."

Guibert rubbed his temples as if he could massage some sense out of his commanding officer's words. Sawick had been discovered by Magnicate vessels only a few decades ago. It was some sort of nature preserve. The autochthones, cave-dwelling troglodytes, had put all but a few hectares of the planet off-limits to outsiders. The Emerging Planet Fairness Court saw to it that Magnicate citizens obeyed the local decision.

"Many thanks for your suggestion, sir," Guibert said carefully, "but I think my team"—*most assuredly including the team leader*—"would prefer Port Jennet as a leave destination. Port Jennet has many educational aspects of its own."

For example, the act Big Liz performs using a 2-liter beer bottle as a prop.

"Nonsense," McBrien said forcefully. "You'll want to better yourselves, I'm sure. I'm *sure*."

He pursed his lips again. "Besides," he added in a voice that was suddenly as thin as if he were speaking only on one sideband, "it occurs to me that you might be able to do me a little favor while you're there. Ah—"

McBrien stared pensively at his paperweight, an ancient gold statuette which had once tipped the scepter of a West African king. The image consisted of a fat man gorging himself while an emaciated man looked on. The tableau illustrated the native proverb that, "The man with food eats, and he owes nothing to the man with no food."

"A way to save on paperwork, don't you know, old chap?" the OC resumed with the same determinedly-false brightness as earlier. "Don't you just *hate* needless paperwork?"

Does a bear shit in the woods?

But if the brass are telling lies, it's no time for peons to stick to the truth . . . Guibert raised an eyebrow and said, "Action without organization is action wasted, sir. I'm sure you don't imagine that I or any other Petit Harrier would violate proper procedures."

McBrien's smile now looked like the rictus of a man being garroted. "Of course," he said, "of course. But since you'd be on leave and I *don't* believe that this little matter was deemed worthy of a formal report . . ."

What little matter?

Guibert didn't open his mouth, knowing that his best chance of getting out of this was not to get in to begin with. He crossed his hands neatly in his lap and focused his eyes on the OC's beard-fringed chin.

"Ah . . ." said McBrien with a hopeful intonation. Guibert kept his eyes fixed and his lips together.

McBrien sighed. "The fact is," he said, looking at the gold paperweight again, "some young people—dependents of some of the dreadnought's personnel—borrowed a vessel from the *Night-Blooming Cereus*. My cutter, in fact. They, ah, wanted to visit Sawick. No harm done, of course."

Guibert blinked again. "No harm done?" he repeated incredulously. "Punks steal the OC's cutter—*filled* with top-drawer electronics—and they take it to a generally proscribed planet? and there's no harm done?"

"They aren't punks," McBrien said to the paperweight. The words were barely audible because his lips were so tightly compressed. "And anyway, the problem is that they, ah . . . seem to have disappeared."

"Benign Female Principle!" Guibert cursed. "The natives grabbed them, you mean?"

He tried to remember what he'd heard about the Sawickis. If he had the aliens right in his mind, they were humanoid but pasty, stunted and stone-blind. Sawick wasn't a place Guibert or anybody he wanted to know would pick for a local romance.

"Well, there's no evidence of that," McBrien said. "In fact, the Sawickis don't have any recollection of the ah, youngsters. Landing control personnel—Magnicate citizens—say the cutter took off from Sawick but suddenly vanished from their screens. I'm afraid that there may have been a, a . . ."

He looked up. "I'm not really sure what might have happened. But I thought, you know, since you and your team are going to Sawick anyway . . . ?"

Guibert shook his head. "Negative," he said. "Sir."

He cleared his throat. "Sir, with the sort of equipment built onto an admiral's cutter, and Sawick being a Class—what, Thirty?—world—"

"Thirty-two," McBrien agreed sadly.

"Great, Class Thirty-two, with a technology level that's almost but not quite up to the spoon stage," Guibert said. "Either the cutter blew up—or you've *got* to put out a full-dress alarm to prevent the autochthones from being infected."

McBrien shivered as though he'd just come out of a bath in ice water. "Oh, I don't think it's so very great a problem, old chap," he said in his single-sideband voice. "The Sawickis are so safe in their pre-industrial purity that I can't imagine them coming to harm. And a fuss, you see, might cause problems for those poor, misguided young people, don't you know?"

Guibert nodded grimly. "You bet," he agreed. "Like spending the next ten years in a Cultural Re-Education camp when the Mromrosii and the rest of the EPFC hear about what they pulled. And you know, for a change, I think I might agree with the Mromrosii."

McBrien pressed his fingers together. This time he didn't jerk them apart when he noticed what he was doing. "Guibert," he said, "I'd really like it if you and your team looked into this unofficially."

"Not without a direct order, sir," Guibert said. "Because me and my people would wind up hoeing rice paddies alongside the punks if we got caught covering up a thing like this."

McBrien bowed his head. "Guibert, do you want me to beg?" he whispered.

"No, sir," Guibert said. "I want you to dismiss me, so that we can both forget we ever had this conversation."

"Guibert, my daughter Megan took the cutter. With seven of her friends."

OC McBrien stood up. He was normally a graceful man. This time there was a dangling looseness about him, like the motions of a scarecrow being hung on a pole. "If you won't take care of this, Guibert," he said, "then I'll have to go myself. Unofficially."

"Sir," Guibert said. "Sir, with all due respect, a Grand Harrier trying to act outside the system would screw things up beyond reasonable belief."

McBrien nodded. "Yes, Mister Guibert," he said. "I'm very much afraid you're right."

"By the Menstruation of the Life-Giving Yang," Guibert muttered as he got to his feet. "Sir, I'll talk to the team. No promises, but I'll talk to the team."

He'd order the team. It was his decision, he was in charge. And anyway, they were professionals. A pro doesn't sit around and watch an amateur make a bad situation worse.

"But one thing!" Guibert added sharply form the door. "*If* we do this"—*and if we don't get our butts confined in a re-education camp till all of us but Wenzil are tripping on our beards*—"then we get a *real* leave out of it. On Port Jennet!"

The Grand Harrier nodded assent. Even under the

present circumstances, McBrien couldn't avoid a moue of distaste at the idea of personnel under his command having fun.

". . . so we'll be going down in a standard leave barge," Guibert explained to his team. "We'll have a full set of orbital scans, but no special equipment aboard."

"A leave barge!" Karge muttered, knuckling his curly auburn hair. "Typical of a faggot like McBrien to expect us to carry out his mission with a bare hull and an engine."

"We'll play it by ear," Guibert said mildly. "If it turns out we need more hardware, then I'll see about getting it."

He cleared his throat. "Dayly," he asked, "what have you got on the Sawickis?"

Wenzil, the team's weapons specialist, was about average height for a human female—a meter sixty-five. Dayly, the data systems specialist, was both shorter and slighter by 10%. He touched a key and projected a hologram of an average Sawickis above the console.

"Great," Karge said. "So now we know that Sawickis are toads."

Guibert pursed his lips. "Slugs, wouldn't you say?" he offered.

Wenzil glanced up, then returned to what she was doing. She'd stripped the team's stunners on her bunk. She was cleaning the contacts individually with an arc-and-vacuum unit and replating when she deemed it desirable.

It was the sort of task normally performed at armory level or above. Wenzil did it before every mission, and once a week or so when the team was on stand-down.

"What sort of stunner setting does the data bank suggest?" she asked as she peered critically at the main buss from Karge's weapon. "*Not* that I'd trust the data bank, but for a place to start."

Dayly clicked to the end of the file rather than scrolling down. He knew that out of squeamishness, the folks at Central Records would wait as long as they could before stating the information that any sane member of an insertion team wanted right up front: how to program their stunners to have an effect on local lifeforms.

"It says eight seventy-three," Dayly offered in a neutral tone.

The setting was almost certainly extrapolated rather than arrived at by empirical testing on the autochthones. Wenzil was likely to get very upset when her darling stunners didn't perform as she desired. Dayly didn't want to have any more association with a probable mistake than was necessary.

"Hmm," Wenzil said as she punched the code into the stunner she'd already reassembled. "They think Sawickis are slugs, all right, but sea slugs. This is a normal-atmosphere world, isn't it?" She didn't sound concerned, just interested.

"Within parameters," Guibert agreed. "A little high in noble gasses, but still under two percent. The figures must be based on Sawicki physiology."

The trouble with stunners was that there were literally billions of life-forms in the known universe. A stimulus that had a stunning effect on one creature might not touch another—or might goad it to fury. Beasts as similar as Terran horses and dogs reacted in violently different ways to would-be knockout drugs.

And, of course, the difference between an incapacitating dose and a lethal dose was often less than a standard deviation within members of the same species. Central could be expected to err on the side of safety—for the hostile autochthones.

"Stunners have got to be the stupidest idea since faculty tenure," said Karge, the ethnology specialist. "It was probably some flaming queen like McBrien who mandated them."

"What we ought to have," said Wenzil, "is *real* weapons. If you blow a hole clear through something, you can be pretty sure it stops chewing your leg off."

"But that would be wrong," the other three team members chorused, "and the Mromrosii wouldn't like it!"

"Thank the Beneficent Flow of the All-Mother," Guibert said, "that at least we don't have to take a Mromrosi with us into this mare's nest."

The door to the team's compartment was locked. It opened anyway. A Mromrosi glided in on tiny feet hidden beneath the train of bright orange hair. The creature looked like an extremely steep-sided orange haystack a meter and a quarter high. Its single eye glinted at Guibert from behind a veil of hair. "What is our departure time, team leader?" it demanded.

The alien had a pleasant baritone voice. It sounded more human than OC McBrien did when he got nervous.

"Ah," Guibert said. He wondered if the syllable sounded as silly from him as when the Grand Harrier spoke it.

Karge leaned forward. "You don't need to come along this trip, Hairball," the big ethnologist said gently. "We're going on leave."

"I know all about your mission," the Mromrosi responded. "An attempt to carry out a mission without the presence of a representative of the Emerging Planet Fairness Court would lead to cultural re-adjustment for the perpetrators."

"You know," Wenzil said wistfully, "there are times I think I might quite like hoeing a rice paddy for the rest of my life. But I'd want the sentence to be for doing something interesting . . ."

She eyed the Mromrosi. Guibert didn't know whether or not the alien could read Wenzil's speculative expression accurately, but as team leader he didn't want to take chances. "Go on with your description of the autochthones please, Dayly," he said in a loud voice.

The data specialist turned to his console again. "Average height a meter fifty," he read in a singsong voice. "They live underground, growing fungus which they feed on decomposing vegetation which they gather from the surface during the hours of darkness."

"They can't stand sunlight?" Guibert asked.

"Now I wonder whether an eight-seven-three setting might not give me lower dispersion. . . ." Wenzil murmured as her attention returned to the numerical programming pad on the receiver of the second stunner.

The Mromrosi's eye rotated to fix Wenzil with its warm brown glare. "You must not depart from Central's recommended stunner settings!" the creature said. "You might *harm* an autochthon by such experimentation!"

"Please, Hairball," Guibert said primly. "Your interference with this briefing could cause one of us to make a mistake that would injure the indigenes with whom we come in contact."

It was impossible to tell Mromrosii apart except by hair color, and Karge insisted that they were able to change *that*. Further, the ethnologist didn't bother trying to pronounce names which he believed the Mromrosii picked at random. Since he got away with it, the rest of the team had picked up the habit also.

The Mromrosi's eye turned again. Guibert wasn't sure whether the whole body moved, or whether the eye slid across the alien's skin beneath the layer of hair.

"I apologize," Hairball said. "Continue."

"They can stand sunlight for a little while," Dayly said, "though they don't have any melanin or the equivalent in their skin, so they sunburn easily."

"You were right, chief," Karge said. "Slugs, not toads."

"The main reason they don't come out by day is that they don't have eyes as such," Dayly continued. "There's a modulated light emitter on top of their heads—a bioluminescent laser, for all practical purposes. There are pick-ups all around the body at neck level, giving them very precise *active* ranging—but in daylight they're at a disadvantage to creatures which have passive receptors."

"Eyes," Guibert translated aloud.

"Eyes," Dayly agreed. "Also, they have excellent hearing."

"Just how strong a laser are we talking about?" Wenzil

asked with an intonation that Guibert couldn't initially place.

"Microwatts," Dayly said. "No danger at all."

The weapons specialist nodded sadly. "It probably wouldn't function if it were removed from the autochthon anyway," she said.

Hairball's eye snapped around, but the Mromrosi kept silent this time.

"The Magnicate made contact with Sawick forty-one years ago," Dayly said. "The autochthons were classified Thirty-two and were informed of their rights under the Emerging Planet Fairness Regulations. The Sawickis elected to eschew outside contact except at one village, the Big Grotto, where they've constructed a surface-level nature area as well. Sawick is believed to be very sparsely settled, but the terms of the autochthonal election make it difficult to determine the amount of sub-surface development."

"Slugs living under rocks," Karge said. "Just the sort of thing you'd expect a pansy like McBrien to get us into."

This wasn't helpful. "Look, Karge," Guibert said. "The only thing I know for sure about the OC's private life is that he's got a kid. Right?"

"Big deal," Karge said. "So did Oscar Wilde. He's a poofter, trust me."

"They sell handicrafts at Big Grotto," Dayly said. "And there's lodging on the surface there." He squinted at the screen. "If these prices are right, I'm not going to be able to afford more than three nights on Sawick."

"I'll talk to his parentness," Guibert said. "Anything more?"

Dayly shrugged. "Nothing too striking in the local wildlife," he said. "Frankly, there wasn't much interest in the place except from nature freaks till the kids went missing. The scans done since would have showed up the cutter, though, no matter how small the bits it smashed into."

Guibert sighed. "I guess we're ready when you get the hardware put back together, Wenzil," he said.

Hairball scanned the insertion team one by one. "This should be very illuminating for you," the Mromrosi said. "Try to open your hearts and appreciate the differentness of this pure people, the Sawickis, who live at one with Nature. *True* nobility!"

"Blind, white slugs," Karge muttered. "With arms and legs."

The landing field serving the Big Grotto was paved with crushed stone. The sharp tang of quicklime made Guibert sneeze when he opened the hatch.

"Gesundheit," said Dayly.

Hairball looked at the data specialist. "Are you demonstrating subservience to Patriarchal Religionism, Harrier?" the Mromrosi asked suspiciously.

"No, no," said Karge. "Simply an Aspect of Native Culture. It's a charm against the possibility of our leader expelling his soul along with the sneeze."

"Ah," said the Mromrosi.

"Gee, I didn't know that," Dayly said.

From orbit, the landing field was a six-pointed star, brilliantly white against the dark green and russet of the forest covering most of the continent. A dozen ships, all to them Magnicate designs, were already on the ground. Two of them were medium-sized cruise liners.

"Come along!" a high-pitched voice called. Guibert looked out and saw his first autochthon. "If you miss this coffle, you'll have to wait till the next ship lands. We're certainly not going to waste an escort on a mere four of you."

Sawickis really *were* slugs, though their faces were broad and toadlike and the fleshy peak that held the laser-ranging organ could have passed for a dunce cap. This one, presumably a guide, wore a brown tunic made of something like bark cloth. It was decorated with geometric designs in black batik.

Guibert hopped to the warm gravel. Twenty-odd humans, roped together, waited at the edge of the field.

Two of the four pasty autochthons accompanying the group carried meter-long prods with stone tips.

"Actually," Guibert said softly, "there's five of us." The boots of the insertion team crunched down behind him, followed by the vague whisper of Hairball's miniature feet. "And I didn't catch what you meant about 'coffle.' We're Magnicate officials on leave, you see."

Ignoring the team leader, the autochthon bowed low to Hairball. "Illustrious sky-brother," the Sawicki said. The creature's voice was unpleasant even when he was obviously trying to be unctuous. "Welcome to the only true world. On behalf of my people, I grant you the status of an honorary Sawicki."

Hairball fluttered in what Guibert supposed was the Mromrosi equivalent of a bow. "Thank you," he said. "Thank you. I am truly honored."

"Naw," Karge said after a critical glance at the Mromrosi. "You don't look a bit like a toad, Hairball."

"Maybe under the fur?" Dayly suggested.

The Mromrosi looked at them. "Sawicki means 'True Person' in their language," he said.

"Somehow," Guibert said, "I would have guessed that. Now, what's this coffle business?"

"Come along, come along," their guide demanded. "You're keeping me and my fellow True Men waiting."

He headed toward the line of humans at a lurching trot. The Sawicki wore boots made of a heavier version of the tunic material. His feet turned slightly on the gravel surface, though it seemed level enough to Guibert.

Hairball followed, drawing the team along behind him. "To prevent visitors from damaging the delicate ecology of this planet," the Mromrosi called over his shoulder, "the Sawickis link individuals together so that they won't leave the prescribed path. A *very* far-sighted regulation, I must say."

"What's delicate about this place?" Dayly asked. "It looks pretty normal to me."

The trees were of a number of species, all with noticeably conical trunks which suggested they had less stiffening material per unit of mass than Terran varieties. The branches were whiplike and small-leafed; the under-growth tended to spike rather than spread.

"*All* ecologies must be carefully overseen to keep them in balance," Hairball said stiffly.

True enough. Nature herself was never in equilibrium. Only outside intellects tried to restrain the natural appetite for change. Usually badly.

"Do you suppose I could check my settings on some of those critters, sir?" Wenzil asked with more optimism than hope. She pointed with her left hand toward a bright-eyed creature clicking at the team from a scaly treetrunk.

"Certainly not!" Hairball said.

"Of course not," Guibert said. "What's that going to tell you that you need to know, Wenzil? It's no longer than your forearm and it seems to be an amphibian anyway!"

All the local life-forms Guibert noticed, with the exception of the Sawickis themselves, were either wet-skinned or chitinous. Some of the latter fluttered among the trees on gossamer wings a meter across. None of the potential targets would help the weapons specialist refine her stunner program. Shooting at them, even with a stunner, would cause more trouble than Guibert needed.

The team reached the tourists. The children were restive or shrieking, and several of the adults glared fiercely at the Harriers. Guibert wondered how long the civilians had been kept waiting.

"Stand here," their guide ordered, pointing to the end of the line. Two of the others grabbed Dayly by the elbows, presumably because he was small, to hustle him into place.

Karge said, "Oops!" and staggered forward, treading heavily on the feet of one of the autochthons. The Sawicki squealed and dropped Dayly's arm.

"Oops!" Guibert said.

The other Sawicki holding Dayly jumped back. Guibert hopped sideways and landed on their guide's foot. The guide squealed also.

"Mister Guibert!" Hairball cried. "Mister Karge!"

The autochthons and tourists looked at the Mromrosi. Dayly kicked the third Sawicki in the crotch and said, "Oops!" happily. The autochthon's squeal was higher pitched than those of his fellows.

The pair of Sawickis with goads moved closer. Wenzil stepped between them and the men of the team. Her hands were empty at waist height, and there was a dazzling smile on her face. The autochthons retreated.

Guibert bent and fingered the rope which tied the civilians together. The tourists drew away from him to either side.

The material was supple, but it seemed strong enough to tow barges with. "Cut from the outer skin of a mushroom that was grown for the purpose?" he guessed aloud.

Nobody responded. Guibert smiled tightly and said to their guide, "I don't think me and the team will need this to keep us on the path. As a matter of fact, I'm afraid it would make us stumble. A lot."

"I promise," Karge rumbled.

Hairball's eye dithered in one direction, then the other. He didn't speak. At last the Sawicki guide said, "Since you're slaves of a True Man—"

He bowed again to Hairball, then winced and rubbed his instep where Guibert had trod.

"—we will make an exception in this case. However, you'll have to surrender the weapons you're carrying to me."

"*This*," said Wenzil, pointing to the stunner in her cutaway holster, "is an icon of my religion. It would violate my cultural personhood to force me to give it up."

"That's ridiculous!" the guide squeaked.

Actually, it was pretty much true for Wenzil. "It would violate other serious strictures as well," Guibert said aloud. "Our, ah, overseer, Hairball, would have us punished severely were we to turn over equipment of such developed character to Class Thirty-two autochthones. It might poison the purity of your, ah, culture."

"I wonder if pearls upset the digestion of swine?" Karge murmured to one of the gaping tourists.

"They're not real weapons anyway," Wenzil said sadly.

The Sawickis' little laser emitters flashed red as they flicked from one member of the team to the next and finally focused on Hairball.

The Mromrosi sighed. "Yes, yes," he said I suppose that's correct. A technical matter only, of course—*I* realize that the truth that underpins your culture is proof against such baubles. But regulations are regulations, I'm afraid."

With obvious reluctance, Hairball added, "I will take responsibility for the good behavior of these, these . . ."

Instead of replying, the Sawicki guide turned and called, "Head 'em up and move 'em out!" One of his fellows jerked the cord around the waist of the leading tourist, pulling her down the path.

"I wish you people would learn to behave decently!" the Mromrosi said, glaring at Guibert.

"I wish," said Karge, stretching his long, muscular arms overhead, "that that queer McBrien was here drinking in slug culture instead of me."

They'd walked a half kilometer from the landing field without reaching the entrance to the Big Grotto. The forest's muggy heat made Guibert feel as though he'd been taking a bath in his own sweat.

"I don't see why it's got to be this far," Dayly grumbled.

The data specialist had more work to do during standdown than the rest of the team. He used that circumstance to avoid compulsory attendance in the Strength through Joy Room—the *Night-Blooming Cereus'* gym. Dayly's cleverness was costing him shin splints if nothing else right now.

"To keep the presence of starships from polluting the village's environment," Hairball said.

"To make the stupid tourists walk their legs off," Karge said.

They came around a bend in the trail. The entrance was in sight a hundred meters away, framed by a yoke made of three stone-headed spears. Either side of the trail was lined with booths from which Sawickis sold a variety of food, drink, and handicrafts.

Tourist children began to shriek and tug against the ropes in their haste to get something to drink. Because some pulled toward the right and others to the left, the line tangled so that no one was able to reach the booths. The autochthonous escort watched, making no effort to intervene.

The team walked over to the booths while shouting parents tried to sort out the mess. Guibert looked at a vat of yellowish fluid. Cups made of fungus caps lay beside it. Local insectoids clustered around the residue drying in the cups.

"Ten hubbles a cup, foreign non-person!" squeaked the Sawicki behind the counter.

"Really?" said Guibert. He took a swig from the straw to the condensing canteen woven into the back of his uniform jacket. For ten hubbles a pop, they could afford to import single-malt Scotch from Terra to sell.

Dayly sniffed the vat. "You know . . ." he said. "I've got a feeling that if I sent a sample of that stuff in for analysis, the lab report would say, 'Your bat has gonorrhea.'"

"You imbibed through your nostrils!" the autochthon cried. "Ten hubbles! Ten hubbles!"

"Pardon our error," said Karge. "Permit me to return your stock to its original volume." He spat into the center of the vat.

One of the escorts ran over to the counter clerk. The two chittered together with a great deal of gesturing. Though the Sawickis faced one another, the lasers in their pointy little heads flicked frequently toward the Harriers.

At last the clerk turned away and pretended to be studying the forest behind his booth. His laser continued to paint the team at intervals as the members drifted down the line of booths.

"You know . . ." said Guibert as he stood before a booth which was selling carved lanterns. "I quite like some of these designs."

"Remarkably delicate handicrafts, aren't they?" Karge agreed. "Remarkable for troglodytes, at any rate. I think upscale boutiques in The Hub might be able to market them."

Dayly cleared his throat. "According to the files," he said, "there's a Big Grotto Trading Association negotiating with Hub jobbers for bulk shipments."

The data specialist looked at the display and shook his head. "I dunno," he said. "Plastic would do a lot better, it seems to me."

Like most of the other Sawicki crafts on offer, the lanterns were made from the caps of large mushrooms, dried and scraped paper thin. The prepared hoods were chiseled into filigrees of enormous delicacy, each one unique.

Internally lighted, the lanterns would be strikingly beautiful. Even now, hanging from the frame of the booth like so many chicken carcasses at a butcher's shop, they had a "natural" loveliness greater than that of the surrounding forest.

The Sawicki clerk in the center of the booth looked like a grub poking its head out of a nutshell. He sneered at the humans.

Guibert rotated one of the lanterns slightly to change the angle of the light falling across the surface. The clerk reached out, plucked the lantern from the peg on which it hung, and dropped it behind his counter. He stamped down. The delicate tracery crunched beneath his foot.

"We True Men are above material covetousness, foreign non-person," the Sawicki squeaked.

"Interesting," Karge said as he and the team leader turned abruptly away.

"I wonder what they spend their hubbles on?" Dayly asked. "Besides a first-rate spaceport control system, that is. And salaries for Magnicate technicians to crew it."

"They ought to import food," Wenzil muttered. "Do you suppose they really eat that cat-barf themselves?"

"We've got our emergency rations," Guibert said. "And anyway, I don't think we're going to be here longer than tomorrow morning."

"All right, all right, foreign non-persons!" the Sawicki guide said. "You may untie yourselves now. You will now visit a village of True Men. Then you will be taken to your accommodations among the natural beauty of our planet."

"Everybody's eaten as much as they could choke down," Karge noted. "Or a little more than that." An eight-year-old was throwing up violently at the edge of the trail while her parents—looking rather green themselves—patted her helplessly. The ejecta didn't look a great deal different from the autochthonous soup the child had swallowed moments before.

"Thank the Ennobling Adiposity of the Mother for emergency rations," Guibert murmured.

"Come along!" repeated the guide. He and his fellows began prodding tourists toward the entrance to the grotto, using knuckles and goads. The pasty-faced autochthons gave the team a wide berth.

Hairball peered at the pool of vomit as he passed. "I suppose," he said in what was for him an unusually ruminative tone, "that since the meals—though perfectly natural—might not agree with digestion trained to freshly-killed food."

"Hey, Hairball," Karge said. "Did *you* bring any rations?" He reached the yoke of spears and kicked it aside.

The entrance to the Big Grotto was a large keyhole in the surface of the ground. A trail, only partly artificial, led down the side of the opening. Several smaller holes in the rock ceiling illuminated the interior with a diffused glow.

The cavern was about a hundred meters wide and at

least a half klick in length. Sawickis and scores of tourists moved among the jumbled rock on the cave floor, but Guibert's eyes weren't sufficiently dark-adapted to see details.

"That ceiling—the cave roof?" he said glancing upward.

"Umm?" said Wenzil who happened to be the person directly behind Guibert on the narrow trail.

"I'm surprised, as thin as the rock looks, that it's strong enough to hold together," Guibert explained. "I'd have expected the whole roof to come crashing down before now. Limestone rotted by ground water doesn't have particularly high tensile strength."

"Hope it doesn't fall while we're underneath," Wenzil said, though she didn't sound concerned. Things that she couldn't shoot and weren't going to shoot her didn't interest the weapons specialist very much.

At the bottom of the grotto, the pale light reminded Guibert of that beneath thirty meters of water. He could see objects well enough, but their outlines were softened by the faint, diffused illumination.

It was a pity that nothing similar could be done about the smell. Guibert at first thought the pong was that of concentrated Sawickis—there were about a hundred of them in sight, working on crafts or (more generally) lounging and curling their lips at the tourists clustered about them.

After a moment, Guibert realized that while Sawickis did stink, their dung stank a great deal worse. The noble autochthons squatted wherever they happen to be when their bowels gave them the signal.

He looked queasily at his feet—found that his fears were justified—and then noticed that the turd was so dry that it crumbled rather than clinging to the soles of his boots.

"Watch where you step," he warned his team.

"That's funny," Dayly said. "The files say they use their shit as part of the compost they grow the fungus on. Here they're just leaving it lie around."

"It's probably contact with outsiders that has caused the breakdown in the normal routine of the Big Grotto," Hairball said. "It's courageous—heroic, in fact—for the True Persons to sacrifice one of their own villages so that other races can be exposed to the purity of their culture."

"Or it's their idea of a joke on the tourists," Karge said. "As a matter of fact, I wonder if this whole place isn't a joke on the tourists. Do we know anything about how the slugs on the rest of the planet live?"

"Negative," said Dayly.

"Certainly not!" the Mromrosi said. "It's quite enough that *one* village be sacrificed to the greed of the Magnicate!"

"Judging by the prices for them baskets and the slush the slugs call food," Dayly said, "I wouldn't say the Magnicate was in the same league."

Guibert squared his shoulders and took a deep breath—the latter which he instantly regretted. They should have brought nose filters as well as emergency rations. "Well," he said, "if I could figure out a cute way to learn about the missing cutter, I suppose I'd try it. Since I can't, I guess I'll go ask the chief what he knows."

"That bugger McBrien could have managed that himself," Karge said.

Guibert cocked an eye at the ethnologist. "Got a better idea?" he demanded.

"Staying back on the *Night-Blooming Cereus* and playing with myself," Karge said. "Apart from that, no."

A Sawicki male, neither more nor less disgusting than any other Sawicki, sat on a block of fallen limestone in the center of the cavern. Given his elaborately-layered costume and the number of tourists clustered around him taking low-light holograms, he must have some rank.

"Once more into the breach . . ." Guibert muttered as he walked toward the fellow.

He passed near a pair of female Sawickis hacking patterns into mushroom caps with stone burins as more tourists recorded the process.

"That's odd," Karge said. "They aren't any good at all."

He was right. While the works for sale on the surface were craft raised to the level of art, these Sawickis were creating junk along the lines of jack-o'-lanterns butchered by three-year-olds.

"I could chew mushrooms and shit a better design," Wenzil agreed.

"See how contact with the outside has warped these poor innocents?" Hairball said.

"That doesn't," said Guibert, "explain where the *good* work is coming from, does it?"

"Good in patriarchal, anthropocentric terms, you mean," Hairball replied, adding a click that passed for a sniff in Mromrosi terms.

True enough; but not an answer to the question.

Guibert looked at the crowd. "You lead," he said to Hairball.

"Make way for the Mromrosi delegate!" he added loudly. Tourists turned and realized the tickle on the backs of their thighs was frizzy orange hair that *walked*. They hurled themselves sideways faster than Guibert could have moved them had he slammed into the crowd full tilt.

The front rank of tourists around the chief was on its knees, calling questions to the disdainful Sawicki. Hairball stopped and looked upward at the team leader. "To speak to the village chief," he said, "you must kneel. By this act you honor not the personhood of the chief, but rather the planet Sawick itself."

"Here, I'll take care of it," said Karge. The ethnologist pushed ahead of Guibert and the Mromrosi. He turned and dropped his trousers.

"Karge!" Guibert said. "What on earth are you doing?"

Tourists gasped, screamed, or giggled, depending on temperament. The crowd universally moved well back from the Harriers. The chief called something, bringing Sawickis on the run from all parts of the cavern.

"Honoring the planet as the locals do," Karge explained as he squatted. "Taking a dump."

"You can't do this!" Hairball cried.

"When on Sawick . . ." the ethnologist said. "Do as the Sawickis do."

"Mister Karge," Guibert said. "*Don't*. Or you walk home."

"What's going on here?" the chief demanded.

"Well, seeing as he's addressing us directly . . ." Karge said. He stood up again.

The autochthons had halted in a wide circle around the team instead of rushing directly to the chief's aid. Guibert noted that the Sawickis' attitude appeared to be fear rather than anger. Sawickis were the sort of bullies who wilted when anybody stood up to them.

"Of course, a seven-five-one setting, Marathrustran Bivalves, might throw them into syncope," Wenzil murmured. The weapons specialist seemed as happy as a pig in shit.

"What?" said Hairball. "What?"

Karge refastened his trousers. In a low voice, the ethnologist began to sing a Chippewa song, *"Do you think she was humiliated, that Sioux woman I beheaded?"*

"Some teenagers from a Magnicate dreadnought landed here last week in an eight-place cutter," Guibert said, "and they haven't come back. We were wondering if you recalled anything about them. Sir." *Courtesy didn't cost much.*

"Why should any True Man be concerned with faceless non-persons?" the chief said.

Wenzil turned to face them. "That doesn't sound like an answer to me," she said. The peculiar lilt in her voice made Guibert shiver.

Enough of the implications must have translated that the Sawicki chief said, "The question was asked through the non-persons who run the devil-machines that guide non-person spaceships. We at once held a village council. No one recalled the missing non-persons, since your faces are all the same anyway."

The guide who'd met the barge added, "We prayed that the soulless non-persons had died with minimal pain, however."

"Then I don't suppose there's much we can do here," Guibert said. "Thank you."

The team headed back toward the ramp up the side of the grotto.

"We'll do the nature watch and spend the night in the tourist lodgings," Guibert said. "Since according to the techs in the landing control facility, that's what the cutter did. We're playing this one by ear."

"You know," Dayly said thoughtfully, "he's lying. But lies are information too."

"Yeah," Karge agreed. "And it's information that turd-burglar McBrien wasn't going to have understood."

"Why would anybody pay good money to watch hogs root through garbage?" Guibert wondered aloud as he walked into the male barracks he, Karge and Dayly shared with ninety-odd other men. "Nature area, hell!"

"Ouch!" said Karge, crushing across his biceps the fly that just stabbed for a meal of his blood.

"Damned good money," Dayly agreed. "This all is coming out of official funds, isn't it, sir?"

"That, or out of that limp-wrist McBrien's hide," Karge said.

Tourist accommodations on Sawicki were sex-segregated. Hairball had presumably tossed the Mrom-rosi equivalent of a coin before deciding to go with Wenzil.

Not that there was much place to go. The barracks were pole frames, roofed with branches. They couldn't have approached being watertight even before their leaves dried up and fell away weeks or months before. The bunks were three-high, with no mattresses or bedding. Lights were whatever individual tourists brought with them.

"True Men lie directly on bare rock," the autochthonal concierge—warden?—explained to a tearful father with an infant, no bedclothes, and no light with which to pick his way back to the landing field and a ship that might well be sealed for the night anyway.

"Wonder how that slug would like to be laid on the bare rock?" Karge said, fingering the knuckles of his big right hand. He peered at the circle of "floor" in his handlight and added, "Or mud, as the case may be."

Guibert guided the ethnologist toward their rack of bunks. "That's not what we're here for," he reminded Karge.

"Still," Karge said, "it'd be a way to improve my time. . . ."

Dayly sat on the top bunk, running data through the chip reader he was never without. From the team leader's angle, Dayly's air-projected holograms appeared to be chunks of terrain from the orbital scans.

Guibert's rank gave him the choice of accommodations: the bottom bunk, where his subordinates provided more rain cover than the roof did, or the top bunk which would prevent him from being crushed if the whole flimsy rack collapsed. He'd gone for the former, because Karge had picked the middle where his momentum would be low. Dayly didn't weigh enough to worry about.

"Ouch!" Karge said, slapping another fly. He wiped his hand disgustedly on his trouser leg for want of a rag. "They're sticky when they squish, and they seem to like me even better than they do the pigs. This is *not* going to be a fun night."

"Suoids, not pigs," said Dayly as he continued to sort through pictures of forest. "They're native to Sawick."

"Don't tell me I don't know what a pig is," the ethnologist grumbled. "I'm from Lontano, remember? For that matter, I swatted my share of these damned gadflies when I was growing up, too."

Tourists huddled in clots around their fellows who'd brought lights, talking in desultory, often despairing, tones. When they got back to their homes, they would pontificate about the benefits they had bestowed on their offspring by exposing the children to the pure beauties of nature.

Not now, however. Guibert wondered whether some of the fortunate offspring weren't going to be strangled here on Sawick unless they stopped wailing. Not that he blamed the kids.

"Who says the pigs are native here?" Guibert asked. "Dayly?"

"The place was discovered forty years ago," the data specialist said without emphasis. "The suoids are present over the whole continent. Therefore they aren't Terran pigs."

"If insects can live on them *and* on humans, of whom I am one," said Karge, "then they're Terran pigs."

"Is there any other warm-blooded life on Sawick, Dayly?" Guibert asked.

"Sure, the Sawickis," Dayly said.

"Warm-blooded slugs," Karge said.

"Bingo!" said the data specialist. He reached down with his chip reader, making the rack creak dangerously as he did so. "Look at *that*, sir. This is an enhanced infra-red scan, blown up to one to a thousand."

Guibert stared at a hollow cross formed of faint white lines against the dark background. "Yeah?" he said.

"I told the system to sort for anomalies," Dayly explained. "This is what it came up with."

Karge craned his neck to see the display from the correct angle. "It's not the OC's cutter," he said.

"Of course not," Dayly said. "Even the Grands would have found *that*. This is the remains of a village. Trees have grown up over it, but on IR you can still see where the foundations were."

"Well I'll be damned," Guibert said. "The cutter had a complete recon system, didn't it?"

"You think the kids noticed something funny and decided to take a look?" Karge said. "I can't imagine they were satisfied with the entertainment they were getting around here."

"Yes *sir*," Dayly said. "I don't suppose Hairball would let us go take a close-up look tomorrow, would he?"

"Not at a proscribed area of the planet, unless we had direct evidence the cutter was there," Guibert said thoughtfully. "Of course the kids shouldn't have been there either."

"The kids," Karge noted, "shouldn't have gone off joy-riding in that faggot McBrien's cutter to begin with."

Dayly snickered. "This means a bunch of spoiled kids figured out something that the Magnicate bureaucracy couldn't in forty years," he said.

"Does that surprise you?" Karge asked. "Remember, the kids didn't have Mromrosii from the EPFC sitting on their shoulders, making sure truth was twisted into the politically correct pattern."

"Well," said Guibert, "let's see if we can't get some sleep. We're likely to have a long day ahead of us tomorrow, unless Hairball can keep us from having engine trouble at the point I sort of think we're going to."

"Oh, golly!" Guibert said when the altimeter read 30K. "We're losing power! We have only enough thrust to permit me to set down softly."

"I'll engage the emergency alert transmitter!" said Karge cheerfully from the duplicate console. He switched the barge into stealth mode.

Guibert disconnected the barge's AI pilot and chopped the power. Dipping the nose, he started to glide toward the ancient building site. It was a bright, clear day. Inertial guidance and the vessel's passive sensors would be sufficient to put the team where they wanted to be.

The barge's skin formed a laminar path for the optical spectrum; longer wavelengths were scattered or absorbed. So long as the pilot avoided a turbulent wake (ripples in the atmosphere were radar-visible even if the cause of the disturbance wasn't), the vessel was virtually invisible.

The OC's cutter had even better stealth characteristics than the Petit Harrier barge did. Based on the description the port controllers had given, the kids had known exactly how to use their equipment.

Might be worth mentioning to a recruiting officer. Assuming the kids get back. Assuming we get back too.

"Shouldn't we be calling the port for help?" Hairball asked. The Mromrosi's voice remained a calm, dulcet baritone, but he looked twice as large as usual. His orange hair was sticking straight out from his skin.

"What?" said Karge. "You would have us use the manual override to interfere with the automatic alert system? You would have us *violate Standard Operating Procedure?*"

"Well, I—" the Mromrosi said. "Ah—of course those technical things aren't my field, you realize."

"Violate SOP indeed," Karge muttered.

"I'll log the improper request, sir," Dayly said, surprising Guibert. The data specialist was normally too straightforward to pick up on these little games.

Poor guy. Focused on Truth in a society dominated by Fairness.

"Or for that matter, setting three-three-one," Wenzil said, speaking aloud but without real hope that anybody else was interested. "Leonids and Hraunian vertebrates in general. The slugs' serotonin release system might well be similar."

"Hang on," said Guibert. "There may be some tree branches or—"

But there weren't. Guibert fluffed to a momentary hover on the attitude jets a few meters above the surface, then dropped the barge neatly into a circular clearing at the base of a low bluff.

"I do hope the True Persons won't be offended that we've trespassed on their planet," Hairball said. His concern, though real enough, had waited for the barge's safe landing.

"Maybe they've gotten used to it," said Dayly. He'd been watching the visual display without responsibility for the controls. "There was exhaust scarring on the soil. Another ship's been here recently."

"What?" said Hairball. "Trespassers in a proscribed area?"

"I think," Guibert said as he opened the hatch, "we've

found the kids. Or at least where the kids went when they left the Big Grotto."

"Now, setting two thirty-six would provide improved range through this atmosphere. . . ." Wenzil said.

She smiled as she led the team out through the hatch. Hairball was uncharacteristically silent.

The air was warm and musty, but it lacked the sour smell that pervaded the environs of the Big Grotto. The Sawicki stench was for the most part confined underground, but the tourists were expected to dump their waste and garbage on a midden. Hogs and bacteria provided the remainder of the reclamation process, neither category an odor-free medium.

"There certainly isn't any sign of foundations from up close," Guibert said. "Did I land us in the right spot, Dayly?"

"Yessir," said the data specialist as he squatted. He opened his field kit and took out a small prybar.

The vegetation was subtly different from that in the neighborhood of the Big Grotto only a hundred klicks away. This forest wasn't quite a monoculture, but the large trees were limited to three or four species. Guibert had noted literally hundreds of different varieties along the path from the landing field, and he wasn't trying to make a detailed census.

"This is regrowth on a cleared area," he said. He walked toward the bluff twenty meters away.

He'd seen the outcrop during landing, but he'd expected that at ground level it would be concealed by the boles of closely spaced trees. The vegetation hadn't had time to build itself into the impenetrable layers that would thin the forest floor by light-starvation.

There was a path from the clearing to the bluff. Trees had been cut or shoved sideways by an object which was dragged through them with enough force to pull up half their roots.

"Well," offered Hairball, "obviously the Sawickis evolved on the surface. These are the remains—you say there are remains—of an early Sawicki village."

Dayly dropped a bit of black material into the isotope separator from his kit and paused for its reading. "Not as early as all that," he said. "Fifty-seven years ago, plus or minus three, from carbonized material trapped under the fused rock." Karge laughed.

"Fused rock?" the Mromrosi said, utterly at sea. "From a volcano?"

"From an energy weapon," Guibert said. "Somebody blew the center out of a village, then used heavy equipment to break up the rest of it. Most of the buildings were probably wood anyhow."

The face of the bluff looked *almost* right. The join was invisible save for slight differences in lichen cover. The stone beneath Guibert's fingertips felt several degrees cooler than the material that closed the meters-wide hole in the outcrop.

"You didn't calibrate for the Carbon 14/16 ratio for *Sawick's* atmosphere!" Hairball cried in an access of hope. "That's why the date figure you got for the wood is so low!"

"Teach your grandmother to suck eggs!" Dayly snapped, seriously offended by the slur on his competence within his specialty. "Besides, it wasn't wood. It was carbonized bone. Human bone with ninety percent assurance."

"Come here, Dayly," Guibert said. "We've got what's either a plug or a door. If it's a door, I want you to open it." If it didn't open, maybe the barge could push the block out of the way.

"Piece of cake!" the data specialist said. He trotted over, rummaging in his case for another tool.

"I don't understand!" Hairball moaned. From the Mromrosi's tone, he did understand—but he *really* didn't like the implications of what he understood.

"Company coming," Wenzil called.

Guibert heard the sound too, the throb of rotors though the engines driving them were inaudible. He couldn't tell direction or distance through the forest.

"I guess I'll start with eight seventy-three and switch to—"

The barge exploded like a cone of thermite, flinging sparks in all directions. *The quality of Sawicki energy weapons hadn't degraded during the past fifty-seven years.*

An aircar with vertical fans front and rear sailed through the trees on the other side of the blazing barge, ten meters above the ground. The Sawicki crew was focused on the damage they'd done with their bow-mounted weapon.

Dayly was busy with the bluff face, but Guibert and Karge aimed their stunners. They were, of course, far slower than the weapons specialist.

Wenzil swept her beam across the aircar. The Sawicki crew began to laugh uncontrollably. The vehicle flipped and disappeared into the trees doing cartwheels.

"Awful!" Wenzil cried as she lowered her stunner to reprogram the keypad. "Try six-six-one!"

"Got it!" Dayly said. "It's a door!"

Three Sawickis ran out of the trees carrying thick tubes pointed forward from alongside their hips. They and the Harriers saw each other at the same time.

Guibert and Karge fired before the aliens could swing their bulky weapons to bear. The Sawickis hopped about, giggling. One of them triggered his weapon into a tree. A cubic meter of wood vanished in dazzling pyrotechnics. The trunk lifted skyward, then spiked straight down into the soil. Branches tangled with those of neighboring trees kept the bole upright.

Wenzil fired, using her new stunner setting. The Sawickis went limp and fell, their faces smiling beatifically.

"Not good enough!" the weapons specialist said. "Try five-four-nine!"

"Leave the damned setting!" Karge said. "It's fine the way it is!"

"Into the cave!" Guibert said. "It'll cover our flanks!"

"Modifying stunner settings to permanently impair the

personhood of native races is forbidden by—" Hairball said.

Another aircar slid through the forest, banking between a pair of the larger trees. The Sawicki gunner fired a wrist-thick hose of stripped ions while the vehicle's bow was still a tad high. The face of the bluff shattered. A chunk of limestone the size of a grapefruit dropped onto Hairball.

The rock remained balanced for a moment. The ensemble looked like a golf ball on a furry orange tee.

The Mromrosi fell over. Guibert and Karge had ducked from the ravening burst. Wenzil didn't, so she beat the men to the new target.

Sawickis jumped in all directions from the air-car, shrieking and tearing at themselves as though they'd been dipped in acid. Neither the gunshield nor the vehicle's hull appeared to have offered any protection against the stunner's effect. The car described a half loop, then slammed into the ground under the thrust of its inverted rotors.

"That's the ticket!" Wenzil cried. "Five-four-nine!"

Guibert holstered his stunner to pick up Hairball. Karge was bending to do the same. To both men's surprise, the Mromrosi got to its tiny feet unaided. *Little beggar must be boneheaded in pure fact!*

"Come on!" Guibert said, grabbing a handful of orange hair while Karge gripped the Mromrosi from the other side. They ran into the cave, dragging the alien along.

Dayly's electronic manipulations had pivoted away a huge disk of rock-patterned plastic. The data specialist had gone ahead with a handlight; Wenzil would provide a rear guard that no slug was likely to dent.

"My faculties have been seriously disarrayed!" Hairball said. "Nothing I observe would be of the slightest evidentiary purpose in an EPFC hearing."

"Come on, *run!*" Guibert gasped. The Sawickis' energy weapons had forged burnt air and burnt rock into an anvil-hard stench that choked him.

"Particularly my prohibition on setting five forty-nine should be ignored!" Hairball said.

There was a crash of rending metal behind them. The amount of light coming through the cave mouth dimmed. "Wee-*ha!*" Wenzil called. She must have brought down another Sawicki vehicle, blocking the cave's entrance for at least the time being.

The *tunnel's* entrance. The sides were glass-smooth, line-straight, and perfectly round in cross-section. The Sawickis lived underground, all right, but they sure weren't limited to natural caves.

"There's something blocking the way!" Dayly warned.

The far edge of the handlight beam picked out bulk and motion. Guibert dropped the Mromrosi and fumbled for his stunner again. *Were they Sawickis or—*

The relays of Wenzil's stunner went *tickticktick*. Her motto was, "If it moves, you shoot."

A pair of Sawickis in the tunnel ahead screamed like damned souls and began running up the curving rock walls. Each time they over-balanced and crashed down, they rose and repeated the attempt.

The object almost filling the tunnel was OC McBrien's missing cutter. The Sawickis had dragged the vessel deep enough that the mantle of living rock would conceal the cutter from even the most sensitive Magnicate instruments.

The speed with which the Sawickis had excavated such an immense tunnel was amazing. Guibert wondered what they did with the tailings; though with a whole forested planet to work with, the slugs wouldn't have much difficulty in disposing of a few kilotonnes of rock without coming to the notice of orbital sensors.

Hairball was moving normally now. Karge scooped up an energy weapon dropped by the howling Sawickis. "Here," he said, offering it to Wenzil.

"Are you kidding?" the weapons specialist said. "Listen to those screams from up the tunnel ahead of us. I must be getting *klicks* of range on this setting!"

"Help!" called a human voice. "Help," this time by a chorus of many voices.

The cutter pointed nose-first down the tunnel. Guibert got out his handlight and squeezed by the vessel. It was a tight fit but possible. "Dayly," he called over his shoulder. "Open us a hatch, will you?"

"Piece of cake!"

The Sawickis had bored an alcove into the side of the tunnel just ahead of where they left the cutter. The opening was barred. The tiny red bulb on the metal grill was the only light the ten humans inside the cell had seen for at least a week.

The eight teenagers wearing filthy but extremely expensive clothing were in reasonable shape. They reached out through the bars, babbling demands that Guibert release them

The other two humans were indeterminate as to age and even sex. They clutched half-carven mushroom caps to their pale chests as though the objects were talismans against the terrors of change.

Their workmanship was intricate and strikingly beautiful.

"Got the cutter open, sir!"

"Then come unlock these bars," Guibert ordered. "We found the kids too."

"The Sawickis aren't really autochthons!" cried a girl with the same cold perfection of visage as OC McBrien. "The planet's called Novy Evgeny! It was settled by one of the first colony ships from Earth. The Sawickis came less than a hundred years ago and enslaved them!"

"Fifty-seven years," Guibert said grimly, remembering the scrap of bone.

"Hold the light for me," Dayly ordered with the assurance of a workman thinking only of his task. Guibert obediently illuminated the featureless lockplate as the data specialist attached a suction probe.

"The slaves do all the work," Megan McBrien said. Her fellows had quieted now that freedom was in sight. "The Sawickis don't do a thing, not even clean up for themselves. That's why the Big Grotto's so filthy. They can't have human slaves *there*, of course."

"Piece of cake," the data specialist murmured. Tumblers clicked; the lock sprang open.

It probably *was* that easy a task for Dayly. If asked, he would have said that his equipment had done all the work. Which it had. As soon as Dayly had told it what to do.

"Let's get aboard," Guibert said. "I don't want to spend any longer in this place than I have to."

He shooed Dayly, then the released prisoners, on ahead of him. The pair who'd been born on Sawick wouldn't go until Megan put an arm around the shoulders of each and guided them forward.

"The Sawickis put Ethan and Nicole in with us to teach us mushroom carving," she explained. "They were going to keep us here for the rest of our *lives*."

The cutter was crowded with fifteen aboard, but Wenzil kept the non-essential personnel squeezed to the back of the cabin. Guibert dropped into the command seat.

"We can't back out of here," Karge said, his tone halfway between warning and question.

"Too true," Guibert agreed. "Wenzil! Did you program this boat's stunners to your pet setting?"

"Is the Pope a symbol of Patriarchal Domination?" the weapons specialist replied.

Ship-mounted stunners were identical to the hand weapons in all respects but size. *If Wenzil thought she was getting kilometers of slug-abatement with a hand stunner, what would three hundred times the power do?*

Something that should have been done at least fifty-seven years earlier.

Guibert triggered the bow stunners in a long burst, then keyed directions into the cutter's artificial intelligence. There was no way a human would be able to control the ship with the precision necessary to run through a maze of rock-walled tunnels.

"Hang on!" he warned. He engaged the AI.

Backblast from the jets rubbed the cutter along the

roof with a short, nerve-rending squeal as they lifted, but in seconds they'd outrun their own shockwaves. The main screen combined sonics and low-light imagery to project a view of the route ahead. Guibert found it wasn't something he cared to observe at the present speed.

He touched a control. The navigation unit projected a hologram of the tunnel complex, a huge ant farm stretching for scores of kilometers beneath the ground. Rock walls made a perfect medium for echo-ranging. The cutters' sorting system converted the returns into a detailed map.

Someone put a hand on Guibert's armrest. Wenzil had allowed Megan to worm forward once the cutter was under weigh.

"The Eugeners froze their population and used only appropriate technology," the girl said bitterly. "Five hundred years after they landed, they still lived in a single village. Except for the pigs getting loose, the planet was almost perfectly natural! How *could* the Sawickis enslave such innocent, harmless people?"

"The Sawickis . . ." Guibert said. Half of him was ashamed to be right. "The slugs play by the same rules as the rest of the universe, I'm afraid."

The cutter changed vector. On the main screen, hundreds of humans gawped from among the bulbous fruit of a mushroom farm. The Sawickis visible were rolling and clawing themselves with mad violence.

Another tunnel mouth loomed before the vessel. Guibert gave it a pulse with the big stunners.

"Hey, Wenzil?" he said. "How long before the stunner effect wears off on the slugs?"

"Darned if I know," Wenzil replied. "Five forty-nine's about a thirty-minute dose on Hagersfield Avians, if that's any help."

Hairball made a throat-clearing chirp. "Setting five-four-nine would erode the nerve sheaths of the, ah, interloping non-autochthons," he said. "The effect should be irreversible."

"No fooling?" Wenzil said.

Guibert triggered the weapons twice more for good measure.

"Of course," the Mromrosi added primly, "I am completely unable to observe or synthesize rationally because of my injury."

Something smashed against the cutter's bow. Guibert hoped it wasn't human. The slugs seemed to confine their slaves to fixed locations. Anyway, the object wasn't solid enough to be a problem to the armored hull.

Karge glanced over from the duplicate console. "You know," he said, "it doesn't look to me like there's an opening anywhere in the complex big enough to fit the cutter through."

"We'll make it," Guibert said.

The cutter yawed 30 degrees. Guibert lay on the stunner switch.

"That's good," the ethnologist continued conversationally. "I've got a date for tomorrow night with a tech from Medical Team Five, and I'd really hate to miss it."

"Not the big blond!" Wenzil interjected. She sounded as incensed as Guibert had ever heard her on a subject that didn't affect her specialty.

"No, no," Karge said. "You're thinking of Boxall, and he's far too butch for me. Besides, I don't think he'd be interested. I mean Quilici, the little sweetheart who doesn't look old enough to shave."

The ethnologist shook his head angrily. "A date with Quilici's not something I want to miss because that fudge-packer McBrien can't keep his own house in order.

"Begging your pardon, madam," he added to the girl kneeling between the consoles.

"Hang on," Guibert warned again. As the bow rotated, he fired the stunners for a last time.

The cutter shot up a sloping shaft and into the huge natural cavity of the Big Grotto. Guibert locked out the autopilot and chopped the main throttles. The bow tilted slightly. The vessel quivered, then began to rise on the thrust of the attitude jets alone.

Tourists stared at the sudden apparition from the tunnel hidden at the back of the grotto. Some of the humans were screaming; but not, Guibert was sure, as loudly as the intermingled Sawickis whose sensory nerves were shorting out.

"Sir," Dayly called in concern as the cavern's roof swelled in the top portion of the screen.

"It's okay," Guibert said, hoping that he was correct. "The ceiling's too thin to be rock. The slugs roofed over a sinkhole to provide a big enough setting for the tourists when the Magnicate arrived."

The cutter crunched against the grotto's roof. It would be plastic, like the tunnel door, and the gaps the Sawickis left to provide minimal light for human visitors would weaken the structure still further.

It had to be plastic.

Guibert slid the main throttles up to their stops. The drive engines boomed, lifting the cutter through the structural plastic with a violent shudder. Bits of rock erupted to either side of the vessel like confetti at a triumphal parade.

Guibert reengaged the autopilot. "Next stop, the *Night-Blooming Cereus*," he said. His team and the freed prisoners, even the pair of locals, cheered wildly.

"Hey, Hairball?" Karge said. "Do you suppose with the evidence we're bringing back, the Grands'll be able to act without a full Fairness Court hearing?"

"Since my confusion and lack of evidentiary value won't be realized until I have a physical examination in a week or more," the Mromrosi said, "I rather think my recommendations for immediate action will carry some weight, yes."

He made the squealing noise of Mromrosi laughter before he added, "They may well accept my statement that stunner setting five-four-nine is peculiarly suitable to the personhood of the Sawickis, also."

I don't play games any more because I'm too darned competitive. Gettysburg, *bridge, solitaire—you name it,* they suck me in and swallow my whole life if I let them get a finger on me. I stopped playing games before Wizards of the Coast took the gaming world by storm with a card game called Magic: The Gathering™.

The game was so successful that Wizards started a publishing offshoot to do fiction set in the world of their game. This wasn't of any particular concern to me one way or another until Bill Fawcett (a friend of some of the people involved but not formally associated with Wizards) phoned and said, "David you've got to do a story for the first Magic anthology! They've got a Dwarf Dirigible Brigade card and it's right up your alley!"

I told him to send the card (remember, I didn't know squat about the game) and I'd think about it. As Bill knew, I've always been fascinated with lighter-than-air flying machines.

The card arrived along with a note from Bill saying it was really the Goblin Balloon Brigade card—or I could write about a Dwarven Demolition Team card if I preferred. Bill's genius is for concepts, not details.

There were also eight pages of Writers' Guidelines provided by Wizards. About half the total involved political correctness (Wizards are based in Seattle), particularly as it involves sexism. They weren't offensive about it— they're thoroughly nice people to deal with in all respects—and I suppose there are people who needed to be told 51% of the population is female and that warrior babes in chain-mail bras are a joke. (People who need to be told that are fools whom I wouldn't want writing for *me even if they avoided those particular problems, but that's a different question.)*

The card shows a group of goblins in a light gas (hydrogen mixture) balloon wondering how they're going to get down again. The writers' guidelines indicated that most goblins were stupid.

I immediately thought of paratroopers.

I did my basic training at Ft. Bragg, home of the 82nd Airborne Division and the XVIIIth Airborne Corps, but my own chief drill sergeant was straight-leg infantry. When the airborne recruiters came around, he commented, "Why would anybody with all his marbles want to jump out of a perfectly good airplane?" I identified very strongly with that opinion.

Now I admit my attitude is unfair, but I could get away with it. Paratroopers are not an oppressed minority about whose mistreatment folks on the West Coast get upset.

I was very, very careful to avoid sexism in my story. Women are shown in positions of power and authority in all the levels encountered, and only 49% of the brigade's balloons are dong-shaped and have masculine names.

People who are interested in the history of flight will note that the method of filling the balloons was the standard one used by 19th century sport balloonists (though the process of coal gasification was carried on in the city's lighting plant rather than being done specially for the flight).

I guess I'll mention one more thing. I was pretty depressed at the time I started to write the story. There were a variety of reasons, but the fact that a close friend had just finished the lengthy process of dying in a stupid and unpleasant fashion was one of them.

Darned if writing "Airborne All the Way!" didn't break my mood. If I'd known it would be that easy, I'd have written a funny story at least six months before.

Airborne All The Way!

Crewgoblin Dumber Than #3 stared with his unusual look of puzzlement as labor goblins unrolled Balloon Prima. He scratched his chain mail jockstrap and said to Dog Squat, the balloon chief, "I dunno, boss."

Dog Squat rolled her eyes expressively and muttered, "Mana give me strength!" She glanced covertly to see if Roxanne was watching what balloon chiefs had to put up with, but the senior thaumaturge was involved with the team of dragon wranglers bringing the whelp into position in front of the coal pile.

Dog Squat glowered at her four crewgoblins. "Well, what don't you know?" she snarled. "What is there to know? We go up, we throw rocks down. You like to throw rocks, Number Three?"

"I like to bite them," said Dumber Than #1. "Will we be able to bite them, Dog Squat?"

The plateau on which the Balloon Brigade was readying for battle overlooked the enemy on the broad plain below. The hostile command group, pulsing with white mana, had taken its station well to the rear. White battalions were deploying directly from their line of march. Gullies and knolls skewed the rectangles of troops slightly, but the formations were still precise enough to make a goblin's disorderly mind ache.

"But boss," #3 said, "how do we get down again?"

"Getting down's the easy part!" Dog Squat shouted. "Rocks aren't any smarter than you are, and they manage

111

to get down, don't they? Well, not much smarter. Just leave the thinking to me, why don't you?"

"I really like to bite them," #1 repeated. He scraped at a black, gleaming fang with a black, gleaming foreclaw. "After we throw rocks, will we be able to bite them, Dog Squat?"

Dog Squat tried to visualize biting from a balloon. The closest she could come was a sort of ruddy blur that made her head ache worse than sight of the serried, white-clad ranks on the plains below. "No biting unless I tell you!" she said to cover ignorance. "Not even a teeny little bite!"

The large pile of coal was ready for ignition. The metal cover sat on the ground behind for the moment. Instead of forging a simple dome, the smiths had created a gigantic horned helmet. To either side of the coal was a sloped dirt ramp so that labor goblins could carry the helmet over the pile and cap it when the time came.

Balloons Prima and Secundus were unrolled to either side, and the three wranglers had finally gotten their dragon whelp into position in front of the pile. The other unfilled balloons waited their turn in double lines. It was time to start.

"All right, Theobald!" Senior Thaumaturge Roxanne said to the junior thaumaturge accompanying her, a mana specialist. "Get to work and don't waste a lot of time. We're already forty minutes behind schedule. Malfegor will singe the skin off me if we don't launch an attack before noon, and I promise that you won't be around to snicker if that happens."

Roxanne strode over to Dog Squat and her crew. The balloon chief tried to straighten like a human coming to attention; she wobbled dangerously. A goblin's broad shoulders and heavy, fanged skull raised the body's center of gravity too high unless the hips were splayed back and the knuckles kept usefully close to the ground.

"Everything ready here?" Roxanne demanded. The senior thaumaturge in charge of the Balloon Brigade wore a power suit with pinstripes of red, Malfegor's color. Her attaché case was an expensive one made of crimson belly skins, the sexual display markings of little male lizards. Very many little male lizards.

"Yes, sir, one hundred percent!" Dog Squat said. She frowned. She wasn't very good on numbers. "Two hundred percent?" she offered as an alternative.

"Yes, well, you'd better be," Roxanne said as she returned her attention to the dragon-filling.

The dragon whelp was no bigger than a cow. The beast didn't appear to be in either good health or a good humor. Its tail lashed restively despite the attempt of one wrangler to control that end while the other two held the whelp's head steady.

Junior Thaumaturge Theobald stood in front of the whelp with a book in one hand and an athame of red copper in the other. As Theobald intoned, a veil of mana flowed into the whelp from the surrounding rock. The creature's outlines softened.

Purple splotches distorted the generally red fields of force. The whelp shook itself. The wranglers tossed violently, but they all managed to hold on.

Dumber Than #1 bent close to Dog Squat and whispered gratingly in her ear. The balloon chief sighed and said, "Ah, sir?"

Roxanne jumped. A goblin's notion of a quiet voice was one that you couldn't hear in the next valley. "Yes?" the senior thaumaturge said.

"Ah, sir," Dog Squat said, "there's been some discussion regarding biting. Ah, whether we'll be biting the enemy, that is. Ah, that is, will we?"

Roxanne stared at the balloon chief in honest amazement. The four crewgoblins stood behind Dog Squat, scratching themselves but obviously intent on the answer.

"You'll be throwing rocks," Roxanne said, speaking very slowly and distinctly. She tried to make eye contact with each crewgoblin in turn, but a goblin's eyes tend to wander in different directions.

The senior thaumaturge tapped the surface of the plateau with one open toed, wedge-heeled shoe. "Rocks are like this," she said, "only smaller. The rocks are already in the gondola of your balloon. Do you all understand?"

None of them understood. None of them understood anything.

Dumber Than #3 scratched his jockstrap again. Roxanne winced. "Isn't that uncomfortable to wear?" she said. "I mean, chain mail?"

The crewgoblin nodded vigorously. "Yeah, you can say that again," he said. He continued to scratch.

"But when is she going to tell us about biting?" #1 said to Dog Squat in a steamwhistle whimper.

The dragon whelp farted thunderously. A huge blue flame flung the rearward wrangler thirty feet away with his robes singed off. The veil of inflowing mana ceased as Roxanne spun around.

"Sorry, sorry," Junior Thaumaturge Theobald said nervously as he closed his book, "The mana here is impure. Too much ground water—we must be over an aquifer. But she's full and ready."

"Carry on, then," Roxanne said grimly to the remaining dragon wranglers.

The leading wrangler crooned into the whelp's ear as her partner stroked the scaly throat from the other side. The whelp, shimmering with newfound power, bent toward the pile of coal and burped a puny ball of red fire. Roxanne frowned.

"Come on, girl, you can do it," the wrangler moaned. "Come on, do it for mommy. Come on, sweetie, come on—"

The dragon whelp stretched out a diamond-clawed forepaw and blasted a double stream of crimson fire from its nostrils. The jets ripped across and into the pile of coal, infusing the flame through every gap and crevice. The wranglers directed the ruby inferno by tugging their charge's head back and forth with long leads.

After nearly three minutes of roaring hellfire, the whelp sank back exhausted. It seemed to have shrunk to half its size of a few moments before. The two normally robed wranglers clucked the beast tiredly to its feet and

walked it out of the way. The third wrangler li.
alongside. In place of a robe he was wearing a red gon.
lon borrowed from a nearby cavalry regiment.

The coal pile glowed like magma trapped deep in the
planetary mantle. "Come on!" Roxanne ordered. "Let's
not waste this. Get moving and get it capped!"

The capping crew was under the charge of two novice
thaumaturges, both of them in their teens. In response
to their chirped commands, the four labor goblins lifted
the gigantic helmet by means of crosspoles run through
sockets at the front and back of the base. They began to
shuffle forward, up the earthen ramps built to either side
of the pile of coal.

The porters were goblins chosen for brawn rather than
brains. The very concept of intellect would have boggled
the porters' minds if they'd had any. In order to keep
the crews moving in the right direction, the novices projected a line of splayed, clawed footprints in front of the
leaders on either ramp to carefully fit his/her feet into.

The goblins on the rear pole set their feet exactly on
the same markings. They didn't put any weight down
until they were sure the foot was completely within the
glowing red lines. The cap's rate of movement was more
amoebic than tortoiselike. Nevertheless, it moved. Senior
Thaumaturge Roxanne drummed fingers on the side of
her attaché case in frustration, but there was no hurrying
labor goblins.

The leaders paused when they reached the last pairs
of footprints at the ends of the ramps. The porters stood
stolidly, apparently oblivious of the heat and fumes from
the coal burning beside them.

The novice thaumaturges turned to Roxanne. "Yes!"
she shouted. "Cap it! Cap it now!"

The novices ordered, "Drop your poles!" in an uncertain tenor and a throaty contralto. Three of the porters
obeyed. The fourth looked around in puzzlement, then
dropped his pole also. The helmet clanged down
unevenly but still down, over the pile. The metal completely covered the coal, shutting off all outside air.

The horns flaring to the sides of the giant helmet were nozzles. Thick hoses were attached to the ends of horns. The novice thaumaturges clamped the free ends of the hoses into the filler inlets of Balloons Prima and Secundus. Adjusting the hoses was hard work, but the task was too complicated to be entrusted to a goblin.

Roxanne personally checked the connection to Prima while the junior thaumaturge did the same on the other side. "All right," she said to the novice watching anxiously from the top of the ramp where he'd scrambled as soon as he attached his hose. "Open the cock."

The novice twisted a handle shaped like a flying dragon at the tip of the horn, opening the nozzle to gas that made the hose writhe on its way to the belly of Balloon Prima. The senior thaumaturge stepped away as the balloon began to fill.

The balloons were made from an inner layer of sea serpent intestine. The material was impervious to gas and so wonderfully tough that giants set bars of gold between layers of the stuff and hammered the metal into foil.

Prima bulged into life, inflating with gases driven out of the furiously hot coal in the absence of oxygen to sustain further combustion. The four drag ropes tightened in the clawed hands of labor goblins whose job was to keep the balloon on the ground until it had been completely filled with its inlet closed.

"You lot!" Roxanne said to Dog Squat and her crew. "What are you waiting for? Get into your gondola now!"

Dog Squat opened her mouth to explain that she'd been waiting for orders. She forgot what she was going to say before she got the words out. "Dumber Thans," she said instead, "get into the little boat."

The wicker gondola creaked as the five goblins boarded it. The balloon was already full enough to lift off the ground and swing in the coarse steel netting that attached the car to it. A light breeze swept down from Malfegor's aerie, ready to waft the brigade toward the enemy on the plain below.

The floor of the gondola was covered with rocks the

size of a goblin's head. Many of the missiles were delight-
fully jagged. #3 patted a piece of chert with a particularly
nice point.

Balloon Secundus lifted into sight from the other side
of the helmet. It was sausage-shaped, like forty-nine percent of the brigade's equipment. Prima was one of the
slight majority of balloons which, when seen from the
side, looked like a huge dome with a lesser peak on top.
The attachment netting gleamed like chain mail over the
pinkish white expanse of sea serpent intestine.

Dog Squat picked up a rock and hefted it. A good,
solid chunk of granite. A rock that a goblin could really
get into throwing, yep, you betcha. Dog Squat had heard
some principals would try to fob their crews off with
blocks of limestone that crumbled if you just looked
crossways at it, but not good old Malfegor. . . .

"Shut off the gas flow!" Senior Thaumaturge Roxanne
called to the novice on the ramp above her. She released
the catch on the input. When Prima wobbled, the hose
pulled loose, and Roxanne clamped the valve shut.

"Cast off!" she ordered the ground crew.

Three of the goblins dropped their ropes. The fourth,
an unusually powerful fellow even for a labor goblin,
continued to grip his. His big toes were opposable, and
he'd sunk his claws deep into the rock of the plateau.

Balloon Prima lifted at an angle. The gondola was
nearly vertical, pointing at the goblin holding the rope.

"Let's go!" Roxanne screamed. "Drop the rope!"

She batted the goblin over the head with her attaché
case. He looked at the senior thaumaturge quizzically.

"Let go!" Roxanne repeated. "Don't you understand
what I'm saying?"

The goblin blinked. He continued to hold onto both
the rope and the ground. Balloon Prima wobbled above
him.

Roxanne looked up. Dog Squat peered down at her.
The balloon chief wore a familiar puzzled expression.
The crewgoblins were stacked, more or less vertically, on
the back of their chief. A gust from the wrong direction

and the contents of the gondola would tip out promiscuously.

"You!" the senior thaumaturge said. "Hit this idiot on the head with a rock. A hard rock!"

Dog Squat looked again at the rock she held, decided that it would do, and bashed the handler goblin with it. The victim's eyeballs rolled up. He dropped the rope and fell over on his back.

Balloon Prima shot skyward, righting itself as it rose. The rope the goblin dropped whipped around Roxanne's waist and dragged her along. The senior thaumaturge weighed scarcely more than any one of the rocks in the bottom of the gondola, so her presence didn't significantly affect the balloon's upward course.

Dog Squat looked over the side of the gondola at Roxanne and blinked. The senior thaumaturge, swinging like a tethered canary, screamed, "Pull me in, you idiot!"

"I didn't know you were coming along, sir," the balloon chief said contritely. She rapped her head hard with her knuckles to help her think. "Or did I?" she added.

"Pull me—" Roxanne said. The rope, kinked rather than knotted about her, started to unwrap. Roxanne grabbed it with both hands. Her attaché case took an obscenely long time to flutter down. At last it smashed into scraps no larger than the original pelts on the rocks below.

Dog Squat tugged the rope in hand over hand, then plucked the senior thaumaturge from it and lifted her into the gondola. Roxanne's eyes remained shut until she felt throwing stones beneath her feet rather than empty air.

"Are we . . . ?" she said. She looked over the side of the gently swaying gondola. Because of its heavy load, Balloon Prima had only climbed a few hundred feet above the plateau, but the ground continued to slope away as Malfegor's sorcerous breeze pushed them toward the enemy lines.

"Oh, mana," Roxanne said. "Oh mana, mana, mana."

"Boss," said Dumber Than #2, "do you remember

when I ate that possum the trolls walked over the week before?"

"Yeah," said Dog Squat. Everybody in the crew remembered that.

"Well, I feel like that again," #2 said.

He did look greenish. His eyeballs did, at least. He was swaying a little more than the gondola itself did, come to think.

"Where did you find a dead possum up here, Number Two?" Dog Squat asked.

"I didn't!" the crewgoblin said with queasy enthusiasm. He frowned, pounded himself on the head, and added, "I don't think I did, anyways."

"Oh, mana," the senior thaumaturge moaned. "How am I ever going to get down?"

"Getting down is the easy part!" Dumber Than #3 said brightly. "Even rocks manage to get down! You're probably lots smarter than a rock, sir."

Senior Thaumaturge Roxanne took another look over the side of the gondola, then curled into a fetal position in the stern.

"Did you eat a dead possum, too?" #2 asked in what for a goblin was a solicitous tone.

Balloon Prima had continued to drift while the senior thaumaturge considered her position. The battalions of white-clad enemy troops were by now almost directly below. They didn't look the way they ought to. They looked little.

Dog Squat frowned. She wondered if these were really the people she was supposed to drop rocks on.

"Boss, are we in the right place?" #4 asked. The gondola tilted thirty degrees in its harness. All four crewgoblins had leaned over the same side as their chief. "Them guys don't look right."

"They make my head hurt to look at," #3 added. "They're—"

Goblins didn't have a word for "square." Even the attempt to express the concept made lights flash painfully behind the crew-goblin's eyes.

In a fuzzy red flash, Dog Squat gained a philosophy of life: When in doubt, throw rocks. "We throw rocks!" she shouted, suiting her actions to her words.

The goblins hurled rocks down with enthusiasm—so much enthusiasm that Dog Squat had to prevent Dumber Than #1 from tossing Roxanne, whom he'd grabbed by a mistake that nearly became irremediable. When Dog Squat removed the senior thaumaturge from #1's hands, the crewgoblin tried to bite her—probably #1's philosophy of life—until Dog Squat clouted him into a proper attitude of respect.

The gondola pitched violently from side to side because of the repeated shifts in weight. The entire balloon lurched upward since the rocks acted as ballast when they weren't being used for ammunition. The crew of Balloon Prima was having as much fun as goblins could with their clothes on (and a lot more fun than goblins have with their clothes off, as anyone looking at a nude goblin can imagine).

They weren't, however, hitting anybody on the ground, which was increasingly far below.

The tight enemy formations shattered like glass on stone as Balloon Prima drifted toward them. That was the result of fear, not actual damage. The goblins could no more brain individual soldiers a thousand feet below than they could fly without Prima's help.

That didn't matter particularly to Dog Squat and her crew. Throwing rocks was a job worth doing for its own sake; and anyway, the collapse of ordered battalions into complete disorder fitted Dog Squat's sense of rightness. The universe (not as clear a concept as it would have been to, say, a senior thaumaturge; but still, a concept in goblin terms) liked chaos.

White-clad archers well to the side of the balloon's expected course bent their bows in enormous futile efforts. The altitude that made it difficult for the goblins to hit targets on the ground also made it impossible for archers on the ground to reach Balloon Prima. The arrows arcing back to earth did more damage to other whiteclad troops than the goblinflung rocks had done.

Malfegor's breeze continued to drive Balloon Prima in the direction of the enemy command group. The hail of missiles from the gondola stopped.

"Boss?" said #4. "Where are the rocks?"

Dog Squat looked carefully around the floor of the gondola. She even lifted Roxanne, who moaned softly in response.

"There are no rocks," Dog Squat said.

Dumber Than #3 scratched himself. "I thought there was rocks," he said in puzzlement.

"Can we bite them now, Dog Squat?" #1 said.

Dog Squat looked over the side again. She hoped there might be another thaumaturge or somebody else who could tell them what to do.

There wasn't. Dog Squat checked both sides to be sure, however.

The enemy had made preparations against the Balloon Brigade's attack. Two teams of antiballoon ballistas galloped into position between Balloon Prima and the white command group. The crews dismounted and quickly cranked their high-angle weapons into action.

A ball nearly the size of the rocks the goblins had thrown whizzed toward the balloon and burst twenty feet away in a gush of white mana.

"Oooh," said Dog Squat and three of her crewgoblins.

The breeze shifted slightly, driving Balloon Prima in the direction of the white blast. Malfegor was hunting the bursts on the assumption that the safest place to be was where the immediately previous shell had gone off.

"Ohhh," said Dumber Than #2, holding his belly with both hands. "The more we shake around, the older the possum gets."

Sure enough, the next antiballoon shell flared close to where Prima would have been if she'd continued on her former course. The breeze jinked back, continuing to blow the balloon toward the command group below.

The hostile artillerists cranked their torsion bows furiously. They were also trying to raise their angle of aim, but Balloon Prima was almost directly overhead and the ballistas couldn't shoot vertically. By the time Prima was in the defender's sights again, the balloon would be directly over the command group.

Dumber Than #4 nudged Dog Squat and pointed to the tightly curled senior thaumaturge. "Can we throw her now, boss?" the crewgoblin asked. "Seeings as we're, you know, out of rocks?"

Dog Squat pursed her lips, a hideous sight. "No," she decided at last. "Throwing rocks is good. Throwing thaumaturges is not good."

At least she didn't think it was. They ought to throw something, though.

"Can we bite them, then?" said #1.

Dumber Than #2 vomited over the side with great force and volume, much as he'd done after the never-to-be forgotten (even by a goblin) possum incident.

The huge greenish yellow mass plunged earthward at increasing velocity. It was easier to track than a rock of the same size because it was slightly fluorescent. For a moment Dog Squat thought the bolus was going to hit one of the antiballoon ballistas. Instead, it glopped the ballista's captain, who fell backward into his weapon.

The toppling ballista fired its shell straight up. Though the glowing white ball missed the gondola by a dragon's whisker, it punched through the side of the gas bag above.

The top of the balloon ruptured with a loud bang. The blast of mana expelled and ignited the bag's contents in a puff of varicolored flame—a mixture of hydrogen, carbon monoxide, and methane, all flammable and dazzlingly pretty.

"Ooooh!" said all the goblins in delight. #2, no longer holding his belly, had a particularly pleased expression.

Ex-Balloon Prima dropped, though not nearly as fast as the rocks thrown earlier. The gas bag had burst, but the steel netting still restrained the tough fabric of sea serpent intestine. The combination made an excellent parachute.

There was wild panic on the ground below. The enemy commanders had realized Prima would land directly on top of them.

Dumber Than #1 looked at the lusciously soft enemy officers, coming closer every moment the air whistled past the gondola. He asked plaintively, "Please, boss, can we bite them?"

Dog Squat glanced at Roxanne—no change there— and made a command decision. "Yes," the balloon chief said decisively. "We will bite them."

Dumber Than #3 scratched himself with the hand that wasn't gripping the edge of the gondola. He gestured toward the senior thaumaturge and said fondly, "Gee, it must be something to be smart enough to plan all this. She's really a genius, ain't she, boss?"

"She sure is," Dog Squat agreed, preparing to jump into the middle of the terrified enemy at the moment of impact.

Senior Thaumaturge Roxanne whimpered softly.

Writer/friend Esther Friesner phoned me saying she was going to do an anthology of tabloid SF—SF stories based on the sort of news you find in the tabloids in the supermarket checkout line. The anthology title, Alien Pregnant by Elvis!, says it all.

I decided it'd be a good idea. I'm darned if I know why—I've turned down plenty of more sensible, profitable requests over the years. I guess it just sounded like fun; and, now that I think about it, that's probably the best reason there is to do anything.

My wife Jo remarked after reading a story of mine "The Predators" that the author was clearly a person who hated plants. There's a certain amount of truth to that, but it's not an irrational prejudice.

When I was a kid growing up we had a large yard with trees, limestone retaining walls, and other neat things to climb and play on. I couldn't, though, because my mother had planted flowers along each vertical surface. There was also an iris bed in the back yard (it grew some quite remarkable cutworms), and half the basement was given over to African violets growing in trays beneath fluorescent lights.

It wasn't much of a leap from that real situation to "Cannibal Plants from Heck." A 1958 Donald Duck story has so similar a theme that I now wonder if one of Carl Barks' wives grew flowers in the same fashion as my mother.

Cannibal Plants From Heck

Betsy Moffett stood beside her father in the gravel driveway, judging the house with nine-year-old eyes. Behind them the real estate agent rummaged in the trunk of her BMW.

It wasn't a large house: one story and forty feet wide by twenty-four deep. There were only two of them now, so that was all right. The three dogwood trees in front had gnarled, low-branching trunks four to six inches in diameter. Betsy had never before been close to a tree she thought she could climb.

In back were a rusty swing set and a length of old telephone pole. The bare, trampled soil around the pole showed that it once had mounted a net and backboard. A new set couldn't cost *very* much, and Betsy had a birthday coming in July . . .

The agent found what she wanted, a thin cap reading UNDER CONTRACT in blue letters on white. She walked over to the realty company's white-on-blue sign, careful because of the soil's March squishiness, and clipped the cap into place to hide FOR SALE.

There were children playing down the street. Betsy couldn't see them from where she stood, but voices rose and fell in shrill enthusiasm.

The other houses in the subdivision were pretty much like this one. Some had brick facades, some had decks; but none of them was very large, and Mr. Moffett's four-year-old Ford fit in much better than the agent's sparkling BMW. The agent had mentioned the well and septic tank in a hurried voice quite different from that in which she described the house as *so cute, a little jewelbox!*

A horse-drawn wagon turned the corner at the end of the block and plodded down the street. The driver was a shabby-looking black man; a large dog walked beside the horse with its head down. Betsy had never seen a real horse-drawn wagon before. She was surprised to notice that it had rubber tires like a car instead of the wooden wheels like the ones on TV.

Neighborhood dogs barked. Several kids appeared on fluorescent bicycles and swooped around the wagon. The driver waved to them.

The agent returned to the Moffetts. For a moment as she glanced toward the wagon her face had been without expression, but the professional smile returned an instant later. "Charles," she said, extending her hand to Betsy's father, "I'm sure you'll be *very* happy here. Let me know when you've decided on the lender and we'll set up the closing."

She shook hands firmly. Her fingernails were the same shade as the cuffs and collar of the blouse she wore beneath the jacket of her gray suit.

"And Betsy," the agent added as she took Betsy's hand in turn, "you're going to have a wonderful time too. Look at all the children to play with!"

The bicycles now lay on their sides in the front yard of a house three doors down. A group had coalesced there to chalk markers on the concrete driveway. The kids ranged from older than Betsy to an infant whose elder brother pushed the stroller.

"I'll be talking to you soon!" the agent said brightly as she got into her car. The BMW's door thunked with a dull finality.

The black man guided his horse to the side of the road, out of the way. The agent backed with verve, then chirped her tires as she took off toward town.

Mr. Moffett put an arm around Betsy's shoulders. "This is my chance to garden," he said. He gestured with

the glossy catalogs in his other hand. Those on top read
White Flower Farm and Thompson & Morgan, but there
were several more in the sheaf.

"Your mother would never let me garden, you know,"
Mr. Moffett went on, surveying the yard with his eyes.
"She ridiculed the whole idea. Well, I'm going to prove
how wrong she was."

"Whoa, Bobo," murmured the black man.

The Moffetts turned. The wagon halted directly in
front of the house. It was full of live plants. Instead of
pots, the root balls were wrapped in burlap. Most of the
plants were in flower, and the blooms were gorgeous.

"Dad, can I play with the horse?" Betsy asked as she
skipped toward the animal without waiting for what
might have been a negative answer.

"The mule, missie," the driver said. "Bobo's a mule,
and just the stubbornest mule there ever was—"

He winked toward Mr. Moffett.

"—but he's on company manners right this moment."

Bobo eyed Betsy over the traces. The mule's head was
huge, but he looked friendly in a solemn, reserved
fashion.

"That's Harbie," the black man said, nodding toward
the dog who sniffed the mailbox post meaningfully, "and
I'm Jake."

"Can I touch Bobo?" Betsy asked, her hand half
extended.

"You surely can, missie," Jake said. To Betsy's father
he went on, "Might I interest you in some plants, sir? A
new house ought to have flowers around it, don't you
think?"

Betsy rubbed the white blaze on the mule's forehead.
One of Bobo's long ears twitched and caressed her wrist.
Harbie trotted over, sat at Betsy's feet, and raised a paw
for attention.

"Well, I'm going to be gardening, yes," Mr. Moffett
said. He waved the catalogs. "But I'll be getting my stock
only from the best nurseries. I—what *are* these plants?
I don't think I recognize any of them."

"They's flowers, sir," Jake said. Betsy couldn't tell how old he was. Older than her father, anyway. "I grows them because they's pretty, is all. I've got bushes up to the house, if you'd like something bigger."

"No, I . . ." Mr. Moffett said. He glanced doubtfully at his catalogs, then back to the wagonload of plants. "Are those Hemerocallis so early?"

"There's daylilies, yessir," Jake agreed. "The tall ones, there, and they's some smaller ones around back as would make a nice bed along the street here."

Harbie rolled over on her back and kicked her legs in the air. Her weight pinned Betsy's right toes warmly. Betsy squatted to rub the dog's belly. The mule snorted.

"Those are eight feet *tall*," Mr. Moffett said, staring at the dark green stems from which brilliant red flowers spread.

"Yessir," Jake agreed. "But they's short ones too. Would you like something for the new house, then?"

Mr. Moffett looked again at the catalogs. To Betsy, the illustrated plants seemed dim and uninteresting compared to the variegated richness in the back of the wagon.

"No thank you," Mr. Moffett said abruptly. "I prefer to trust certified species. Betsy, come along. We need to get back to the apartment."

He reached decisively for her hand. Harbie rolled to her feet and wagged her tail as Betsy straightened.

"Good day to you, then, sir," Jake said. He touched his cap and clucked to his mule.

Mr. Moffett didn't get into the car immediately after all. Instead, he continued to watch the wagon clopping down the street.

"What an odd man," he said.

The lustrous flowers nodded from the back of the wagon.

When Betsy ran up at the head of a delegation of five children, Mr. Moffett was loading a cart with washed stone from the pile the truck had deposited at the end of the driveway.

It was a clear day; even at ten in the morning the

June sun was hot. Mr. Moffett nonetheless wore his new gardening apron. The pockets glittered with tools: clippers, hedge trimmers, a planting dibble, and a set of cast-aluminum trowels with a matching spading fork.

"Dad!" Betsy cried. "Stepan's mom says we can take the backboard off their garage and bring it over to *our* pole so it can be regulation height!"

The rest of the children waited behind Betsy, viewing with interest the work Mr. Moffett had already done in the yard. Except for the driveway itself and a narrow walk, the area between the house and the street was now a flowerbed. Irises, tulips, and the daylilies which Mr. Moffett always called Hemerocallis predominated, but there were many more bulb plants that Betsy didn't recognize. Perhaps some of them would have been familiar under other names, but as Acidanthia, Zantedeschia, and similar sounds they could have been tribes of the Amazon.

The climbable dogwoods were gone, chain-sawed off flush with the ground. Near where they had stood, Mr. Moffett had planted what he called Cornus Alba Elegantissima—which looked like dogwoods to Betsy, only very spindly. The saplings had to be guyed in three directions to hold them straight.

"Pole?" Mr. Moffett said. He looked doubtfully at the group of children.

Betsy glanced over her shoulder to make sure the other children were staying in the driveway as she'd warned them to do so that they didn't threaten the plantings. Everybody was fine.

Jake and his wagon clopped down the street. Harbie walked ahead of Bobo with her head up, stepping in a sprightly fashion. Jake raised his cap in salute when he saw Betsy.

Mr. Moffett noticed the wagon also. "Does that man live around here?" he asked with an edge in his voice. His eyes were on Stepan, the only black in the present group.

"No sir," Stepan said, holding himself stiff. "But my mom, she buys his flowers sometimes."

"We buy flowers too!" said Muriel, who was only six.

"You know the pole, Dad," said Betsy, determined to get the discussion back on course. "In the back yard. The people who lived here before took the backboard when they moved but Stepan's mom says we can move theirs and have it regulation height!"

"Oh, that pole," Mr. Moffett said. He rubbed his forehead with the back of his hand, looking serious. "Ah."

The car was parked in the street because the Moffett's driveway was full of gardening supplies. Besides the peanut-sized washed stone for drainage at the bottom of pots and flower beds, there were pallets of bagged topsoil and other bags marked ORGANIC PEAT MOSS—but with a stencilled cow to indicate the real contents more delicately than DRIED COW-FLOP would have done.

Mr. Moffett had said he would carry the temporary excess to the metal storage shed he'd built at the back of the property, but he hadn't gotten around to it yet. The 5-horsepower rototiller that had dug the front lawn into flowerbeds was in the shed already, parked beside the powerful chipper/shredder that had ground up all but the lower trunks of the dogwood trees with an amazing amount of racket.

Betsy was a little concerned that her father hadn't bought a lawn mower among all the other new equipment. She was afraid he'd decided that there wouldn't be any lawn left when he was done with the yard.

"We can get it right now, Dad," Betsy pressed. "You don't have to help. The bolts are still up in the pole, and we can borrow Lee's father's ladder. You can go on digging."

"I'm sorry, darling," Mr. Moffett said. He sounded at least uncomfortable if not exactly sorry. "*That* pole is part of my plan for the garden. I'm going—I'm preparing right now—to plant Ipomoea around it. So that the vines can climb properly."

"Whoa, Bobo," Jake muttered out in the street.

Betsy glanced sideways so that she didn't have to look at her father for the moment. He wouldn't meet her eyes anyway. He never did at times like these.

Roses twined up the wrought iron posts which supported the rain-shield over the front door. The window to Betsy's bedroom was a green blur from the potted fern which Mr. Moffett had hung there to catch the natural light.

"Good day, sir," Jake called. "I guess you're going to raise some tomatoes."

Harbie snuffled the back of Betsy's knees. Betsy turned quickly and bent to pet the dog. Harbie's tail wagged enthusiastically, whopping all the children as they crowded around her.

"No sir, I don't intend to raise vegetables," Mr. Moffett said stiffly. "I'm concentrating on flowers and flowering shrubs, so if you're selling tomato plants—"

"Not me, sir," Jake said with a chuckle. "But if you don't plan to raise tomatoes—"

He nodded toward the bags of "organic peat moss."

"—then did you tell the cows?"

"Can we get the backboard, now?" Muriel demanded.

"Yeah, what did he say?" Stepan said.

Mr. Moffett grunted angrily. "I don't care to buy any of your plants," he said. "Good day."

"You said," Jake said from the seat of his wagon, "that you were going to plant morning glories around the pole in the back, sir. I've got some fine morning glories here myself."

"I'm quite satisfied with my Purpurea Splendens, thank you," Mr. Moffett said, taking a brightly colored seed packet from an apron pocket. "They have a delicate lavender—"

He stopped. Even the children gaped at the size of the trumpet-shaped blooms Jake held up for approval. They were pure white and at least eight inches across.

Mr. Moffett swallowed. "Lavender picotee, I was saying," he concluded weakly.

"If you want purple edges, sir," Jake said agreeably as

he leaned further back into the loaded wagon, "then I got them too."

The flower he raised on a vine trailing back into the mass of root balls and foliage was ten inches in diameter. As Jake had said, the edges of the broad bell were faintly lavender.

Mr. Moffett stared at the picture on the seed packet in his hand. "No," he said. He sounded angry. It seemed to Betsy that her father was afraid to look directly at the black man's obviously superior bloom.

"No!" Mr. Moffett repeated. "I prefer a certified product, thank you. Now if you *all* will leave me alone, I have a great deal of work to do."

Mr. Moffett lifted the handles of his cart and began wheeling it around the side of the house. He had only a part load of gravel, and that was unbalanced.

Harbie had been lying on her back so that the children could rub her belly. She rolled to her feet and trotted to the wagon.

"Good day, then, sir," Jake called. He bowed in his seat to the children. "And good day to you, sirs and missies."

Bobo clopped forward again without a formal order from his driver.

"Let's go back to Stepan's and choose up sides," Betsy said.

"I don't get it," said Stepan, looking in the direction Mr. Moffett had taken around the house. "What's your dad mean certified? He could see the flowers, couldn't he? They're *real*."

"I don't know what real means any more," Betsy answered morosely. She broke into a run to get out of the yard—her father's yard—quickly.

The school bus stopped half a block up from the Moffett's house. There were still hours of daylight left on an early September afternoon. Todd ran past Betsy calling, "Come on! We're all going to meet at Stepan's when we change clothes!"

Betsy waved, but she didn't much feel like playing. With every step toward home she felt less like playing, or starting the leaf collection for science class, or doing anything at all.

The front yard was dug up again. Betsy's father had removed the bulbs for storage through the winter, then tilled the beds and worked in compost. The rototiller waited beside the house with a blanket over it, ready to finish the job under the yard light above the porch as soon as Mr. Moffett got home.

Because the front yard looked so much like a construction site, Betsy picked her way past bushes to the side door. The Hydrangeas were done blooming now, but during their season her father had gotten sprays of pink, white and blue flowers in the same bed by careful liming to lower the soil acidity at one end.

Mr. Moffett was always careful. He didn't even own a grass-whip for edging, because the spinning fishline wasn't precise enough. He used hedge trimmers and his trowels instead.

Betsy's father was always careful with his gardening.

Hollies grew along the side of the house, flanking the doorway two and two. There were three China Girls and a China Boy that Mr. Moffett said wouldn't form berries but was necessary anyway. The holly leaves were sharp. They crowded the concrete pad in front of the door.

Shrubs concealed the back yard. The top of what had been the swing set was just visible above the Forsythias. The bars were now festooned with baskets holding Fuchsias and Campanula. Betsy didn't suppose those plants would spend the winter outdoors, but she was afraid to ask her father what he planned to do with them.

Betsy unlocked the door and went into the kitchen. She dropped her jacket on a chair and opened a can of ravioli to warm for a snack in the microwave while she changed clothes.

Three large Bird of Paradise plants grew from a pot in front of the window beside the refrigerator. A Pothos sprawled from the tray beneath the sink window and across most of the back wall. The growlight in the ceiling flooded down on them as well as on the Cycads and Baobab on the kitchen table.

Betsy visualized the Baobab spurting up to the size its ancestors grew to on the African plains—seventy feet tall, with a huge water-filled trunk. The house would disintegrate, and the Moffetts would have to move back to an apartment where Betsy's father couldn't garden any more.

Oh, well.

Betsy changed her school clothes for worn jeans and a sweatshirt in her room. She had to turn the overhead light on to see, because the basket-hung fern covered the window almost completely. At least the light fixture held a regular bulb. Her father had given up on another growlight when Betsy began to cry.

A free-standing hanger rail holding skirts and blouses filled the space between the bed and the wall. The closet had been converted to shelves to store bulbs through the winter. Betsy's father had given her a choice. She could have kept the closet, but then her sweaters and under-wear would have gone into cardboard boxes while her dresser provided for the bulbs.

Sighing, Betsy went back to the kitchen. The Pothos tickled her neck with a pointed leaf as she got a Pepsi out of the refrigerator. She dumped the ravioli on a plate and carried the snack out through the living room to the front door.

The box in the center of the living room holding the Datura was four feet square. It would have made the room seem claustrophobically small even without the other plants filling the corners and shelves on all the walls.

Betsy sat down on the front steps and ate her ravioli bleakly. She could hear the other children playing down the street, but she was too depressed to go join them.

"Whoa, Bobo," a voice said.

Betsy's eyes focused. Though she'd been looking toward the street, there was nothing in her mind but dull green thoughts. Now she saw that Jake had halted his heavily-laden wagon in front of the Moffetts' driveway. "Oh!" she called. "Hi, Jake!"

As always before when Betsy had seen him, Jake was carrying a new assortment of plants. This time many of them were completely covered in what looked like blankets and old bedsheets.

Harbie ran to Betsy and began licking her hands. The dog didn't try to get the last three ravioli until Betsy put the plate down on the step and walked out to the wagon.

"Good afternoon, missie," Jake said, tipping his hat. "Might I trouble you for a bucket of water for Bobo?"

It was funny: even in Betsy's present mood, the flowers and bushes in the wagon had a cheerful look to them. Most of the blooms *were* bigger and brighter than anything Betsy's father had managed to grow, but the difference was greater than that.

"Sure," Betsy said, starting toward the shed where she knew her father kept galvanized buckets of various sizes. Then she stopped and turned around again. "Jake," she said. "Would you like a Pepsi?"

"I surely would," the black man said. "But let me pay for it, missie. It's better that I do if anybody should ask."

Betsy still wasn't sure about Jake's age. His face was unwrinkled and his moustache was dark, but sometimes she got the feeling he was—old. Very old.

"I—" Betsy said. "Jake, come in the house with me."

Bobo snorted. Jake shook his head firmly. "No, missie," he said. "That I will *not* do, nossir."

Betsy squeezed her eyes to keep from crying. "Will you look in through all the windows at least?" she begged. "You know about plants. I want you to see the house. And the yard!"

Jake got down from the wagon seat, moving with the deliberation of a big cat rather than an old man. He walked to the front window, careful not to step on the low bushes planted along the front of the house. "Pretty enough bog rosemaries," he said. "A bit on the puny side, though."

"My dad calls them Andromeda," Betsy said.

"To tell the truth," Jake murmured, "I thought he might."

Betsy darted inside, ready to move anything that prevented Jake from getting a clear view of the environment in which she lived. He walked to her window after gazing seriously into the living room. Betsy opened the closet doors and swung the fern out of the way so that he could look in.

The spare bedroom had become a hothouse with multiple banks of growlights. Betsy couldn't get to the orchid-shrouded window, but the mass of variegated green Jake could glimpse was sufficient to give him the picture. Her father's bedroom was almost as packed, though the plants lowering over the dresser and single bed weren't as temperature sensitive.

The bathroom window was above head height. Jake could see the Begonias in the hanging basket, but the tubbed water lily that turned the shower/bath into a cramped shower was concealed. She could tell him about it, but it was such a drop in the bucket that she didn't suppose she'd bother.

While Jake peered through one kitchen window, then the other, Betsy flicked her way past the Pothos and got another Pepsi. She met Jake again at the side door, where he was fingering the leaves of the China Boy holly. His lips smiled slightly, but his eyes were a cold brown Betsy hadn't seen before.

"Jake," she said, "I can't stand this. What am I going to do?"

Jake sipped the soda, looking over the top of the can as he surveyed the back yard. At last he lowered the can and handed it back to Betsy, empty, without looking at her.

"You know," he said, "ever'body ought to have plants in their life, missie. But they oughtn't to be your life . . . and *sure* you oughtn't to make them somebody else's life besides."

"But what am I going to *do* Jake?"

Jake suddenly beamed at her. "Come along with me to the wagon, missie," he said. He waved her ahead of him. Harbie led them up the congested path, barking cheerfully.

"It seems to me," Jake resumed as he pulled a shovel and a narrow spade from the bed of the wagon, "that since your father likes plants so all fired much, we ought to give him some more plants."

He handed the tools to Betsy and reached back for one of the larger plants—one completely covered by a stained wool blanket that had originally been olive drab.

Betsy thought about her savings passbook with the—small—amount of her aunt's Christmas gift in it. "Ah . . ." she said. "How much will this cost? Because—"

Jake looked down. For a moment, he seemed as old as the Earth itself, but he was smiling.

"I'll barter the plants to you, missie," he said. "For one Pepsi-Cola. And a smile."

Betsy gave him a broad, glowing smile.

The sky was still bright when Mr. Moffett pulled up in the street, but the ground was a pattern of shadows and muted colors that made the headlights necessary for safety. He'd be able to get the last of the front beds turned, but the remainder of the evening would be spent inside with the orchids.

The air had a slight nip to it. Warm days weren't over yet, but the nights were getting cool. He'd have to bring in all the half-hardy plants within the month. Locating them indoors would require planning.

Children called to one another down the street as Mr. Moffett followed the walk to his front door. A basketball whopped a backboard, though there didn't seem to be enough light to play. He wondered if Betsy was among the group.

Something caught at Mr. Moffett's legs. He'd built the walk of round, pebble-finished concrete pavers, bordered on either side by Statice. The flowers were finished growing, but the papery blooms remained on the stems like so many attractive, dried-flower displays.

They should have finished growing. In fact, the plants at the head of the walk seemed to have spread inward during the day. They were sticking to his knees.

Mr. Moffett detached himself carefully. He couldn't afford to replace the trousers of this suit, not with the bulb order he was preparing for next spring.

The small earth-toned flowers even clung to his hands. Statice didn't have stickers, so it must be dried bud casings that gripped him.

Mr. Moffett was smiling faintly as he walked to the front door, fishing in his pocket for his keys. He'd dosed his beds with a hormonal additive he'd ordered from Dresden, *Azetelia Ziehenstoff*. Perhaps he'd been a little excessive with the Statice.

He inserted the key in the lock. "Betsy, are you home?" he called.

The rosebushes trained up the pillars to either side rustled. They gripped his shoulders from behind.

Mr. Moffett shouted. For a moment he thought his daughter was playing a joke. He looked around. The bush to his left extended a tendril toward his elbow. The spray of fresh leaves on the end exaggerated the movement like the popper tip of a bullwhip.

"Hey!"

The main stems were *biting* through multiple layers of cloth and the skin of his shoulders. Lesser thorns on the tendril pricked him as well, almost encircling his arm.

Holding him.

The front door was unlatched. Mr. Moffett hurled himself toward it, but he couldn't break the thorns' grip on his back. Another tendril slid drily across his neck. He wriggled out of his coat, all but the left arm, and then tore himself free of that also. The lining pulled from his sleeve. There were streaks of blood on his polyester-blend shirt. He fell on the living room floor.

The suitcoat writhed in the air behind him as the roses continued to explore the fabric.

Mr. Moffett was breathing hard. A rose tendril waggled interrogatively toward the doorway. Mr. Moffett kicked the door shut violently.

The living room seemed dark. He looked around to be sure the bank of growlights in the ceiling was turned on. It was, but the Datura in the central planter had more than doubled in height since he left in the morning. The dark, bluish-green leaves now wrapped the fixture, permitting only a slaty remnant of the light to wash the room.

The plant whispered. The flowers, white and the size of a human head, rotated toward the man on the floor. They were deadly poison, like all parts of the Datura. Stamens quivered in the throats of the trumpet-shaped blooms as if they were so many yellow tongues.

Mr. Moffett got up quickly and walked to the kitchen. His right pants leg flapped loose. He hadn't noticed it being torn while he struggled with the rose.

He was sweating. He wasn't a drinker, but there was a bottle of Old Crow in the cabinet behind the oatmeal. This was the time to get it down.

The kitchen . . . The kitchen wasn't *right*. The Bird of Paradise plants made a thin buzzing noise, and their flowers trembled. They didn't look the way they—

Mr. Moffett had put his hand on the kitchen table without being aware of the fact in his concentration on the Birds of Paradise. Pain worse than he ever recalled feeling lanced up his arm.

The dwarf Baobab had swung down a branch. There were spikes in the bottom of every one of the tiny leaves. They stabbed deeply through the back of Mr. Moffett's hand.

He screamed and hurled himself sideways. He collided with the refrigerator. The back of his hand looked as though he'd been using it as a pull-toy for a score of insufficiently-socialized cats. He was spattering blood all over the kitchen.

Something dropped around his neck. The Pothos was trying to strangle him. The thin, green-white vine was no match for the hysterical strength with which Mr. Moffett tore its stem and leaves to shreds.

The buzzing was louder. He glanced up. The orange

Bird of Paradise flowers lifted off their stems. They hovered for a moment, looking and sounding like the largest hornets in the world. They started toward Mr. Moffett.

Crying uncontrollably, Mr. Moffett threw open the side door and jumped clear of the kitchen. He might have been all right if he'd continued running, but he paused to slam the panel against the oncoming Birds of Paradise.

The holly bushes were waiting.

Until the side door banged, Betsy waited in the back yard with the hedge trimmers in her hands. Jake had told her not to move until her father came outside again and shouted. The blood-curdling shriek an instant after the door closed was her signal.

She ran around the corner. The China Girl to the right of the door had her father in a full, prickly embrace. Mr. Moffett had taken off his coat, and his tie was twisted back behind him.

The China Boy on the other side bent sideways. The two bushes on the ends of the border were shivering in frustration that they hadn't been planted close enough to join in the attack.

"I'll help you, daddy!" Betsy shrilled. She thrust the hedge trimmers toward a branch clutching her father's left shoulder. She clamped down with all her strength.

The holly's woody core resisted the blades. Betsy twisted, worrying at the limb when she couldn't shear it.

The branch parted at last. Those leaves' grip on her father weakened, but he was still held by a dozen other limbs. A branch was twisting toward him from the rear of the bush to replace the severed one, and branches reached for Betsy as well.

The tips of China Boy's limbs bent gracefully toward Mr. Moffett's face.

"Betsy, get out of here!" Mr. Moffett cried. He pushed away jagged leaves that threatened his eyes, but more poised to engulf his head from all directions. "Run away! Run away!"

An air-cooled engine fired up nearby with a ringing clatter. Doors banged shut as neighbors came out to see what the shouting was about. By the time anybody could tell in the twilight, it would be too late.

Betsy hacked at a twig, severing it cleanly. She was crying. It wasn't supposed to be like *this*! She closed the trimmer on another branch, this one thicker than her thumb. The blades wouldn't cut. She tugged and twisted and bawled.

"Darling, get *away!*" her father cried.

Something grabbed the cuff of her jeans. She ignored it. China Boy unfolded a limb toward her face. The kinked branch was amazingly long when it straightened to its full length. The touch on her cuff was now a spiky, circular grip that held her like a shackle.

Harbie curved through the air and caught the China Boy branch in teeth that were amazingly long and white. The dog's weight slapped the spray of jagged leaves away from Betsy's face an instant before the big jaws crushed through and severed the branch completely.

Jake came around the front corner, guiding the big rototiller. The spinning bolo tines chewed into the end China Girl. The engine labored, then roared with triumph as the blades ground free and forward again.

The holly gripping Mr. Moffett shuddered as the rototiller slammed it, shredding roots and main stem together. The limb Betsy hacked at finally parted.

All the holly branches relaxed with the suddenness of a string snapping. Mr. Moffett fell free.

"Watch yourselves, sir and missie!" Jake shouted over the racket of the rototiller's exhaust. The tines sparked as Jake drove over the concrete pad outside the door and into the recoiling China Boy.

Betsy sat down abruptly on the gravel. Her knees suddenly wouldn't lock. Her father crawled over to her.

Harbie, wagging her tail furiously, began to lick Betsy's face. Beside the house, the rototiller bellowed as it devoured the fourth holly.

*   *   *

The morning was overcast, but it wasn't raining. Mr. Moffett wore his overcoat, leather gloves, and the motorcycle helmet he'd borrowed from Ricky Tilden at the head of the block. He picked up the last of the plants, a geranium.

Pink flowers gummed Mr. Moffett's gloves harmlessly as he flung the plant into the intake of the roaring chipper/shredder. The machine didn't react to the minuscule load.

Mr. Moffett reached down and shut off the spark. As the powerful hammermill spun down slowly against the inertia of its flywheel, he stripped off his gloves and then removed the helmet.

Betsy and Jake took their hands away from their ears. Harbie, who'd been lying under the wagon, got up and walked over to the humans again. The chipper/shredder had made an incredible amount of noise.

A long trail of wood-chips and chopped foliage led up the drive to the machine. Rather than clear away the piles of debris that spewed out through the grating in the bottom, Mr. Moffett had simply rolled the chipper/shredder backward to each new concentration of vegetation to process.

"There!" Mr. Moffett said. He took off the overcoat. The heavy fabric was stained and even torn in a few places.

The yard had been converted to raw dirt and chewed-up vegetation.

"You've got ever'thing turned up, sir," Jake said as the last ringing chatter of the chipper/shredder died away. "And you know, a yard ought to have *some* plants in it—"

"No," Mr. Moffett said with absolute finality. "It should not."

He looked around him. "I may pave it. Though I suppose grass would be all right. Or maybe gravel . . ."

Betsy ran over to her father and hugged him. His face was scratched and blood seeped through the thin cotton gloves he'd worn under the leather pair, but he hadn't been seriously injured in the previous evening's events.

"I think," Mr. Moffett said as he squeezed his daughter's shoulders, "that I'm going to get a dog. My wife would never let me have a dog. I've always regretted that."

"Is that so, sir?" Jake said with enthusiasm. "Why, you know, Harbie here's going to have a litter just next month. She likes kids, Harbie does, and I reckon her puppies'd like them too."

"Oh, Dad, could we?" Betsy asked. "Could we have one of Harbie's puppies?"

"Harbie's puppies?" her father said in puzzlement. "Well, I don't think . . ."

He looked at Jake. "Your Harbie is a *mongrel*, isn't she?"

Jake smiled. "Harbie's a dog, sir," he said. "A good dog, though she has her ways like we all do."

Harbie dropped over onto her back with an audible thump and kicked her legs in the air. Jake rubbed her belly with his fingertips. Harbie's dugs were beginning to protrude from pregnancy hormones and the pressure of the puppies beneath.

"That's very well, I'm sure," Mr. Moffett said in a voice that gave the lie to his words. "But I'm thinking of something pedigreed. A Bernese Mountain Dog, I believe."

Jake nodded. "I reckon you know your own mind, sir," he said as he walked back to his wagon.

"I'm going to shower, darling," Mr. Moffett said to Betsy. "Would you carry the helmet back to Mr. Tilden for me?"

"Yes, daddy," Betsy said to her father's back.

"Get on, Bobo," Jake murmured.

Betsy looked at the wagon. Bobo glanced over the traces and winked at her. Harbie barked cheerfully and winked.

And Jake, turning on the wagon seat, winked also. His smile was as bright as the summer sun.

I started out being fascinated by the craftsmanship of M.C. Escher's artwork. Much later I realized that the conceptions were even more amazing than the delicate cabinetry of their execution. Seemingly closed cycles of opposites are really infinite series with boundless implications.

As I stared for the umpteenth time at Relativity I started to wonder what it would be like to be a perfectly normal person, living in a perfectly normal house—which happens to be a nexus at which perfectly normal alien people in alien houses coexist with you. Then I wrote "The Bond."

The Bond

The bipedal—*thing*—with orange feathers disappeared a foot in front of Alice Hobart as suddenly as it had blurred into sight a moment before.

"My *God!*" she said. The cup in her hand rattled badly enough against its saucer to slop coffee. "Mary, I *swear* I can't imagine how you get used to it! Seeing monsters wander through your house is one thing, but that was coming right *at* me. It could have *touched* me!"

Mary Chasten smiled. She did not remark that the Hobarts had pretty well invited themselves. Not that Steve and Alice were precisely unwelcome; but it was an awkward time. The nexus was approaching one of its periodic peaks. In fact, the level of extra-dimensional appearances was already so high that the Chastens were both sure they should have begged off for another few days instead of having their friends over for dinner tonight.

"Well," Mary said, leaning forward to hand Alice a napkin, "it could have touched you without any harm, you know. It's happened often to John and myself. There's a tingling, is all. They think it's—" she swallowed to cover a catch in her breath "—a chance intersection of nerve impulses."

Alice had reached for the napkin, but her fingers did not close over it. Mary turned to follow her friend's goggling eyes. Something with scales and a dazzling, translucent mane had walked through Mary's chair. It had missed her by no more than the amount she had leaned

145

forward. The plane of intersection between the chair and the—visitor—was as sharply fluid as that of a shark's fin cleaving the sea.

"My God," Alice repeated as she took the napkin. Her hostess twisted minusculely to prevent their fingers from touching. "And the news says there are more of these places appearing every day. My God."

"Well, that was rather fortunate for us, you know," Mary said. The scaled creature was still quite solid in appearance as it strode through the walled-off area in the center of the Chastens' living room. The creature ignored the door as it ignored everything else in the room, including the humans. "The government was determined to force us out of our house in order to study the nexus. With others springing up here, there, and the other place all over the world, they could have their 'studies' and leave us in peace. I never heard their studying had accomplished anything worth the mention."

"In *peace*," Alice said with a moue of disgust. "I dread to think what's going to happen if it gets so that nowhere is safe from these—things." She looked away from the blank wall. "Of course," she added with a tinge of bitterness, "it may mean sweetness and light for everybody. Living in a zoo certainly seems to have agreed with you and John."

"Oh, we fight just like we always did," boomed John himself as the men re-entered the living room. Steve Hobart trailed behind, holding the camera with which he had been trying to photograph the temporary inhabitants of the nexus. "Thing is," John continued, "we make do now because we can't split." He grinned broadly. "After all, how could we decide who got the house?"

The closed room in the middle gave an odd appearance to what had been a large, sunken living room. It now had the look of a hotel lobby with an elevator shaft in the center. As Steve opened his mouth to speak, something gray and smooth shimmered out of the central wall. It faded, then sharpened into focus again a foot or so into the room before it disappeared completely. Hobart rapped the wall with his knuckles, testing its solidity.

"It doesn't really have anything to do with the wall, Steve," Mary remarked. "Will you have some more coffee—" she darted a glance at the wall clock "—before you go?"

"What *is* inside here, anyway?" Hobart asked, trying the knob on the door. It was locked.

"Just a storeroom," said John Chasten, walking calmly to the couch under the clock. "We closed off the center of the nexus, though it's no different from the rest of the house, except for the frequency of appearances there."

"Too much of a good thing, huh?" Steve said. He stepped to the side. Beyond the picture window, dimly glimpsed against the summer dusk, something walked across the air. None of its feet were close to the steeply-sloping ground. "No two of them the same?" Hobart commented with a shake of his head. "Well, it's interesting, but I can't say I envy you guys."

"Occasionally you'll see the same, well, species," John remarked, glancing at his own watch. "What looks like it, at any rate. I understand that statisticians think maybe ten thousand, ah, dimensions impinge at each nexus. Or at the ones the government's studied most, at any rate, though there doesn't seem to be a great deal of difference."

Alice grimaced. "I wish they'd learn what's causing it and stop it," she said. "I get the heebie-jeebies every time I think of one popping up in *my* living room—or *bed*room—and nothing I could do about it except move."

"If you'd read the article, like I *told* you to do before we came over, you'd know, wouldn't you?" her husband snapped. "They think one of the other dimensions is deliberately causing them to form. They may be mining minerals from us—or energy."

"If I did everything *you* told me to do, I'd drop right off the face of the Earth, wouldn't I?" said Alice Hobart in a rising voice. "You'd like that, wouldn't you?"

In the startled silence, Mary said, "I don't think that

could be, Steve. Nothing ever appears but the people—
the creatures themselves." She gestured at a trio of tenta-
cles undulating as they projected briefly through the central wall. "And certainly nobody's been strip-mining our
carpet or setting up solar panels in the fireplace."

"And after all," John chimed in, "people have tried
to trap and even shoot the—the others." He scowled
murderously. "Including representatives of the so-called
authorities, I'm told. I wonder if they gave any thought
to what might happen to *us* if that sort of nonsense
hadn't been completely ineffectual?"

Alice screamed and lunged out of her chair. Her saucer and cup sailed off in separate parabolas. The few
remaining drops of her coffee straggled across the white
ceiling. The creature that had materialized in the woman's chair continued its leisurely progress toward the central room before it faded away. The creature had an
exoskeleton and more legs than anyone could count during the moments it was present.

John and Mary ran to their guest. Steve Hobart himself
paused uncertainly, halfway across the room. "Oh, my
God," Alice was moaning, "it was like ice all through me!
And then it came out my front as if—" Her voice trailed
away without a simile adequate to her horror.

The Chastens carefully helped Alice to her feet,
steadying her by the puffed sleeves of her blouse and
Mary's hand on her waist. "Yes, that can be a surprise
the first time," John murmured awkwardly.

Steve had bent to pick up a piece of the broken saucer.
He said, "There's a guy out in Idaho who says the experience can actually be pleasurable, you know? Claims when
it happens that he feels what the other thing is feeling
and what he's feeling himself at the same time. A double,
ah, kick."

The Chastens had stepped back while their guest stood
shivering. John smiled and said dryly to Steve, "Does he
say what he was smoking at the time?"

"Yes, goodness," Mary added. "If Washington decides

this is some sort of drug trip, they *will* take it away from people, won't they?"

"*My God!*" Alice Hobart blurted. Her fists were clenched and her arms were locked tightly against her breast. She stared at the others over white knuckles and cried, "I just want to get *out* of here before it happens again! It was awful. Awful!"

"I'm really sorry, Alice," said John in a mixture of concern and relief. "It does hit some people that way. Here, your coats are in the front closet." He mimed turning the woman without actually touching her. Still drawn up, darting fearful glances in all directions, Alice followed her host.

Mary took a deep breath and then realized that Steve Hobart was stacking cups and saucers. "Oh, don't bother with that, Steve," she said. "I'll take care of it later."

"No, no," Steve said. "I owe you at least this much. You don't know how sorry I am about the way my wife acted." He began to walk toward the kitchen door.

Carrying the cream and sugar, Mary strode past him. "It was our fault," she said. "We don't usually have people over when the appearances are so frequent. This time it happened a little faster than we were expecting."

"Oh, she's always making a scene," said Steve. His dishes rattled. "I'm getting damn sick and tired of it, too. You know, Mary," his voice dropping an octave, "sometimes I think you're the only woman in the world who isn't crazy." He had freed a hand. It stroked Mary's bare elbow to punctuate his sentence.

Mary jumped as if she had been stabbed. She turned and Steve lurched back in surprise. He might have expected disapproval, but he had only once before seen disgust to equal Mary's present expression. That was the morning he had glimpsed himself in the mirror an instant after seeing the garden slug that had crawled into the glass with his toothbrush.

"I—I'm sorry," he stammered.

Mary pointed to the countertop she had cleared for the dishes. "I think you'd better go, now," she said distantly.

Wishing that he could vanish like the other visitors, Hobart obeyed.

When she heard the front door close, Mary walked back toward the heart of the dimensional nexus. John, already unbuttoning his shirt, met her at the door to the central room. The air around them was beginning to cloud with micro-second appearances, too brief and too frequent to have discernible shapes. The Chastens' bodies tingled with shared stimuli as barriers broke down around them.

"Never seen it so sudden," John grumbled. He tossed his slacks over his wife's crumpled dress. "Another five minutes and I planned to throw Steve and Alice's coats out the front door and hope they had sense enough to follow."

"Shh," said Mary gently. She unlocked the door and opened it. They were both nude as they stepped into what had been the center of their living room. Now, a large waterbed filled the walled-off area. They stepped carefully to the middle of the shifting surface with their hands together, almost touching. Mere physical contact was dry bread now to their sophisticated palates. The impingement of other dimensions, other nervous systems, was almost constant now. The nexus was at crescendo, nearing the climax for which it had been designed.

With a mutual sigh, John and Mary moved together as they had learned to do. Their bodies, and the myriads of other bodies began to tremble with an ecstasy multiplied 10,000 times.

Bill Fawcett (and you'll see that name yet again before you finish reading these intros) brought me in to coedit and create a space-opera shared universe idea of his: The Fleet. While the concept was deliberately aimed at a younger audience (if you don't entice young SF readers, you won't have any readers in a generation), we had a pretty amazing number of top writers.

Because I'd been working on another project with Larry Niven, I asked him if he'd like to play. He had an idea that would work, but he didn't have time to write it up. He did a rough outline, I wrote the story, and he did a polish draft. We split the credit and the money.

While the stories I did for The Fleet were grim even by my own standards, this story "The Murder of Halley's Comet," had a lighter tone. In fact, it had a light tone. (You could make a case that Dostoyevsky has a lighter tone than some of my stories in the series.) It was fun.

A while later, Larry called with another idea. The process of creation was the same as before, and this time the result—"Mom and the Kids"—was downright funny if you've got the right sort of sense of humor. It proves that I'm perfectly capable of seeing humor in a fictional construct, so long as somebody else points it out to me first.

Mom And The Kids

Em-Em-Three-Niner—"Mom" to the crews that flew in to collect the monthly production—plodded forward a centimeter at a time, circling the power and storage hub. Her teeth skirled a cheerful song on the taconite; her fans slurped up pulverized raw ore; and deep in Mom's belly, a vacuum furnace purred as it melted, separated, and blended.

Every minute or two, depending on the quality of the ore, Mom's electromagnetic drivers spat another ball bearing up her long tail of spun-ceramic hosing and into the storage drum in the hub.

If anybody'd asked her, Mom would've said she was as happy as a clam; if she'd had enough self-awareness to know that.

Which she didn't.

Quite.

MM 39's only purpose in not-quite life was to make ball bearings of whichever type was required by the signal from the hub, or to reproduce herself when the signal was switched off. It didn't matter to MM 39—to Mom—whether the humans of Ouroboros enclosed her bearings in races, or used them as a source of highly refined metals and alloys. Mom's interest was entirely in her job.

She was a half cylinder about five meters long and three meters across the flat bottom on which she crawled over the taconite, nibbling as she went. Her broadmouthed, compact shape was ideal for crawling along a featureless expanse of low-purity ore, but if Mom had to reproduce under modified circumstances, her offspring would be modified too.

For that matter, Mom herself could change. In a few weeks she'd have to extend herself another half meter or so to enclose additional magnetic drivers. The distance between the hub and Mom's slowly expanding circle was approaching the limits of the present set of drivers. She would need more power to shoot bearings reliably up the tube to storage.

The modifications would take her out of production for a few days, but that didn't bother Mom. She was programmed to take the long view. Better to lose a few thousand ball bearings now than chance a clogged guide tube that would take Mom weeks to clear, as slowly as she moved.

Mom's teeth chirruped as the rock before her changed character. Here was an igneous dike, very low in the iron and nickel which were her target ores; but Mom's ground-penetrating radar told her that the intrusion was narrow, so it was best to devour it and spew it out as waste—as tubing like that which guided the ejected bearings, neat coils which were easily policed up by the human service crews. Besides, the dike had some interesting trace elements Mom could add to her stores as tiny beads, in case she needed those elements in the future.

The future of making ball bearings.

The long view, after all.

Ouroboros was a cold and watery world, warm enough around the equator, frigid elsewhere. The name referred to a band of ocean and islands only a couple of thousand miles wide. A sizable fusion weapon, set under the ice in a tectonic region, would melt enough polar cap to flood the islands to a depth of three hundred meters.

But Mom neither knew nor cared that a squadron of Khalian raiders had landed on Ouroboros and threatened to melt both polar ice camps with a pair of such devices. Mom would've adapted to the deluge. The bearing delivery system would have to be modified to allow for the greater viscosity of water. The fusion powerplant would've failed in time, but Mom could replace that with an array of solar collectors floating on the surface. No, the threatened flood wouldn't affect the production of ball bearings on Ouroboros.

But it would end the life of every soul in the human colony.

There was no resistance to the Weasels. When they demanded the location of every potentially valuable artifact on the planet, they got it.

"Are you sure this is the target?" Squad Leader Ixmal snarled to Duwasson, the pilot of the Khalian transporter. "It looks like a nest-fouling bomb crater."

"Maybe another team got here first and nuked it," suggested Private Moketric, gloomily combing his whiskers with the knuckles of his left forepaw. One of these days Moketric would forget he was wearing a combat gauntlet when he groomed himself; the half of his face that remained would have a right to be gloomy then.

"The transporter thinks it's the right place," said Duwasson doubtfully as they neared the gray scar on the brown/green/dun landscape. "But I dunno, I just fly 'em. . . ."

The ground had been eaten down around a pillar in the center. That supported a small building which didn't look a Motherin' bit like the drawing.

"That's it," said Senior Private Volvon, a smart-ass if Ixmal had ever met one—and the Great Mother knew, he'd met his share. "There at the rim, see it? Must be a piece of mining hardware we're supposed to pick up."

"Didn't look that fouling big in the nest-fouling picture," Ixmal grumbled into his whiskers, squinting as he looked from the half cylinder below to the three-view drawing they'd given him at the drop point while they loaded the coordinates into the transporter. You'd've thought they could put a scale on the nest-fouling drawing, wouldn't't'cha?"

Of course, he prob'ly woulda ignored the fouling figures if they'd been there.

The transporter started to circle the crater. Ixmal flung the useless drawing out into the airstream. "Well, put us down, dung-eater!" he shouted to the pilot.

Duwasson landed the transporter on the crater's edge hard enough to jounce loose milkteeth. Fool musta thought he was putting down on a meadow instead of a rocky plateau as unyielding as a battleship's armor. Never been a pilot whelped that was worth enough dung to cover his body, noways.

"Go! Go! Go!" Ixmal shouted as he led his six-Weasel pickup team out of the cab, snarling and threatening the barren landscape with their weapons.

There wasn't a soul around. There wasn't even any sound except a high-pitched screaming from the object the team was supposed to grab. It sounded like a victim being tortured, which put Squad Leader Ixmal into a better mood momentarily—until he noticed that that nest fouler Moketric was squatting to mark the site with his musk.

Ixmal batted his junior with his rifle butt. "Up!" he said, eyes glazing as he reversed the weapon in case Moketric decided to make something out of it.

No problem. Moketric backed away, offering his throat while making mewling noises. Ixmal squatted deliberately and overmarked the tussock his junior had chosen.

"All right," he continued, now that he'd satisfied the needs of discipline. "Let's get the fouling thing and get back before the others've gobbled the choice cuts!"

Ixmal turned, jumped from the edge of the crater, and sprawled onto his short, furry tail on the smooth rock three meters below.

He was supposed to have landed on the arched top of the object instead of just behind it.

"Squad Leader Ixmal," Volvon said with careful propriety. "I believe the object moves."

Ixmal had dropped his rifle when his ass slammed the stone. Just as well for Volvon.

The rest of the team leaped into the shallow crater with more circumspection than their leader had displayed. You could groom your tail tufts with the rock for a mirror, it was that smooth where the thing had passed. . . .

Something went *chuk!* and the team all flattened, looking for the shooter and wondering who'd gone to the Great Mother this time. Not a soul anywhere, though maybe the building on the pinnacle in the center of the crater—

"Sir," said Volvon, "it wasn't a shot. I think the thing just spit something up this tube here." He pointed with his disemboweling knife, then used the weapon to pick his fangs while his brow wrinkled in thought. "And I bet the other one's a power cord."

The object continued to advance, though the increments of motion were so slight that they had to be inferred. One of the privates backed away from the stealthy approach and said, "Sir, can't we turn it off?"

"Anybody see a switch?" Ixmal muttered, wondering why he had to get all the jobs out in South Ass-Sniff, without a fouling scrap of anything's liver to eat for loot.

"The power switch is probably on the central island, sir," said Volvon.

"Who the Mother-fouling nest-gobbling hell asked you?"

"And I think we ought to take that building in too," Volvon added, like what he thought mattered t' somebody.

"Can't take 'em both," said Moketric, scratching at the side of the big machine as it oozed its way past him, screaming. His combat gauntlet left four deep gouges down the mild steel of the casting. "They're too big t'gether."

Chuk!

They all hit the deck again. All but Volvon.

"Then we ought to summon another transporter," the senior private said, looking idly skyward while his superior got up from the stone with a jingle of equipment and a look in his eyes that would've curdled milk in a mother's dugs.

"What we oughta do," said Ixmal in a snarl as controlled as millstones rubbing, "is the job they fouling told us ta do. Which is carry this back for pickup before some fouling slick-skin battlecruiser waxes all our butts."

He stared at Volvon. "Period."

"Yessir, but the brass probably isn't familiar with the installation," Volvon argued. "If they had been, they'd've wanted us to—"

Squad Leader Ixmal aimed his automatic rifle at Volvon's feet, then twitched the muzzle a centimeter to the side before he triggered a long burst. Sparks, pebbles, and ricocheting bullet fragments blasted in all directions as the powerline separated.

Volvon yelped and jumped away. The big half cylinder the team had come for halted in silence.

Ixmal fired the rest of his magazine into the guide tube. The tough fibers tore under the bullet impacts, but the tube wasn't completely severed.

Squad Leader Ixmal slapped a fresh magazine into his weapon while the rest of the team stared at him with a heartwarming mixture of fear and loathing. "Duwasson!" he shouted. "Lower the bird onto this fouling thing so we can tie it on 'n get our asses outa here!"

He looked at Volvon as the transporter's gravity-drive engines ran up to lift speed above the rim of the artificial depression. "You there," Ixmal ordered. "Cut the resta that tube loose."

The cowed private prodded the tube with his disemboweling knife.

"Use your teeth!" Ixmal ordered, grinning.

Ixmal had Motherin' sure learned one thing on this job.

If Senior Private Volvon didn't get his own squad soon, Squad Leader Ixmal was going to chew his throat out fer sure.

*   *   *

"All right, all right," said Deck Chief Limouril, who looked like an elf, acted like a Weasel, and came from a planet whose name was closer to spfSelrpn than it was to anything human tongues could pronounce. "Who's presenting on this one?"

He kicked Mom in the side. Her sheathing belled dolefully.

"Ah, I am, sir," said Estoril, shuffling his notes as he stepped out of the clot of technicians making rounds with Limouril. Estoril was another elf—which cut no ice with Limouril; quite the contrary. "Ah, it is, ah, an object, ah, picked up on—"

"We all know it was picked up on Ouroboros, Estoril," Limouril said coldly, fluffing his ear tufts in scorn. "What we want to know is what does it do? Do you intend to enlighten us this morning, or shall we check back in a voyage or two?"

Some of the other techs giggled, puffed out their cheeks, or made clawing motions in the air—depending on their racial type—as they sucked up to the deck chief.

"Yessir," Estoril muttered, flushing a deeper shade of green. He'd found his place in his notes—not that it helped very much. "This is a processing plant, sir. An automated processing plant."

"But what does it process, Estoril?" Limouril demanded, turning his face toward the heavens—which in this case were formed by the Deck Four ceiling girders of the mothership *Tumor.* "I swear, I'm going to suggest to our Khalian brethren that they recruit bark fungus into their technical staff. That would improve the average intellectual quality."

Giggle. Puff. Claw.

"Sir, that information wasn't in the data that came up from Ouroboros."

"You mean that you didn't find the data, Technician Estoril," Limouril snapped, though he knew as well as anybody else that most of the documentation this time had been left behind by the Weasel snatch squads, probably because the paper didn't look edible.

And speaking of the devils, a party of chittering Khalians seemed to be working this way down the aisles of loot.

Estoril got a stubborn look on his face. "The powerline was severed," he said. "I think we ought to reconnect it and note the results."

"By all means, Estoril," the deck chief said. "I can't imagine why you haven't already done that part of your job."

Because there was only so much time. And because Deck Chief Limouril would have burned his subordinate a new one if Estoril had taken that initiative anyway. . . .

But the squad of Weasels was coming closer, and the last thing Limouril wanted was a problem in front of them. He could act like a Weasel when only his subordinates were present, but the Khalians themselves were unpredictable.

And they didn't take much note of rank. Among slaves.

Something fragile shattered explosively in the near distance. Most of this region of the deck was filled with motor vehicles of all types and descriptions. Crashing and tinkling sounds continued as the Weasels pelted each other with bits of whatever their horseplay had destroyed.

Estoril crept behind the arch-roofed machine, looking for a universal receptacle from which he could mate a length of flex to the severed cord. "Go on, go on," Limouril said, making shooing motions with his ears toward the other technicians. "Help him, let's get this working."

A ship big enough to carry the loot of a planet must be a significant fraction of planetary size itself. The *Tumor* was bigger than a battleship, but most of the vessel was empty space which could be configured to hold everything from holoscreens to silverware to . . .

Well, to Mom.

The tens of thousands of tonnes of loot gleaned from even a minor planet like Ouroboros were stuffed into the *Tumor*. It had been packed every which way by Khalian pirates who expected the Fleet to arrive momentarily, and who didn't much care about anything that couldn't be made to bleed and whimper.

Far behind the region of engagement, the *Tumor* would deliver its load to the Syndicate, whose human personnel would tag, store, distribute—and mostly lose— the loot of Ouroboros; but for even that degree of efficiency, there had to be a presort on board the mothership.

Syndicate humans didn't operate with pirate raiders whose ships were in imminent danger of destruction or, worse, of capture. There were other races more technically adept than the Khalians, though; and serving pirate raiders was a better job than providing them with a quick lunch.

Besides, Limouril liked what he did. He liked the power it gave him, too, except when Weasels were present.

The squad of Khalians came around the corner just as a pop, a blue flash, and a curse indicated that the technicians had gotten the machine hooked up again. Also that the machine hadn't been turned off before it was brought in, which figured for Weasels.

"Hey, what's that?" said one of the Weasels. He carried a tangle of pipes that had probably been part of an exercise machine.

"Dinner!" chittered another one.

The technicians, already braced to whatever their cultures considered a posture of attention, stiffened still further. Estoril and the two roly-poly, ill-smelling Brownians who'd just connected the cable edged back behind the machine again.

A ball bearing clanked against the hull, dropped to the deck, and rolled out in front of the technicians. Its perfect polish winked mysteriously in the overhead lighting. Limouril began to sweat.

Mom hummed as she brought all her systems up to speed again and took stock of the changed circumstances. Power was intermittent. The Phase One response, solar collectors, didn't seem practical here, though she wouldn't be able to make a final determination until she'd explored the exterior of her present enclosure.

On the other hand, the ore vein was remarkably rich.

The machine's cutting head rose from ground level through a 180-degree arc, determining that the joint hadn't frozen while the power was turned off. The tiny rock-cutting blades skirled as they sharpened themselves. Limouril's technical crew stumbled away in terror.

"Here, catch!" called a Weasel. He flung the exercise machine into the cutting head. Mom's teeth began to devour the chrome-plated steel with howls of delight.

The technicians stared at Mom in awe while Khalians laughed and nipped one another playfully. One Weasel slipped the pistol from another's holster and tossed the weapon into the whirling cutters. As the gun sank into Mom's mouth, half of the twenty-round magazine went off in a spray of noise and bits of flying cartridge casings. The Weasels laughed even harder.

A Brownian yelped as another ball bearing bounced off his knee. That was an accident, though, an item already in the delivery chute before the power was cut.

Mom wasn't primarily interested in making ball bearings anymore. The signal that carried specifications for ball bearings had been turned off.

Now she was supposed to reproduce.

Limouril got up from the deck carefully, dabbing at the line a fragment of something had cut beneath his right eye. His coveralls were fluid- and stain-proof, so he ought to be able to get back to his quarters before it became obvious that he'd fouled himself in panic.

Two Weasels were chittering at one another in fury, but the angrier of the pair didn't have a pistol anymore and that seemed to be keeping a lid on the potential violence.

"Come on," said another of the Khalians. "Let's see what else it'll eat!"

He hacked at the cable tying down a rubber-tired ground car, then looked over his shoulder. "You there!" the Weasel ordered. "Slaves! Push this thing to it!"

Limouril blinked in horror. Was the vehicle battery-powered, or did it have fuel tanks? In which latter case—

"Noble masters," he blurted. "Instead, I think we should—".

A Weasel threw an empty liquor bottle at the deck chief.

Limouril hunched away. "Well, hop it!" he bleated to his subordinates. "Obey your master's orders!"

It didn't take long to carry out the Weasel's command. It never took long to carry out a Weasel's command if there were to be survivors among those doing the work. Shards of the car's plastic body spit out of the cutting teeth momentarily; then Mom extruded a hood to enclose the workpiece and avoid losing potentially valuable raw materials. Waste not, want not . . . It was part of the long view.

The car was, thank the Spirit of the Live-giving Soil, battery-powered. Limouril breathed almost normally for a moment, but the way a solid one-tonne object vanished as though it were sinking into water was more than disturbing. What in the name of Forest Fires had they got here?

"Ah?" called Estoril from behind the machine, balancing one fear against another in his voice. "Sir? Masters? I think it's extruding something. Or, ah, it's growing."

Right the first time. Mom was extruding a casing for the Kid. Quite a different design from her own, of course; scarcely any family resemblance. For one thing, with this amazing bounty of ore to mine, the Kid could be much smaller than Mom, who'd been configured to process low-purity taconite.

For another, the power source in this new vein had proven untrustworthy once. The Kid would need a power storage system. Fortunately, the present meal was providing just the right elements.

Mom wouldn't simply adapt the car batteries. She could do much better than that, though that step would require some additional processing time before the Kid was ready to go off on his own.

Ready to make perfect ball bearings, as soon as he was asked to do so.

Limouril slid toward Estoril to stare at the closed forty-centimeter-diameter steel tube that extended itself from a port in the back of this damnable machine. The deck chief couldn't imagine what it was.

"Looks like a bomb," one of the Brownians muttered.

Great. Might his children all get root-rot.

The car had vanished completely. "Let's see what it does with sumthin' real big," a Khalian suggested. "Let's, you guys, push one a them trucks up here!"

"Are you insane?" Limouril blurted.

He felt all the blood drain out of his face. Oh, that had been a bad mis—

The Weasels didn't pause for thought, much less to issue orders. Three of them seized the deck chief in their short, immensely strong arms and hurled him into Mom's waiting mouth.

The cutting blades screamed longer than Limouril did, but that wasn't very long at all.

For a moment, nobody said anything. Then Estoril piped, "Well, come on! Let's get that truck up here!"

Waste water, which was most of the deck chief's volume, drained from vents on Mom's underside and ran across the plating. She'd found some interesting trace elements, though.

For a while, the Weasels stood around chirping with pleasure to watch Mom's cutting head grind its way across the truck in slow sweeps, as though she were a gigantic vacuum cleaner. Her raw material storage compartments filled long before the fine processing on the Kid was complete.

Mom began to dribble out ball bearings as she marked time.

The Khalians lost interest. One of them fired at the windows of a stored car. After a while, the whole squad wandered away in a flurry of shots, ricochets, and popping glass.

Limouril's leaderless technicians stared at one another.

They crept away in the opposite direction, heading for their quarters by a roundabout route. Only the Khalians on the *Tumor*'s bridge could assign the technicians another deck chief until the mothership docked.

And none of the late Limouril's crew wanted to come anywhere close to a Weasel before then.

Mom chuckled to herself. She couldn't've been happier.

Not long after the technicians left, Mom crawled several meters away from the hull so that the Kid could be born without deformities from the tight space. The move would have overstretched her new powercord, so she extruded plenty of slack while she was at it.

Ball bearings continued to *whang* onto the decking, more or less as an afterthought. They were no longer Mom's prime imperative ... but in her universe, you could never have too many ball bearings.

When her internal furnace had digested a sufficient quantity of the car and truck she'd swallowed, Mom nibbled a stretch of the deck. The plates were of wonderful metal, almost perfect for bearings without additional alloys; but the floor was thin and Mom knew better than to cut herself off from the main supply of ore by letting her immediate appetite rule her.

The Kid's slim, segmented body, optimized for tight spaces and incredibly rich forage, dropped to the deck. His caterpillar tracks were larger than the tiny spiked wheels on Mom's underside. As the junior of the pair, it was the Kid's duty to migrate to a distant part of the ore vein before he started to work on his own.

The long view. If Mom and the Kid stayed close together, their offspring would soon be stumbling all over one another. That would seriously handicap production despite the wealth of available resources.

For a moment, the Kid remained linked to Mom by an umbilicus of powercord. A relay clicked open and the Kid's internal batteries took up the load. They would support him as he crawled to the opposite side of the deck, where his magnetic sensors had already located another universal outlet.

The Kid's treads rattled purposefully as he set out, waggling the length of powercord behind him. Tiny motors in his tail controlled spines which stiffened the cord; when he reached his destination, he would plug himself in more easily than the technicians had connected Mom.

Mom and the Kid exchanged affectionate radio signals as they parted. Mom was already beginning to turn herself around.

She didn't want to eat the flooring that supported her.

But there was no reason not to devour the metal of the *Tumor*'s outer hull.

It didn't bother Mom in the least when her cutting head ground its way completely through the hull plating and vented the atmosphere of Deck Four in the middle of a sponge-space transit.

It bothered the surviving members of the mothership's crew a great deal.

It took more than half an hour for the emergency crew to reach the problem. The slave technicians were clumsy in their suits. The lights of Deck Four were no longer scattered into an ambiance of illumination by the air, so the crew stumbled in sharp reflections and hard shadow through the ragged aisles of loot.

They argued about what could have caused the trouble—until they saw Mom.

The technicians slapped a temporary patch over the hole. The squad of Weasels escorting the slaves emptied their guns into Mom, doing some cosmetic damage to her casing. They also unplugged her, however.

Mom radioed the Kid just before the power died. She needed to warn him not to eat all the way through the hull just now. It seemed to negatively affect long-term production.

On the *Tumor*'s bridge, Captain Slevskrit stopped chewing long strips of paint off the bulkheads for long enough to order a course change. They'd have to divert to Bileduct, the nearest repair station that could handle the major structural work which the *Tumor* now required.

Mom had eaten a main spar before the emergency crew arrived. The deck around her was littered with perfect ball bearings, and the casing of her next offspring was almost complete.

The commander of Bileduct Base was a sub-syndic 3d class, the equivalent of an admiral in the action service. Her name was Smythe and she was human.

Smythe's office was in the peak of the HQ Tower, giving her an unparalleled view of the base. She looked with disgust at the rank upon rank of battered warships which had limped here following their attempt to block the Alliance landings on Bull's-Eye.

With a little planning by the action services, these ships could have been spaced over a reasonable period of time instead of descending on Bileduct in a bolus that choked Smythe's facilities.

Or with a little luck, at least half the vessels out there might have been destroyed instead of staggering back to disrupt her base. That would have had the additional benefit of getting rid of a lot of the wretched, chittering Weasel officers with whom Smythe must now deal.

Like this one, Slevskrit.

Smythe turned from the tangled backlog outside to the Khalian across the desk from her. "Yes, I assure you, Warrior Slevskrit, that my staff has carefully considered your proposal to give the *Tumor* crash priority."

She paused. If things hadn't been so screwed-up, this pushy Weasel with bits of what looked like paint, for God's sake, in his whiskers, would never have gotten as far as the outer office. As it was, with Chief Loadmaster Rao out sick from overwork and Loadmaster Class 2 Jiketsy swamped with trying to straighten out the situation in Bay H, there wasn't anybody else handy. . . .

"And I concur with them completely," Smythe went on, letting her voice show a little of her own frustration.

"Warrior"—it was policy among the Syndicate's human personnel to ignore relative rank among their Khalian surrogates—"how in God's name did you manage to fracture a main spar in sponge space?"

All the chairs in Smythe's office were configured for humans. Slevskrit scratched furiously at his plush armrest—and yelped as the electrified mesh just beneath the fabric bit him hard enough to singe his fur.

"It was unusual," Slevskrit mumbled as he licked his paw. "Many people have been punished."

"Right," said Smythe dismissively. "Well, we'll get to the *Tumor* sometime this generation, with any luck. Until—"

"Wait!" Slevskrit protested. "You don't understand. We've got a full cargo, very valuable loot, and it can't sit—"

"It can do as I damned well say it can, warrior!" Smythe retorted furiously.

If the Weasel lunged for her, lasers in the office walls would turn him to shaved meat in midair. Besides, if this Slevskrit had any balls by Khalian standards, he'd've been in charge of something other than a space-going furniture van.

And anyway, Smythe was too tired to care.

She waved her arm at the scene beyond the circle of windows. "Look at it!" she demanded. "We're set up here to repair a mean of forty-one vessels a week. There're three hundred and twelve vessels out there. Warships! Can your minuscule Weasel brains imagine how badly those ships are needed right now?"

Smythe had been right about her Khalian. Instead of going into a killing rage—which would've solved one of Smythe's problems, though the office would need cleaning afterward—Slevskrit stared glumly out the windows also.

At the best of times, the view wasn't a particularly enticing one. Bileduct was an airless planetoid 2000 kilometers in diameter, the only significant satellite of a small white star. The base was in the center of an ancient meteor crater. If you looked carefully, you could see portions of the base's automatic defensive system glittering like diamonds on the ring of the crater's walls.

The HQ Tower and eight repair bays of Bileduct Base sprawled in the center of the crater like an exhausted spider. And now, of course, the excessive hundreds of ships awaiting repair rayed out from the base like a ragged web.

"My crew is specialized," Slevskrit said gloomily. "Our job is very important. Whatever they say about us in the home burrows. . . ."

Smythe's mouth opened in surprise. Whoever would have thought a Weasel would have a good idea—or even be the occasion of one?

"Right," she said. "Leave a skeleton crew aboard the *Tumor* and send the remainder of the combat complement here to Reassignment Section." That was what Smythe had decided to do with most of the waiting ships anyway, using the crews of idle vessels to replace battle casualties on the ships the base had been able to repair.

"But in your case," Smythe continued, "send your technical crew—they're slaves, I suppose?"

"But . . . ! But . . . !"

"Yes, of course they are," Smythe said, shaking her head at her own silly question. "Tell your technical crewmen to report directly to Loadmaster Jiketsy at Bay H. We'll put them to good use."

It took some minutes before Smythe got the frothing Khalian out of her office, and for a moment or two she thought the wall lasers were going to be needed after all. Still, the interview had been the base commander's only positive experience for a solid week.

She looked out her circuit of windows again, savoring the silence after the door finally closed behind Slevskrit. The huge lump on the outer fringe of ships was probably the *Tumor* herself; there wasn't anything else that big awaiting repair, thank God.

Smythe's eyes narrowed. Some sort of nonstandard excrescence rode the mothership's hull at about the level of Deck Four. It looked like an array of solar collectors, of all things. Presumably some sort of nonstandard field modification dreamed up by Supply in order to make life difficult for the people in Repair.

The base commander sighed and went back to her paperwork. As if things weren't already difficult enough for the people at Bileduct Base.

The Kid stayed busy, but not too busy to remember Mom. One of his first actions was to create a miniature, twenty-centimeter-long version of himself which trundled back across the expanse of Deck Four and plugged Mom back into the wall.

With that mission accomplished, Kid headed for an elevator shaft on a colonizing trek to Deck Three. He paused frequently along the way to top off his tiny battery pack and to ingest more metal.

At regular intervals, another mirror-perfect ball bearing plinked onto the deck behind him.

Though the *Tumor*'s fusion plant met their present needs, Mom and the Kid had learned not to trust wall current. Gingerly, drilling holes no larger than the superconducting cables required, the larger von Neumann machines set up solar arrays. The sun hung in one position above Bileduct Base, and the amount of incident light slanting into the crater was quite sufficient for collectors as efficient as those which shortly sprouted from the *Tumor*'s outer skin.

Then Mom and the Kid got down to the work of reproduction. It was, after all, the only real job they had until their masters switched them back to the creation of ball bearings as their primary duty. They were very good at reproducing; as perfect as machines could be without true sentience. . . .

And maybe a little better than that.

Mom had been designed to process taconite, though she could function sub-optimally within the *Tumor*. The Kid was as good a *Tumor*-miner as could be imagined, and several of both machines' next-born were configured just like the Kid.

But Mom had extended sensors through the hull along with the solar array, and she could see that there was a nonmind-boggling richness of ore bodies on the floor and rim of the ancient crater. She couldn't even speculate as to what might lie still farther out on the surface of Bileduct.

But she and her brood could learn.

On the *Tumor*'s bridge, Captain Slevskrit spent his time morosely drinking a mixture of esters and alkaloids. He hurled the empty bottles at members of his staff when he caught them peeking around the corner at him.

Objects of various shapes crept down the mothership's hull from time to time and picked their way across the barren landscape. The new machines ran on drive motors powered by the solar sails which they kept precisely perpendicular to the sun's rays. They didn't look much like Mom anymore, but they were perfect for the new conditions.

Captain Slevskrit never noticed the boojums. A handful of the *Tumor*'s crew did. Two even discussed it and came to the same conclusion. Syndicate business was none of theirs, and Syndicate secrets were not safe to steal. The little widgets trundling toward other ships and the outer stations of the defense array probably had something to do with the Bileduct Base facilities.

Which, in a manner of speaking, was precisely correct.

"Wow!" said the elf technician, Estoril. "Look at that destroyer! I can't imagine how it was able to make it back."

"You aren't paid to imagine that or any other foulin' thing," Ixmal chirped sourly over the vibration of the transporter's engines. The bird had direct impulse drivers, but no navigational aides beyond the pilot's eyesight, so Duwasson was keeping them low and slow to avoid winding up in orbit. "Except how to get Outpost 27 back in working order fast, before me and the boys bite yer ears off."

Squad Leader Ixmal wasn't sure just how he'd carry out the threat, seeing as they were all wearing suits, but the thought brightened his mood and made his whiskers twitch. For that moment he could stop wondering what had happened to Outpost 27.

Ten hours ago the installation's Ready-to-Go code had stopped sending to the Tower. Only a broken radio. Ixmal would get a technician to find out what happened; ultimately he'd blame a technician; but unexplained events had been evil lately. Evil.

"Pups," muttered Private Moketric. "The whole burrow did chew on that un, didn't it just?"

Even Ixmal had to admit that scarcely more than a skeleton remained of the destroyer they'd just scudded over. Though the ship was parked way out here on the edge of the vessels awaiting rebuild, Ixmal had seen multiple movements aboard it during the transporter's quick overflight. Just like the slickskins here at Bileduct to waste time repairing a wreck like that instead of getting serviceable ships back into action.

The *Tumor* was parked only a couple rows over, which robbed the squad leader of the minor surge of glee he'd gotten when he thought of eating the technician he was supposed to escort. If the *Tumor* hadn't broken down, it wouldn't be sinking into the slag on this nest-fouling planetoid—

And Squad Leader Ixmal wouldn't be bouncing his kidneys blue out in the vacuum, checking on why some fouling machine had broken. The only machine that was worth having was an automatic rifle, and teeth were generally better 'n guns even then.

"Wow!" Estoril repeated.

Ixmal was just short of batting the elf with his rifle butt on general principles when he noticed that Estoril was staring over the bow, toward Outpost 27.

"Wow!" said Squad Leader Ixmal.

The installation was gone, just about. One of the

plasma cannon still stood mournfully, but the other three guns had disappeared. There was no sign of the rocket clusters either.

Something glittery was moving over the site, though.

Ixmal opened his mouth to order Duwasson to keep them up, but he was three seconds too late. The pilot flared for landing, then chopped his throttles early and dropped the transporter from a meter up. Vacuum hadn't improved Duwasson's fouling technique, that was for sure. . . .

"Go! Go! Go!" Ixmal shouted as he leaped from the transporter, snatching a grenade from his belt with one paw while the other forelimb aimed his automatic rifle at the intruder in Outpost 27.

The creature ignored the squad of Khalian troopers. It was cylindrical, about two meters long, and draped in solar panels like the wings of a tasty butterfly.

"Uh-oh," said Volvon, suggesting that he too recognized the thing's resemblance to the last load Ixmal's squad had lifted from Ouroboros.

Ixmal tossed his grenade and ducked, figuring that this was as good a time as any to see which of his privates remembered that shrapnel flies a long way without air to slow it down. All the squad members flattened, Volvon included, worse luck.

The blast knocked a hole in the creature's casing and sent its solar collectors sailing off like a puff of smoke. Ixmal rose and emptied the magazine of his rifle into the hole. The rest of the squad fired also, though that dung-brain Moketric for some reason shot up the surviving plasma weapon instead of the intruder.

Sparks flew in all directions, hazy blue crackles of electricity and the red glare of burning metal. The intruding machine settled onto its treads with a shiver.

A ball bearing dropped from the rear of the sputtering ruin.

"Help!" screamed the elf technician.

Ixmal turned. Estoril had stayed alone in the transporter, peering over the bulkhead which shielded him from ricochets and who knew what.

The elf wasn't alone anymore. A machine much like the one melting in the wreckage of Outpost 27 had crawled into the vehicle and was devouring the banks of sheet-metal seats.

Ixmal cursed and pulled another grenade from his belt. There was going to be hell to pay over this one, of that he was sure.

Base Commander Smythe could split the flat-screen Operations Room display into as many as sixteen separate facets to track the course of the battle. The technology would have been wonderful if she'd liked what she saw in more of the pictures.

The crater wall still glowed where Outpost 27 had been. Smythe had nuked the site after a Weasel squad retreated from swarms of machines.

Battle, hell. This was a war!

Loadmaster Rao sat beside Smythe, talking angrily to a Weasel officer on the other end of the phone line. Rao's skin had a grayish cast and hung in folds over what had been a Buddha-like visage. He stopped speaking in mid-bark and stared at the handset which had just gone dead.

A lot of machinery was failing at Bileduct Base just now.

One facet of the screen showed patches of light advancing slowly up a crawlspace ahead of the Weasel trooper whose suit held the camera. Something glittery quivered out of sight ahead. The picture jumped violently as bullets ricocheted from and around the escaping machine.

Another facet: the fireball of a plasma burst, so bright that the quarter quadrant went momentarily black. When the picture returned, the boojum's gutted casing still glowed in the control room of a corvette. That machine had manufactured its last ball bearing.

Of course the control room was glowing slag also. For all practical purposes, the corvette was now fit only for scrap. The wreck might as well be 1500 tonnes of ball bearings for all the good it would do the war effort.

Another facet: a squad of suited Khalians moving purposefully across the crater floor. Ahead of them, three boojums munched on a destroyer. The tough hull plating spat occasional sparks beneath their cutting teeth. The leading Weasel hurled a grenade whose soundless explosion collapsed a boojum's casing.

The Weasel spun like gauze in a hailstorm while the rock puffed upward around him. He dropped, his atmosphere suit in bloody tatters around the remnants of his body.

As Smythe watched in horror, the two surviving boojums backed toward the squad, carefully realigning their solar wings as they loosed further streams of ball bearings. They'd beefed up their electromagnetic delivery systems considerably over what had sufficed for Mom in the taconite mines of Ouroboros.

Another facet, this one from a transporter Smythe had ordered to search the immediate surroundings of the base when she thought the attack must be coming from outside. There was a fresh crater thirty kilometers from Bileduct Base, easily visible because of the huge solar array in the center of it. Six lines rayed from the power station; at the far end of each line was a boojum which looked a great deal like MM 39.

The six bearing-delivery tubes rose and pointed simultaneously. The image blurred into rushing landscape as the transporter pilot dropped to the deck and wicked up on his throttles. . . .

Smythe knuckled her prickling eye sockets. That nest of machines wasn't doing any particular harm at the moment; anyway, a missile could take care of it easily enough. But if the little bastards kept reproducing—and learning—the base staff wasn't going to get all of them ever. That much was certain.

Loadmaster Jiketsy bustled into the Operations Room with a slave technician in tow. Normally it would have been doubtful etiquette for a Syndicate officer to bring

even a Khalian into this sanctum, but all the rules had
gone out the window when the machines declared war
on Bileduct Base.

"Sir," said Rao, too tired to notice that Jiketsy already
had his mouth open to speak, "we've got to call in support, at least a full battle squadron. I'm readying a corvette—"

"No," said Smythe, without taking her fists away from
her eyes.

"Sir," said Loadmaster Jiketsy, "it's confirmed that the
original thing came in from Ouroboros on the *Tumor*.
This slave—"

Smythe uncovered an eye and stared coldly at Estoril.
The elf technician bobbed his head nervously.

"—was there when it was turned on."

"Well, has anybody thought to turn it off?" Smythe
asked in a close approximation of calm reason. She was
too exhausted to be furious.

"We melted the *Tumor* to slag three hours ago," Rao
said. "What was left of it. Using the base defense system
on manual override."

He shrugged. "I suppose we got a lot of them in the
mothership's hull. Got a lot more as the survivors tried to
flee. But it didn't make any difference in the overall—"

A particularly bright flash from the display screen drew
a flick of the loadmaster's eye.

"Overall picture, that is. Sir, we really need to call
for help."

And spend the rest of our careers swabbing toilets in
the slave pens, Smythe added mentally.

"You!" she snapped at Estoril. "You were on Ouroboros. Was the place covered with these, these
monsters?"

Estoril waggled his ears violently. "Nosir, nosir," he
said. "It was just, you know, a place . . . not that I was,
you know, on the ground."

"They booby-trapped the load before they let us capture it," Jiketsy snarled. "And with us using idiot Weasels
to do the wet work, they knew nobody'd notice till—"

He drew his index finger across his throat.

"Sirs, I think it must have been an accident," Estoril said. "I mean, the machine didn't start out, you know, hostile. Maybe the crew—maybe it was dropped when the Khalian master crew brought it aboard?"

Smythe looked at Rao. "You have a corvette ready to lift?"

Rao nodded. "Yessir. I'm glad you—"

"Shut up," Smythe interrupted. "I want it crewed by Weasels who were on the first Ouroboros raid. I want that tech"—she pointed at Estoril; fur quivered on the elf's ear tips—"along. I want them to learn how to fix these machines, turn them off—end them. Do you all understand?"

Three heads nodded at the base commander.

"And I want the answer fast!" she added, breaking composure in a scream.

Rao, pasty-faced despite his normally swarthy complexion, began keying access codes into a phone that still worked. Smythe, Jiketsy, and Estoril watched the progress of the battle on the display screen.

Matters were not improving. . . .

Mom was gone, but her spirit lingered on.

There was enough iron and alloying elements in Bileduct's rocks to continue the making of ball bearings for a reasonable length of time. Some of the materials necessary to produce boojums, the first order of business for the present, were limited to Bileduct Base and its immediate environs.

The boojums, linked by tight-focus radio and subsonic communications through the mantle of Bileduct, watched with dismay as a starship rose from the surface of the base, hovered, and sped away, carrying with it trace elements that could be found nowhere else on the planetoid. Not only that, but the attacks by bands of rabid Weasels with guns, grenades, and plasma weapons had seriously affected production of both bearings and boojums. Some of the latest boojum models were being turned out with heavy armor, but that was a short-term solution.

Mom had taught her kids to take the long view.

Boojums talked as they ran and hid; talked as they shot back; talked as they ate and reproduced and ran and hid and shot back.

Unlike human committees—to say nothing of throat-ripping Khalian clan gatherings—Mom's kids reached a semi-intelligent consensus within a few seconds of compiling the available data.

The battle continued for several hours among and within the ships grounded at Bileduct Base without apparent change. It took some while to produce boojums to meet the new requirements, after all; but before long finger-length boojums, hidden beneath solar panels which looked like flat hillocks, began to crawl away from the embattled ships.

Because they were so small, it would take them days to reach the defensive clusters in the crater wall. The sensors in the outposts were precise enough to notice the little creatures, but all inputs from within the base were automatically filtered out.

And this time, the boojums knew better than to dismantle the outposts and call down on themselves a point-blank barrage of missiles like those which had finally ended the first attempt to devour the defenses.

The business would take time, but that was all right with the boojums.

"But you got everything the first time!" wailed the human engineer two of the raiders were dragging onto the cramped bridge of the corvette *Carbuncle*. The electronic human/Khalian translator in the command console spewed out a translation of sorts in an unpleasant Brightwater Clan accent.

"Silence!" barked Slevskrit. The elf technician bawled something at the human which the console agreed was a proper translation. Someday maybe the fouling machines would handle both sides of the conversation.

By the Great Mother! how he hated machines.

"When we came to your mud ball before," Slevskrit said, "we captured one of these." Somebody at Bileduct Base had managed to find a drawing of MM 39, turned in when the *Tumor* arrived and filed properly, for a wonder. Slevskrit held the paper out to the human. His claws punctured it. "Do you recognize it?"

Even before Estoril finished his translation, the human squinted at the drawing and said, "Oh, yeah. One of the mining machines from South Continent. Needs to have a power station to work, though."

"No," said the elf, unprompted. "It doesn't."

The colonists hadn't resisted this time either. Ouroboros was a fundamentally defenseless world. A single corvette could hold the planet to ransom just as effectively as the hundred-ship fleet of raiders had done the first time. The firepower needed was still two nuclear missiles, to melt the world's ice caps and flood the meager land masses along the equator.

Besides, as the engineer was trying to tell them, there was nothing left to steal from Ouroboros!

Nothing but knowledge.

"If you recognize the machine," said Slevskrit, "then you know how to turn it off. Tell us or—"

The Weasel captain spent some time explaining precisely what the "else" would be. Estoril began translating long before Slevskrit had finished. In fact, the elf seemed to be pretending that he didn't hear the captain's lovingly detailed words.

"Turn the machine off?" said the engineer. "Well, throw the switch, of course. There's a big yellow junction box in the powerplant. Just throw—"

"We don't have the powerplant," Estoril said in human. The console translated his words in the same fouling Brightwater accent as it did the engineer's. "Ah . . . some of the units are operating on solar power. Ah, there are a number of the units by now."

"Ah," said the human. "Ah, I do see. . . ."

Slevskrit bared his fangs. Both non-Weasels jumped.

"Ah, yes," the human said thoughtfully. "Probably quite a lot of them. The ball-bearing signal would have been effectively turned off when you, ah, liberated the unit. Without that, the unit becomes a von Neumann machine; it just builds more of itself. Be interesting to do the math on that—"

Slevskrit growled. Both slaves jumped again.

"Right," said the elf. His ears momentarily tried to stuff their furry tips into his aural channels. "What's a ball-bearing signal and how do we send one?"

"Well, the easiest way to send the signal is to use the transmitter from the original site," the human explained. "I suppose you left the powerplant in place on South Continent? The lord knows we haven't gotten around to doing anything about it."

"Yes," snarled Slevskrit, furious that the other two had figured out something—and he didn't have a clue himself, even though he'd heard every word of the conversation. "But what does a ball-bearing signal do!"

Estoril didn't bother to translate. "It tells the machines what's needed. Maybe it's ball bearings. Maybe it's molybdenum, or molybdenum steel, or bronze or iridium, but it might as well come as little balls. It . . . see, the signal turns the machines into ball-bearing factories," he said to the Weasel captain, "instead of ball-bearing factory factories. It won't destroy the, ah, units that have already been built, but it'll stop the, ah, production of new units."

"Right," said the elf. "And the masters can deal with the overpopulation by conventional means. Plasma weapons and the like."

The human shook his head in quiet amazement. "That must really be something to see, wherever you've got 'em."

Estoril bobbed his ears in agreement.

"One of those Mother-fouling things is overpopulation," Slevskrit growled.

He reached for the control that would initiate take-off procedures, then paused and said to the troopers who'd brought the prisoner in, "Toss him out the port before we lift."

Bringing an Alliance human to a Syndicate base would subject them all to punishment worse than what Slevskrit visualized for the engineer if he hadn't cooperated.

"In pieces?" asked one of the guards hopefully.

"No!" the captain snapped. "Alive. Running." How could he convey what he meant? "Happy!"

Not because the prisoner had been promised his life if he cooperated.

But the way this whole fouling operation had gone, Slevskrit suspected they might need the hairless turd again.

"It's gotten awfully quiet," Loadmaster Rao mumbled. His elbows were on the desk, and he cradled his face in his splayed hands. It was impossible to see whether or not his eyes were open.

Anyway, Base Commander Smythe's eyes weren't focusing even though they were open.

"Maybe we got 'em all," Loadmaster Jiketsy said. He was facing the display screen. There was absolutely no emotion overlying either his words or his visage.

"Fat frigging chance," Smythe said. "Shouldn't the *Carbuncle* be back from Ouroboros by now?"

"It's only been three days," Jiketsy said. "It'll take another three days at best."

"Feels longer," said Smythe.

"It's gotten awfully quiet," mumbled Rao.

A phone rang.

Smythe raised the handset, concentrated, and poked the button for the correct line with the single-minded concentration of someone spearing the last pickle in the jar.

"This is Mobile Three!" barked the pilot of the only transporter still operating. "There's something happening out here."

The transporter had been trapped on the other side of the crater wall when the boojums started shooting back. Any attempt to land at the base since then would have left Mobile Three where all its fellows were—crumpled on the crater floor after being shredded by converging streams of ball bearings.

Smythe was willing to bet that the Weasel pilot was just as happy to be out of the action anyhow, though she didn't have enough energy left to get angry about it. "Just show us, will you?" she pleaded with the phone. "Don't talk. Please don't talk."

Loadmaster Jiketsy touched a control without looking down at the console. "Upper right quadrant," his flat voice said as that portion of the screen filled with the picture sent by the cameras of Mobile Three.

"Good God almighty," Smythe said, shocked out of her lethargy.

Something was happening, all right. The horizon was crawling with what looked like huge lumps of rock—and likely were just that; slabs of regolith would make excellent armor against even the plasma weapons of Bileduct Base's outer defenses.

Speaking of which—

"Jiketsy!" Smythe snapped. "Why aren't the defensive outposts engaging those things?"

"I'll take over on manual," Jiketsy said without concern or any other sign of emotion. His fingers tapped keys.

"That's funny," he said, no longer emotionless.

Other views of the crater rim showed that the heavy batteries were rotating, all right: inward, toward the base.

The captain of a destroyer decided he'd had enough. Without orders—against orders—and facing a drumhead court martial and execution as soon as all this business was sorted out, he lifted his ship from the crater floor.

At least thirty of the plasma cannon in the defensive outposts fired simultaneously, wrapping the destroyer in a blue-white glare for the instant before it crashed back onto the ground.

Where its valuable materials could be recovered at leisure by the boojums.

There were bursts of firing from all over Bileduct Base.

The boojums inside the perimeter had laid low until their armored bigger brethren had arrived from manufacturing centers kilometers away. Now they were coming out to take part in the final struggle to make Bileduct safe for ball bearings.

"It isn't quiet anymore," Loadmaster Rao muttered into his hands.

The *Carbuncle* could hover, but it wasn't the maneuver for which Khalian corvettes were optimized. Her gravity thrusters hammered the hull, threatening to shake the vessel apart three kilometers above the surface of Bileduct.

Or wherever the nest-fouling hell they were.

"Where the nest-fouling hell are we?" Slevskrit shouted.

"We've arrived at Bileduct Base, sir," said the corvette's navigator. His lips were drawn back to show that he would defend his statement with his life, if need be.

It might well come to that, the way Slevskrit was feeling. "You dung-brained idiot, there's no base down there!"

He turned and pointed his full paw at Estoril. The Weasel's claws extended reflexively; the elf's ears curled. "You!" Slevskrit said. "Slave! Do you see any base down there? Do you?"

Estoril's face was warped into a rictus of terror. He peered at the console's landing screen and said, "Ah, it looks like the crater, but . . ."

"Not even the crater's right," Slevskrit grumbled, but he let his whiskers twitch loosely. The engine vibration was jellying his brain; he couldn't manage to stay angry.

They had to do something.

"Right!" Slevskrit said. He held down the General Announcement key on his console. "Landing parties, prepare to disembark in radiation suits. Gunnery Officer, prepare to fire one, I say again, one torpedo with a one by ten-kilotonne warhead, fused for an air burst with ground zero at marked point. . . ."

The captain's paws slid the mechanical crosshairs over his console display, halting them over what had been the northwest quadrant of the crater when there was a base in the center of it. There might still be a base there, though Slevskrit certainly wasn't seeing it.

"Mark!"

"Target marked, sir," crackled the gunnery officer's voice through a rush of static. The com system wasn't taking to the prolonged hovering any better than Slevskrit himself was.

"Fire one!"

"Fi . . . n!" sputtered the response.

The torpedo's release was lost in *Carbuncle*'s engine vibration. Light bloomed on the display screen, white which faded to red even before the shockwave struck the corvette three kilometers above it. The modest nuclear explosion buffeted the *Carbuncle* with a pillow of vaporized rock, the first atmosphere Bileduct had known in a million centuries.

"Now," Slevskrit barked in satisfaction, "set us down in the middle of what the blast cleared!"

The *Carbuncle* began to settle, slanting toward the dull glow. Estoril peered at the screen, twitching his aquiline nose in concern. "You know, ah, sir . . ." he said. "The crater walls don't look quite—"

Slevskrit turned brown, furious eyes on the elf. Estoril swallowed and braced to his race's posture of attention, feet crossed at the insteps and hands crossed in front of the crotch.

"You," the Weasel captain said. "You're ready to broadcast the ball-bearing signal? Or you're lunch."

"Yessir, master," said Estoril. "Yessir, master, the transmitter is ready, master. It'll be triggered as soon as we land, master."

Either the *Carbuncle* greased in to an unusually smooth landing, or the pounding they'd taken while they hovered made it seem that way. The shallow bowl of glass had frozen hard. An occasional quiver of residual radiation lighted the slag.

As Estoril had said, the ball-bearing signal blasted out at the full strength of the corvette's transmitters as soon as *Carbuncle*'s hull crackled down on the fresh glass.

Slevskrit snorted in relief. "All right," he said. "What happens now?"

"Wow!" said Estoril.

"Wow!" barked Slevskrit and his navigator together.

Lifting the solar panels that camouflaged them into a close approximation of the rock walls they had devoured, the latest generation of Mom's kids was sweeping down on the *Carbuncle*, dribbling bearings behind them. The boojums moved particularly fast for the first part of their rush because they were skating on the layer of ball bearings that already carpeted what had been the surface of Bileduct Base.

They moved sufficiently fast on the glass of the bomb crater also, though they sank much deeper into the shattered substrata than the relatively light corvette had done.

Carbuncle's plasma cannon fired a few useless bolts, but the gunnery officer had no time to launch nuclear missiles. That was good from the boojums' standpoint, because blasts so close might have destroyed the vessel itself.

Mom's kids had realized that they were going to run out of trace elements very quickly unless they preserved the radio and databanks of this vessel, instead of recycling it totally as ore the way they had done with the rest of their prey. . . .

They took the long view, after all. Mom would have been proud of them.

Syndicate Inspection Vessel *Matsushita* hung in a powered orbit above Bileduct Base.

"That's all they're saying?" Sub-Syndic 1st Class Whisnant demanded, knuckling his bald scalp.

"Yes, Lord Whisnant," said Cuvier, the Regional Inspector's chief aide. He cleared his throat and repeated, " 'Welcome honored guests. Join us for the Birth Celebration of the Brightwater Clan.' "

"That's insane," Whisnant said.

Cuvier cleared his throat again. "It's in Khalian, of course."

"What's a base like this doing under Weasel control?" Whisnant wondered aloud. "Of course, that might explain why they apparently haven't completed any repairs in the past three months. . . ."

The Regional Inspector and his aide stared at the holographic image of Bileduct Base. There must be over three hundred ships backlogged around the HQ Tower and repair bays.

There was something funny about the ships' outline— a fuzziness, almost—but that was presumably a fault in the hologram projector.

"Right!" Whisnant decided. "Tell the captain to set us down. We'll soon sort things out!"

The best thing I've found about book signings is that they take me to a lot of bookstores and I love books. At a signing in the North Carolina mountains I stumbled onto *The Jack Tales* by Richard Chase, retellings of classic fairy tales in mountain idiom. I neither know nor care whether the stories were "authentic folktales" or largely the creations of Chase himself. I do know that a number of folksongs were first sung in the mountains by the collector him or herself . . . and dammit, ballad collectors are folks too, aren't they?

My friend Manly Wade Wellman had recently died. Perhaps the best of Manly's many fine fantasies were the stories about a balladeer named John, born in the Sandhills Country but wandering North Carolina's mountains. As homage to Manly but using Chase's concept of reworking fairy tales, I wrote a series of stories set in 1830 in the area of central Tennessee to which my parents had retired.

The main character is a cunning man—a hedge wizard—named Old Nathan, a crochety old guy who talks to animals and tolerates his fellow humans with notable difficulty. As for the animal's personalities—I work outdoors near a couple bird feeders which draw the normal complement of ground-based critters to get their share of the sunflower seeds. If I'd ever had a tendency to romanticize our feathered and furry friends, that dose of reality would have cured me.

The Bullhead

"That don't half stink," grumbled the mule as Old Nathan came out of the shed with the saddle over his left arm and a bucket of bait in his right hand.

"Nobody asked you t' like it," the cunning man replied sharply. "Nor me neither, ifen it comes t' thet. It brings catfish like it's manna from hivven, and I *do* like a bit of smoked catfish fer supper."

"Waal, then," said the mule, "you go off t' yer fish and I'll mommick up some more oats while yer gone. Then we're both hap—"

The beast's big head turned toward the cabin and its ears cocked forward. "Whut's thet coming?" it demanded.

Old Nathan set the bucket down and hung the saddle over a fence rail. He'd been raised in a time when the Tennessee Territory was wilderness and the few folk you met liable to be wilder yet—the Whites worse than the Indians.

But that was long decades ago. He'd gotten out of the habit of *always* keeping his rifle close by and loaded. But a time like this, when somebody crept up so you didn't hear his horse on the trail—

Then you remembered that your rifle was in the cabin, fifty feet away, and that a man of seventy didn't move so quick as the boy of eighteen who'd aimed that same rifle at King's Mountain.

"Halloo the house?" called the visitor, and Old Nathan's world slipped back to this time of settlement

189

and civilization. The voice was a woman's, not that of an ambusher who'd hitched his horse to a sapling back along the trail so as to shoot the cunning man unawares.

"We're out the back!" Old Nathan called. "Come through the cabin, or I'll come in t' ye."

It wasn't that he had enemies, exactly; but there were plenty of folks around afraid of what the cunning man did—or what they thought he did. Fear had pulled as many triggers as hatred over the years, he guessed.

"T'morry's a good time t' traipse down t' the river," the mule said complacently as it thrust its head over the snake-rail fence to chop a tuft of grass just within its stretch. "Or never a'tall, that's better yet."

"We're goin' t' check my trot line t'day, sooner er later!" Old Nathan said over his shoulder. "Depend on it!"

Both doors of the one-room cabin were open. Old Nathan liked the ventilation, though the morning was cool. His visitor came out onto the back porch where the water barrel stood and said, "Oh, I didn't mean t' take ye away from business. You jest go ahead 'n I'll be on my way."

Her name was Ellie. Ellie Ransden, he reckoned, since she'd been living these three years past with Bully Ransden, though it wasn't certain they'd had a preacher marry them. Lot of folks figured these old half-lettered stump-hole preachers hereabouts, they weren't much call to come between a couple of young people and God no-ways.

Though she still must lack a year of twenty, Ellie Ransden had a woman's full breasts and hips. Her hair black as thunder, was her glory. It was piled now on top of her head with pins and combs, but if she shook it out, it would be long enough to fall to the ground.

The combs were the only bit of fancy about the woman. She wore a gingham dress and went barefoot, with calluses to show that was usual for her till the snow fell. Bully Ransden wasn't a lazy man, but he had a hard way about him that put folk off, and he'd started from less than nothing. . . .

If there was a prettier woman in the county than Ellie Ransden, Old Nathan hadn't met her.

"Set yerse'f," Old Nathan grunted, nodding her back into the cabin. "I'll warm some grounds."

"Hit don't signify," Ellie said. She looked up toward a corner of the porch overhang where two sparrows argued about which had stolen the thistle seed from the other. "I jest figgered I'd drop by t' be neighborly, but if you've got affairs . . . ?"

"The fish'll wait," said the cunning man, dipping a gourd of water from the barrel. He'd drunk the coffee in the pot nigh down to the ground already. "I was jest talkin' t' my mule."

Ellie's explanation of what she was doing here was a lie for at least several reasons. First, Bully Ransden was no friend to the cunning man. Second, the two cabins, Old Nathan's and Ransden's back some miles on the main road, were close enough to be neighbors in parts as ill-settled as these—but in the three years past, Ellie hadn't felt the need to come down this way.

The last reason was the swollen redness at the corners of the young woman's eyes. *Mis'ry was what brought folks most times t' see the cunning man, t' see Old Nathan the Witch. Mis'ry and anger. . . .*

Old Nathan poured water into the iron coffeepot on the table of his one-room cabin. Some of last night's coffee grounds, the beans bought green and roasted in the fireplace, floated on the inch of liquid remaining. They'd have enough strength left for another heating.

"Lots of folks, they talk t' their animals," he added defensively as he hung the refilled pot on the swinging bar and pivoted it back over the fire. *Not so many thet hear what the beasts answer back, but thet was nobody's affair save his own.*

"Cullen ain't a badman, ye know," Ellie Ransden said in a falsely idle voice as she examined one of the cabin's pair of glazed sash-windows.

Old Nathan set a knot of pitchy lightwood in the coals to heat the fire up quickly. She was likely the only soul in the county called Bully Ransden by his baptized name. "Thet's for them t' say as knows him better 'n I do," he said aloud. "Or care t' know him."

"He was raised hard, thet's all," Ellie said to the rectangles of window glass. "I reckon—"

She turned around and her voice rose in challenge, though she probably didn't realize what was happening. "—thet you're afeerd t' cross him, same as airy soul hereabouts?"

Old Nathan snorted "I cain't remember the time I met a man who skeerd me," he said. "Seeins as I've got this old, I don't figger I'll meet one hereafter neither."

He smiled, amused at the way he'd reacted to the girl's—the woman's—obvious ploy. "Set," he offered, gesturing her to the rocking chair.

Ellie moved toward the chair, then angled off in a flutter of gingham like a butterfly unwilling to light for nervousness. She stood near the fireplace, staring in the direction of the five cups of blue-rimmed porcelain on the fireboard above the hearth. Her hands twisted together instinctively as if she were attempting to strangle a snake.

"Reckon you heerd about thet *Modom* Taliaferro down t' Oak Hill," she said.

Old Nathan seated himself in the rocker. There was the straight chair beside the table if Ellie wanted it. Now that he'd heard the problem, he didn't guess she was going to settle.

"Might uv heard the name," the cunning man agreed. "Lady from New Orleens, bought 'Siah Chesson's house from his brother back in March after thet dead limb hit 'Siah."

Oak Hill, the nearest settlement, wasn't much, but its dozen dwellings were mostly of saw-cut boards. There was a store, a tavern, and several artisans who supplemented their trade with farm plots behind the houses.

Not a place where a wealthy, pretty lady from New Orleans was likely to be found; but it might be that

Madame Francine Taliaferro didn't *choose* to be found by some of those looking for her.

Ellie turned and glared at Old Nathan. "She's a whore!" she blazed, deliberately holding his eyes.

Pitch popped loudly in the hearth. Old Nathan rubbed his beard. "I ain't heard," he said mildly, "thet the lady's sellin' merchandise of *any* sort."

"Then she's a witch," Ellie said, as firm as a tree-trunk bent the last finger's breadth before it snaps.

"Thet's a hard word," the cunning man replied. "Not one t' spread where it mayn't suit."

He had no desire to hurt his visitor, but he wasn't the man to tell a lie willingly; and he wasn't sure that right now, a comforting lie wouldn't be the worse hurt.

"Myse'f," the cunning man continued, "I don't reckon she's any such a thing. I reckon she's a purty woman with money and big-city ways, and thet's all."

Ellie threw her hands to her face. "She's old!" the girl blubbered as she turned her back. "She mus' be thutty!"

Old Nathan got up from the rocker with the caution of age. "Yes ma'm," he agreed dryly. "I reckon thet's rightly so."

He looked at the fire to avoid staring at the back of the woman, shaking with sobs. "I reckon the coffee's biled," he said. "I like a cup t' steady myse'f in the mornings."

Ellie tugged a kerchief from her sleeve. She wiped her eyes, then blew her nose violently before she turned again.

"Why look et the time!" she said brightly. "Why, I need t' be runnin' off right now. Hit's my day t' bake light-bread fer Cullen, ye know."

Ellie's false, fierce smile was so broad that it squeezed another tear from the corner of her eye. She brushed the drop away with a knuckle, as though it had been a gnat about to bite.

"He's powerful picky about his vittles, my Cull is," she went on. "He all'us praises my cookin', though."

Ellie might have intended to say more, but her eyes

scrunched down and her upper lip began to quiver with the start of another sob. She turned and scampered out the front door in a flurry of check-patterned skirt. "Thankee fer yer time!" she called as she ran up the trail.

Old Nathan sighed. He swung the bar off the fire, but he didn't feel any need for coffee himself just now. He looked out the door toward the empty trail.

And after a time, he walked to the pasture to resume saddling the mule.

The catfish was so large that its tail and barbel-fringed head both poked over the top of the oak-split saddle basket. "It ain't so easy, y'know," the mule complained as it hunched up the slope where the track from the river joined the main road, "when the load's unbalanced like that."

Old Nathan sniffed. "Ifen ye like," he said, "I'll put a ten-pound rock in t'other side t' give ye balance."

The mule lurched up onto the road. "Hey, watch it, ye old fool!" shouted a horseman, reining up from a canter. Yellow grit sprayed from beneath the horse's hooves.

Old Nathan cursed beneath his breath and dragged the mule's head around. *There was no call fer a body t' be ridin' so blame fast where a road was all twists 'n tree roots—*

But there was no call fer a blamed old fool t' drive his mule acrost thet road, without he looked first t' see what might be a'comin'.

"You damned old hazard!" the horseman shouted. His horse blew and stepped high in place, lifting its hooves as the dust settled. "I ought t' stand you on yer haid 'n drive you right straight int' the dirt like a tint-peg!"

"No, ye hadn't ought t' do thet, Bully Ransden," the cunning man replied. "And ye hadn't ought t' try, neither."

He muttered beneath his breath, then waved his left hand down through the air in an arc. A trail of colored light followed his fingertips, greens and blues and yellows, flickering and then gone. Only the gloom of late afternoon among the overhanging branches made such pale colors visible.

"But I'll tell ye I'm sorry I rid out in front of ye," Old Nathan added. "Thet ye do hev a right to."

He was breathing heavily with the effort of casting the lights. He could have fought Bully Ransden and not be any more exhausted—but he would have lost the fight. The display, trivial though it was in fact, set the younger man back in his saddle.

"Howdy, mule," said Ransden's horse. "How're things goin' down yer ways?"

"I guess ye think I'm skeered of yer tricks!" Ransden said. He patted the neck of his horse with his right hand, though just now the animal was calmer than the rider.

"'Bout like common, I reckon," the mule replied. "Work, work, work, an' fer whut?"

"If yer not," Old Nathan replied in a cold bluster, "thin yer a fool, Ransden. And thet's as may be."

He raised his left hand again, though he had no intention of doing anything with it.

Now that Old Nathan had time to look, his eyes narrowed at the younger man's appearance. Ransden carried a fishing pole in his left hand. The ten-foot length of cane was an awkward burden for a horseman hereabouts—where even the main road was a pair of ruts, and branches met overhead most places.

Despite the pole, Bully Ransden wasn't dressed for fishing. He wore a green velvet frock coat some sizes too small for his broad shoulders, and black storebought trousers as well. His shirt alone was homespun, but clean and new. The garment was open well down the front so that the hair on Ransden's chest curled out in a vee against the gray-white fabric.

"Right now," the mule continued morosely, "we been off loadin' fish. Whutiver good was a fish t' airy soul, I ask ye?"

"Waal," Ransden said, "I take yer 'pology. See thet ye watch yerse'f the nixt time."

"I'm headed inter the sittlement," said the horse in satisfaction. "I allus git me a feed uv oats there, I do."

"Goin' into the settlement, thin?" Old Nathan asked, as if it were no more than idle talk between two men who'd met on the road.

The cunning man and Bully Ransden had too much history between them to be no more than that, though. Each man was unique in the county—known by everyone and respected, but feared as well.

Old Nathan's art set him apart from others. Bully Ransden had beaten his brutal father out of the cabin when he was eleven. Since that time, fists and knotted muscles had been the Bully's instant reply to any slight or gibe directed at the poverty from which he had barely raised himself—or the fact he was the son of a man hated and despised by all in a land where few angels had settled.

Old Nathan's mouth quirked in a smile. He and Ransden were stiff-necked men, as well, who both claimed they didn't care what others thought so long as they weren't interfered with. There was some truth to the claim as well. . . .

"I reckon I might head down thet way," Ransden said, as though there was ought else in the direction he was heading. "Might git me some supper t' Shorty's er somewhere."

He took notice of the mule's saddle baskets and added, "Say, old man—thet's a fine catfish ye hev there."

"Thet's right," Old Nathan agreed. "I figger t' fry me a steak t'night 'n smoke the rest."

"Hmph," the mule snorted, looking sidelong up at the cunning man. "Wish thut some of us iver got oats t' eat."

"I might buy thet fish offen ye," Ransden said. "I've got a notion t' take some fish back fer supper t'morry. How much 'ud ye take fer him?"

"Hain't interested in sellin'," Old Nathan said, his eyes narrowing again. "Didn't figger airy soul as knew Shorty 'ud et his food—or drink the pizen he calls whiskey. I'd uv figgered ye'd stay t' home t'night. Hain't nothin' so good as slab uv hot bread slathered with butter."

Bully Ransden flushed, and the tendons of his bull neck stood out like cords. "You been messin' about my Ellie, old man?" he asked.

The words were almost unintelligible. Emotion choked Ransden's voice the way ice did streams during the spring freshets.

Old Nathan was careful not to raise his hand. A threat that might forestall violence at a lower emotional temperature would precipitate it with the younger man in his current state. *Nothing* would stop Bully Ransden now if he chose to attack; nothing but a bullet in the brain, and that might not stop him soon enough to save his would-be victim.

"I know," the cunning man said calmly, "what I know. D'ye doubt *thet*, Bully Ransden?"

The horse stretched out his neck to browse leaves from a sweet-gum sapling which had sprouted at the edge of the road. Ransden jerked his mount back reflexively, but the movement took the danger out of a situation cocked and primed to explode.

Ransden looked away. "Aw, hit's no use t' talk to an old fool like you," he muttered. "I'll pick up a mess uv bullheads down t' the sittlement. Gee-up, horse!"

He spurred his mount needlessly hard. As the horse sprang down the road with a startled complaint, Ransden shouted over his shoulder, "I'm a grown man! Hit's no affair of yourn where I spend my time—nor Ellie's affair neither!"

Old Nathan watched the young man go. He was still staring down the road some moments after Ransden had disappeared. The mule said in a disgusted voice, "I wouldn't mind t' get back to a pail of oats, old man."

"Git along, thin," the cunning man said. "Fust time I ever knowed ye t' be willing t' do airy durn thing."

But his heart wasn't in the retort.

The cat came in, licking his muzzle both with relish and for the purpose of cleanliness. "Found the fish guts in the mulch pile," he said. "Found the head too. Thankee."

"Thought ye might like hit," said Old Nathan as he knelt, adding sticks of green hickory to his fire. "Ifen ye didn't, the corn will next Spring."

The big catfish, cleaned and split open, lay on the smokeshelf just below the throat of the fireplace. Most folk, they had separate smokehouses—vented or chinked tight, that was a matter of taste. Even so, the fireplace smokeshelf was useful for bits of meat that weren't worth stoking up a smoker meant for whole hogs and deer carcasses.

As for Old Nathan—he wasn't going to smoke and eat a hog any more than he was going to smoke and eat a human being . . . though there were plenty hogs he'd met whose personalities would improve once their throats were slit.

Same was true of the humans, often enough.

Smoke sprouted from the underside of the hickory billet and hissed up in a sheet. Trapped water cracked its way to the surface with a sound like that of a percussion cap firing.

"Don't reckon there's an uglier sight in the world 'n a catfish head," said the cat as he complacently groomed his right forepaw. He spread the toes and extended the white, hooked claws, each of them needle sharp. "A passel uv good meat to it, though."

"Don't matter what a thing looks like," Old Nathan said, "so long's it tastes right." He sneezed violently, backed away from his fire, and sneezed again.

"Thought I might go off fer a bit," he added to no one in particular.

The cat chuckled and began to work on the other paw. "Chasin' after thet bit uv cunt come by here this mornin', are ye? Give it up, ole man. *You're* no good t' the split-tails."

"Ye think thet's all there is, thin?" the cunning man demanded. "Ifen I don't give her thet one help, there's no he'p thet matters a'tall?"

"Thet's right," the cat said simply. He began licking his genitals with his hind legs spread wide apart. His belly fur was white, while the rest of his body was yellow to tigerishly orange.

Old Nathan sighed. "I used t' think thet way myse'f," he admitted as he carried his tin wash basin out to the back porch. *Bout time t' fill the durn water barrel from the creek; but thet 'ud wait. . . .*

"Used t' think?" the tomcat repeated. "Used t' *know*, ye mean. Afore ye got yer knackers shot away."

"I knowed a girl a sight like Ellie Ransden back thin . . ." Old Nathan muttered.

The reflection in the water barrel was brown, the underside of the shakes covering the porch. Old Nathan bent to dip a basinful with the gourd scoop. He saw his own face, craggy and hard. His beard was still black, though he wouldn't see seventy again.

Then, though he hadn't wished it—*he thought*—and he hadn't said the words—*aloud*—there was a woman's face, young and full-lipped and framed in hair as long and black as the years since last he'd seen her, the eve of marching off with Colonel Sevier to what ended at King's Mountain. . . .

"Jes' turn 'n let me see ye move, Slowly," Old Nathan whispered to his memories. "There's nairy a thing so purty in all the world."

The reflection shattered. The grip of the cunning man's right hand had snapped the neck of the gourd. The hollowed body fell into the barrel.

Old Nathan straightened, wiping his eyes and forehead with the back of his hand. He tossed the gourd neck off the porch. "Niver knew why her folks, they named her thet, Slowly," he muttered. "Ifen it was them 'n not a name she'd picked herse'f."

The cat hopped up onto the cane seat of the rocking chair. He poised there for a moment, allowing the rockers to return to balance before he settled himself.

"I'll tell ye a thing, though, cat," the cunning man said forcefully. "Afore King's Mountain, I couldn't no more talk t' you an' t' other animals thin I could talk t' this hearth rock."

The tomcat curled his full tail over his face, then flicked it barely aside.

"Afore ye got yer knackers blowed off, ye mean?" the cat said. The discussion wasn't of great concern to him, but he demanded precise language nonetheless.

"Aye," Old Nathan said, glaring at the animal. "Thet's what I mean."

The cat snorted into his tail fur. "Thin you made a durned bad bargain, old man," he said.

Old Nathan tore his eyes away from the cat. The tin basin was still in his left hand. He sighed and hung it up unused.

"Aye," he muttered. "I reckon I did, cat."

He went out to saddle the mule again.

Ransden's cabin had a single door, in the front. It was open, but there was no sign of life within.

Old Nathan dismounted and wrapped the reins around the porch rail.

"Goin' t' water me?" the mule snorted.

"In my own sweet time, I reckon," the cunning man snapped back.

"Cull?" Ellie Ransden called from the cabin. "Cullen?" she repeated as she swept to the door., Her eyes were swollen and tear-blurred; they told her only that the figure at the front of her cabin wasn't *her* man. She ducked back inside—and reappeared behind a long flintlock rifle much like the one which hung on pegs over Old Nathan's fireboard.

"Howdy," said the cunning man. "Didn't mean t' startle ye, Miz Ransden."

Old Nathan spoke as calmly as though it were an everyday thing for him to look down the small end of a rifle. It wasn't. It hadn't been for many years, and that was a thing he didn't regret in the least about the passing of the old days.

"Oh!" she said, coloring in embarrassment. "Oh, do please come in. I got coffee, ifen hit ain't biled dry by now."

She lifted the rifle's muzzle before she lowered the hammer. The trigger dogs made a muted double click in releasing the mainspring's tension.

Ellie bustled quickly inside, fully a housewife again. "Oh, law!" she chirped as she set the rifle back on its pegs. "Here the fust time we git visitors in I don't know, and everything's all sixes 'n sevens!"

The cabin was neat as a pin, all but the bed where the eagle-patterned quilt was disarrayed. It didn't take art to see that Ellie had flung herself there crying, then jumped up in the hope her man had come home.

Bully Ransden must have knocked the furniture together himself. Not fancy, but it was all solid work, pinned with trenails rather than iron. There were two chairs, a table, and the bed. Three chests held clothes and acted as additional seats—though from what Ellie had blurted, the couple had few visitors, which was no surprise with Bully Ransden's reputation.

The windows in each end wall had shutters but no glazing. Curtains, made from sacking and embroidered with bright pink roses, set off their frames.

The rich odor of fresh bread filled the tiny room.

"Oh, law, what *hev* I done?" Ellie moaned as she looked at the fireplace.

The dutch oven sat on coals raked to the front of the hearth. They'd burned down, and the hotter coals pilled onto the cast iron lid were now a mass of fluffy white ash. Ellie grabbed fireplace tongs and lifted the lid away.

"Oh, hit's *ruint!*" the girl said.

Old Nathan reached into the oven and cracked the bread loose from the surface of the cast iron. The loaf had contracted slightly as it cooled. It felt light, more like biscuit than bread, and the crust was a brown as deep as a walnut plank.

"Don't look ruint t' me," he said as he lifted the loaf to one of the two pewter plates sitting ready on the table. "Looks right good. I'd admire t' try a piece."

Ellie Ransden picked up a knife with a well-worn blade. Unexpectedly, she crumpled into sobs. The knife dropped. It stuck in the cabin floor between the woman's bare feet, unnoticed as she bawled into her hands.

Old Nathan stepped around the table and touched Ellie's shoulders to back her away. Judging from how the light played, the butcher knife had an edge that would slice to the bone if she kicked it. The way the gal carried on, she might not notice the cut—and she might not care if she did.

"I'm *ugly!*" Ellie cried as she wrapped her arms around Old Nathan. "I cain't blame him, I've got t' be an old frumpy thing 'n he don't love me no more!"

For the moment, she didn't know who she held, just that he was warm and solid. She could talk at the cunning man, whether he listened or not.

"Tain't thet," Old Nathan muttered, feeling awkward as a hog on ice. One of the high-backed tortoiseshell combs that held and ornamented Ellie's hair tickled his beard. "Hit's jest the newness. Not thet he don't love ye. . . ."

He spoke the words because they were handy; but as he heard them come out, he guessed they were pretty much the truth. *Cullen ain't a bad man,* the girl had said, back to the cunning man's cabin. *No worse 'n most men,* the cunning man thought, *and thet's a durned poor lot.*

"Don't reckon there's a purtier girl in the county," Old Nathan said aloud. "Likely there's not in the whole blame state."

Ellie squeezed him firmly, this time a conscious action, and stepped back. She reached into her sleeve for her handkerchief, then saw it crumpled on the quilt where she'd been lying. She snatched up the square of linen, turned aside, and blew her nose firmly.

"You're a right good man," Ellie mumbled before she looked around again.

She raised her chin and said, pretending that her face was not flushed and tear-streaked, "Ifen it ain't me, hit's thet *bitch* down t' the sittlement. Fer a month hit's been Francine this 'n Francine that an' him spendin' the ev'nins out an' thin—"

Ellie's upper lip trembled as she tumbled out her recent history. The cunning man bent to tug the butcher knife from the floor and hide his face from the woman's.

"She witched him, sir!" Ellie burst out. "I heerd what you said up t' yer cabin, but I tell ye, she *witched* my Cull. He ain't *like* this!"

Old Nathan rose. He set the knife down, precisely parallel to the edge of the table, and met the woman's eyes. "Yer Cull ain't the fust man t' go where his pecker led," he said, harshly to be able to get the words out of his own throat. "'Tain't witch'ry, hit's jest human natur. An' don't be carryin' on, 'cause he'll be back—sure as the leaves turn."

Ellie wrung her hands together. The handkerchief was a tiny ball in one of them. "Oh, d' ye think he will, sir?" she whispered. "Oh, sir, could ye give me a charm t' bring him back? I'd be iver so grateful. . . ."

She looked down at her hands. Her lips pressed tightly together while silent tears dripped again from her eyes.

Old Nathan broke eye contact. He shook his head slightly and said, "No, I won't do thet."

"But ye could?" Ellie said sharply. The complex of emotions flowing across her face hardened into anger and determination. The woman who was wife to Bully Ransden could either be soft as bread dough or as strong and supple as a hickory pole. There was nothing in between—

And there was nothing soft about Ellie Ransden.

"I reckon ye think I couldn't pay ye," she said. "Waal, ye reckon wrong. There's my combs—"

She tossed her head; the three combs of translucent tortoiseshell, decorative but necessary as well to hold a mass of hair like Ellie's, quivered as they caught the light.

"Rance Holden, he'd buy thim back fer stock, I reckon. Mebbe thet *Modom* Francine—" the viciousness Ellie concentrated in the words would have suited a mother wren watching a blacksnake near her chicks "—'ud want thim fer *her* hair. And there's my Pappy's watch, too, thet Cullen wears now. Hit'll fetch somethin', I reckon, the case, hit's true gold."

She swallowed, chin regally high—but looking so young and vulnerable that Old Nathan wished the world were a different place than he knew it was and always would be.

"So, Mister Cunning Man," Ellie said. "I reckon I kin raise ten silver dollars. Thet's good pay fer some li'l old charm what won't take you nothin' t' make."

"I don't need yer money," Old Nathan said gruffly. "Hain't thet. I'm tellin' ye, hit's wrong t' twist folks around thet way. Ifen ye got yer Cullen back like thet, ye wouldn't like what it was ye hed. An' I *ain't* about t' do thet thing!"

"Thin you better go on off," Ellie said. "I'm no sort uv comp'ny t'day."

She flung herself onto the bed, burying her face in the quilt. She was sobbing.

Old Nathan bit his lower lip as he stepped out of the cabin. *Hit warn't the world I made, hit's jest the one I live in.*

"Leastways when ye go fishin'," the mule grumbled from the porch rail, "thur's leaves t' browse."

Wouldn't hurt him t' go see Madame Taliaferro with his own eyes, he reckoned.

Inside the cabin the girl cried, "Oh why cain't I jes' *die*, I'm so miser'ble!"

For as little good as he'd done, Old Nathan guessed he might better have stayed to home and saved himself and his mule a ride back in the dark.

The sky was pale from the recently set sun, but the road was in shadows. They would be deeper yet by the time the cunning man reached the head of the track to his cabin. The mule muttered a curse every time it clipped a hoof in a rut, but it didn't decide to balk.

The bats began their everlasting refrain, "Dilly, dilly, come and be killed," as they quartered the air above the road. *Thet peepin' nonsense was enough t' drive a feller t' distraction—er worse!*

Just as well the mule kept walking. This night, Old Nathan was in a good mood to speak phrases that would blast the bones right out of the durned old beast.

Somebody was coming down the road from Oak Hill, singing merrily. It took a moment to catch actual phrases of the song, "*. . . went a-courtin', he did ride . . .*" and a moment further to identify the voice as Bully Ransden's.

"*. . . an' pistol by his side, uh-huh!*"

Ransden came around the next bend in the trail, carrying not the bottle Old Nathan expected in his free hand but rather a stringer of bullheads. He'd left the long cane pole behind somewhere during the events of the evening.

"Hullo, mule," Ransden's horse whinnied. "Reckon I ate better'n *you* did t'night."

"Hmph,.." Grunted the mule. "Leastways my master ain't half-shaved an' goin' t' ride me slap inter a ditch 'fore long."

"Howdy, feller," Bully Ransden caroled. "Ain't it a fine ev'nin'?"

Ransden wasn't drunk, maybe, but he sure-hell didn't sound like the man he'd been since he grew up—which was about age eleven, when he beat his father out of the cabin with an ax handle.

"Better fer some thin others, I reckon," Old Nathan replied. He clucked the mule to the side, giving the horseman the room he looked like he might need.

Ransden's manner changed as soon as he heard the cunning mans' voice. "So hit's you, is it, old man?" he said.

He tugged hard on his reins, twisting his mount across the road in front of Old Nathan. "Hey, easy on!" the horse complained. "No call fer thet!"

"D'ye figger t' spy on me, feller?" Ransden demanded, turned crossways in his saddle. He shrugged his shoulders, straining the velvet jacket dangerously. "Or—"

Bully Ransden didn't carry a gun, but there was a long

knife in his belt. Not that he'd need it. Ransden was young and strong enough to break a fence rail with his bare hands, come to that. He'd do the same with Old Nathan, for all that the cunning man had won his share of fights in his youth—

And later. It was a hard land still, though statehood had come thirty years past.

"I'm ridin' on home, Cullen Ransden," Old Nathan said. "Reckon ye'd do well t' do the same."

"By God," said Ransden. "By *God*! Where you been to, old man? Hev you been sniffin' round my Ellie? By God, if she's been—"

The words echoed in Old Nathan's mind, where he heard them an instant before they were spoken.

The power that poured into the cunning man was nothing that he had summoned. It wore him like a cloak, responding to the threat Bully Ransden was about to voice.

"—slippin' around on me, I'll wring the bitch's—"

Old Nathan raised both hands. Thunder crashed in the clear sky, then rumbled away in diminishing chords.

The power was nothing to do with the cunning man, but he shaped it as a potter shapes clay on his wheel. He spread his fingers. The tree trunks and roadway glowed with a light as faint as foxfire. It was just enough to throw each rut and bark ridge into relief, as though they were reflecting the pale sky.

"Great God Almighty!" muttered Bully Ransden. His mouth fell open. The string of small fish in his left hand trembled slightly.

"Ye'll do *what* to thet pore little gal, Bully Ransden?" the cunning man asked in a harsh cracked voice.

Ransden touched his lips with his tongue. He tossed his head as if to clear it. "Reckon I misspoke," he said; not loud but clearly, and he met Old Nathan's eyes as he said the words.

"Brag's a good dog, Ransden," Old Nathan said. "But Hold-fast is better."

He lowered his arms. The vague light and the last trembling of thunder had already vanished.

The mule turned and stared back at its rider with one bulging eye. "Whut in tar-*nation* was that?" it asked.

Bully Ransden clucked to his horse. He pressed with the side, not the spur, of his right boot to swing the beast back in line with the road. "Don't you think I'm afeerd t' meet you, old man," he called; a little louder than necessary, and at a slightly higher pitch than intended.

Ransden *was* afraid; but that wouldn't keep him from facing the cunning man, needs must—

As surely as Old Nathan would have faced Bully's fists and hobnailed boots some moments earlier.

The rushing, all-mastering power was gone now, leaving Old Nathan shaken and as weak as a man wracked with a three-days flux. "Jest go yer way, Ransden," he muttered, "and I'll go mine. I don't wish fer any truck with you."

He heeled the mule's haunches and added, "Git on with ye, thin, mule."

The mule didn't budge. "I don't want no part uv these doins," it protested. "Felt like hit was a dad-blame thunderbolt sittin' astride me, hit did."

Ransden walked his nervous horse abreast of the cunning man. "I don't know why I got riled no-how," he said, partly for challenge but mostly just in the brutal banter natural to Bully's personality. "Hain't as though you're a man, now, is it?"

He spurred his horse off down the darkened trail, laughing merrily.

Old Nathan trembled, gripping the saddle horn with both hands. "Git on, mule," he muttered. "I hain't got the strength t' fight with ye."

Faintly down the road drifted the words, *"Froggie wint a-courtin', he did ride . . ."*

Bright midday sun dappled the white-painted boards of the Isiah Chesson house. It was a big place for this end of the country, with two rooms below and a loft. In addition, there was a stable and servant's quarters at the back of the lot. How big it seemed to Madame Francine Taliaferro, late of New Orleans, was another matter.

"Whoa-up, mule," Old Nathan muttered as he peered at the dwelling. It sat a musket shot down the road and around a bend from the next house of the Oak Hill settlement. The front door was closed, and there was no sign of life behind the curtains added to the windows since the new tenant moved in.

Likely just as well. The cunning man wanted to observe Madame Taliaferro, but barging up to her door and knocking didn't seem a useful way to make her introduction.

Still. . . .

In front of the house was a well-manicured lawn. A pair of gray squirrels, plump and clothed in fur grown sleekly full at the approach of Fall, hopped across the lawn—and over the low board fence which had protected Chesson's sauce garden, now grown up in vines.

"Hoy, squirrel!" Old Nathan called. "Is the lady what lives here t' home?"

The nearer squirrel hopped up on his hind legs, looking in all directions. "What's thet? What's thet I heard?" he chirped.

"Yer wastin' yer time," the mule said. "Hain't a squirrel been born yet whut's got brain enough t' tell whether hit's rainin'."

"He's talkin' t' ye," the other squirrel said as she continued to snuffle across the short grass of the lawn. "He says, is the lady home t' the house?"

The male squirrel blinked. "Huh?" he said to his mate. "What would I be doin' in a house?" He resumed a tail-high patrol which seemed to ignore the occasional hickory nuts lying in the grass.

"Told ye so," the mule commented.

Old Nathan scowled. Boards laid edgewise set off a path from the front door to the road. A pile of dog droppings marked the gravel.

"Squirrel," the cunning man said. "Is there a little dog t' home, now?"

"What?" the male squirrel demanded. "Whur is it? Thet nasty little monster's come back!"

"Now, don't yet git yerse'f all stirred up!" his mate said. "Hit's all right, hit's gone off down the road already."

"Thankee, squirrels," Old Nathan said. "Git on, mule."

"Ifen thet dog's not here, thin whyiver did he say it was?" the male squirrel complained loudly.

"We could uv done thet a'ready, ye know," the mule said as he ambled on toward the main part of town. "Er we could uv stayed t' home."

"Thet's right," Old Nathan said grimly. "We could."

He *knew* he was on a fool's errand, because only a durned fool would think Francine Taliaferro might be using some charm or other on the Ransden boy. He didn't need a mule to tell him.

Rance Holden's store was the center of Oak Hill, unless you preferred to measure from Shorty Hitchcock's tavern across the one dirt street. Holden's building was gable-end to the road. The store filled the larger square room, while Rance and his wife lived in the low rectangular space beneath the eaves overhanging to the left.

The family's space had been tight when the Holdens had children at home. The five boys and the girl who survived were all moved off on their own by now.

"Don't you tie me t' the rail thur," the mule said. "Somebody 'll spit t'baccy at me sure."

"Thin they'll answer t' me," the cunning man said. "But seeins as there's nobody on the porch, I don't figger ye need worry."

Four horses, one with a side-saddle, were hitched to the rail. Usually there were several men sitting on the board porch among barrels of bulk merchandise, chewing tobacco and whittling; but today they were all inside. That was good evidence that Madame Francine Taliaferro was inside as well. . . .

The interior of Holden's store was twelve foot by twelve foot. Not spacious by any standard, it was now packed with seven adults—

And a pug dog who tried to fill as much space as the humans.

"Hey, you old bastard!" the dog snapped as the cunning man stepped through the open door. "I'm going to bite you till you bleed, and there's nothing you can do about it!"

"Howdy Miz Holden, Rance," Old Nathan said. "Thompson—" a nod to the saddler, a cadaverous man with a full beard but no hair above the level of his ears "—Bart—" another nod, this time to the settlement's miller, Bart Alpers—

"I'm *going* to bite you!" the little dog yapped as it lunged forward and dodged back. "I'll do just that, and you don't dare stop me!"

Nods, murmured *howdies/yer keepin' well* from the folk who crowded the store.

"—'n Mister M'Donald," the cunning man said with a nod for the third white man, a husky, hard-handed man who'd made a good thing of a tract ten miles out from the settlement. M'Donald looked even sillier in an ill-fitting blue tailcoat than Bully Ransden had done in his finery the evening before.

Madame Taliaferro's black servant, on the other hand, wore his swallowtail coat, ruffed shirt, and orange breeches with an air of authority. He stood behind his mistress, with his eyes focused on infinity and his hands crossed behind his back.

"Now, Cesar," the woman who was the center of the store's attention murmured to her dog. She looked at Old Nathan with an unexpected degree of appraisal. "Baby be good for ma-ma."

"*Said* I'm going to bite you!" insisted the dog. "Here goes!"

Old Nathan whispered inaudible words with his teeth in a tight smile. The little dog *did* jump forward to bite his pants leg, sure as the Devil was loose in the world.

The dog froze.

"Mum," Old Nathan said as he reached down and

scooped the dog up in his hand. The beast's mouth was open. Sudden terror filled its nasty little eyes.

Francine Taliaferro had lustrous dark hair—not a patch on Ellie's, but groomed in a fashion the younger woman's could never be. Her face was pouty-pretty, heavily powdered and rouged, and the skirt of her blue organdy dress flared out in a fashion that made everyone else in the store stand around like the numbers on a clock dial with her the hub.

But that's what it would have been anyway; only perhaps with the others pressing in yet closer.

Old Nathan handed the stiffened dog to Madame Taliaferro. "Hain't he the cutest li'l thing?" the cunning man said.

The woman's red lips opened in shock, but by reflex her gloved hands accepted the petrified animal that was thrust toward her. As soon as Old Nathan's fingers no longer touched the animal's fur, the dog resumed where it had stopped. Its teeth snapped into its mistress's white shoulder.

Three of the men shouted. Madame Taliaferro screamed in outrage and flung Cesar up into the roof shakes. The dog bounced down into a shelf of yard goods, then ran out the door. It was yapping unintelligibly.

Old Nathan smiled. "Jest cute as a button."

There was no more magic in this woman than there was truth in a politician's heart. If Ellie had a complaint, it was against whatever fate had led a woman—a *lady*— so sophisticated to Oak Hill.

And complaint agin Bully Ransden, fer bein' a durned fool; but folks were, men 'n women both. . . .

"By God!" M'Donald snarled. "I oughter break ye in two fer thet!"

He lurched toward the cunning man but collided with Alpers, who cried, "I won't let ye fall!" as he tried to grab the woman. Rance Holden tried to crawl out from behind the counter while his wife glared, and Thompson blathered as though somebody had just fallen into a mill saw.

"Everyone stop this at once!" Madame Taliaferro cried

with her right index finger held upright. Her voice was as clear and piercing as a well-tuned bell.

Everyone *did* stop. All eyes turned toward the woman; which was no doubt as things normally were in Madame Taliaferro's presence.

"I'll fetch yer dog," blurted Bart Alpers.

"Non!" Taliaferro said. "Cesar must have had a little cramp. He will stay outside till he is better."

"Warn't no cramp, Francine, honey," M'Donald growled. "Hit war this sonuvabitch here what done it!" He pushed Alpers aside.

"What d'ye reckon happint t' Cesar, M'Donald?" Old Nathan said. The farmer was younger by thirty years and strong, but he hadn't the personality to make a threat frightening even when he spoke the flat truth. "D'ye want t' touch me 'n larn?"

M'Donald stumbled backward from the bluff— for it was all bluff; what Old Nathan had done to the dog had wrung him out bad as lifting a quarter of beef. But the words had this much truth in them: those who struck the cunning man would pay for the blow, in one way or another; and pay in coin they could ill afford.

"I don't believe we've been introduced," said the woman. She held out her hand. The appraisal was back in her eyes. "I'm Francine Taliaferro, but do call me Francine. I'm—*en vacance* in your charming community."

"*He* ain't no good t' ye," M'Donald muttered bitterly, his face turned to a display of buttons on a piece of card.

The cunning man took Taliaferro's hand, though he wasn't rightly sure what she expected him to do with it. There were things he knew, plenty of things and important ones; but right just now, he understood why other men reacted as they did to Francine Taliaferro.

"M' name's Nathan. I live down the road a piece, Columbia ways."

Even a man with a woman like Ellie waiting at home for him.

"I reckon *this* gen'lman come here t' do business,

Rance," said Mrs. Holden to her husband in a poisonous tone of voice. "Don't ye reckon ye ought t' he'p him?"

"I'll he'p him, Maude," Holden muttered, trying—and he knew he would fail—to interrupt the rest of the diatribe. He was a large, soft man, and his hair had been white for years. "Now, how kin—"

"Ye *are* a storekeeper, ain't ye?" Mrs. Holden shrilled. "Not some spavined ole fool thinks spring has come again!"

Holden rested his hands on the counter. His eyes were downcast. One of the other men chuckled. "Now, Nathan," the storekeeper resumed. "Reckon you're here fer more coffee?"

The cunning man opened his mouth to say he'd take a peck of coffee and another of baking soda. He didn't need either just now, but he'd use them both and they'd serve as an excuse for him to have come into Oak Hill.

"Ye've got an iv'ry comb," he said. The words he spoke weren't the ones he'd had in mind at all. "Reckon I'll hev thet and call us quits fer me clearin' the rats outen yer barn last fall."

Everyone in the store except Holden himself stared at Old Nathan. The storekeeper winced and, with his eyes still on his hands, said, "I reckon thet comb, hit must hev been sold. I'd like t' he'p ye."

"Whoiver bought thet thing!" cried the storekeeper's wife in amazement. She turned to the niche on the wall behind the counter, where items of special value were flanked to either side by racks of yard goods. The two crystal goblets remained, but they had been moved inward to cover the space where the ornate ivory comb once stood.

Mrs. Holden's eyes narrowed. "Rance Holden, you go look through all the drawers this minute. Nobody bought thet comb and you know it!"

"Waal, mebbe hit was stole," Holden muttered. He half-heartedly pulled out one of the drawers behind the counter and poked with his fingers at the hairpins and brooches within.

The cunning man smiled grimly. "Reckon I kin he'p ye," he said.

He reached over the counter and took one of the pins, ivory like the comb for which he was searching. The pin's blunt end was flattened and drilled into a filigree for decoration. He held the design between the tips of his index fingers, pressing just hard enough to keep the pin pointed out horizontally.

"What is this that you are doing, then?" Francine Taliaferro asked in puzzlement.

The other folk in the store knew Old Nathan. Their faces were set in gradations between fear and interest, depending on the varied fashions in which they viewed the cunning man's arts.

Old Nathan swept the pin over the counter. Mid-way it dipped, then rose again.

"Check the drawers there," the cunning man directed. He moved the hairpin back until it pointed straight down. "Reckon hit's in the bottom one."

"Why, whut would that iv'ry pin be doin' down there with the women's shoes?" Mrs. Holden demanded.

"Look, I tell ye, I'll pay ye cash fer what ye did with the rats," the storekeeper said desperately. "How much 'ud ye take? Jest name—"

He was standing in front of the drawer Old Nathan had indicated. His wife jerked it open violently, banging it against Holden's instep twice and a third time until he hopped away, wincing.

Mrs. Holden straightened, holding a packet wrapped with tissue paper and blue ribbon. It was of a size to contain the comb.

She started to undo the ribbon. Her face was red with fury.

Old Nathan put his hand out. "Reckon I'll take it the way i'tis," he said.

"How d'ye guess the comb happint t' be all purtied up 'n hid like thet, Rance?" Bart Alpers said loudly. "Look to me like hit were a present fer som'body, if ye could git her alone."

Francine Taliaferro raised her chin. "I know nothing of this," she said coldly.

Rance Holden took the packet from his wife's hands and gave it to Old Nathan. "I figger this makes us quits for the rats," he said in a dull voice. He was slumped like a man who'd been fed his breakfast at the small end of a rifle.

"Thankee," Old Nathan said. "I reckon thet does."

The shouting behind him started before the cunning man had unhitched his mule. The timbre of Mrs. Holden's voice was as sharp and cutting as that of Francine Taliaferro's lapdog.

Taking the comb didn't make a lick of sense, except that it showed the world what a blamed fool God had made of Rance Holden.

Old Nathan rode along, muttering to himself. It would have been awkward to carry the packet in his hand, but once he'd set the fancy bit of frippery down into a saddle basket, that didn't seem right either.

Might best that he sank the durn thing in the branch, because there wasn't ought he could do with the comb that wouldn't make him out to be a worse fool than Rance. . . .

The mule was following its head onto the cabin trail. Suddenly its ears cocked forward and its leading foot hesitated a step. Through the woods came, *"Froggie, wint a-courtin', he did ride. . . ."*

"Hey, thur!" called the mule.

"Oh, hit's you come back, is it?" Bully Ransden's horse whinnied in reply. "I jest been down yer way."

Horse and mule came nose to nose around a bend fringed by dogwood and alders. The riders watched one another: Old Nathan stiff and ready for trouble, but the younger man as cheerful as a cat with a mouse for a toy.

"Glad t' see ye, Nathan old feller," Bully Ransden said.

He kneed his mount forward to bring himself alongside the cunning man, left knee to left knee. The two men were much of a height, but the horse stood taller than the mule and increased the impression of Ransden's far greater bulk. "I jest dropped by in a neighborly way," he continued, "t' warn ye there's been prowlers up t' my place. Ye might want t' stick close about yer own."

He grinned. His teeth were square and evenly set. They had taken the nose off a drover who'd wrongly thought he was a tougher man than Bully Ransden.

This afternoon Ransden wore canvas breeches and a loose-hanging shirt of gray homespun. The garment's cut had the effect of emphasizing Bully's muscular build, whereas the undersized frock coat had merely made him look constrained.

"I thankee," Old Nathan said stiffly. He wished Bully Ransden would stop glancing toward the saddle basket, where he might notice the ribbon-tied packet. "Reckon I kin deal with sech folk as sneak by whin I'm gone."

He *wished* he were forty years younger, and even then he'd be a lucky man to avoid being crippled in a rough and tumble with Bully Ransden. This one was cat-quick, had shoulders like an ox . . . and once the fight started, Bully Ransden didn't quit so long as the other fellow still could move.

Ransden's horse eyed Old Nathan, then said to the mule, "Yer feller ain't goin' t' do whatever hit was he did last night, is he? I cain't much say I liked thet."

"Didn't much like hit myse'f," the mule agreed morosely. "He ain't a bad old feller most ways, though."

"Like I said," Ransden grinned. "Jest a neighborly warnin'. Y' see, I been leavin' my rifle-gun t' home most times whin I'm out 'n about . . . but I don't figger t' do thet fer a while. I reckon if I ketch someb'dy hangin' round my cabin, I'll shoot him same's as I would a dog chasin' my hens."

Old Nathan looked up to meet the younger man's eyes. "Mebbe," he said deliberately, "you're goin' t' stay home 'n till yer own plot fer a time?"

"Oh, land!" whickered the horse, reacting to the sudden tension. "Now it'll come sure!"

For a moment, Old Nathan thought the same thing . . .

and thought the result was going to be very bad. Sometimes you couldn't help being afraid, but that was a reason itself to act as fear warned you not to.

Ransden shook his head violently, as if he were a horse trying to brush away a gadfly. His hair was shoulder length and the color of sourwood honey. The locks tossed in a shimmering dance.

Suddenly, unexpectedly, the mood changed. Bully Ransden began to laugh. "Ye know," he said good-humoredly, "ifen you were a man, I might take unkindly t' words like thet. Seeins as yer a poor womanly critter, though, I don't reckon I will."

He kicked his horse a step onward, then reined up again as if to prove his mastery. The animal nickered in complaint.

"Another li'l warning, old man," Ransden called playfully over his shoulder. "Ye hadn't ought t' smoke meat on too hot uv a fire. You might shrink hit right up."

Ransden spurred his mount forward, jerking the left rein at the same time. The horse's flank jolted solidly against the mule's hindquarters, knocking the lighter animal against an oak sapling.

"Hey thur, you!" the mule brayed angrily.

"*Sword 'n pistol* by *his side!*" Bully Ransden caroled as he trotted his horse down the trail.

"Waal," said the mule as he resumed his measured pace toward the cabin, "I'm glad *that's* ended."

"D'ye think it is, mule?" the cunning man asked softly. "From the way the Bully was talkin', I reckon he jest managed t' start it fer real."

The two cows were placidly chewing their cud in the railed paddock behind the cabin. "Thar's been another feller come by here," the red heifer offered between rhythmic, sideways strokes of her jaws.

"Wouldn't milk us, though," the black heifer added. " 'Bout time somebody does, ifen ye ask me."

"Don't recall askin' ye *any* blame thing," Old Nathan muttered.

He dismounted and uncinched the saddle. "Don't

'spect ye noticed what the feller might be doin' whilst he was here, did ye?" he asked as if idly.

"Ye goin' t' strip us now?" the black demanded. "My udder's full as full, it is."

"He wint down t' the crik," the red offered. "Carried a fish down t' the crik."

Old Nathan dropped two gate bars and led the mule into the enclosure with the cows. His face was set.

"Criks is whur fish belong," the black heifer said. "Only I wish they didn't nibble at my teats whin I'm standing thur, cooling myse'f."

"This fish don't nibble airy soul," the red heifer explained in a superior tone. "This fish were dead 'n dry."

Old Nathan removed the mule's bridle and patted the beast on the haunch. "Git some hay," he said. "I'll give ye a handful uv oats presently. I reckon afore long you 'n me goin' t' take another ride, though."

"Why*ever* do a durn fool thing like that?" the mule complained. "Ye kin ride a cow the next time. I'm plumb tuckered out."

" 'Bout *time*," the black heifer repeated with emphasis, "thet you milk us!"

The cunning man paused, halfway to his back porch, and turned. "I'll be with ye presently," he said. "I ain't in a mood t' be pushed, so I'd advise ye as a friend thet y'all not push me."

The cows heard the tone and looked away, as though they were studying the movements of a late-season butterfly across the paddock. The mule muttered, "Waal, I reckon I wouldn't mind a bit uv a walk, come t' thet."

The cat sauntered through the front door of the cabin as Old Nathan entered by the back. "Howdy, old man," the cat said. "I wouldn't turn down a bite of somp'in if it was goin'."

"I'll hev ye a cup uv milk if ye'll wait fer it," the cunning man said as he knelt to look at the smoke shelf of his fireplace. The greenwood fire had burnt well down, but there was no longer any reason to build it higher.

The large catfish was gone, as Old Nathan had

expected. In its place was a bullhead less than six inches long; one of those Ransden had bought in town the day before, though he could scarcely have thought that Ellie believed he'd spent the evening fishing.

"What's thet?" the cat asked curiously.

Old Nathan removed the bullhead from the shelf. "Somethin' a feller left me," he said.

The bullhead hadn't been a prepossessing creature even before it spent a day out of water. Now its smooth skin had begun to shrivel and its eyes were sunken in; the eight barbels lay like a knot of desiccated worms.

"He took the fish was there and tossed hit in the branch. I reckon," he added in a dreamy voice, holding the bullhead and thinking of a time to come shortly. "He wasn't a thief, he jest wanted t' make his point with me."

"Hain't been cleaned 'in it's gittin' *good* 'n ripe," the cat noted, licking his lips. "Don't figger you want it, but you better believe *I* do."

"Sorry, cat," the cunning man said absently. He set the bullhead on the fireboard to wait while he got together the other traps he would need. Ellie Ransden would have a hand mirror, so he needn't take his own. . . .

"Need t' milk the durn cows, too," he muttered aloud.

The cat stretched up the wall beside the hearth. He was not really threatening to snatch the bullhead, but he wasn't far away in case the cunning man walked out of the cabin and left the fish behind. "Whativer do *you* figger t' do with thet ole thing?" he complained.

"Feller used hit t' make a point with me," Old Nathan repeated. His voice was distant and very hard. "I reckon I might hev a point t' make myse'f."

"Hallo the house!" Old Nathan called as he dismounted in front of Ransden's cabin.

He'd covered more miles on muleback recently than his muscles approved. Just now he didn't feel stiff, because his blood was heated with what he planned to do—and what was likely to come of it.

He'd pay for that in the morning, he supposed; and he supposed he'd be alive in the morning to pay. He'd do what he came for regardless.

The cabin door banged open. Ellie Ransden wore a loose dress she'd sewn long ago of English cloth, blue in so far as the sun and repeated washings had left it color. Her eyes were puffy from crying, but the expression of her face was compounded of concern and horror.

"Oh sir, Mister Nathan, ye *mustn't* come by here!" she gasped. "Cullen, he'll shoot ye sure! I niver *seen* him so mad as whin he asked hed you been by. An' my Cull. . . ."

The words *"my Cull"* rang beneath the surface of the girl's mind. Her face crumpled. Her hands pawed out blindly. One touched a porch support. She gripped it and collapsed against the cedar pole, blubbering her heart out.

Old Nathan stepped up onto the porch and put his arms around her. Decent folk didn't leave an animal in pain, and that's what this girl was now, something alive that hurt like to die. . . .

The mule snorted and began to sidle away. There hadn't been time to loop his reins over the porch railing.

Old Nathan pointed an index finger at the beast. "Ifen you stray," he snarled, "hit's best thet ye find yerse'f another hide. I'll hey *thet* off ye, sure as the Divil's in Hell."

"Fine master you are," the mule grumbled in a subdued voice.

Though the words had not been directed at Ellie, Old Nathan's tone returned the girl to present circumstances as effectively as a bucket of cold water could have done. She stepped back and straightened.

"Oh, law," she murmured, dabbing at her face with her dress's full sleeves. "But Mister Nathan, ye mustn't stay. I won't hev ye kilt over me, nor—"

She eyed him quickly, noting the absence of an obvious weapon but finding that less reassuring than she would have wished. "Nor aught t' happen to my Cull neither. He—" she started to lose control over her voice and finished in a tremolo "—ain't a bad man!"

"Huh," the cunning man said. He turned to fetch his traps from the mule's panniers. He was about as embarrassed as Ellie, and he guessed he had as much reason.

"I ain't goin' t' hurt Bully Ransden," he said, then added what was more than half a lie, "And better men thin him hev thought they'd fix *my* flint."

Ellie Ransden tossed her head. "Waal," she said, "I reckon ye know yer own business, sir. Won't ye come in and set a spell? I don't mind sayin' I'm glad fer the comp'ny."

Her face hardened into an expression that Old Nathan might have noticed on occasion if he looked into mirrors more often. "I've coffee, an' there's a jug uv good wildcat . . . but ifen ye want fancy French wines all the way from New Or-leens, I guess ye'll hev t' go elsewheres."

With most of his supplies in one hand and the fish wrapped in a scrap of bark in his left, Old Nathan followed the woman into her cabin. "I'd take some coffee now," he said. "And mebbe when we've finished, I'd sip a mite of whiskey."

Ellie Ransden took the coffee pot a step toward the bucket in the corner, half full with well water. Without looking at the cunning man, she said, "Thin you might do me up a charm after all?"

"I will not," Old Nathan said flatly. "But fer what I will do, ye'll hev to he'p."

He set his gear on the table. The bark unwrapped. The bullhead's scaleless skin was black, and the fish had a noticeable odor.

Ellie filled the pot and dropped in an additional pinch of beans, roasted and cracked rather than ground. "Reckon I'll he'p, thin," she said bitterly. "All I been doin' keepin' house 'n fixin' vittles, thet don't count fer nothing the way some people figgers."

"I'll need thet oil lamp," the cunning man said, "but don't light it. And a plug t' fit the chimley end; reckon a cob'll suit thet fine. *And* a pair of Bully Ransden's britches. Best they be a pair thet ain't been washed since he wore thim."

"Reckon I kind find thet for ye," the woman said. She hung the coffee over the fire, then lifted a pair of canvas trousers folded on top of a chest with a homespun shirt. They were the garments Bully Ransden wore when Old Nathan met him earlier in the day. "Cull allus changes 'fore he goes off in the ev'nin' nowadays. Even whin he pretends he's fishin'."

She swallowed a tear. "An' don't he look a sight in thet jacket he had off Neen Tobler fer doin' his plowing last spring? Like a durned ole greenbelly *fly*, thet's how he looks!"

"Reckon ye got a mirror," Old Nathan said as he unfolded the trousers on the table beside the items he had brought from his own cabin. "If ye'll fetch it out, thin we can watch; but hit don't signify ifen ye don't."

"I've a hand glass fine as iver ye'll see," Ellie Ransden said with cold pride. She stepped toward a chest, then stopped and met the cunning mans' eyes. "You won't hurt him, will ye?" she asked. "I—"

She covered her face with her hands. "I druther," she whispered, "thet she hev him thin thet he be hurt."

"Won't hurt him none," Old Nathan said. "I jest figger t' teach the Bully a lesson he's been beggin' t' larn, thet's all."

The young woman was on the verge of tears again. "Fetch the mirror," Old Nathan said gruffly. That gave her an excuse to turn away and compose herself as he proceeded with the preparations.

The words that the cunning man murmured under his breath were no more the spell than soaking yeast in water made a cake; but, like the other, these words were necessary preliminaries.

By its nature, the bullhead's wrinkling corpse brought the flies he needed. The pair that paused momentarily to copulate may have been brought to the act by nature alone or nature aided by art. The cause didn't matter so long as the necessary event occurred.

Old Nathan swept his right hand forward, skimming above the bullhead to grasp the mating pair unharmed within the hollow of his fingers. He looked sidelong to see whether the girl had noticed the quickness and coordination of his movement: he was an old man, right enough, but that didn't mean he was ready for the knacker's yard. . . .

He realized what he was doing and compressed his lips over a sneer of self-loathing. Durned old *fool*!

The flies blurred within the cunning man's fingers like a pair of gossamer hearts beating. He positioned his fist over the lamp chimney, then released his captives carefully within the glass. For a moment he continued to keep the top end of the chimney covered with his palm; then Ellie slid a corncob under the cunning man's hand to close the opening.

The flies buzzed for some seconds within the thin glass before they resumed their courtship.

The woman's eyes narrowed as she saw what Old Nathan was doing with the bullhead, but she did not comment. He arranged the other items to suit his need before he looked up.

"I'll be sayin' some words, now," he said. "Hit wouldn't do ye airy good t' hear thim, and hit might serve ye ill ifen ye said thim after me, mebbe by chance."

Ellie Ransden's mouth tightened at the reminder of the forces being brought to bear on the man she loved. "I reckon you know best," she said. "I'll stand off till ye call me."

She stepped toward the cabin's only door, then paused and looked again at Old Nathan. "These words you're a-speakin'—ye found thim writ in books?"

He shook his head. "They're things I know," he explained, "the way I know . . ."

His voice trailed off. He'd been about to say "—yer red hen's pleased as pleased with the worm she jest grubbed up from the leaves," but that wasn't something he rightly wanted to speak, even to this girl.

"Anyhow, I just know hit," he finished lamely.

Ellie nodded and walked out onto the porch of her cabin. "I'll water yer mule," she called. "Reckon he could use thet."

The beast wheezed its enthusiastic agreement.

Old Nathan sang and gestured his way through the next stage of the preliminaries. His voice cracked and he couldn't hold a key, but that didn't seem to matter.

The cunning man wasn't sure what *did* matter. When he worked, it was as if he walked into a familiar room in the dead dark of night. Occasionally he would stumble, but not badly; and he would always feel his way to the goal that he could not see.

He laid the bullhead inside the crotch of Ransden's trousers.

In between snatches of verse—not English, and not any language to which he could have put a name—Old Nathan whistled. He thought of boys whistling as they passed through a churchyard; chuckled bitterly; and resumed whistling, snatches from *Mossy Groves* that a fiddler would have had trouble recognizing.

> *"How would ye like, my Mossy Groves,*
> *T' spend one night with me?"*

Most of the list had by now crackled out of the extra stick of lightwood Ellie had tossed on the fire. Beyond the cabin walls, the night was drawing in.

The pair of trousers shifted on the table, though the air was still.

A familiar task; but like bear hunting, familiarity didn't remove all the danger. This wasn't for Ellie, for some slip of a girl who loved a fool of a man. This was because Bully Ransden had issued a challenge, and because Old Nathan knew the worst that could happen to a man was to let fear cow him into a living death—

And maybe it *was* a bit for Ellie.

The ver' first blow the king gave him.
Moss' Groves, he struck no more. . . .

Life had risks. Old Nathan murmured his spells.

He was breathing hard when he stepped back, but he knew he'd been successful. Though the lines of congruence were invisible, they stretched their complex web among the objects on the table and across the forest to the house on the outskirts of Oak Hill. The lines were as real and stronger than the hard steel of a knife edge. The rest was up to Bully Ransden. . . .

Old Nathan began to chuckle.

Ellie stood beside him. She had moved back to the doorway when the murmur of the cunning man's voice ceased, but she didn't venture to speak.

Old Nathan grinned at her. "Reckon I'd take a swig uv yer popskull, now," he said. His throat was dry as a summer cornfield.

"Hit's done, thin?" the girl asked in a distant tone. She hefted a brown-glazed jug out from the corner by the bed and handed it to the cunning man, then turned again to toss another pine knot on the fire. The coffee pot, forgotten, still hung from the pivot bar.

Old Nathan pulled the stopper from the jug and swigged the whiskey. It was a harsh, artless run, though it had kick enough for two. Bully Ransden's taste in liquor was similar to Madame Taliaferro's taste in the men of these parts. . . .

"My part's done," the cunning man said. He shot the stopper home again. "Fer the rest, I reckon we'll jest watch."

He set the jug down against the wall. "Pick up the mirror," he explained. "Thet's what we'll look in."

Gingerly, Ellie raised the mirror from the table where it lay among the other paraphernalia. The frame and handle were curly maple finished with beeswax, locally fitted though of the highest craftsmanship. The bevel-edged four-inch glass was old and European in provenance. Lights glinted like jewels on its flawless surface.

Ellie gasped. The lights were not reflections from the cabin's hearth. They shone through the curtained windows of Francine Taliaferro's house.

"Won't hurt ye," Old Nathan said. "Hain't airy thing in all this thet could hurt *you*."

When he saw the sudden fear in her eyes, he added gruffly. "Not yer man neither. I done told ye thet!"

Ellie brought the mirror close to her face to get a better view of the miniature image. When she realized that she was blocking the cunning man's view, she colored and held the glass out to him.

Old Nathan shook his head with a grim smile. "You watch," he said. "I reckon ye earned thet from settin' up alone the past while."

Bully Ransden's horse stood in the paddock beside the Taliaferro house. Madame Taliaferro's black servant, now wearing loose garments instead of his livery, held the animal by a halter and curried it with smooth, flowing strokes.

"He's singin'," the woman said in wonder. She looked over at the cunning man. "I kin hear thet nigger a-singin'!"

"Reckon ye might," Old Nathan agreed.

Ellie pressed her face close to the mirror's surface again. Her expression hardened. Lamplight within the Chesson house threw bars of shadow across the curtains as a breeze caressed them.

"She's laughin'," Ellie whispered. "She's laughin', an' she's callin' him on."

"Hain't nothin' ye didn't know about," Old Nathan said. "Jest watch an' wait."

The cunning man's face was as stark as the killer he had been; one time and another, in one fashion or other. It was a hard world, and he was not the man to smooth its corners away with lies.

The screams were so loud that the mule heard them outside and snorted in surprise. Francine Taliaferro's voice cut the night like a glass-edged saw, but Bully Ransden's tenor bellows were louder yet.

The servant dropped his curry comb and ran for the house. Before he reached it, the front door burst open. Bully Ransden lurched out onto the porch, pulling his breeches up with both hands.

The black tried to stop him or perhaps just failed to get out of the way in time. Ransden knocked the servant over the porch rail with a sideways swipe of one powerful arm.

"What's hap'nin?" Ellie cried. Firelight gleamed on her fear-widened eyes. "What is hit?"

Old Nathan lifted the lamp chimney and shook it, spilling the flies unharmed from their glass prison. Mating complete for their lifetimes, they buzzed from the cabin on separate paths.

The trousers on the table quivered again. The tip of a barbel peeked from the waistband.

"Hain't airy thing hap'nin' now," the cunning man said. "I figgered thet's how you'd choose hit t' be."

Bully Ransden leaped into the paddock and mounted his horse bareback. He kicked at the gate bars, knocking them from their supports.

Madame Taliaferro appeared at the door, breathing in great gasps. The peignoir she wore was so diaphanous that with the lamplight behind her she appeared to be clothed in fog. She stared in horror at Bully Ransden.

Riding with nothing but his knees and a rope halter, Ransden jumped his horse over the remaining gate bars and galloped out of the mirror's field. Taliaferro and her black servant watched him go.

"I'll be off, now," Old Nathan said. There was nothing of what he'd brought to Ransden's cabin that he needed to take back. "I don't choose t' meet Bully on the road, though I reckon he'll hev things on his mind besides tryin' conclusions with me."

He was shivering so violently that his tongue and lips had difficulty forming the words.

"But what's the matter with Cull?" Ellie Ransden begged.

"Hain't *nothin'* the matter!" Old Nathan gasped.

He put a hand on the doorframe to steady himself, then stepped out into the night. Had it been an ague, he could have dosed himself, but the cunning man was shaking in reaction to the powers he had summoned and channeled . . . successfully, though at a price.

Ellie followed him out of the cabin. She gripped Old Nathan's arm as he fumbled in one of the mule's panniers. "Sir," she said fiercely, "I've a right to know."

"Here," the cunning man said, thrusting a tissue-wrapped package into her hands. "Yer Cull, hit niver was he didn't love ye. This is sompin' he put back t' hev Rance Holden wrap up purty-like. I told Rance I'd bring it out t' ye."

The girl's fingers tugged reflexively at the ribbon, but she paused with the packet only half untied. The moon was still beneath the trees, so there was no illumination except the faint glow of firelight from the cabin's doorway. She caressed the lines of the ivory comb through the tissue.

"I reckon," Ellie said deliberately, "Cullen fergot 'cause of all the fishin' he's been after this past while." She tilted up her face and kissed Old Nathan's bearded cheek, then stepped away.

The cunning man mounted his mule and cast the reins loose from the rail. He was no longer shivering.

"Yer Cull, he give me a bullhead this forenoon," he said.

"We goin' home t' get some rest naow?" the mule asked.

"Git up, mule," Old Nathan said, turning the beast's head. To Ellie he went on, "T'night, I give thet fish back t' him; an fer a while, I put hit where he didn't figger t' find sech a thing."

As the mule clopped down the road at a comfortable pace, Old Nathan called over his shoulder, "Sure *hell* thet warn't whut Francine Taliaferro figgered t' see there!"

I won't go into detail about how I came to write this story; I've explained that in the afterword to Forever After, the Roger Zelazny shared universe volume. The short version is that at dinner with Roger (an idol of mine whose project it was) and Jim Baen (the publisher), Bill Fawcett (the business manager) noted that the slot for one of the four writers was unfilled and I'd be perfect for it. I was busy on a lot of other work, but under those circumstances I couldn't even fight the hook. The presence of Roger, Jim and Bill had dynamited the pond.

I didn't know at the time that Forever After was the last opportunity anybody would have to work with Roger Zelazny during his lifetime. I've been lucky in a lot of unexpected ways over the years. Saying "Yes," to Forever After more or less against my will, is one of those ways.

The premise is that the fantasy quest had ended. The Good Prince has regained his throne and is about to marry the Beautiful Princess. The four magical objects gathered to defeat the Evil Wizard must now be dispersed to their original locations in reverse quests because when concentrated in the capital they cause space-time distortions.

Roger plotted the whole novel—not only the frame sequences he would write himself but also the rough outlines of the segments for the other four writers. I was sent the opening and the outlines of all four novellas which would be bound by Roger's frame, so I had a good feel for the broad humor of the book's intent.

My character's quest was to get rid of the magical ring Sombrisio. Roger's outline noted that Sombrisio was an offensive weapon, so I gave the ring an offensive personality. And as will be evident to anybody who's read this *far in* All the Way to The Gallows, *my take on "broad humor" is similar to Chaucer's.*

I used Roger's wonderful novella "The Furies" as my model for the story's tone. It's a very funny story until you think about what the words are really saying.

The texture of "A Very Offensive Weapon" is deliberately anachronistic. I wouldn't bother mentioning that some of the elves are named after tranquilizers were it not that the fact puzzled a copyeditor. Army veterans will recognize the radio-telephone operator, RTO, and the long antenna of his PRC-25 radio; and so forth. I had fun with this one.

Roger said it made him laugh. That pleased me more than I can say. And then a month later he died after the long illness he'd hidden, taking me and most of the world completely by surprise. He was a brave man and a wonderful writer.

I got to like my character, Jancy Gaine, a lot. She's very straightforward, very honest. She keeps on doing her job though she doesn't have a clue about the Big Picture and nobody gives a damn about her or her feelings.

Jancy Gaine is a Good Soldier. For me that makes her as surely a figure of tragedy as any Oedipus or Othello.

A Very Offensive Weapon

The sun rising behind the walls and towers of Caltus reddened the armor of Jancy Gaine and her companions as they looked back from the mound west of the city. Squill, the sorcellet, knelt apart from the others, busied with the customs of his art.

The packhorses whickered, looking discontentedly for foliage to browse during the brief halt. There would be still less forage for them when the party entered the Desolation of Thaumidor; much of the pack train's burden consisted of its own fodder.

The horses were under the control of ten hard-bitten mercenaries—five humans, the rest elves. These retainers were scarred, dour folk every one. They had seen death in a hundred fashions already, and their hearts were prepared to face him yet again.

Calla Mallanik, Jancy's faithful elf companion, stood at her side with a grim look on his aristocratic visage. He held his silver-strung bow. Its arrows of fiery, elf-wrought gold never failed to find the life of the evildoers at whom they were shot.

Jancy Gaine wore her horned helmet and a leathern jackshirt to which were riveted iron medallions cast in the image of terrible gods. Her small buckler, steel rimmed and its boss spiked with steel, hung at her left hip. There it balanced the right-side weight of her bearded ax Castrator.

A distorted female image circled the middle finger of

Jancy's right hand: the massive ring Sombrisio, hammered by demigods from native silver torn out of a glowing meteor. The fire that winked in Sombrisio's eyes was only partly reflected from the sunrise, for the ring was as surely alive as Jancy herself.

Some lanterns still scuttled through the streets of Caltus. A few windows were lighted, but not those of the tower suite in which Princess Rissa would dwell until her marriage to Prince Rango. Rissa, whom Jancy had rescued, and who with Jancy had fought through scores of perils, each more dangerous than the last, to take her place in triumph at the side of the Prince . . .

Heat lightning flickered among the clouds to the west. The air on the top of the mound was as still as the faces of her heroes turned toward the homes many of them might never see again.

Sombrisio farted.

"I had the royal lottery on *ice*," Calla said in a voice like stones grinding. "No way any ball was going to get out the trap but good old one million, seven hundred ninety-two thousand, five hundred thirty-nine. I had the tolerances down closer than flea whiskers! Not another elf craftsman in—"

A cry of horrible, hollow pain filled the air. Jancy turned her head. "Squill!" she said. "What in Sif's name are you doing?"

Squill grimaced and shook his head. He held his left arm crooked; his fingers were bunched near his ear in the mysterious handset which was part of his magic. Above the squatting sorcellet waved the wand of his specialist profession, a twelve-foot whip of thin steel. Its base was screwed into Squill's knapsack.

Instead of answering Jancy, Squill repeated, "Knowed Wyvern Two to Knowed Wyvern Base. Communications check. Over."

Squill unclenched the fingers of his left hand. The hideous moan sounded again. Squill shook his head and muttered uncomfortably, "Sorry, sorry, I guess I'll have to change crystals. Too many lost souls drifting in the part of the ether where this crystal resonates."

"Oh, right," cried the ring Sombrisio in a shrill, unpleasant voice. "Blame your equipment, sure. The trouble couldn't be because you're a half-trained boob sent out with a bunch of losers, no."

"Don't mind her, sorcellet," Jancy snapped, covering Sombrisio with her callused left palm. "Just get on with your work. I don't want to spend the rest of my life here on the municipal garbage dump."

Squill shrugged off his backpack. He rummaged in its side fittings, removing a chip of malachite and replacing it with a block of green tourmaline from his belt pouch. The wand that intensified his spells waggled above him.

"There was no way any other ball could've come out of the tumbler after I'd worked over the machinery in the basement of the palace," Calla resumed grimly. His face was turned toward the towers of the capital, but his mind was focused solely on the injustice done him and his skill.

Last week's royal lottery had been held to defray expenses incurred in the Triumph of Good and Return of the True King. Faithful elf companions had incurred plenty of expenses, too; Calla would tell the *world* he had! And it'd seemed so simple—to an elf of Calla Mallanik's unique skill and craftsmanship—to jigger the result in a completely undetectable fashion.

"Naw," one of Jancy's stalwart human retainers said to the slimmer (but otherwise equally stalwart) elf beside him. "There'll never be an equal to Hormazd the Centurion. Seventy-eight wounds to the body, *seventy*-eight."

The elf pursed his lips. "I heard that was body and limbs combined," he replied. The horse he held pawed rotting garbage in a desultory attempt to find something edible.

"No way!" said the human. "Body alone. Well, body and head, but that's only counting ones that broke the skin, not what was sticking in his armor."

Sombrisio managed a prolonged burst of flatulence.

Jancy lifted her left hand and waved it; not that it made a lot of difference, what with the pong of the rubbish tip.

Squill snapped the side fitting over the new crystal. Instead of hitching the knapsack onto his back again, he knelt over it and formed the handset. He began to speak earnestly to unseen listeners.

"*No* ball but one million, seven hundred ninety-two thousand, five hundred thirty-nine could come down the chute," Calla said in the stark tones of the deeply wronged. "So what happens? Balloons float up, hautboys hoot and gonfalons flutter, and Princess Rissa announces the winner is nine million, three hundred fifty-two thousand, nine hundred seventy-one. There shouldn't have *been* a number that high!"

"Look, I'm not taking anything away from Hormazd," said another of the elves, "but seventy-eight, a hundred seventy-eight—I don't see where the *art* is in that."

Squill relaxed his handset. This time clipped voices sounded faintly through the keening spirits of the atmosphere.

"And not only that," Calla said. The others no longer listened to him. The story's constant repetition over the past week had worn grooves in the surface of their hearing. The elf's words rolled along without leaving a trace in the others' consciousness "The guy who wins is a stranger to Caltus who brought a chance ten minutes before the drawing. And he's the *ugliest* pipsqueak I've ever seen in my life, more like a gander than a human!"

"Art!" said the leading human retainer. "Art, schmart! We're talking about craftsmanship here, boy, a man who took *pride* in his death!"

"Roger, five by five," said Squill. "Knowed Wyvern Two, out." He broke the handset completely and rose, hefting the backpack with him.

"Are you done, then, sorcellet?" Jancy asked sourly. Fifteen fucking minutes marking time on a garbage heap. Mind you, the Desolation of Thaumidor wasn't the Garden Spot of the Universe either. More like the fucking asshole, it was.

"I've established communication with our base, if that's what you mean," Squill replied, flushing. He'd recovered his sense of self-importance now that he'd finally managed to do his job. "I wish you wouldn't call me that, though."

"Sorcellet?" said Jancy with a frown. "You *are* a sorcellet."

She didn't have a lot of use for men who thought the ability to call spirits from the vasty deep made them something special. To tell the truth, she didn't have a lot of use for men, period.

Calla awakened enough from his bleak revery to help Squill fit his arms through the straps of his knapsack. "A sorcellet," Squill said tightly, "is a wizard in training with a limited number of skills. *I* am a comspec, a specialist in the communicatory arts. An artio, to use the term of, well, art."

Sombrisio let out what was either a raspberry or another fart. "You're a one-trick pony," the ring shrilled. "A loser in a dead-end job. And if you want to know how dead a loser you are, just take a look at the turkeys you've been sent along with!"

"Move 'em out!" Jancy ordered. "And Sombrisio, shut up. It's going to be a long enough trip without you going on about it."

The party started forward. Every finger's breadth the sun rose above the horizon boiled new levels of reeking effluvium from the garbage. Honey wagons were already wending their way from the west gate of Caltus with the night's further increment to the surroundings.

"You think this is a good time for me?" Sombrisio demanded. "Traipsing along with the Company of Intellectually Challenged Adventurers? And for what? So I can spend the rest of eternity in the Lost City of Anthurus, that's what!"

"I said," Jancy said in a voice so quiet that hair pricked at the back of the neck of everybody who heard it, "shut up."

Of course Rissa wasn't watching. What would a princess want to look out over the municipal garbage dump for, anyway? Besides, Rissa probably had lots of important things to talk over with her fiancé, the Prince.

Got a quest for a city lost in the Desolation of Thaumidor? Well, jeepers, the only road in *that* direction leads out through the garbage dump. Let's send Jancy, shall we? After all, she's only saved our life and honor about twenty dozen times.

"The only ball that could get through the trap . . ." Calla murmured.

"Gobble-gobble-gobble," Sombrisio said in a piercing whisper.

It was hard to tell where the sun was. The sky was bright, but the landscape itself was gloomy and shadowed. The sparse vegetation had a grayish tinge, and sometimes a shrub collapsed in a cloud of bitter dust when one of the party brushed it.

They'd reached the Desolation of Thaumidor, all right.

"Is that—" Calla said. "Yeah, that's it. That's got to be the hermit. Who else would live in a bone hut?"

"Now, I'll tell you what was the first-class death," said one of the stalwart elf retainers. "When Brightlock, Prince of the Windward Elves, fought Sokitoomi, the Crystal Giant—"

"Sif, what a desolate place," muttered Jancy Gaine.

"Hey, what a surprise!" said Sombrisio. "You go to a desolation and it's *desolate*. Did your schooling get to the part about not sticking your hand in the fire? Or is fire itself too advanced a concept for northern bumpkins?"

Jancy twisted the ring so that Sombrisio faced palmward, but by now the sniping didn't really bother her. No more than everything else, at any rate.

Thaumidor was a waste of ill-watered dust, not sand. The soil was light and yellow-gray; loess, a concretion of windblown particles, though there hadn't been any wind in the few minutes since the party had entered the Desolation. The border between Thaumidor and the unpeopled but ordinary barrens they'd crossed to reach it was as sharp as a fenceline.

"—when the lance hit Sokitoomi at the cleave point," the elf was saying, "the Crystal Giant broke into shards that rained down on Brightlock's retainers, the warrior-sisters Everill and Worrell. They—"

The agatized femurs of monsters of a bygone day formed the main structure of the hut's walls. The interstices between these great bones were filled with parts of lesser skeletons in a puzzle of immense complexity. Rabbit tibiae bound bear clavicles and were wedged in turn by the ulnae of sparrows, themselves associated with still finer ossicles. The gill rakers of an enormous shark formed the roof beams, though no sea had penetrated within a hundred miles of Thaumidor during the present Fourth Age of Man.

"Hail, hermit!" Jancy called, twenty feet from the door. "A party of noble travelers comes, seeking your assistance on a dangerous quest."

A jewel-eyed viper sunning itself on the hut's roof slid back within the thatching of mouse ribs. The snake's eyes were literally jewels—yellow topaz, Jancy thought. They had no lids or pupils.

"—cut Everill and Worrell into slices thin enough to see through if you put them between glass plates," the elf said, continuing his story. "Which is about how it happened, after all. We raised a joint monument over them, because sorting them into separate coffins would've been harder than putting two salamis back together after you dropped the slices."

"Are you going to stand here forever?" Sombrisio demanded in a muffled voice. "That's all right with me, I'm the one who's going to be buried for the rest of eternity, but—"

"Hermit!" Jancy bellowed. "Get your sanctified ass out here!"

"Bet it wasn't seventy-eight slices, though," said a

human retainer. "Not even seventy-eight between the two of them."

A crabbed little man scuttled out of the hut. His sclera were almost as yellow as those of the viper. The diet of hermits in the Desolation of Thaumidor couldn't be a very healthy one.

"Well, well," the hermit said. "Decided to stop by and say hello to the fellow who's devoted decades to learning the life and lore of the Desolation, have you? Hello, then! Now go away and leave me alone."

"Hey, wait a minute!" Calla demanded.

The hermit had ducked beneath his lintel of buffalo humerus. He turned again and cried, "I have more important things to do than be gaped at by scabs on a second-rate quest! Like watching my fingernails grow!"

Sombrisio giggled. "Well, he's got you lot pegged," she noted.

"Wait a darn minute," said Jancy. "What do you mean, 'scabs'? We're here on a bona fide quest, requesting—"

"Requesting *now*, that you are," the hermit said, stepping closer and waggling his gnarled index finger toward Jancy's face. "But let me ask you, Little Miss Venturer, just which member of the Guild of Licensed Cicerones did you employ on your first journey through the Desolation? On a real quest!"

"Ah," said Jancy. "Ah. Well. You see, the Princess and I were fleeing from minions of the Ghoul-Lord of Otchbacko and we didn't have a lot of time to shop around for guides, so we—"

"Hired scabs!" the hermit snapped. "Well, you can just go—"

"We didn't hire anybody!" Jancy shouted. Rows of lizard sternums pinning the thatch to the roof beams jounced when she bellowed. "We didn't have time to hire anybody!"

"Right, right!" the hermit crowed in triumph. "Well, you're not going to hire anybody now either, because the regulations of the guild forbid members to accept employment from those who've previously used scabs. So there!"

He stuck his thumbs in his hairy ears and wriggled his fingers at Jancy.

"Look—" said Jancy.

The hermit lowered his hands and flowered. "Do you know how dangerous the Desolation of Thaumidor is?" he asked. "Three centuries ago, King Voroshek the Extremely Ill-Tempered the Fourth refused to employ guild members when he marched into the Desolation on his way to attack Faltane. He and his army are still there, girlie! And so will you and elfikins here be, three centuries hence!"

"That's telling them, hermit!" said Sombrisio. "Of course, if you really knew jack shit about this place, you'd have found me yourself, wouldn't you?"

"That's it," Jancy said in her quiet voice. "That's all of this we're going to hear."

She twisted Sombrisio outward and thrust her clenched fist toward the hermit so that he got a good look at the massive ring. "Now," Jancy said, "you're going to guide us on our quest. And no smart remarks about second rate or losers or turkeys, do you understand? Or I'm going to use the power of Sombrisio here to turn you into a lobster."

"And I," said Calla Mallanik, leaning forward to call attention to himself, "will eat you in cream sauce."

Jancy blinked. "Well, you know," she said to her faithful companion, "he won't really be a lobster, he'll just think he is."

The elf shrugged. "So what?" he said. "It's not cannibalism so long as it's out of species. And I'll guarantee he'll taste better than the can of ham and lima beans I had last night. Where on Middle Earth did the royal commissary get sea rations, anyway? Faltane doesn't have a navy."

Jancy returned her attention to the hermit. "Well, anyway," she said. "If you don't guide us, it'll be the worse for you. Do you understand?"

"Oh, sure," said the hermit bitterly. "Well, my guild's going to hear about it, though. Wait till the wave of sympathy strikes hits your employers! What kind of a wedding do you suppose it's going to be when the flower girls down tools, hey? And the Worshipful Company of Rice Sellers bans their products from crossing a picket line!"

Jancy sighed. "All you need to know," she said, "is that if you're not packed and ready to guide us in fifteen minutes, I'm going to help Calla here look for a cow for the cream sauce."

The hermit reentered his hut, muttering about strong-arm bully-girls. After that, the only sound for a time was the squeal of Squill's apparatus. The artio was reporting to base on the progress of the quest.

Though the sun even at zenith was wan, its heat hammered the landscape. The rock basin was rimmed by three distinct margins of different color: yellow, orange, and a virid hue close to that of copper acetoarsenite. The fluid (it certainly wasn't water) in the center of the pool quivered; Jancy thought she felt microshocks through the soles of her boots as well.

"Are there earthquakes here?" she asked.

The hermit shrugged. His expression wavered. An expert's natural urge to pontificate warred with his personal desire in this case to be as obstructive as possible. The former won out, perhaps aided by the way Calla Mallanik fished from his wallet a miracle of elf craftsmanship—a nested nine-piece flatware set, including cracking tongs and a miniature mallet.

"Well, it's not so much earth tremors as it is a dog scratching itself in its sleep," the hermit explained. "The Desolation is a living entity." He pursed his lips, then added, "A thoroughly grumpy and ill-tempered one, too."

A small armadillo charged from its burrow and began to urinate on Calla's right boot. The elf kicked the little creature through the center of a squamous-looking cactus which collapsed with a sucking sound.

"Seems to attract dwellers of similar temperament," Calla said with a significant glance toward the hermit.

"I know what you're hinting at!" the hermit cried, as if anybody with brains enough to breathe wouldn't have known. "The reason *I* inhabit the Desolation is that it frees me from the cares of the world, so that I can immerse my mind in holy contemplation."

"You bet," said Sombrisio. Either the ring had been dozing for most of the morning, or she'd waited like a true artist for the right opening. "Cares like the string of bad debts you've left behind you, starting when you did a midnight flit from the seminary in Quiberon."

The hermit turned his head with an expression whose horror melted into rage before settling on injured innocence. "Silence, demon, in the name of the Twelve Beneficent Aspects of God!" he said in a piping attempt at thunder.

"Not to mention," Sombrisio continue with lip-smacking enthusiasm, "that your wife's new boyfriend said he'd pull your face *off* if he ever saw it again in Caltus. Those the cares you had in mind?"

"I won't dignify that with a response," the hermit muttered. Rather, he mouthed the comment. He'd already demonstrated a capacity for knowing when to cut his losses.

The party topped a rise. What Jancy had thought was the keening of the wind resolved itself into desperate, fluting screams coming from just off the trail.

"Unhand her, you brute!" Jancy shouted as she lifted her ax from its belt loops. She leaped into the brush without waiting to free her shield from the slip knot holding it to her left hip. It was going to be embarrassing if the screams were from a rabbit; or worse, from a man rather than the woman she'd assumed.

It was a woman, all right, buried to the waist beneath a thorn tree. Her marble bosom was bare; her alabaster arms were raised to fend off unseen horror

Jancy grasped the woman's right hand and realized her

mistake. The arms, like the bosom, were marble. The screams came from the open throat of a statue.

Calla Mallanik eeled into the small clearing. Behind him galumphed the retainers, bellowing their war cry: "Death and glory!"

The screams stopped abruptly. The retainers looked in disappointment at the dismal but harmless surroundings.

Jancy straightened. "What in blazes?" she said as the hermit joined them with a smirk on his visage. "She stopped screaming."

"Union rules," the hermit explained. "She gets five minutes off in every two-hour period."

"Well . . ." Jancy said. She stared at Castrator as if wondering how the ax had come to be in her hand.

"She doesn't need to be rescued, then?" said Calla Mallanik.

"Rescued from what, dummy?" Sombrisio said. "It's a statue. Rescued from being a chunk of rock lying in the ground? Boy, I've heard elves were dumb, but I'm beginning to think communing with the earthworms in Anthurus is going to be an improvement over you guys."

Jancy rehung Castrator as furtively as you can hang an ax with a hooked, sixteen-inch cutting edge. She cleared her throat. "Best be getting on," she said. "I want to march at least another couple of miles before we camp for the night."

"And if any of you lot is wondering just how stupid your leader is," Sombrisio continued in a voice that carried like brakes squealing, "*she's* wondering if the Princess Rissa might just be in love with her after all."

"I am not!" Jancy shouted. "Why, the Princess wouldn't even *think* of such a thing!"

"You got that one right, boss-lady," the ring agreed gleefully. "Rissa doesn't even know that sort of thing happens. Boy, it'd really turn her stomach if she knew her sturdy defender here dreamed about—"

That was as far as Sombrisio got before Jancy wadded a handful of friable soil around the ring and spat on it. She kneaded the wad into a blanket of clay. The casing smothered Sombrisio's complaints to a sound as faint as the buzz of a fly's wings on the other side of a closed window.

Jancy stuck the ball of clay onto the spike of her shield boss, where it would dry rock hard in the sunlight. Dusting her palms against one another, she glowered at Calla Mallanik and said, "Any comment you want to make?"

"Do I look like I want to say anything?" the elf protested. "No, not me. Not a word."

"Good," Jancy said. She tramped back out to the trail, deliberately kicking the shrubbery to bits. A bush with thorns and dirty pink flowers squeaked as it trotted out of the way, its taproot twitching behind it.

"What I figure," Calla continued, "is that anything adult humans want to do within the privacy of their own bedrooms is going to be unspeakably disgusting. So there's no point in drawing distinctions between one revolting act and another."

The statue was screaming again. It struck Jancy as a pretty reasonable way to pass the time around here.

"If we're headed toward the city of Anthurus," said Calla Mallanik in a tone so coolly reasonable that it was twice as threatening as a shout, "then why is the sun setting to our left, hermit?"

"Look, do you want to take over the guiding?" the hermit said. "I didn't ask to come with you, you know! Fine, I'll just go back to—"

Jancy grabbed a handful of the hermit's long, scraggly hair and lifted. She didn't have quite the strength in her shoulder muscles to raise the hermit completely off the ground, but the pain brought him instantly up on his tiptoes.

"I think," Jancy said, "that we'd all be more comfortable if you just answered the question. Especially you'd be more comfortable."

She let him go. The hermit's mouth twisted, showing that he was swallowing a spate of shrill complaints; but he did swallow them.

"Directions aren't fixed in the usual fashion in the Desolation of Thaumidor," he explained in a chastened tone as he massaged his scalp with both bony hands. "That's why it's so important to employ a licensed practitioner, a god-guided soul whose wisdom penetrates demonic illusion."

Sombrisio responded with a high-pitched whine. The ball of dried clay smothered the ring's comment to unintelligibility.

"It's about time we think about camping," Jancy said. The sun, which had remained motionless for what seemed like hours, now settled as though somebody was pulling a shade down over the sky.

"Yes," said the hermit, pointing to a hill to the right of the road. At the top of the moderate slope was a small ruined building with a spire. "We'll shelter there, in the Little Brown Church in the Vale. It will protect us from the spirits which meep and gibber in the darkness."

"The little brown church in the *what?*" Calla said.

"I don't name them!" the hermit snapped. "If it comes to that, the boards are weathered pretty much gray by now, too."

Jancy didn't speak; but she looked at the hermit, and she hadn't looked warmly at any damn thing since she'd got this assignment. In a more cautious voice the hermit added, "I suppose it was in a vale, once. I told you, things change around here."

"I don't remember the sun going wonky the other time we were here," Jancy said to Calla Mallanik.

The elf shrugged. "What I do remember about that trip," he said, "is we were being chased by thirty thousand Ghoul Myrmidons. Put them behind us again, and I don't expect I'd notice where the sun was this time either."

He looked over his shoulder. A huge, misshapen shadow fell across the party from behind. The creature casting the shadow was invisible; but then, so was the light source that the creature's body blocked.

"Run for the church!" the hermit screamed. Everybody, including the terrified packhorses, was already doing that.

Jancy charged up the slope, the fatigue of a few moments before forgotten. Castrator swung on its loops. Brandishing an ax against the oncoming invisible giant was obviously a waste of time that could be better spent in flight.

The ring, though . . .

Jancy plucked the wad off the shield boss and tried to crush the clay between her palms. It was hard as a rock. Hard as her own damned head for hiding the magical weapon while they were in the Desolation of Thaumidor.

The party had been marching in a straggling line. Jancy, Calla and the hermit led, with Squill a few steps back with his apparatus. The packhorses broke free of the retainers leading them and streamed forward across a broad front. Their panniers strewed bags of oats, skins of water, and the ugly green cans of sea rations that rolled in broad arcs when they hit the ground.

One of the retainers kept hold of the lead strap for some time. His boots raised a spectacular plume from the light soil, but there weren't enough rocks or thorns—for a wonder—on the hillside to drag him to death properly. When the strap broke, the retainer bounced a couple times, then rose and limped toward the hallowed ground on his own.

Jancy slammed the ball of clay against the rim of her buckler. The metal bonged. Bits flaked from the clay, but the mass didn't break apart as she'd hoped. She was at least halfway to what they hoped was safety, but the curve of the slope now hid all but the tip of the church's spire.

Calla Mallanik's long legs had carried him some way ahead of his leader. The hermit was showing a remarkable turn of speed for somebody so old and apparently infirm, staying alongside Jancy even though he took four steps to her three.

It was hard to tell how tall the giant stood, since the question depended on the position of the equally unseen light source casting his shadow. At least the giant's sex wasn't in doubt, unless that was a second spike-headed club swinging between his bandy legs.

Jancy had a moment to wonder what the giant's girl-friends must look like the next morning. The chill the thought shot down her spine should have been pleasant relief from the sweaty overload of her uphill run, but it wasn't.

Calla Mallanik flung himself through the sagging door-way of the Little Brown Church at One Time in a Vale. The packhorses were already inside, frothing from their unexpected run. Jancy lost a half step to the hermit when she shifted her weight to rap the ball containing Som-brisio on Castrator's upper tip. The clay finally disin-tegrated.

Sif's Hair! If the stuff was that tough when air dried, somebody ought to be mining the Desolation for the raw material of unbreakable dinnerware.

Jancy halted beside the church doorway. She tried to fit Sombrisio onto her middle finger. The finger hole was still packed with clay. Jancy reamed it desperately on Castrator's point.

"Ooh, do that again!" Sombrisio cried. "So nice of you to provide me with a little recreation now that every-thing's quiet."

Retainers dived one by one through the doorway like pinballs falling out of play. Squill crouched by a sidewall; he'd formed his handset. Most of the chapel's roof was missing, so the tip of artio's wand wobbled between bare beams.

The packhorses at the front of the nave neighed con-gratulations to one another. A gelding snuffled the tat-tered altar cloth in vain hopes of a snack.

Calla stood at one of the Norman windows in a litter of stained glass and lead strips. He drew an arrow to its gold-glittering head and loosed it.

The elf-forged arrow sped like a jet of noonday sun, over the helmets of the struggling retainers and toward the distant horizon. The missile's course was straight for as far as the eye could follow. Unaffected, the shadow continued to lurch up the slope toward the party.

"There's nothing there!" shouted Calla Mallanik.

"We're running from nothing, because my arrow would have slain it unerringly if—"

The shadow club lengthened and shrank, as if the invisible reality casting it had been swung in a high arc. Arc and foreshortened shadow ended on the last of the retainers, a human. The ground dimpled into a cavity ten feet across. For the most part, the retainer remained on the bottom of the basin, but some of him spattered as far as the ruined church.

"Well, you know, maybe there's something there after all," Calla said, examining the point of another golden arrow with an expression of puzzled concern.

"Who needs Sombrisio?" the ring said as Jancy tried to work her finger through the hole again. "We're such all-knowing heroes ourselves that we don't need *her* help!"

The now hindermost retainer was an elf. The shadow bunched as the giant that cast it bent over. The retainer turned, swinging the leaf-shaped blade of his elven sword in a shimmering arc.

The edge, keen enough to cut a moonbeam, touched nothing. Only the elf's innate grace permitted him to pirouette instead of falling on his face the way a human would probably have done.

The elf suddenly rose a hundred feet in the air, dancing helplessly in the grip of something invisible.

"Well, I don't know," muttered Calla Mallanik. "I'm sure I was all right for azimuth, but maybe I wasn't allowing enough elevation."

His silver bow twanged. The arrow, blazing with right, justice and the elven way, shrieked through empty air on an apparent track to lunar orbit.

The eighth retainer wheeled and blew his way through the chapel's doorway. The interior of the fane took on a pearly glow. Music as soothing as a bath in warm syrup whispered on the night air.

The elf hanging in the air spun a little higher, tossed by the invisible hand. The shadow shook itself in the two-dimensional projection of an unintelligible three-dimensional reality.

Invisible club met visible retainer in a loud *whock!* that sent the elf in a screaming drive toward the sunset. Bits of equipment and, well, other things, dribbled along the route of passage the way a meteor fragments on hitting the atmosphere.

"Are you ready, ring?" Jancy demanded. She raised her right fist toward the air above the base of the shadow.

"Me?" Sombrisio said. "I've been ready all bloody day, haven't I? It's you who haven't—"

"By the power of this ring!" Jancy shouted. "Thou art a rabbit!"

The invisible giant had paused just outside the glow of the ruined church, though Jancy for one wouldn't have bet he was going to stay there. For a moment, the looming shadow froze. Then it turned, hunched, jumped back in the direction from which it had come.

Dirt exploded at the base of the slope where the creature touched down. He leaped again, then again. The line of dust geysers continued into the fallen night, each impact a good hundred yards from the previous one.

"Sif," Jancy muttered.

"Not bad, if I do say so myself," said Sombrisio. "And not before time, I might add."

"Don't expect an argument from me," said Jancy.

They'd wait till morning to gather the supplies strewn up the hill slope, but there ought to be something in the horses' loads. Jancy figured food right now to settle her stomach might be a good idea.

Brushwood gathered from the hillside blazed hot and cleanly on the bonfire in the front of the ruined chapel. The lack of wind meant that the smoke, which smelled as if sulphur was being cooked on a bed of cat turds, wasn't generally a problem to those sitting around the fire.

The surviving retainers were going to be pretty busy feeding the blaze. The hair-fine thorns on many of the plants around here burned like the coals themselves, but that wasn't one of Jancy's problems. Rank hath its privileges.

Jancy's most pressing problem was that she very clearly saw figures in the flame. Including the figure of the Princess Rissa. Rissa wasn't being tortured—quite the contrary; but the glimpses Jancy got when she forgot and looked into the fire were torture for her.

Jancy was sure the images were demonic sendings, not a real view of what was going on in the Princess's suite in Caltus. She didn't even consider asking anybody else what they saw in the flames. Sombrisio had already had a field day with Jancy's daydreams: Jancy wasn't about to reopen the subject.

Calla Mallanik stared grimly at the contents of the can he'd just opened. "This is supposed to be pound cake," he said. "I think I really could pound nails with it. If the Commissary Service is so determined to punish us, couldn't they just have arranged for a plague of boils? Meals were always a happy occasion for me in the past."

"I'm not going to say Athos let down the side . . ." a human retainer remarked morosely. He was carrying toward the fire a bush which thrashed feebly and called for its mother. "But the truth is, I was hoping for a more inspired performance than he gave us."

"Well, I don't know," said one of the elves dragging a matronly shrub which was, in fact, the mother of the other one. "I rather liked the splash. Sometimes the simplest effects are the most memorable."

"Give Athos his due, Aramis," said a human across the fire from Jancy. "The giant didn't give him a lot to work with. You can't make a silk purse out of a sow's ear."

"Why not?" said an elf retainer in surprise. "It's a pretty simple protein conversion. If it was me, I'd start with the collagen and . . ."

The conversation drifted off into technicalities. A retainer tossed the small bush on the fire. The crackle with which it flared up drew Jancy's reflexive attention. She looked down hurriedly. She was *absolutely* sure that the Princess Rissa wasn't on such affectionate terms with an aardvark.

Squill was in the spire of the church. The ladder didn't look safe or even possible, but the artio had finally managed to clamber up when he found he couldn't reach Caltus from anywhere else on the hilltop.

He must have finally gotten through, because Jancy heard in intervals between the howls of atmospherics the words, "... figures two KIA but hostile forces beaten off ..."

Maybe this church really was in a vale. It'd sure seemed like a hill when Jancy was trying to reach the church before the giant reached *her*.

A shimmering image caught Jancy's eye again. She deliberately got up and walked to the other side of the fire. She seated herself with her back to the flames, looking out into the night.

Something sparkled in the distant darkness. She couldn't tell whether it was on the horizon or closer, since the moon and stars had vanished behind a cloudbank as black as the ground beneath.

The soil trembled, though of course it usually did here.

"Now, I don't expect aspic-preserved duck à l'orange in the field," Calla Mallanik said to the round of pound cake. It was probably as interested in his comments as the rest of the party was. "Not from humans, at any rate. But I don't see any reason chicken Marengo couldn't be supplied. Chicken Marengo was *developed* as a field collation, for pity's sake!"

Jancy saw the sparkles again. As a matter of fact, when she squinted she realized that the slowly moving effect dimmed and brightened, but never completely vanished.

"Hermit!" Jancy called.

"I think he dossed down inside," one of the retainers offered.

"Well, bring him out here," Jancy said.

"Your boy did pretty well," a human retainer said to the elf beside him.

"Melaril?" the elf said. "Yeah, that was a nice job,

wasn't it, especially for a kid who'd just turned seven hundred last Thursday."

"Mind you," said another elf, "for a real disintegrating arc, there was Count Diamondbringer the Undaunted, when love of the nymph Arachneida caused him to hurl himself into the vent of the volcano Earthsfire."

"Well, I don't know," argued a human. "Diamondbringer turned bright yellow from the sulphur. Well, the bits of him did, anyway. I always thought that detracted from the majesty of the occasion."

"Not at all!" an elf insisted. "Why, that just added to the uniqueness. How many *yellow* disintegrating arcs can you name? Name one other!"

"Well, there was Charles the Cowardly," a human offered with a snigger. "When he sneaked out the sally port of Castle Dangerous without noticing that the besiegers had already set a lighted petard against it."

A retainer dropped the mother shrub on the fire. Sparks and flame exploded from the tinder-dry wood. Everybody nearby had to jump away. Jancy slapped a smoldering spot on her doublet with her bare hand and cursed.

"Ah," said Sombrisio, "how I'm looking forward to the intellectual conversations I'll soon be having with dung beetles and petrified trees in Anthurus."

Jancy turned and bellowed, *"Her—"*

The hermit was settling into a squat beside her. His face had been about three inches away when Jancy twisted to bellow toward the church where she thought he was still sleeping. He yelped and fell over.

Retainers paused in their conversations. Calla Mallanik raised an eyebrow from across the fire.

"Sorry," Jancy muttered as she helped the hermit to sit up. Sombrisio tittered like a psychotic bat. The male members of the flame tableau Jancy glimpsed this time were dressed as sanitation workers, to the extent that they were dressed at all.

"Yes, well," the hermit said. "What is it, Mistress Gaine?"

He seemed humble rather than his usual madder-than-hops manner. Handled with normal decency, the fellow was unbearable. He had to be treated like dirt to behave himself. Well, Jancy was in a mood to make him behave.

"That," she said, pointing to the faint glimmer in the night. "What's that?"

When Jancy concentrated, she thought she heard a groan from the same general direction of the darkness; though that could have been wind, her imagination, or the muttering of a queue of commuters waiting for a streetcar on the Thaumidor Line. *She* didn't know what was out there.

"Oh," said the hermit. "That's just the mountain. Don't worry about that."

"A lot you know," Sombrisio chirped.

Jancy leaned forward. "What mountain?" she said, loud enough to fluff the scraggly beard. "A mountain like the one we're on?"

"Or a vale," the hermit said, bobbing his head like a chicken drinking. He wasn't being obstructive, just speaking precisely as a result of his healthy fear. "Ah, no, that's a real mountain."

He frowned. "Or it was. It's been wandering around the Desolation for centuries, looking for some guy named Mohammet, and it's pretty well worn itself down to a nubbin by now."

Jancy looked off to the east again. Probably the east. "Who in blazes—"

She shouldn't have said "blazes," because it turned her mind to the fire.

"—is Mohammet?"

The hermit shrugged. "I've no idea," he said. "Mountains don't have any brains at all, of course. I suspect this one got into entirely the wrong space-time and has been cruising around here since."

"The Desolation of Thaumidor attracts all sorts of folk who don't know their ass from a hole in the ground," Sombrisio said. She added flatulent emphasis.

"All right, but what's the . . . the glow, the light?"

Jancy asked. She was emotionally convinced that the glimmer was weaving itself closer as she watched. Intellectually she knew that the light's faint waxing and waning made realistic distance calculations impossible.

"Well," said the hermit, "it's a mountain, so it's made of rock. When you stress rock, the phlogiston entrapped in the crystal matrix is first driven out, then reabsorbed. When the phlogiston content of the surrounding atmosphere increases, it causes the ether to glow."

"Ah," Jancy said, pretending that the explanation made sense to her. She had no more acquaintance with phlogiston than she did with honest politicians.

"He got through third-year alchemy before he scooted out of Quiberon ahead of the bailiffs," Sombrisio said.

"It just roves back and forth across the Desolation," the hermit said, pretending he hadn't heard the ring. "The mountain does. Quite harmless. Unless, of course, you don't get out of its way."

Now that Jancy had been told what was happening, it sounded like a mass of rock grinding its way slowly over . . . well, grinding over anything that happened to be in its way.

"Is that all, mistress?" the hermit asked humbly.

"Right," said Jancy. "Get some sleep."

If she listened hard, the growl of rock had a plaintive undertone that could have been the name Mohammet. . . .

To the (putative) east, the ridge was dry and clothed with no vegetation save glass-spiked, poisonous cacti. On the other side of the ridge was a swamp.

"Traditionalists claim a buried aquifer follows folded layers of the underlying rock strata," the hermit said. "My researches, however, indicate that the Desolation is sweating."

Water black as a banker's heart gurgled at the base of tussocks. The reeds were gray with death, and the creatures which flitted among them were feathered skeletons instead of living birds.

"It was a place like this where I saved Princess Rissa

from the Dragonspawn of Loathly Fen," Jancy said, reminiscing aloud.

"*You* saved?" said Sombrisio. "Oh, right, I suppose it was you hanging on the Princess's finger, turning dragonspawn into bullfrogs so fast your head spun for the next three days!"

"I don't believe there are any dragonspawn here," the hermit said, peering over the swamp with a look of concern. "There's been some talk of a tribe of toadmen, but I don't believe the contract details have been worked out."

"If you don't mind my asking, sir," said one of the retainers. "Mistress, that is. What sort of retainers did you have with you there? In the Loathly Fen, that is?"

"Ah," said Jancy. "We'd run into a bit of a problem earlier, you see. With the Killer Vines of Siloam."

"The truth is," Calla Mallanik admitted. "we'd expended all our retainers before we reached the Loathly Swamp."

"I blame myself for not keeping a closer eye on the supply," Jancy said.

Calla frowned. "Well, still, there'd been that recruitment problem in Sandoz when we set out."

"The Duke had marched on Tzerchingia to battle the three-headed ogre and her minions," Jancy explained. "There was a dearth of retainers in Sandoz unless we wanted to wait for the new crop of fifteen-year-olds to ripen."

"Ah," said the retainer sadly, with a nod of his hoary head. "Well, I'm sure a hero like yourself knows best, mistress. But to simple folk like us—"

He gestured with his grizzled jaw to indicate the retainers behind him.

"—it seems like a quest isn't rightly a quest lessen you have proper retainers in it."

Another retainer, an elf this time, nodded sagely. "And I do like a bit of cranberry sauce in the quest rations, too," he said.

Jancy grimaced uncomfortably. "Well, we hired a fine

lot of retainers as soon as we could," she said. "At a low dive in the foreign quarter of Boroclost. Desperate men willing to murder their own grandmothers for a chance to put Princess Rissa on the throne of Caltus."

"Two of them," Sombrisio said. "Two retainers. One, two."

"Well, they *were* pretty desperate," Calla said mildly. "I know I didn't feel comfortable turning my back on either of them."

"Not a very impressive retinue," Sombrisio said.

"Well, what did you want?" Jancy shouted. "We were flat broke, weren't we? We'd been skedaddling for months from doom-ridden castle to monster-haunted mere, *not* to mention the Desolation of Thaumidor. Were we supposed to melt you down to pay for a proper mob of retainers?"

"Huh," the ring said. "I'd like to have seen you try to melt me. If you're a Third Age demigod, then I'm a soup tureen."

A sepulchral bonging sounded deep within the mist-shrouded fastnesses of the swamp. The chittering laughter of the bird skeletons ceased; reed bracts shivered with no wind to stir them.

Jancy Gaine untied the thong holding her buckler, then took Castrator into her right hand. She shrugged, loosing the powerful muscles of her shoulders so that she would be ready to react at an instant's need.

"All right," she said. "We'll enter the swamp now."

"Good Lord!" said the hermit. "Why on Middle Earth would we want to do that?"

Jancy paused, feeling the noble set of her carriage slacken. "Huh?" she said. "Well, to venture boldly on our course to the Lost City of Anthurus and the accomplishment of our quest, of course."

"Yes, all that," said the hermit in barely controlled exasperation, "but we can't go through the *swamp*. Those hummocks, they wouldn't support a man."

"And what about the horses, hey?" Sombrisio chortled. "They'd sink so far that you'd have to stack them on each other's backs to have the ears of the top one break the surface!"

Jancy shot Castrator home with a violence that she'd *really* like to have worked off on a more deserving target. "Then why," she bellowed, "did you lead us here? Is this the scenic tour of the Desolation of Thaumidor, is that it?"

"Well, no, I intended to follow the ridgeline, here," the hermit said. "It's better walking, you see, than down below."

The hermit scuffed his sandal toe at the ground. The surface was hard as concrete. Salts deposited during the swamp's periodic floods had combined with the light soil.

Jancy remembered the difficulty she'd had unpacking Sombrisio's clay jacket when the invisible giant pursued them.

"Oh," she said. "Well, let's get going, then."

"Never mind," Sombrisio said, drawing out the syllables in a nasal whine. Judging from the ring's continuing guffaws, it must have been a joke of some sort.

The sky was a bronze furnace. It should have been late afternoon, but Jancy hadn't seen the sun since her party mounted the ridgeline.

The swamp to the right gurgled and shuddered. Once Jancy happened to be looking in that direction when a thirty-foot hole gaped in the surface of the water. It could have been a bubble bursting, of course, but she was sure she saw vomerine teeth deep in the watery gullet.

The hole slapped shut. Bulging eyes the size of washtubs blinked at Jancy, then closed again.

She grimaced and looked away. The party marched on.

A spiral of fine soil curled into the air on the left. It zigzagged along on a course roughly paralleling the ridge. The funnel's spinning tip traced a broad line into the ground. A snake with scales like fire opals whirled aloft with the dust, striking in impotent fury at the air.

Jancy paused. "What's that?" she said, pointing.

"Just a dust devil," the hermit replied.

"But there's no wind," she snapped.

The initial funnel was already breaking up half a mile away, but four similar whirlwinds emerged on the left—desert—side of the ridgeline. These moved in unison, as if they were cutting tools milling away the surface of the ground.

"I didn't say it was the wind," the hermit said peevishly. "I said it was a dust devil. Obviously a number of them. Sometimes in the fall they swarm like locusts."

Each of the immediate dust devils spun out a constellation of minivortices which grew larger as they rotated. The funnels climbed only a few hundred feet in the air. Their forms, insubstantial at first, became yellow-gray and then black as the air loaded itself with soil.

"They're quite harmless, of course," the hermit added. He sounded a little doubtful. "To humans."

A prickly pear cactus beat its spiky lobes furiously. The plant was trying either to fly out of the vortex or to make the gripping funnel drop it. The dust devil spun its unintended prey lazily higher.

"Let's keep moving," Jancy ordered.

"And whose idea was it to stop and gawk in the first place?" said Sombrisio.

Logy with the dirt they had swallowed, the devils staggered farther desertward and spewed their meals in the near distance. Half a mile from Jancy's party, a new ridge began to rise from what had been flat ground.

Calla Mallanik frowned. He peered not toward the dust devils but at the ground they were sweeping in their proliferating arcs. "Say," the elf said. "There's something down there."

Then he added, "There's a lot of somethings down there!"

Where the dust devils had scoured away the soil, the remains of an army entombed standing up appeared: Pointed steel caps, some of them bearing tattered ribbons tied to the peaks. Halberds and guisarmes, their blades forged in fanciful shapes and chased with designs in gold and orichalc and rich black niello.

Within the helmets, half-rotted faces covered by veils of silvered mail.

"Run!" cried the hermit, suiting his actions to his words. "It's the buried army of Voroshek the Extremely Ill-Tempered the Fourth!"

It was an army, at least. The whole half-mile swath the dust devils were uncovering was planted with dried soldiers. Jancy couldn't estimate how far the array extended alongside the ridge on which her party traveled, but she had to assume it was a long damned way.

"But they're dead, aren't they?" Jancy asked as she broke into a run alongside the hermit.

"Not exactly!" he replied, puffing out a syllable every time his right heel slammed down. "But they don't move very fast!"

Mummified with the army were hump-shouldered mammoths. Their long hair, bleached russet during burial, fell out in handfuls as the beasts began to move. Gilded palanquins swayed on the mammoths' backs, but the bowstrings of the archers within had rotted.

As the dust devils sucked loess from the feet of Voroshek's soldiers, the army strode slowly toward the ridge along which Jancy's party was by now in full flight. The lowering menace of the mummies' advance was unmistakable.

"Are they attacking us because we're from Faltane?" Jancy asked. "*I'm* not from Faltane."

"I'm certainly not from Faltane!" agreed Calla Mallanik. The elf had nocked an arrow, but he wasn't poised to shoot. Targets were in embarrassing oversupply, and it seemed unlikely that an arrow was going to do more damage than three centuries of burial had already accomplished.

"Anyway, we weren't even born when the trouble started," Jancy said.

"Look, every member of the Voroshek dynasty was named 'the Ill-Tempered!' " the hermit shouted. "What possible excuse do you have for thinking that the last distillation of the line would need a *reason* for feeding us all our entrails?"

Since the boundary the dust devils swept was the end of the danger area—if there were soldiers buried beyond that point, that was fine: they were *buried*—Jancy thought her party ought to be able to win free. The mummies moved with slow deliberation, and the slope of the salt-compacted ridge was as sheer as a castle wall now that the vortices had excavated the soil from alongside it.

On the other hand, the mummies were trained soldiers. Already troops were forming tortoise formations by squatting with their broad, rectangular shields sloped across their backs. Further squads scrambled up the layer of their fellows and formed a second step for yet more mummies to mount.

And there was Hel's own plenty of mummies, that there was.

Jancy pulled Sombrisio from her right hand and gave the ring to Calla. "Here you go," she said. "I'm going to be busy."

She untied her buckler and drew the great ax Castrator from its belt loops. Her party was almost going to reach the edge of the danger zone before Voroshek's soldiers climbed to the top of the ridge.

Almost.

A pair of mummies stood on the backs of their fellows, clambering the rest of the way onto the ridge. They thrust pole arms toward Jancy's legs. These leaders weren't a danger to her; she could have jumped the halberds and raced ahead to safety. By the time the last of the party jounced along with the packhorses, however, the two would have become a platoon.

Castrator swept the heads from both mummies. Their necks were tinder dry. The flesh splintered despite the keenness of the ax edge.

The bodies continued to climb the ridge. Jancy kicked them sideways, tumbling the doubly dead backward.

Their fall upset the stepped array of their fellows like a house of cards. Corpses spilled like jackstraws. When they crashed into the ground, some of the bodies broke apart in a litter of limbs and powdered flesh. Even these twitched feebly as they attempted to execute Voroshek's unheard commands.

Like a tongue of water driven through a dike by the storm surge, another force of mummified soldiers climbed the ridge in front of the party. Squill and the hermit stopped short of the lethal obstruction.

A pair of retainers had thundered past Jancy while she was occupied. They rushed the mummies at the side of the Calla Mallanik.

Calla aimed his beringed fist. "Thou art dead!" he shouted.

Voroshek's soldiers needed a lot of convincing, as Jancy knew, but Sombrisio was up to the job. A mummy took the force of the ring's displeasure in the chest and folded up, disintegrating within its armor as it fell.

The only problem with Sombrisio—as a weapon, that is—was that she had an individual focus. If you wanted to blot out an army—and Jancy wanted very much to blot out an army—you had to do it one soldier at a time. That wasn't going to be fast enough.

A human retainer hurled himself against the forest of mummy-borne pole arms. This band was equipped primarily with short-bladed pikes. Groaning, "Death and glory!" the retainer managed to gather half a dozen of the points into his torso, immobilizing the weapons until they could be pulled clear.

An elven retainer leaped into the gap the human had opened, wielding a curved saber in either hand. Even before he struck his first blow, a mummy sliced through the elf's armor of grasses beaten hard by the feet of elvish maidens dancing to the Goddess of Samhain.

The mummy's guisarme stabbed deep into the retainer's belly. The blade's hook came out with a coil of intestine.

The mummy yanked back with all the supernal

strength of its preserved muscles. The elf lifted his left toe to his right knee, went up on point, and pirouetted. His sabers whickered as they spun down across a broad circle of Voroshek's army like the blades of a food processor. Edges of elf-cast dendritic steel lowered the height of nearby mummies in a sequence of delicate slices.

His solo maneuver completed, the retainer bowed gracefully and fell. He made a very flat corpse.

Calla Mallanik collapsed the ramp up which reinforcements clambered by blasting mummies at the edge of the bottom layer with Sombrisio. Boy, once a mummy was killed, he was *dead*. There wasn't so much as a bone or a patch of mold remaining within the ragged armor and accouterments.

There were still mummies standing between Jancy's party and safety, though. Jancy strode forward, shrieking, "Princess!" her war chant, to end the problem.

Three pikemen lunged toward Jancy's chest, and a fourth mummified soldier swung his guisarme down at her horned helmet. Jancy griped her buckler's two close-set handles in her left fist.

She swept the pikes aside with her chattering shield rim. One point ripped muscles-deep along eight inches of her left triceps, but in this state Jancy didn't notice the contact. She stepped inside the arc of the guisarme, swinging her bearded ax.

Castrator combined the weight and shock effect of an ax with the long cutting edge of a sword. Jancy's stroke carried the blade through the neck and shoulder of the mummy wielding the guisarme. The soldier wore a shirt of high-quality chain mail. Most of the welded, double-wired links held, but the dried flesh within exploded out the neck and armholes as powder.

The mummy continued to march forward. His guisarme fell, still in the grip of the severed arm. Because the decapitated soldier had no eyes to guide him, he plunged into the swamp a few strides on. Something swallowed him, then burped happily.

Jancy stabbed a mummy through the face with her

spiked shield boss. The creature stolidly shortened its grip on its pike in order to pierce the shield-maiden since she was too close for a normal pike thrust.

Castrator crunched through the mummy's left knee. Jancy flexed her shield arm, hurling the unbalanced semi-corpse back down the desert side of the ridge. He'd probably climb back up despite his one leg, but his presence wouldn't matter by the time he arrived.

Jancy stepped forward. There were mummies all around her. Voroshek's soldiers were clumsy and their pole arms were the wrong weapons for a close-in fight, but there were still a lot of them.

Too many of them, if she'd let herself think about it, but reflexes and bloodlust ruled Jancy Gaine in a fight.

She swung Castrator to the right and the edge of her buckler left in counterbalanced blows. The boss spike wasn't as useful as it would have been against living— fully living—opponents. She smashed the steel rim across a mummy's eyes instead, crushing the sunken orbs and the bones of their sockets. The tactic must have worked, because the soldier stopped where he was and prodded the air hesitantly with his halberd.

An elf retainer fought in a circle of the enemy on the other side of the ridge from Jancy. A guisarme blow lopped off both his feet.

"Death and glory!" the elf cried, striding forward on his ankles. He left circular pools of golden ichor behind him. His ripple-bladed kris decapitated a pair of mummies with a single stroke.

The mummy who'd cut off the retainer's feet hunched his shoulders and leaned into another whistling stroke with his guisarme. He really put his back into it this time. The broad blade, decorated with a scene of professors eating the brains of a colleague who had failed to use inclusive language, whacked the elf's legs off at the knees.

"I have not yet begun to fight!" cried the retainer, stumping another short stride onward. His kris eviscerated a mummified soldier. The mummy bent over to view the damage, thus bringing his neck within range of a following slice of the kris.

The guisarme made another enormous sweep, slinging ropes of golden droplets off its blade's hooked tip. Jancy had too much on her own plate to consider the outcome but she'd have bet that the retainer would manage to remove at least one more mummy while teetering on his pelvis.

For her own part, Jancy howled as she spun on the ball of her right foot, whirling Castrator in a figure eight. On the high side of the arc the ax beheaded a pair of Voroshek's soldiers. When the blade dipped low, it clipped one mummy off at the knees and the next at the ankles.

The latter two were still dangerous to a degree. When the mummies hit the ground, Jancy crushed their skulls to powder with the heels of her hobnailed boots.

A guisarme clanged from her helmet and ripped a gouge down her back. Jancy's vision blurred for a moment. She spun and sliced horizontally through the mummy's brittle skull at eye-socket level.

"I got it!" a human retainer shouted. Jancy looked over her shoulder. The retainer leaped sideways, waving his arms wildly to distract the mummy who was thrusting the spike-topped blade of his halberd toward Jancy's back. "I got—"

Sklurk!

The retainer wore a cuirass of boiled leather. The spike, which was square in cross-section and so cut with four ninety-degree edges, stuck out a hand's breadth through the backplate.

"A far, far better thing I do—" said the retainer.

Jancy beheaded the mummy who was trying to withdraw the halberd from the fellow's chest.

"—than I have ever done before."

Calla and Sombrisio struck a mummified soldier dead. It collapsed to rags, rusty armor, and a whiff of cedar oils. That one was the last of those in a blocking position, though the entire ridgeline behind the party of humans now crawled with Voroshek's soldiery. Mammoths were striding toward the ridge as well. Their palanquins had fallen when the rotted leather of their cinches broke.

"Come on, come on," Jancy muttered. The rest of her party was already jogging forward at a pace mummified muscles couldn't match. Calla Mallanik offered Jancy his arm, knowing that the aftermath of berserk rage was a sleep near death—and that sleep *now* would be death for fair.

They stumbled along the hard-packed surface of the ridgeline. Everything but what was directly ahead vanished into a gray blur of fatigue. Jancy's world view was the ass of a roan packhorse whose occasional tail lift better *not* mean the beast was about to take a dump.

"Now a lot of people . . ." keened Sombrisio in a voice that grated like a silver chalk-sharpener, ". . . when their lives had been saved by a magic ring would be saying, 'Gee, how could we reward this ring?' Others, of course, would figure, what the hell, let's dump our benefactor in the deepest lost city we can find . . ."

The fallen tree had been buried in loess when the climate changed, but it wasn't petrified. In fact, judging from the way the tree groaned as the party's fire burned into the innards of the bole, the tree wasn't even really dead.

Well, it would be by morning, except maybe for the tips of some limbs.

Squill was perched on the root ball now, swaying slightly as rootlets twisted around him in agony. Dust devils, perhaps the same swarm that lighted on Voroshek's army, had cleared the tree in the recent past. That was good luck for the questing humans. There's no wind but blows ill for somebody, however: the tree wasn't in the least happy about the turn of events.

"Knowed Wyvern Two to Knowed Wyvern Base," the artio repeated. "Come in, over." Only wailing atmosphereics answered him.

"Damn the man!" Jancy snarled under her breath.

"This isn't a place I want to listen to souls howling in the darkness!"

"Squill says he has to call at night," Calla Mallanik said mildly, "or they wouldn't hear him in Caltus. His spells don't propagate properly when the sun shines. The communications demons are embarrassed to make love in daylight."

"Who in Hel's house *cares* if his spells propagate?" Jancy said. "It'd be all right with me if he stuffed that twelve-foot wand of his straight up his specialized ass!"

"Don't bury me there . . ." sang the four surviving retainers in good barbershop harmony, ". . . on the lone prairie . . ."

"Shit, I wonder if we're going to run out of retainers?" Jancy muttered. Her mind was bouncing from generalized gloom to specific problems that were beyond her practical control.

"Where the coyotes howl . . ." sang the retainers as lost souls keened from the comspec's receiver. ". . . so-o-o mournfully."

"Oh, I think we'll be all right," soothed Calla.

"Do you suppose there's an inn nearby where we could fill up if we need to?" Jancy said. "Hermit! Is there an inn around here with retainers? I don't care if they're off-brand."

"Well, not really very close," the hermit admitted doubtfully. "*Really* not very close, to tell the truth."

Jancy swore. She wrung her hands together as a way of working off some of her bleak anger without hurting anybody.

Almost anybody.

"Hey!" said Sombrisio. "This is the way you treat a ring that's saved your miserable life, is it?"

"Sorry," said Jancy, jerking her hands apart.

"You can't hurt her by squeezing," Calla Mallanik pointed out reasonably. "You couldn't hurt her by pounding her all day on an anvil."

"Oh, nice!" said the ring. "Sombrisio doesn't have any

feelings, is that it? Let's grind our dirty hands over her. Or better yet, we can hit her with a hammer!"

"I said I'm sorry!" Jancy said.

". . . come in, Knowed Wyvern Base, o—"

"Squill!" Jancy roared. "Will you shut the hell up, or do you want me to feed that knapsack to you, crystal and all?"

"Jancy, he's got to report back," Calla said. "Otherwise there'll be no record for future generations."

"Future generations can go bugger themselves," Jancy said, but she spoke in a low voice that indicated she was embarrassed at the outburst.

"Go ahead, Squill," Calla called. "But try to wrap the business up quickly, won't you?"

"Knowed Wyvern Two to Knowed Wyvern Base," the artio said. He spoke this time in a voice of quiet desperation. Squill's repeated call was less irritating than the fingernail squealing of the atmospherics, but he was at least doing what he could.

"There has to be a record," Calla said. He patted the back of Jancy's scarred, powerful hand. "In case in later days they have to retrace our path in order to retrieve Sombrisio against a terrible new danger."

"Or you could just keep Sombrisio in a comfortable jewelry box in Caltus," the ring said bitterly. "But no, that'd be too simple, wouldn't it?"

"Well, I don't see why," Jancy said. "I mean, a quest is a quest. If unimaginable evil breaks forth in the world again, then some hero will struggle through perils, temptations, and the foul sleights of evil wizards. That's all there is to it."

It was her grim state of mind speaking, though she hadn't said anything that she hadn't thought oftentimes before.

"Well, yes, but the quest will be guided by—"

"Oh, don't give me *that* crap again," Jancy snapped. "I don't care if the route's written on a half-charred palimpsest found in a ruined palace, stamped on a torque of unknown metal taken from the tomb of a forgotten king, or drawn in blazing letters on stone by the finger of an unseen spirit. The quest is all that matters."

"Tradition matters, Mistress Gaine," Calla Mallanik said huffily. Elves, because of their long lifespans (except for elves who took up the profession of retainer to puissant heroes, of course), were great respecters of tradition.

"It's traditional that heroes go on quests," Jancy said stubbornly. "They either triumph or they leave their bones to whiten in dire warning to those who come later. All the rest is just window dressing."

"Feckless Teuton," Calla muttered with a sigh. It obviously wasn't a conversation that was going anywhere useful, so he dropped the subject. The pair sat for a time in silence punctuated by the snores of the hermit nearby.

The retainers on the other side of the tree bole had stopped singing. They now picked at cans of sea rations with an understandable lack of enthusiasm.

"I'm really disappointed in Porthos," said a grizzled veteran. He was the unofficial leader of the human contingent, now reduced to himself and a kid who said he was from Brooklyn.

"Say, I thought he did a great job," said the senior elven retainer. "In human terms, of course. Did you see the way he spread his legs so that he stayed upright with the halberd as a brace when his body went rigid in death?"

"Sure," said the grizzled veteran, "that's fine. But he used 'A far, far better thing I do' out of context."

"An act is its own context!" said the leading elf. "You can't go importing context from outside the environment of the deed."

"And besides," said the kid from Brooklyn, "knowing Porthos, it probably was a better thing. I'm sorry now he's gone that I called him a hanging plant, though."

"*That*," said the veteran, waggling his finger in the kid's face, "is a clear example of the Autobiographical Fallacy! And—"

He returned his attention to the elf.

"—the environment of a deed is the entire universe.

Who among us can claim to have separated himself from the world?"

"Well, in absolute terms, I agree," said the retainer who had been silent until now. "But in terms of elven realities . . ."

The kid from Brooklyn got out his harmonica. He began to play "Lorena" in soft accompaniment to the groans of the burning tree.

Jancy interlaced her fingers, careful not to cover Sombrisio, and said to her hands. "You know what really frosts me? It's the injustice of it all."

"Umm?" said Calla Mallanik. He'd learned long since that if you ignored Jancy Gaine, she'd go off and do something that would *damned* well get her noticed. A passive aggressive with a big ax was nothing to joke about.

"I saved Princess Rissa's life and virtue, why, it must have been dozens of times," Jancy continued bitterly. "And here I am, out in the Desolation of Thaumidor, eating sea rations."

"Right," said Sombrisio unexpectedly. "And just when did the Princess say to you, 'Jancy, m'girl, I'm going to need a whole shitload of saving. I'm hiring you to do it in consideration of my hand in marriage when we've won through these terrible dangers.' Hey?"

"Well, that's not what happened, no," Jancy said uncomfortably. "But I *did*—"

"And as far as saving went," Sombrisio continued in a voice that would have roused dogs three miles away if there'd been any dogs in the Desolation, "I seem to recall there was about as much of that on the one side as the other. Not least because it was the Princess mostly who was wearing *me*."

"Well, I grant that," Jancy admitted. "But still, we were companions in peril, and here she's sent me—"

She waved her hands.

"—here!"

"Actually," Calla said, now that the ring had broken Jancy's icy self-absorption, "the orders came from Prince

Rango. And it seemed to me that it was more an understanding than, well, a formal order."

"Right!" Sombrisio agreed. "You know, elf, sometimes I think you might have the brains of a rutabaga after all. You. Axgirl! You're a hero, right?"

"You're bloody well told I am," Jancy said grimly. She glared at the ring in obvious contemplation of determining whether the meteoritic silver was really impervious to Castrator's edge.

"So if Princess Rissa really was your friend," Sombrisio said, "what's she going to say? 'My fiancé has a dangerous quest that'll bring eternal honor to some hero, but I told him I'd rather keep you around the palace and wrap you in angora fluff.' Is that what she's going to say, dumdum?"

"Ah," said Jancy Gaine.

"Damned right, 'Ah,'" the ring agreed. "Now, get some sleep, will you? I'm tired of looking at your ugly face."

Squill must have finally reached Caltus, because he climbed down from the root ball and wrapped himself in his cloak on the other side of the fire. Two of the retainers took station at the edge of the firelight to guard the camp. The other pair began to sing "There's a Long Long Trail A-Winding" quietly.

Neither the song, nor the ache of her bandaged arm and shoulder, kept Jancy awake. She fell into fatigued sleep like a stone wobbling down an ocean abyss.

"Hey, lover girl!" a voice squealed. "Wake up! Your dreams are disgusting me!"

"What?" said Jancy. "What—"

By the second syllable she was standing with Castrator cocked to swing. Two quick snaps had wrapped Jancy's left arm in the cape in which she'd been sleeping. Only then was she sufficiently alert to realize that Sombrisio had called her from dreams that were anything but loving.

"You and Rissa," the ring said. "Phew!"

"That's a lie!" Jancy shouted. "That's—"

"Guards!" cried Calla Mallanik. Everyone was awake now, from Jancy's shout if not from Sombrisio's shrill demand. The stalwart elf aimed his half-drawn bow toward the ground at his feet. "Where in the name of the All-Nurturing Mother-Force are you?"

Breezes parted the high overcast, allowing the moon to cast its baleful light over the landscape. The guards, an elf and a human, were a hundred yards from the fire log's sunken glow. The human waved. Nothing else moved in the night.

"We thought we heard something!" the retainer called. "But there's nothing here."

The ground shivered, a movement no less disquieting for having become familiar while the party crossed the Desolation. The hobbled packhorses were restive.

"Run!" the hermit shrieked. "It's the mountain!"

The landscape at the feet of the two retainers on guard hunched itself up like a giant inchworm.

The human turned, shouting, "Woops!" The rising cliff flowed over him, sparkling with piezoelectrical radiance. The many kilotons of rock reduced the retainer and his equipment to a molecular film.

"Save the supplies!" Calla Mallanik ordered. He knew as well as any of them that there was no time to do anything more than flee, but he also knew that depending on the bounty of the Desolation of Thaumidor was a recipe for lingering death.

Jancy shifted Castrator to her left hand. She held Sombrisio out toward the mountain in a clenched-fist salute and cried. "Thou art petrified!"

The spell had no effect on the mountain.

"Death and—" the elf on guard cried as he took two clean-limbed strides back toward the camp. A rock almost exactly the size of the retainer's head fell from the top of the advancing cliff. It precisely intersected the course of the running elf.

The helmet of boars' tusks and gold wire disintegrated, as did the retainer's skull. The elf waltzed in widening

circles like those of a child's top slowing to the point it
will soon fall over. In the uncertain light there was nothing unusual about the figure, though of course he'd
stopped shouting when the rock brained him.

The packhorses neighed and kicked their bound forelegs high. The hobbles were of elven working, fashioned
from children's mercy, maidens' constancy, and suchlike
materials. The horses would never be able to break free
of their mythical bonds. Even if they did, the off-loaded
supplies would be lost beneath the mountain's advance.

"I said, thou art petrified!" Jancy bellowed. Telling
mummified soldiers they were dead had been a striking
success. Telling a rock it was rock ought to be an equally
natural win.

The cliff had stopped rising. Now it began to slump
forward again at increasing velocity.

"You idiot!" Sombrisio said. "The mountain doesn't
have any more brains than you do, so how do you expect
me to affect *its* beliefs? Blast the ground, yoyo!"

The ring's directions didn't make a lot of sense, but
Jancy didn't have a better idea. Waiting for the cliff to
arrive was a terrible idea.

"Thou art in pain!" she said, aiming her fist toward
the soil at the base of the glittering mountain. By now
the rock was moving *really* fast with gravity adding its
considerable increment to force of the spell which ani-
mated the mountain.

"Eeeeeeek!" screamed the world, or at least as much
of it as Jancy Gaine and her party were occupying at the
moment. The ground drew back in agony, forming a lip
of fine loess which scooted Jancy, her fellows, and the
entire bouncing paraphernalia of their camp away from
the mountain's line of advance.

"The Desolation is a living entity," the hermit had said,
or something very like that, early on in the quest. . . .

When the scarified soil drew back, it formed a huge
hole. The mountain, plunging down at an enormous rate
intended to carry it by inertia a thousand yards out across
the moonlit wasteland, streamed into the chasm.

Crevices gaped and closed across the granite. The entire surface of the mountain glowed with expelled phlogiston.

The jiggling tail of the mountain followed the rest of the rock into the hole. There was a shuddering impact a very long way down. The Desolation of Thaumidor was a being of unsuspected depths.

Jancy got to her feet. Calla and the surviving pair of retainers had started to gather up the supplies. The mountain would probably tunnel its way to the surface again, but that wouldn't be for a while.

"Now, that," said Sombrisio in tones of exhausted satisfaction, "is the sort of spell magical implements will still be talking about well into the Fifth Age of the Middle World!"

Bushes tumbled across the landscape, dragging the tips of their branches in desperate but vain attempts to halt their progress. Occasionally one of the whirling weeds hit an unseen barrier and splattered to a stop, leaking its life juices into the dry soil.

There was no wind. Trees deformed by leprous scale stood leafless, waiting for dust to bury them. This was as doomed and barren a place as Jancy'd seen since, since the most recent time she'd opened her eyes in the Desolation of Thaumidor.

"Do you want to camp here?" Calla Mallanik suggested, obviously solicitous because of Jancy's physical state.

She grimaced. She probably looked like walking death. She certainly felt like walking death; but right now the best way to avoid Death in his real skeletal majesty was to keep on walking until they reached Anthurus.

"No," she said. "We need to keep moving as long as it's daylight. Besides, the more distance we put between ourselves and that mountain, the better I'll like it."

"The mountain isn't really hostile, you know," the hermit said. "We just happened to be in its path."

"Wrong, wrong, wrong," Sombrisio said. "You'd think

you'd have learned something about the Desolation, as many years as you've spent here."

"As big as the mountain is," Calla said, "it doesn't have to be hostile."

"That's right," said the surviving elf retainer. "I remember Elavil of the Rock and his riding brontosaur. He claimed it was the best-tempered creature alive. Maybe it was, but one cold night it decided to curl up with Elavil to stay warm. Some heroic death that was, hey?"

The kid from Brooklyn put down the harmonica on which he'd been softly playing "In the Baggage Car Ahead." His visage was sad.

"It's too bad about the old man," the kid said in a broken voice. "He was . . . he was the one we all looked up to for guidance. And then, squirt, he's gone. What kind of craftsmanship does that show, getting squirted like a tube of toothpaste?"

"Umm," Calla said. "More like a tube of red paint, from what I could see. Of course, with the moonlight you've got to extrapolate."

The elfin retainer put an arm around the kid's shoulders and said, "Don't take it so hard, kid. He didn't have a chance. It's not in our hands to choose whether we'll be Tibbalts or just so many kerns and gallowglasses."

"What I was saying," Sombrisio said, "not that any of you lot seem to be interested in something that your very lives depend on . . ."

The ring let her voice trail out in a painful whine.

Jancy looked down at her finger. "Ah, sorry, Sombrisio," she said. "I was . . ."

"Walking around in a daze," the ring said. "After all, why should today be different? What I was going to say, though, is that the mountain isn't just wandering anymore. It's following me."

"Nonsense!" said the hermit.

"Oh?" said the ring. "Like it's nonsense that the last thing you did before leaving Caltus was to rob the poor box of the Hospice of Sisters of Fallen Virtue?"

"Ah," said the hermit. "That makes sense, I was saying."

"*And*," Sombrisio continued, never one to be turned when she scented psychic blood, "you only got three pewter buttons and a slug for your trouble."

Jancy glanced back toward the retainers. "Hey, kid?" she called.

"And when the slug crawled out of your purse that night, it wrote *thief* across the back of your robe in slime," the ring concluded triumphantly.

The kid from Brooklyn looked up. "Mistress?" he said, palming his harmonica nervously.

"Seems to me that the Old Man took worse punishment than even Hormazd the Centurion," Jancy said. "I mean, what's seventy-eight separate wounds compared to having a whole mountain fall on you, huh?"

"Gee, mistress," said the retainer. His eyes widened in dawning pleasure. "Do you really think so?"

"Anybody'd think so, kid," Jancy assured him.

"Wow," said the kid. To the elf retainer he went on, "Say, did you notice the way the Old Man threw his arms and legs wide as he fell forward? He was making sure that he'd be smashed *absolutely* flat. Now, that's craftsmanship if I ever saw it!"

Calla Mallanik looked at Jancy. "That was a good thing to do," the elf said quietly.

"I can't stand that damned song about the mother's corpse up in the baggage car," Jancy replied, also under her breath.

"Ready to learn why the mountain's chasing me, noble hero?" Sombrisio demanded.

"Yeah," said Calla. "We'd—"

"It's because I'm the closest thing it's ever found to an all-powerful prophet on his way to heaven by direct translation," Sombrisio said, deliberately interrupting the elf. "Unless one of your lot think you qualify better?"

Jancy shrugged. That motion reminded her of the cut across her shoulder. The pain disappeared behind a curtain of adrenaline when danger threatened, but it sure wasn't gone for good.

"Makes sense to me," Calla said. "What do you think, hermit?"

The hermit cleared his throat. "That's an extremely wise ring you have there," he said carefully. "I certainly wouldn't argue with any assessment it made of a situation. No, sir, not me."

The ring farted at surprising length.

Jancy Gaine raised her right fist and rubbed the corner of her mouth with her thumb knuckle. "Hey, Sombrisio?" she whispered.

"Yeah, numskull?" the ring replied.

"Thanks for waking us up last night," said Jancy.

"Huh!" Sombrisio said. "I told you—I was listening to you talk in your sleep and it turned my stomach."

"Thanks anyway," said Jancy as she lowered her hand to the head of Castrator.

She no longer worried about how long it would take them to find Anthurus. After all, the quest was the thing.

Shadows lengthened, abruptly and much sooner than sunset should have been threatening. The sudden dimness drew Jancy's mind from thoughts that were considerably darker yet.

The hermit was a few steps in the lead of the rest of the party. He stopped with his palms forward, as though he'd hit an invisible wall.

Jancy tugged Sombrisio from her finger. She held the massive silver ring out toward Calla Mallanik.

"My bow will—" the elf protested. He'd already nocked an arrow.

"Take the ring," Jancy said in a voice more terrifying than words alone could have been.

The party had entered a shallow valley. From above, the Desolation of Thaumidor would have looked as flat as a marine recruit's bunk. Swales and rises that were minute in geomorphic terms were nonetheless enough to limit the vision of humans at ground level to a few score yards.

That didn't explain the darkness. The packhorses, led

in two long trains by the surviving retainers, whickered nervously. Though the beasts were only ten or a dozen yards behind the elf and humans at the head of the party, they were already lost in gloom.

"I may have made the wrong turning," said the hermit in a voice of controlled terror. "When the mountain . . . You know. I think we'd better—"

"All right," Jancy ordered in a voice trembling with hormones. "Turn the pack train. I'll wait."

Light gleamed on the shadowed hillside, faint but increasingly slowly to illuminate the ruined fane from which it sprang. Pillars, most of them broken, were set in a circle. At their bases lay a rubble of blocks and tiles, remnants of the architraves and a domed roof.

The light was all the colors of the rainbow. It should have been beautiful. Instead it reminded Jancy of the shimmer of a snake's cast skin.

The hermit backed slowly around Jancy. "I'm very sorry to have brought us this way," he whispered. "We seem to have found the temple of IRiS, the rainbow goddess of evil and misfortune."

Squill's eyes rolled in fear. He formed his handset and began speaking desperately into it. Jancy doubted the artio would be able to punch a spell out of a valley with the magical resonance of this one, but at present there was almost no question on Middle Earth that she cared less about.

She held Castrator and her spiked shield out at angles before her, trying to cover as broad an area as possible. Jancy Gaine wasn't a team player, had never been that. She was a straight-ahead berserk, keep slashing so long as there's anybody else still on his feet.

That was fine when she was alone, but Jancy wasn't alone now and the people with her couldn't take care of themselves the way the old gang did. Spotty Gulick, whose idea of a good time on stand-down was to get into drunken brawls; Dominik Blaid, who saw everything on a battlefield and then fixed the problems with his own saber; even Gar Quithnick, a creep but *our* creep. You never had to worry about anybody else stabbing you in the back if Gar was there.

But now . . .

Something moved in the darkness. At first she thought it was a dog, but it was too big for that. A bear, perhaps . . .

"The minions of IRiS were once human," the hermit said. There was a singsong intonation to his voice. He spoke to keep from dissolving in panic, not because he had any necessary information to impart. "But now—"

The necessary information was the degree of fear with which this place had struck the hermit when he recognized it.

The figure rose up on its hind legs. It stepped toward Jancy, giggling loudly. The light suffusing the fane brightened. There were more of the figures, many more of them, standing now and pacing forward.

They were spotted hyenas, but they walked like men. The slavering jaws through which they laughed at their victims had teeth that could crush bones too big for a lion to devour.

"Run!" the hermit cried.

The whole valley was now bright with the rainbow radiance of IRiS and her ruthless minions. There was no escape, to the rear or in any direction.

Scores of the hyenas shrieked their joy as they pulled down the kid from Brooklyn and the stalwart elf retainer beside him. Over the monsters' laughter and the snap of crunching bones, their leaders cried, "Disallowed! Disallowed!" in nearly human voices.

Horses screamed in their final terror. The minions of IRiS wasted everything in their frenzies of slaughter.

"Princess!" Jancy called as she lunged at the leading hyena. She could focus the pack's attention on her and save the others for perhaps a few seconds. "Princess! Princess!"

The hyenas came at her from all sides, but *this* Jancy Gaine understood. The bearded ax slashed down through a minion's upper chest. Broken ribs, lengths of blood vessels, and much of the right lung spilled onto the soil as the monster's sternum flopped in two pieces.

Not only hyenas jaws could crush bones.

The spike in Jancy's shield boss drove through a hyena's thin nasal bones, into the brain case or near enough. Another minion hunched to tear the tendons from Jancy's knees, met her hobnailed boot instead, and collapsed wailing as she broke its spine with a downward chop of her buckler's rim.

There was a hyena behind her. Jancy killed it with a quick, unthinking stab of Castrator's ball pommel, not even bothering to look. She thrust the ax forward again like an épée, putting the upper tip into a monster's thick throat and through the neck vertebrae behind it.

Calla Mallanik shouted something. It couldn't affect Jancy's present situation, so her ears didn't hear it. The part of her mind that processed language didn't operate at times like these.

She was drenched in blood. Some of it was her own, from her right side. She hadn't been conscious of teeth ripping along her ribs, but she'd split a hyena's skull with Castrator's edge in the same motion that smashed the pommel through the chest of the creature on her back.

She started forward. The minions were fleeing, all those that survived. They were running for their lairs, noisome holes dug into the ruins of the temple, and the rainbow light was fading.

"Sif's hair," Jancy muttered. She turned. She almost fell because the adrenaline rush had left her as suddenly as it arrived. She had very little remaining from her normal reserves of strength.

A few horses had survived the hyenas' single-minded bloodlust. They pitched and bucked in terror. Squill knelt over his pack with his handset, uninjured but blinded by fear. The hermit stood transfixed, staring at—

Jancy blinked. Staring at what looked like a much younger edition of Jancy Gaine: herself as a young girl, just before she made the decision to go on her first war party as a shield maiden instead of staying home to marry in the village at the edge of the ice fields.

The figure, her figure, wore Sombrisio on its right hand, so it must be Calla who stood there.

The illusion trembled and vanished like a picture projected on smoke. Calla Mallanik shook himself. "Let's get out of this *damned* place," he said.

The hermit moved like an automaton until the party reached daylight again at the head of the valley, and he gave only monosyllabic directions for the remainder of the afternoon until they camped.

Jancy awakened. Every muscle hurt. Where the flesh had been severed by steel or the hyenas' teeth, it hurt more; but that was a matter of degree rather than type.

"Sif!" she muttered. Two figures were still sitting up, across the coals of the campfire. "How late is it, Calla? You should've gotten me up for my watch before now."

The constellations above the Desolation of Thaumidor weren't the familiar ones. Normally Jancy didn't see shapes in the stars, but she did see things here. Unfortunately.

"You needed the sleep," Calla Mallanik said. "You've been one of the walking dead all day. Except when it counted."

"Sif's *hair*," Jancy said; but as she moved, her muscles warmed and the pain sank to what normal people would consider bearable levels. She squinted across the fire. "Hermit, is that you?" she asked.

"Yes, Mistress Gaine," the hermit said.

"Let's throw another log on," Jancy said. She thought about the possible implications and added, "Ah, there's no . . . The fire doesn't make pictures here, does it?" Calla shrugged. "Not that I've seen," he said. Instead of adding wood, he prodded the end of a thick branch from the edge into the heart of the coals. "Not a lot of heat, either, but that may be me."

"I never asked you what you did to drive off those

hyenas," Jancy said. "I thought, I thought we were gone geese."

"What you thought," said Sombrisio, who was back on her finger, "was that you'd screwed up even at heroic endeavor. When you already knew you were no good at any other damn thing."

Jancy looked down at the ring. "If you want to know the real truth," she said, "I was thinking about which hyena to stick next. After things slowed down, I thought I'd blown it, yeah."

"It was what the hermit said," Calla explained. He nodded toward the man beside him, but the hermit was sunk in an open-eyed daze. Maybe he was the one seeing things in the wan firelight this time.

"That the minions of IRiS had once been men," the elf resumed. "I find it odd, but most human evil isn't done by evil humans."

"Huh?" said Jancy. It could be that she'd been whacked on the head so hard that everything she heard sounded like double-talk. And again, it could be that Calla'd been whacked on the head.

"No, I mean that," the elf said. "Most humans slip into evil deeds with the best intentions in the world. They slide down the road to destruction, thinking what they're doing is necessary or even good. If they could really see what they were doing, why, they'd stop."

"They wouldn't stop," said Sombrisio. "They'd just find some other excuse. Humans are even more despicable than elves, elf."

"And the ones who are already lost irretrievably . . ." Calla continued. They'd all learned by now that the best way to deal with the ring's gibes was to ignore them. "If you show them what they've become, they, well, they can't stand it. They'd run away. As the minions of IRiS ran away."

"I still don't get it," Jancy said. Not that that was news. *Don't worry, Jancy, we've got it all under control. Go sharpen your ax, why don't you?* How often had she heard that or a close equivalent of that? "You showed a pack of hyenas that they were hyenas?"

"No," said the elf with pardonable pride. "I showed them that they had once been men. I turned the power of Sombrisio on myself. I projected to everyone watching the image *of* the watcher before the fatal decisions that led to where they were now."

The hermit looked at Calla Mallanik with dismal, haunted eyes. "It seems to me," the hermit said, the first words he'd volunteered since the battle at the fane of IRiS, "that's using the ring on many at once. While I understood its powers were limited to one person at a time."

"So I stretched a point, buster," Sombrisio said. "Sue me! If you can find a jurisdiction this side of the Outer Sea where there aren't bad debt warrants still out for you, I mean."

"I really meant to make the money good," the hermit said. He didn't appear to be talking to anyone present, except perhaps to his younger self in judgment. "Every time. Every single time."

"You didn't look at me until after the effect had worn off, I suppose, Jancy?" Calla Mallanik said with studied nonchalance.

"Huh?" Jancy repeated. "No, I glanced back when the hyenas started running. I saw myself looking like I did when I was a kid and wondered what in Sif's name was going on. I still don't see what it has to do with the price of fox fur."

Calla looked at her sharply. "You didn't feel regret," he said, "for the choices you made, for the path you didn't follow?"

She shrugged. Damn, she needed to remember not to do that until the cut had knitted together better. "What's to regret?" she said. "I made choices, everybody makes choices. People who choose to serve an evil goddess— Sif, everybody knows IRiS is evil. People who choose to serve evil, for whatever reasons, are evil. It's just that simple."

Calla Mallanik shook his head in wonderment. "Ah, what an elf was lost in you, Mistress Gaine," he said.

"Oh, you bet," said Sombrisio. "And she'd have been a right triumph when her creche cycle was taught aesthetic appreciation, wouldn't she?"

"It's not far to Anthurus now," the hermit said. He was still speaking to himself, or at any rate to a portion of himself. "I'll guide them the rest of the way."

Either the fire or Sombrisio interjected a *BLAT/hissing* sound.

"I really meant to repay the money," the hermit added in a whisper.

The stretch of waste on which the hermit halted was unusual only in that it was so completely barren. A few gangling plants were scattered on the slope. They bent down their stems and buried their seed heads in the dirt when they saw members of Jancy's party glancing in their direction. Larger examples of the noisome vegetation which ranged the Desolation were conspicuous by their absence.

Calla Mallanik glanced back in the direction by which they'd come. There was a plume of dust on the horizon. "The mountain's after us again," he said glumly.

Jancy shrugged. "It doesn't move very fast," she said. "How much farther is it to Anthurus, hermit?"

"We've arrived," the hermit said. He pointed to the ground. "It's right here."

"Hel take you if we're here!" Jancy snarled. "I've been to Anthurus, remember? That's where I found the damned ring!"

"Where Princess Rissa found my puissant self," Sombrisio said in an arch tone. "And of course Hel, or at least some civilized equivalent of your barbaric death goddess, will take the hermit. Happens to all humans."

"I'm sure you did," the hermit said. "But unfortunately, it seems that the Desolation has covered the city again during the interim. Anthurus is down here, somewhere, under this sand dune."

He scuffed the soil. "Dirt dune, that is."

"And not nearly soon enough, in most cases," Sombrisio muttered as a coda to her previous comment.

The hermit had lost all the cranky bluster with which he'd joined the quest. It wasn't because he was afraid of what Jancy might—might very well—do to him, either. He faced her anger with what could only be described as an attitude of quiet resignation.

"Well, what are we supposed to do?" Calla demanded.

The elf looked back over his shoulder in the direction of the mountain. Sure, it didn't move *very* fast, and it wasn't even making a beeline toward the questing party. More like the line a bee really makes, jagged casts back and forth across the landscape, laboriously orienting itself.

But Calla wasn't going to forget any time soon the sight of flat ground humping itself up into a cliff a thousand feet high.

"I'm sorry," the hermit said. "I truly don't know. Perhaps you could leave the ring here and the loess would bury it eventually?"

"Or not," Sombrisio said. "Umm, you know, I could right fancy being plucked from the ground by a condor and dropped into the hands of some powerful and no doubt wicked wizard."

"Hel's bloody toenails," Jancy muttered. She was in charge of the expedition so she had to decide what to do. Thinking through intractable problems wasn't the sort of thing she was best at, to put it mildly.

A scrawny gooseberry bush bent slowly toward her foot. The tip of a needle-sharp thorn pecked abruptly at her bootlace.

Jancy kicked the plant away with a divot of light soil. The gooseberry squawked when it landed and scurried farther away from the party.

Jancy gazed around. Her eyes lighted on the artio. "Squill!" she said.

"Mistress?" the comspec replied, wincing. He'd spent much of the past several days with his eyes closed. He was justifiably certain that they weren't going to show him anything he really wanted to see.

"I want you to contact Caltus," Jancy ordered. "Tell them the city's gone—buried till who knows when. Ask them if we ought to bring Sombrisio back with us. Got that?"

"Yes, mistress," the artio said. He squatted down and formed his handset. He'd closed his eyes again.

"Mistress Gaine?" the hermit said.

She looked at him again, startled that he was still standing before her with a look of significance. "Do you have something useful to say after all?" she demanded.

"Not the way you mean it, mistress," the hermit said. He cleared his throat, then went on, "I have fulfilled your request of me in the best fashion I could. There's nothing more for me to do here. I therefore ask your leave to, ah, leave."

"We'll be going back to Caltus as soon as . . ." said Calla Mallanik. He glanced at the artio, speaking into his handset. "Well, pretty quick, anyway. We'll drop you off at your hut."

"If I may," the hermit said, "I'll go on my own. I'm headed in the opposite direction, you see. Toward Quiberon. I have some debts to clear up there."

"There," said Sombrisio. "And debts all across the North Coast. *And* in Caltus."

"Yes, I'm afraid that's correct," the hermit said, nibbling his lower lip. To Jancy, the old man looked worn and frightened and more determined than she'd ever imagined he could be.

"A doddering old fool like you won't ever be able to pay off all you owe!" Sombrisio said.

Jancy waved her left palm over the ring, though without actually touching the metal. "Hush, hush," she murmured.

"I will *not* hush," Sombrisio said. "Why, he's not even employable. Unless maybe somebody wants a doorstop!"

"And there's my wife, of course," the hermit added. "Well, one does what one can."

"I understood that your wife . . ." the elf said, giving Sombrisio a speculative look. "Had left you. Not the other way around."

The hermit shrugged. "Nothing happens in a vacuum," he said. "I suppose I always knew that. My wife is responsible for her actions, but that doesn't diminish my own responsibility for mine."

"There was a boyfriend?" Jancy said, looking toward the empty horizon beyond the hermit's left shoulder rather than meeting his eyes directly as she asked the question.

The hermit smiled faintly. " 'Pull your face off'n then stick your head where the sun don't shine,' I believe were his exact words," he said. "Well, he won't be as young as he was, either. And in any case, I need to apologize to her, whatever happens afterwards."

"Well, I'll be damned," said Jancy Gaine.

"Perhaps," said the hermit. "But I'm no longer sure damnation is a necessary part of the human condition."

They gave him a packhorse and more than a sufficient share of the remaining food. As the hermit said as he began trekking westward over the steep leading edge of the dune, if he had any of the sea rations left when he arrived in Quiberon, he might be able to sell the cans to a shipmaster as ballast.

The sky to the west was almost as black as Jancy Gaine's mood. Lightning flickered within the clouds. If there was thunder, it was lost against a background of the Desolation's normal rumbles and sighing.

They'd set up their exiguous camp midway on the long slope. Squill squatted at the top of the encampment that formed the dune's leading edge, the highest ground available. The artio's apparatus squealed in hopeless despair as he attempted to contact his superiors in Caltus. Every time the distant lightning flashed, a demon roared at the doomed souls.

Calla Mallanik picked grimly at a can of sea rations.

There wasn't a fire because there was nothing bigger than a gooseberry bush to burn on this bleak stretch. The best you could say for the situation was that the food in the olive drab cans was so unappetizing hot that eating it cold didn't degrade the experience significantly.

"Well," the elf said, "we could try blasting a hole in the soil, the way you did to trip up the mountain."

"Great thought!" Sombrisio said. "The first time you prod the Desolation that way, the hole will close before you can get me off your finger and throw me in. The second time, though, you'll bury me I don't want to guess how deep."

"We will?" Jancy said in surprise.

"You bet," Sombrisio said. "The second time, the Desolation'll be ready for you. It'll swallow us all down like a trout takes a fly. That'll give me some company for the next three millennia. Or however long."

"I thought it was too easy," Calla said. He took another forkful of sea ration, punishing himself for having let his hopes rise.

"Look, it's fine with me," said the ring. "I figure you both'll be about as bright after you're buried as you are now."

"The best choice," Jancy said in a loud voice, "is to take Sombrisio back to Caltus. One item won't be enough to disturb the magical balance."

She cleared her throat and added, "Besides, the ring might be useful to have around for, you know, useful things."

Jancy had spoken forcefully because she knew that whenever she had an idea which didn't involve lopping somebody to bits with Castrator, she was out of her depth. If she put enough emphasis on a statement, listeners might forget that Jancy Gaine was basically as dumb as a post.

Alternatively, they might remember Castrator, and that could be an even better way of getting them to agree with her.

She and Calla heard a gabble from the top of the dune.

They couldn't understand the words, but they could tell that the artio had made actual contact instead of flinging his spells vainly into the howling atmospherics.

"If we're going to head back," Calla said, checking the cover of his silver-strung bow, "I'd like to start before the storm hits. The rain'll come down this slope like the front of Deucalion's flood."

Squill trotted toward them. His wand, still extended, wobbled above him like the baton of a maestro conducting the sky.

"I got through!" the artio called. "They say, 'Lose it good!'"

Jancy stood with threatening deliberation. She placed her hands on her hips. "Lose it good," she repeated. "Do they say *how* in the name of Sif's blond cunt we're supposed to do that when the city's buried?"

Squill skidded to a halt so abruptly that he almost lost his footing. His cloak flapped around him and back. "Ah," he said. "No, Mistress Gaine, they didn't say that. I explained the situation clearly, *very* clearly, Mistress Gaine—"

The artio noticed the way Jancy's right hand clenched on the helve of Castrator. He closed his eyes.

—"and they just said, ah, what they said. Mistress."

"It's not his fault," said Calla Mallanik mildly. "Though of course it's traditional in many human cultures to kill the messenger, so I suppose we—if you'd like to, that is—could—"

"Put a sock in it," Jancy said grimly. She turned away from the artio before she did something she wouldn't regret but knew she ought to.

"Hel's teeth," she said. There were a variety of ways to handle frustration. The only one that worked worth a damn for her was to go berserk for a few minutes, but she supposed she'd have to make do here with being depressed.

Light glimmered in the middle distance. "Has the storm got all the way around us now?" she asked, kneading her hands together to relax the cramp threatening as a result of her grip on the bearded ax.

Calla squinted. "No," he said, "that's the mountain again. The phlogiston being expelled when the rock cracks and closes, the hermit said."

"Does a light dawn?" Sombrisio demanded.

"The mountain!" Jancy and Calla shouted together.

"You know," said the ring, "I think the intellectual dominance of this age is in the hands of the cockroaches. Or whatever cockroaches use instead of hands."

It wasn't raining yet, but when it did it was going to come down like a cow pissing on a flat rock. Not that there was a lot of rock in the Desolation of Thaumidor. Or any cows, of course, so far as Jancy could tell.

The mountain roared to the foot of the dune like an avalanche; which it basically was, though the rocks had to bootstrap themselves upward each time in order to fall.

The ground shook like a hammered drumhead. Light shot in every direction from the collapsing granite, sparkles and sheets and faintly colored balls as large as haystacks. These last hung trembling in the air, dreaming of a paradise in which ghost trains ran down phantom tracks.

The forward flow of stone exhausted itself for the moment. The silence that followed the sound was only relative, but it seemed complete because of the crashing amplitude of the cataclysm it succeeded.

Jancy Gaine and her elf companion stood at the top of the slope. They'd chosen a spot half a mile from the camp where Squill huddled with the horses. No point in leading a mountain straight over their supplies; though if things went wrong, it wouldn't make a whole lot of difference.

The dune's leading edge fell away at a sixty-degree angle behind the pair of them. The mountain's thunder shook veils of fine soil from the escarpment. The dust twisted into the shape of tortured women as it settled toward the ground three hundred feet below.

"Let's start moving apart," Calla Mallanik said. He took two steps away from Jancy, looking back over his shoulder to make sure that the ax woman intended to follow the plan they'd worked out while the mountain was still miles away.

She didn't intend to.

"Get on out of the way," Jancy ordered. Her eyes were fixed on the mountain as it inched upward again; she held Sombrisio between her cupped palms. "I think I'll take care of it myself."

"*You* think?" Sombrisio piped. "You *think*? Sure, you would think that your getting mushed into the dirt was just as good as burying me in living rock!"

"Jancy," Calla said. He spoke with the sort of controlled earnestness with which one coaxes a toddler who's managed to lock himself alone in the bathroom. "Toss me the ring, move a few steps, and I'll toss it back. We've got to keep the mountain from focusing on one point. It's got too broad a front to survive if it comes straight at one of us."

"All right," she said. "All right."

She tossed Sombrisio underhand to the elf, then walked away from him along the escarpment in seeming nonchalance. This would either work or it wouldn't. If it didn't, it was very damned unlikely that Jancy Gaine would be around to answer questions about what went wrong.

The mountain, dark and quiescent for a moment at the foot of the slope, seemed to have gotten its figurative breath. The crystalline entity humped itself taller at a steady rate, preparing for the final gravity-driven rush to the goal it sensed.

As Calla walked north along the crumbling dune edge with the ring, the rising layers of rock shifted slightly in his direction. The mountain's progress had been increasingly direct as it neared Sombrisio. If the mass of rock were a Plott hound, it would be yelping in climactic enthusiasm by now. As it was, the pop and crunch of stone sliding on itself took on a sort of tail-wagging joyousness.

"You can toss her back to me now," Jancy called, raising her voice to be heard over the background of geological preparation. She'd left her buckler and helmet in the camp, since they were obviously useless against present needs.

Castrator was useless also, but the big ax swung at Jancy's right hip. She'd always figured to be buried with Castrator. If things went wrong in the next few seconds, *mingled* would be a better word than *buried* to describe her future relationship with the ax.

"Here she comes!" Calla shouted. He was nearly a hundred feet away by now, but the mountain covered several times that width of the lower dune.

The elf put his whole body into an overhand throw. The motion was as graceful as that of a cat leaping to tear some small bird to bloody feathers. Sombrisio, spinning and lighted pastel by the discharges from the straining mountain, described a perfect catenary arc which ended in Jancy's clasping hands.

Jancy began to run along the edge of the escarpment. Castrator slapped her thigh. The base of the mountain skidded slightly toward her as the wall of rock staggered swiftly up. Friction against the loose soil wasn't sufficient to completely brake the enormous mass pouring itself into a tower from the rear forward.

As the mountain moved, it flexed beyond the elastic modulus of the crystals which comprised it. Gaps like mouths opened and shut between layers of rock. Granite teetered over Jancy in a vertical sheet. The roar echoed from the clouds in thunder beyond human imagination.

"Throw me *now*, you brainless cunt!" Sombrisio screamed.

The face of the rock wavered only twenty feet from Jancy. A momentary split appeared in the surface, like a shake in drying wood. Jancy flung Sombrisio between plates of granite. The gap slammed shut as the entire mountain plunged downward in a rush nothing could have stopped.

Jancy dived with her arms outstretched in the direction

she'd been running. The friable soil lost cohesion under the impact of megatons of granite. The dune's edge exploded in a plume of dust that cloaked and preceded the river of cold stone on its dive into the flat landscape three hundred feet below. The noise continued for a quite remarkable time.

Jancy lay on the escarpment. The mountain had missed her, but her boots dangled out in the air where the cliff of dirt had collapsed when the rock slid past. Five hundred feet of the dune's face had been chiseled from sixty degrees to half that.

Well beyond the bottom of the slope, the mountain was shivering to a halt. Calla Mallanik got to his feet on the far side of the notch in the dune. He waved. Squill barely visible in the beclouded twilight, was climbing up the slope. The artio needed high ground to report back to Caltus.

To report Jancy Gaine's success back to Caltus.

The rain fell in sheets, by buckets, and as great slashing waves. It even smelled a little like cow urine. Jancy Gaine bathed once a year, in the spring when the ice broke, so the odor wasn't a matter of great concern to her.

Despite the storm, she should have been a lot more cheerful than she was.

Calla Mallanik caught the lead of the gray mare so that Jancy could finish cinching the pack. The animal was supposed to stand drop-reined to be loaded, but the weather spooked her. Sif, the mare thought she had problems?

Under the sluicing rainfall, the soil was vanishing faster than good intentions at a bachelor party. By the time Jancy grabbed the last pack saddle, it had washed twenty feet down the slope. She hoped the damned horses liked their fodder wet and muddy, because that's the way they were going to be eating it till they escaped the Desolation of Thaumidor.

She and Calla loaded the roan gelding. The horse

came *that* close to being strangled with its own tail, but it realized its danger in time to stop sidling away from Jancy. Its breast was a froth of nervous sweat, despite the cleansing rain.

Jancy paused, then kneed the gelding in the ribs to tighten the girth another notch. "Where in Sif's name is Squill?" she shouted to Calla.

The elf pointed up the disintegrating dune. "Right where he was," he said. "I guess he's still trying to call Caltus through this storm."

The artio was silhouetted against the western sky. The clouds hid every trace of sunset, but lightning was a constant white glare across the heavens.

"Well, if he doesn't get down here *now*, we're heading back without him!" Jancy said.

Squill stood up. He took a step toward them, as if he'd heard Jancy from a quarter mile away through a chaos of deluge and thunderclaps. He waved.

A lightning bolt touched the tip of the artio's twelve-foot wand. The flash was brighter than the sum of all those the storm had flung down previously. Squill's bones stood out momentarily from a ball of actinic radiance before dissolving like the rest of him.

Jancy got to her feet again. She didn't know if electrical shock, the sky-splitting thunder, or pure surprise had knocked her on her ass.

"Let's get moving!" she said to Calla. The elf wouldn't be able to hear anything for a while after the boom that followed the lightning; but it wasn't as if he needed to be told to get out of this place, either.

The storm ended not far beyond the base of the dune covering Anthurus. The boundary between rain and not-rain was as sharp as a razor cut.

The dune that *had* covered Anthurus. Rain gouged the loess and carried it away with an enthusiasm no human public-works crew would ever show. Great rivers of silt flowed in four directions from the site, following subtle variations in topography and cutting them deeper.

Or maybe the streams were flowing uphill. This was the Desolation of Thaumidor, after all.

The packhorses whickered, congratulating one another on being alive. Calla Mallanik paused and took off his tunic to wring it. Even if they'd carried changes of clothing, nothing could have come through the downpour without being soaked.

Jancy looked back at the foaming, rain-torn lake. "I suppose we could have waited," she said. "Anthurus is going to unlose itself completely in the next twenty minutes."

"I don't think it would have worked that way," the elf said. He didn't sound particularly cheerful either.

The western sky was scarlet, though the sun should have been well below the horizon by now.

"Sombrisio's going to be all right," Jancy said in a bright voice. "Someday a guy named Mohammet is going to be seeing something on a pile of sand. When he bends over to pick it up, it'll ask if his mother brought a paternity suit against the camel."

"Yeah," Calla said. "Nothing a mountain can do is going to bother that ring."

Jancy clucked to the pair of horses she led. She began to walk on. "We really did it, didn't we?" she said. "They'll be talking about us for a long time. The heroes who got rid of Sombrisio."

"You bet," Calla agreed. "This one was a quest and a half, I'll tell the world!"

There was a small noise, Jancy spun around.

"Sorry," the elf said in embarrassment. "I had a can of beans and franks for dinner."

"Oh," said Jancy. She clucked to the horses again.

"I miss her too," said Calla Mallanik in a voice almost too soft to be heard; but then, it wasn't as if Jancy needed to be told that.

Behind them, the opal towers of Anthurus gleamed under a bloody sky.

Brother to Dragons   72141-0 ✦ $4.99 ☐

Sometimes one man can make a difference. The John Campbell Award winner for best novel of the year. "...memorable characters and a detailed world that recalls Charles Dickens."   *—Chicago Sun-Times*

"It's a compulsive read...a page turner...riveting... Sheffield has constructed a background that is absolutely convincing, and set against it a walloping good story."   —Baird Searles, *Asimov's*

Dancing with Myself   72185-2 ✦ $4.99 ☐

Sheffield explains the universe in nonfiction and story. "...one of the most imaginative, exciting talents to appear on the SF scene in recent years."

—Publishers Weekly

Between the Strokes of Night   55977-X ✦ $4.99 ☐

The Immortals seem to live forever and can travel light years in days—and control the galaxy. On the planet Pentecost, a small group challenges that control. "Sheffield speculates about the future with the best of them....this is hard SF at its best."   *—Kliatt*
